I0770077

ALSO BY JOSEPH JOHN LEE

The Spellbinders and the Gunslingers
THE BLEEDING STONE
THE CHILDREN OF THE BLACK MOON

Novellas
PALE NIGHT, RED FIELDS

THE LEGION OF THE LOST

BOOK THREE OF THE SPELLBINDERS AND THE GUNSLINGERS

JOSEPH JOHN LEE

ECLIPSEBORN PUBLISHING

For you, the reader.
Thank you for finishing the ride with me.

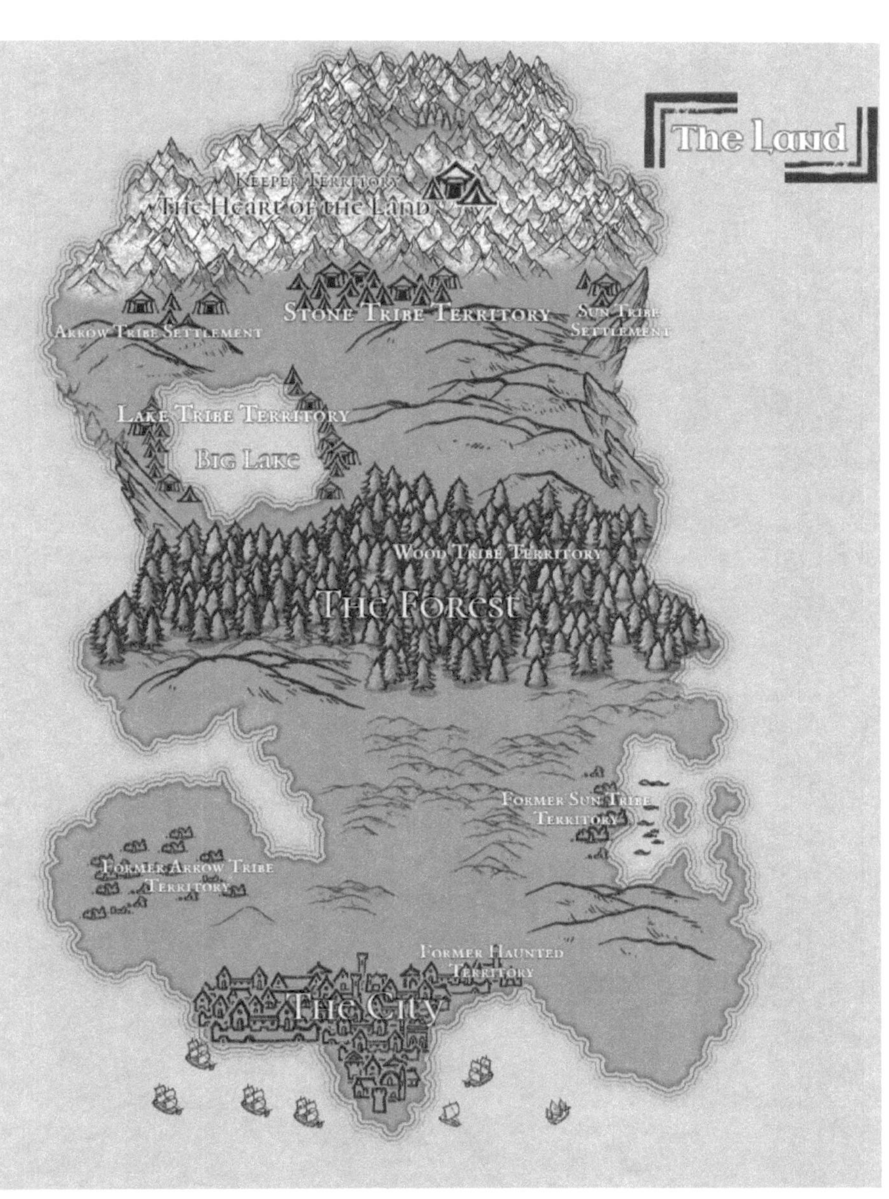

The Land
Keeper Territory
The Heart of the Land
Stone Tribe Territory
Arrow Tribe Settlement
Sun Tribe Settlement
Lake Tribe Territory
Big Lake
Wood Tribe Territory
The Forest
Former Sun Tribe Territory
Former Arrow Tribe Territory
Former Haunted Territory
The City

THE STORY SO FAR

The Bleeding Stone

<u>The Memories That Have Come to Pass</u>

In the year 1534 Anno Salvatoris, an Eclipse struck fear in the hearts of the Stone Tribe. During this Eclipse, an event carrying with it an ill omen, a baby girl was born to the Stone Chief Fannalhen and his wife Dennalhir. The girl was given the name Sennalhat, which in the Stone tongue meant "Child of Light."

Sennalhat, bearing the nickname "Sen," spent much of her childhood carousing with her close friends, Narva and Fann, as well as her older sister, Tez, and younger brother, Brin, unaware of the circumstances resultant from her birth. One day, however, during an adventure through the mountain ranges to the north of the Stone Tribe village, Sen inadvertently triggered a rockslide that horribly broke Fann's arm. Fann's mother, Koelhe, denounces Sen as a "Curseborn" and forbade her son from ever associating with Sen. Perplexed, Sen was given no clarification as to the meaning behind the label from her parents, and as the years go on, her friendship with Fann deteriorated into a rivalry of extreme animosity, often manifesting in Fann berating and bullying Brin. One such occasion led to Sen violently breaking Fann's nose.

Upon reaching eighteen years of age, Sen ventured into the mountain ranges of the Heart of the Land to undergo her Trial, a coming-of-age ceremony whereupon children of the Tribes passed into adulthood and were granted Boons associated with the Animal Deity under whose Sign they were born—either the Bear, the Wolf, or the Owl. Sen, however, still unaware of her being born during an Eclipse, was subjected to a strange non-Trial in which she was belittled by two entities acting as envoys of the Moon, revealing to her the nature of her birth and her status as an Eclipseborn, a being looked upon with disdain in Tribal society for the supposed calamity they were meant to bring. The Eclipseborn were meant to be shunned from society, banished from their Tribes, but due to her parents' intervention, Sen was permitted to remain within her village and Tribe, despite the implications that would inevitably arrive.

The two entities offered Sen a choice between life and death, elaborating no further on the offer. Sen chose neither and instead opted to reflect on the good fortune with which she was blessed to have been permitted to remain among her people. However, at seeing the horror upon the faces of those conducting her Trial, Sen realized that she would never be accepted among her people and admonished her parents for keeping her true nature secret to her. She ventured off on her own until finding herself at a tavern and taking up playing a card game with a stranger, a game based entirely on chance that Sen suddenly won with ease, a consequence of the new power of Luck that was just awakened within her.

THE EVENTS NOW TO COME

In the year 1556 Anno Salvatoris, Brin, accompanied by his family, underwent his Trial. Brin completed his Trial, bestowing upon him the Boon of Memory associated with the Owl, and turned to face his family, but realized Sen had disappeared. Sen was found drinking at a tavern by Fannalhen, who angrily led her back to the Stone Tribe village.

As the family returned to the village and Brin was granted his abilities, Sen once again wandered off to a tavern, where she met with Narva and lamented that she was an outcast for the accident of her birth, admitting her own jealousy at the adulation that Brin was receiving, none of which she was ever able to receive herself.

Meanwhile, as the festivities continued, Fannalhen's celebration at his son's success was interrupted by the Sun Chief Han'e, who came to plead with Fannalhen for the Stone Tribe's assistance in reclaiming the lands of the Sun Tribe. Fifteen years prior, an army of Invaders came from across the eastern sea and claimed for themselves all lands to the south of the Forest, which displaced the Sun and Arrow Tribes while also nearly wiping out the Haunted Tribe. The Sun and Arrow Tribes since relocated and were permitted to settle in the territories belonging to the Stone Tribe. For years, though, Han'e had been attempting to employ Fannalhen and the Stone Tribe to reclaim the Sun lands from the Invaders, but Fannalhen, once again, declined, much to Han'e's frustration.

The next day, Sen was admonished by Tez not only for her frequent drinking but also for her shirking of responsibilities pertaining to Brin. Sen made an unsteady peace with her brother and vowed to him stop drinking after he confessed that he no longer recognized her for the person she became.

Later that evening, Dennalhir encountered two haggard people collapsed at the entrance to the village. Convening with Fannalhen and the rest of the Tribal council, they learn that the two, named Shara and Ran, were once members of the Haunted Tribe who were now slaves of the Invaders, held in a prison camp in the Invaders' City to the south. Fannalhen and his council—which included Koelhe; Tawa, who was Narva's father; Rantalha, a stoic hunter; and Sharrabha, a huntress and liaison to the Keeper Tribe to the north—could not find common ground on which to agree regarding what to do with these runaways and decided to table the discussion for the morning.

However, a party of Invaders led by General Aritz a Mata arrived in the village in the middle of the night, having followed the runaways this far, and first questioned Sen as to their whereabouts over a game of cards, a request that Sen immediately rebuked. Aritz returned later with a greater and more furious intent, and when Fannalhen refused to give Shara and Ran up, Aritz shot him dead and instead stole away Brin and another villager, much to Sen's shock. Feeling she was to blame for her father's death and brother's capture, Sen resolved to go to the Invaders' City to the south and bring Brin back, despite her mother's objections. She left with Narva the next day, determined to prove her worth to the Tribe.

As the Stone Tribe's council, now led by Dennalhir, discussed what to do after Fannalhen's murder. Koelhe indicated her own intentions to claim leadership, pointing to Fannalhen and Dennalhir's supposed disregard and disrespect for Tribal customs after allowing their Eclipseborn daughter to remain in the village and therefore "dooming" the Tribe. Dennalhir banished Koelhe from the council.

Sen and Narva's journey south took them through the Forest, where they encountered the zealously territorial Wood Tribe. Upon meeting with the Tribe's Chieftain, Sen learned that the Invaders passed through the Forest with a bloody and violent disregard for the lives of the Wood Tribe, slaughtering them both times they passed through the Forest. At the same time, Sen began experiencing episodic visions of herself killing her father, the face of Aritz replaced with her own face. Narva attempted to quell her guilt as Sen confessed the degree of blame she placed upon herself for her father's murder and brother's kidnapping.

Sen and Narva reached the Invaders' City and, finding suitable disguises, set out to find the slave camp that was described to Sen by Ran before she left the village. To their surprise, they found a disoriented Brin wandering the streets of the City. They chased after him, but for some reason, Brin opted to return to the slave camp. Though confused at the decision, Sen freed her brother, deciding not to free the countless other Tribespeople who remained chained in the camp despite Narva's protests, and ran for the hills alongside Brin and Narva. Unbeknownst to them, however, a trap is deployed by an Invader soldier, and before they were able to get too far, Narva was shot dead by the Invaders while Sen and Brin were immediately captured and brought back to the City.

Meanwhile, Dennalhir and Tez began to grow suspicious of a possible coup by Koelhe. Tez inadvertently happened across a secret meeting with Koelhe and many of her co-conspirators, who also included Fann, Han'e—who was promised Koelhe's assistance in reclaiming the Sun Tribe territories— and Rantalha. Tez was dragged away by Rantalha, who explained that he could not abide by her parents' dismissal of Tribal customs in allowing her Eclipseborn sister to remain as part of the Tribe. Tez rushed back home to warn her mother, but before they were able to act, they were faced with Koelhe's attack. Though fighting hard against the odds, Dennalhir's loyalists were overrun, Dennalhir was captured, Koelhe installed herself as Chief, and Tez fled alongside Tawa and Sharrabha to recruit the assistance of the Lake Tribe to the west in order to reclaim the Stone Tribe.

Back in the City, Sen and Brin were paraded around the slave camp as a warning to the others not to attempt another escape. Sen and Brin were brought to an alleyway, where they faced an execution via a firing squad of four, but while Sen's innate Luck prevented any of the shots from hitting her, Brin was not so fortunate, and immediately died. While two of the Invader soldiers approach Sen to futilely attempt to shoot her, the other two soldiers turned on their fellows and shot them dead. The soldier who sprang the trap approached Sen and recognized the latent Eclipseborn power of Luck within her. The soldier dispelled an illusion, revealing herself as not only a Tribal woman named Kamataa, but also an Eclipseborn. Disregarding Brin's dead body entirely, Kamataa offered Sen an opportunity to learn from a fellow Eclipseborn.

THE FUTURE YET TO COME

In the year 1581 Anno Salvatoris, Lord Aritz a Mata returned to Ferranda for the first time in years, promising to give a lecture at the University. At the end of his lecture, he was admonished by a student who challenged him on the founding of Ferranda, questioning what happened to the Tribes who had once populated this land. Aritz disregarded the Tribes as little more than wicked spellbinders who could kill people with a single touch and worshipped animals as gods, and that he was glad to have banished them deep into the mountains after he claimed the land for the Acrarian Kingdom.

Upon returning to his Ferranda manor, Aritz found one of his pieces of memorabilia, an ornate flintlock pistol, missing from the trophy shelf within his chambers. In his search for the missing weapon, Aritz noticed a Tribal ornament placed on his desk, weighing down a handwritten letter pledging that the "Harvest" had never been forgotten. Aritz disregarded the letter but was drawn to the ornament, a pendant carved with a rune he recognized as being a Tribal symbol meaning "Memory." Touching the ornament, Aritz was forced to relive a moment at this estate in Acraria where he slaughtered the vast majority of his estate attendants and guards before brutally murdering his wife and children. Judging by comments made by those he killed, Aritz realized that this incident happened after his departure for Ferranda and that someone was framing him.

Before he could pursue that thread further, he heard the hammer of a pistol click behind him. The dissenting student from the lecture showed herself, promising that she was there to claim revenge against Aritz for her family. Aritz began to dismiss her claim, but the student immediately changed form, taking the shape of Aritz knew long ago. Someone who he knew to be dead.

The Children of the Black Moon

THE MEMORIES THAT HAVE COME TO PASS

In the year 1159 Anno Salvatoris, Kamataa underwent her Trial, but was revealed, to her surprise, to have been an Eclipseborn. The Keeper facilitator An Kehzan reacted to her with horror and sent a missive to the Lake Tribe Chief Azantt warning him of this fact. When Kamataa returned to her home in the eastern Lake Tribe, she found her parents, Taanta and Hetren, held in the grips of Fear by Azantt as punishment for keeping an Eclipseborn hidden all this time. Kamataa asserted that she passed not *the* Trial, but *a* Trial, and still had the right to challenge the Chief to a duel atop the Big Lake to assert her place in the Tribe. She emerged victorious against Azantt's champion, but the Chief disregarded the victory and impaled her with his spear and sent her to the depths of the Big Lake. Though it should have killed her, Kamataa washe ashore with her wound already healed, an Eclipseborn ability called the Draw that rapidly mends wound and extends life. Realizing the danger her parents are in, Kamataa rushed home to find Taanta and Hetren brutally killed. In response, Kamataa entered the Chief's house and killed him and his wife, leaving their son to scream for help, which Kamataa did not offer. She then fled the Lake Tribe village.

By the year 1166, Kamataa had been living in solitude in the fringes of the Forest, far from the zealous and watchful eyes of the Wood Tribe. Whilst hunting, she came across a small group wandering through the Forest and made to attack them, but was stopped when the group's leader, Ruhr, recognized her. Ruhr and Kamataa had grown up together in the Lake Tribe, until Ruhr mysteriously left some years before Kamataa's Trial. Ruhr explained he had to leave because it was discovered he was Eclipseborn, and he had since spent the years gathering other expelled Eclipseborn to form a "Tribe" of their own. Kamataa hesitantly joined this "Tribe," and was introduced to a former Stone Tribeswoman named Ziialhan, or Ziia, who also possessed the Eclipseborn ability of the Draw.

In 1216, Kamataa prowled the eastern Lake Tribe in search of marks from whom to steal Tribal pendants, after research done by Ruhr before his passing while hiding amongst the Keepers revealed secrets regarding the nature of the pendants. Kamataa stole the pendants of an old fishmonger and a hunter, watching both have a mental break as their connection to the gods was severed. Though she was to only seize those two pendants, she decided to pay a visit to the Chief's hut, where Azantt's son had grown up to be Chief. She watched him in his bed until her presence at last woke him, at which point she flashed him a sinister smile. Some time later, Kamataa rejoined Ziia on a hill overlooking the Lake villages and produced three pendants. Ziia at first questioned the extra pendant, and then noticed blood on Kamataa's neck.

In 1276, Kamataa was acting as a housekeeper for the western Lake Chief Noanet for the last decade amidst a period of testy relations between the two halves of the Lake Tribe. Though she outwardly professed familial warmth toward Noanet and his family, she was in truth awaiting Ziia's signal from the other side of the Lake to begin a new plan in earnest. When the time arose, Kamataa stole Noanet's pendant and watched him slowly be reduced to a mindless husk, and "accidentally" left an eastern adornment outside the room to frame the eastern Tribe. She met with Ziia outside the village and learned Ziia killed the eastern Chief, and they watched as the two sides of the Tribe emerged from their huts in calls for retribution.

In 1376, one hundred years after the Long War began, Kamataa drafted a peace agreement to be signed by the two Lake Chiefs, Ruwexi and Tenrir, dejected though she was that the Lake Tribe still endured despite her best efforts. Ziia assured her that the peace would not last, and that one day, whenever it may be, the fall of not just the Lake Tribe, but all the Tribes, would come.

In 1546, Kamataa and Ziia overlooked the Invader City, already a marvel even five years after their initial arrival in the Land. Kamataa admitted jealousy at how easily these Invaders subjugated the southern Tribes, but Ziia pointed out an opportunity for them to take advantage of if they wished to see the end of the Tribes, affirming that the enemy of their enemy was their friend.

In 1556, Kamataa patrolled the slave pits in the City when one day she decided to spurn loose two Haunted prisoners: Shara and Ran. She smiled to Ziia, knowing it will at last give Aritz the drive to push past the arboreal barrier of the Forest and finish what he started fifteen years prior.

THE EVENTS NOW TO COME

In the year 1556 Anno Salvatoris, Sen was face-to-face with Kamataa, a fellow Eclipseborn who had taken part in the execution of Sen's brother Brin while using the Tribal power of Illusion to disguise herself as a member of the invading Acrarian guard within the army of Aritz a Mata. Despite Sen's objections, Kamataa repeatedly offered Sen a place among her organization of Eclipseborn, which she called the Children of the Black Moon, asserting that Brin's execution was necessary, much to Sen's shock.

Having nowhere to go, Sen reluctantly accepted an offer to sleep in the barracks which house the Children, where she met the other members of the group while also learning that Kamataa, due to the abilities granted to her by the Moon, was over four hundred years old. She also learned that the members of the Children of the Black Moon were all expelled from their respective Tribes, often under traumatic circumstances, and the organization existed to bring an end to the Tribes.

In the course of her sleep, Sen triggered the recollections housed within Brin's Memory pendant, which Kamataa urged her to keep. After watching a series of Memories from the past few days, Sen realized that both her brother and her father Fannalhen did not hold her in any high regard, with Brin, particularly after his capture at the hands of the Acrarians, bemoaning her as the source of his misery and labeling her with the pejorative term Curseborn.

Realizing that those few who claimed to stand for her did so under false pretenses, Sen agreed to join the Children of the Black Moon, at which point Kamataa revealed to her the source of the taboo regarding Tribal pendants and their inherent boons: the pendants act as a symbiotic link between the wearer and the god to whom they correspond—the Bear, the Wolf, or the Owl—that the longer a person wears their pendant, the greater a dependency they develop to that power. When a pendant is removed, the wearer effectively loses a part of themselves, rendering themselves mindless to varying degrees dependent on the level of "dependency." Thus, Sen was given a number of pendants, while keeping Brin's Memory pendants, for her uses, which she used without fear of reprisal.

Shortly after Sen's commitment to the Children, Aritz ordered his army to ready for deployment to the north, having prepared plans to return to the north of the Land to overtake the remaining Tribal lands. Now under Illusion as an Acrarian soldier, Sen marched north and joins in battle in the Forest against the remnants of the Wood Tribe, but was shocked at the brutality by which the Children of the Black Moon reveled in the violence and carnage. Sen did kill the Chieftain of the Wood Tribe, though only as a mercy in response to his horrific battle wounds, but was too appalled to continue, especially after witnessing Kamataa shoot and kill several defenseless Wood Tribespeople at point blank range with delight.

Meanwhile, Tez, having survived Koelhe's successful coup of the Stone Tribe, journeyed to the west alongside Tawa and Sharrabha to enlist the help of the Lake Tribe to reclaim the Stone village and unite the north against the inevitable return of the Acrarian army, despite knowing the Tribe's propensity for infighting and internal strife. Tez met with the eastern Lake Tribe's chief Tenazt, who would offer the Tribe's help in exchange for Tez's own help, citing the Stone Tribe's lack of assistance in settling the Lake Tribe's own internal wars. Tenazt explained that Barrah, a Wolfsign with the Boon of Stealth, had recently been rendered mindless and his pendant was stolen. He suspected that the western Lake Tribe—who reside on the other end of the Big Lake—were responsible. Despite her frustration at being forced to search for a trinket, Tez realized she has no other options.

When Tez, Tawa, and Sharrabha readied to search the western Lake Tribe, the western Tribe's Chief, Yhaan, arrived and accused Tenazt of the same theft, noting that several of his people had fallen mindless with missing pendants as well. Tenazt claimed ignorance, but Yhaan challenged him to combat, citing Tenazt's ruination of the longest peace the Lake Tribe had known in a long time. Tez offered to champion for Tenazt as a sign of commitment of the Stone Tribe's commitment to Tenazt, but also under the pretense of wanting not to begin negotiations anew with Yhaan should Tenazt fall in combat.

The next day, Tez and Yhaan met in combat, matching each other in prowess. Tez gained an upper hand and was about to deliver a finishing blow before the challenge was interrupted by a messenger from the Wood Tribe, informing the Lake Chiefs of the Acrarian attack on the Forest and the near-extinction of the Wood Tribe. Tez resolved to return to the Stone village to challenge Koelhe, while Tenazt and Yhaan both offered her Lake fighters while they journeyed to the north to enlist the help of the Arrow Tribe for the same purpose.

Tez arrived with her new force of fighters and a large battle breaks out between Tez's loyalists, Koelhe's separatists—led by her son Fann—and the fighters of the Sun Tribe, led by their Chief Han'e, who had become frustrated by Koelhe not following through on her promise to reclaim the Sun lands to the south. In the midst of the battle, Tez fought her way to the hut in hopes of finding her mother, Dennalhir, and met with Rantalha in combat, besting and killing the defector outside her mother's hut. Fann and Han'e were locked in a fiery duel, and as Fann delivered a killing blow to Han'e, the Acrarian army arrived at the Stone village.

Battle shifted from between the factions of the Stone Tribe to focusing on the invading Acrarians. Tez fought her way into her mother's hut to find Dennalhir still alive, though still recovering from her wound suffered during the coup. Their reunion was interrupted by Ziialhan, who attempted to kill Dennalhir, but was stopped and killed by an Acrarian soldier, revealed to be Sen under Illusion. The three were relieved to see each other alive, promising to speak on Sen's company with the Acrarians later, and stepped outside to face the invading army. As they steeled themselves, Tenazt and Yhaan arrived with the Arrow Tribe, who pushed the Acrarians back in a victory for the Tribes.

Resolving that they would be able to defend themselves better in the mountains, the Tribes retreated to the Heart of the Land, meeting the Keepers deep in the True Heart, where the Bear, Wolf, and Owl resided. Sen confessed what she discovered about Brin and Fannalhen to her mother and sister, but they both admonished her for not realizing how much her father and brother truly loved her, and that those moments of frustration and anger were not indicative of how they truly felt about Sen. Sen also shared a moment with Tawa, speaking of Narva's death, with Tawa remarking how much his son loved her, and Sen confessing the same. The Tribes continued their defense preparations.

In the Acrarian camp, Kamataa was granted an audience with Aritz and revealed herself as native to the Land. She asserted her commitment to Aritz by giving him a battle knife imbued with Strength, granting him the power of the Bear should he wield it, if the need for it were to arise. She also asked him if he ever thought himself capable of killing a god.

The Acrarians marched deep into the Heart to meet the Tribes in combat. The Tribes' plan was led astray when Sen realized that they had been infiltrated by members of the Children of the Black Moon, who used Illusion to blend in among the northern Tribes. The Animal Deities, realizing the danger, broke free from their pedestals, the Owl flying off, the Wolf departing through the nearby woods, and the Bear angrily joining the battle. The Bear single-handedly defeated a significant portion of the Acrarian army, impervious to the Invaders' weapons. In a desperate maneuver, Aritz stabbed the Bear with the Strength-infused knife, felling the beast before delivering a killing blow.

As the Bear died, all of the connected Bearsigns, including Dennalhir, Fann, Tez, and many others, fell mindless, as though all of their pendants were removed, because of their loss of connection to the Bear. Standing next to Tez, Sen desperately put Brin's Memory pendant on her sister, the act keeping Tez from falling mindless.

As a stunned hush fell over the battlefield, Sen watched in horror as all of the Tribes' most adept fighters fall just as the Acrarian fighters began to regroup.

THE FUTURE YET TO COME

In the year 1581 Anno Salvatoris, Aritz was admonished by his assailant, a woman using Illusion to bear the appearance of Kamataa's Acrarian disguise, who continued to hold him at gunpoint in his Ferrandan chambers. The woman decried Aritz's "accomplishments" as nothing more than falsehoods serving only to inflate the man's ego and self-importance, destroying his collection of "trophies" in the process. The only thing he *was* responsible for was the complete eradication of the Tribes and their culture from the annals of history, and she promised to topple the empire and history he had created for himself.

Aritz defended his actions and affirmed that no matter what this woman hopes to unearth, none of it would serve a purpose, and history would remember him fondly for his accomplishments regardless. The assailant compared him to a fallen Acrarian scholar who had feigned his research on a supposed war hero who was nothing of the sort, using the comparison to emphasize that even if the world would continue to shine brightly upon Aritz's deeds in this lifetime, generations down the line may eventually feel differently, especially if they were informed of his actions during the Harvest, the details of which she demanded he divulge. Aritz looked at her with confusion, as the idea of the "Harvests" was Kamataa's, and began to question her true identity.

Dismissing the notion as myths and slander, Aritz pressed the assailant on who she really was, to which the woman admitted she had watched Kamataa die and hoped only her visage would have loosened Aritz's tongue. She warned Aritz to speak under the guise as one who *escaped* the Harvests, and was therefore one he should have feared entirely.

She professed that she was one of the lucky ones.

PROLOGUE

HEARD NO MORE

THE YEAR 1581 ANNO SALVATORIS
40 YEARS AFTER THE SETTLING

"Lucky, you say?"

Aritz's ears perked at the admission, the barrel of his flintlock but five paces from his forehead. The clattering of metal pails and heavy footsteps echoed from the lower floor of his manor, the clamor of citizens' revelry and seagulls' cawing sounding from outside the opened windows. Salt air wafted into the room heedless of invitation, the aroma of the inviting sea breeze mingling with the permeating stench of stagnant sweat accumulating in the tense environs.

The woman, this impostor, this phantom wearing Kama's skin, stood unperturbed at arm's length from Aritz, her red hair coming undone from a tight bun and dancing in front of her face in wispy strands. A trail of sweat streamed down the side of her forehead, the heat of the day at last overtaking the interior of the manor.

Her eyes betrayed no fear, no misgivings about what led her to this moment. What led her to mercilessly slaughter Aritz's wife and children. What led her to impersonate a comrade-in-arms, traitor though she was. What led her to stand before him, his own weapon held to his head, with nary a trace of remorse, regret, or recompense.

A savage she is, he thought. *Well and truly, just as the lot of them.*

"How lucky do you feel, earnestly?" Aritz asked, raising an eyebrow.

The woman did not respond. She merely stood with a present scowl, the orange hue of the waning sunlight glowing behind her, casting her expression in a blanket of shadows. The shattered remains of Aritz's trophy shelf crunched and crackled beneath the heel of her boots.

Aritz grunted with affirmation. "Fortune hardly smiles upon you. You're nothing more than a revenant of a people long gone from this world."

"No," his assailant answered, her nostrils flaring. "I am but the long shadow you cast from the moment you took our land from us. I am the remnant of what was lost, and the echo of all the voices yet to come."

"And what voices still remain to sound your supposed battle cry? Hmm?" Aritz licked his lips, the leather of his chair growing hot against his sweat-slickened back. "So few remain who hold fast to their faculties, after all."

The subtlest of winces flashed in the woman's face.

I have you now. "Then I ask once more: how lucky do you feel? How must it feel to be the last among your people, perhaps one of a dwindling number clean of mind and free of will? Do you feel *proud* that your people are little more than mindless husks, that they are relegated to but a vegetative suggestiveness, that they can do no more than follow orders to which they're given without any drive or wherewithal to protest or question? Am I to feel sorrow for you, that atop this pile of heathens and savages, you would deign to say that I am a monster merely for doing as the Savior bid of me?"

The stone expression upon his assailant's face at last began to crack.

Finding comfort in this, Aritz leaned back. He crossed one leg over the other, clasping his fingers together as he rested his elbows upon the armrests, a grin creasing his lips. "The Savior, through me, demanded a use for your people, beasts though they may be, for even the lowly cattle provides us with succor. What you call the 'Harvest,' I would call...a blessing."

"A *blessing*?" the woman responded with incredulity. "You would—"

"*Yes*, I would," Aritz asserted. "Look upon what remains of your people and tell me that those mindless husks, those poor sods with not a thought to carry them, at least are deserving of the release that was provided their brethren. It is a disservice to your people to keep them in that sordid state."

The woman scoffed dismissively. "And I am to *thank* you, then?"

Aritz flashed a wide smile. "Now you understand. I did only that which was necessary, and I would do it again, and again, and *again*." Slowly, he rose to his feet, his hands clasped behind his back. He took a tentative step forward, closing the gap between them by a pace.

The flintlock ever so slightly began to waver in the woman's furious hand, her fingers wrapped tightly along the grip.

He basked in the remaining light, the orange glow illuminating his face while keeping the woman's in the shadows. "I will speak of your Harvest," Aritz said, amusement rising in his throat. "And I will revel in the telling."

CHAPTER ONE

THE DOGS OF WAR

All Sen could do was stifle a sob into her palm.

Silence echoed in substantial volumes across the battlefield, not a word nor cry uttered amongst the gathered combatants. As she surveyed the scene in the canyon, Sen could only assume that what was coursing through her was making its way through both the Tribespeople and Invaders alike.

Shock. Pure, stunning shock.

A god felled by a mortal hand. And the cost that came with it.

She watched as Aritz slowly backed away from the Bear's lifeless body, perhaps even himself riled into complete silence. The General of the Invaders' forces did not seem to take his eyes off the blade he had just driven into the god's skull, the steel glistening with deep-red blood. *I would have thought that bastard to be celebrating,* Sen thought. *But here he is, dumbfounded with the rest of us.* He merely took one halting step backwards after another, the knife quivering in his grip, his teeth gritted. All the arrogance that Sen had ever seen him with, all of it gone in an instant.

The mountainous winds howled their grief, nearer to a scream than a gust. Pellets of heavy snow pelted Sen's face and coat, red falling with the white, the sky itself crying tears of blood. Her hands, raw from the cold, gripped the shaft of her spear tighter, her mind averse to touching the Deatharm that remained sheathed in the holster around her thigh. As wrong as it had felt before, it only felt more so to touch the tool of an Invader. The weapon of a people who had managed to fell the very essence of strength and bravery among the Tribes.

Sen followed the path of the snow as the wind carried it in the direction of the pedestals dedicated to the three Animal Deities. In the chaos of everything, she hadn't realized that the Wolf and the Owl had departed, or retreated, or whatever they may have done. All three pedestals were empty, regardless. The Bear's just felt all the emptier.

And with the host of Bearsign warriors all collapsed before it, their minds broken and frozen in an instant at the god's murder, the scene was simply horrendous.

It provided for an involuntary cease-fire, if only because all present were at a loss for what next to do.

In those initial moments, Sen could hear the slow reloading of the Invaders' Deatharms, but no one shouted orders. No one seemed eager to press a charge against a suddenly handicapped opponent. None of them understood the reasoning for it.

But the same could be said of the remaining Tribespeople, Sen knew.

Kamataa's words kept repeating in her head the longer she stared at the felled Bearsigns. *When one is exposed to the Boon granted to them by their respective Deity, they grow...inseparable from it. It only grows worse the longer they are exposed to it.* To Sen, it stood to reason that no one knew that truth. She wouldn't have believed it herself if not for this moment, if not for all the mindless husks she had encountered in the City's slave camp during her failed rescue attempt of her brother.

This was Kamataa's plan all along. To strike down the gods where they stand, Ziia had said. She managed to make it possible. But how?

A grumble from behind broke her focus from the silent battlefield and back toward her sister. Tez had remained on all fours, still unable to sit back up under her own power. The break from the Bear's connection had clearly sapped her, but not quickly enough that Sen couldn't do anything to stop her sister from losing her mind entirely. As Tez heaved a handful of rasped breaths, a new pendant dangled from her neck. A new connection to a new god. It was the only thing keeping Tez's faculties intact.

For what seemed the first time, it was their brother's turn to protect them. Brin's Memory pendant glinted against the snow gathering atop it, the heavy winds pounding the ornament against Tez's shoulders and chest. When Sen had taken her departed brother's pendant as a memento, Tribal customs and taboos be damned, it never once crossed her mind that it would wind up saving someone's life. How little she had known then. And how little she had anticipated.

Sen gently grasped her sister by the shoulders and helped her up to a seated position. Tez's eyes were still moderately glazed over but seemed to be regaining some clarity and focus. Her gaze was narrowed, trailing off toward the snow falling past Sen's reach, the bruises beneath her eyes still vibrant from the broken nose she suffered during the fight against Koelhe's followers in the Stone Tribe village. Blood spattered and trailed down her face, both her own—primarily from the reopened wound along the bridge of her nose—and that of her fallen foes. She was still breathing heavily but she had started to steady herself. A trembling hand reached up to grasp the new pendant around her neck, a disconcerted and frightened expression strewn across her face.

Tez lifted the pendant to eye level and examined the rune, her eyes growing wide. "S-S-S-Seeennn..." she stammered, anxiety rising in her voice. She turned the ornament towards Sen, nearly to the point of hyperventilating. "What-What-What d-did...what did you..." She tugged hard on the pendant, the chain pulling taut against the back of her neck.

Quickly, Sen grabbed her sister's hands, prying the ornament loose before it could snap. "Tez, stop, stop, stop!" she screamed, afraid to let go. "It's the only thing keeping you alive right now, so leave it!"

A tear escaped Tez's eyes as she listlessly turned her head one direction and the next, unperturbed by the snow squalls turning her skin a raw red. "Why did you, Sen..." she whispered. "Why is it—"

"I'll explain everything later, but I need you to trust me!" Sen released Tez's hands and took her sister by the shoulders once more, forcing her to look upon her in the eyes as best as she could manage. "And I need you to listen. We have to get you somewhere to acclimate. Here is not the place."

Tez blinked unsteadily, squinting off into the distance. "The...the b-b-battle..." She shrugged her shoulders out of Sen's grip, her attention turned to something sticking out of the snow, a steel point still coated in swaths of red. "Sp...spear..."

"Tez, listen to me!" Sen said sharply, the words hissing out of her mouth. "You are in *no* condition for that right now. None of the Bearsigns are. We need to get you out of here."

Flashing a quizzical look, Tez appeared to be concentrating intently on forming her own speech again. "No...Bear...signs?"

Words weren't necessary. Sen could only shake her head.

"But...that...means..." Recognition seemed to return to Tez's mind. The glaze over her eyes was vanishing, the pale complexion of her face disappearing, and a mixture of fear and consternation settled into her brow. "That means...M...Mo...Muh—"

Sen grimaced and slowly turned her head, the battlefield still gripped in the throes of deafening silence. The Invaders had remained frozen, shakily reloading their Deatharms but offering no sign of pressing forward otherwise, while the remaining Tribal fighters huddled about the collapsed Bearsigns, in equal measure to protect those who fell and to stand tall amongst those who remained. Deep within that throng, amidst the mass of shattered minds, Sen could make out the subtle motion of a woman still holding on. Still fighting, despite the state to which she had been reduced.

Clenching her eyes shut, tears welling behind a closed dam, Sen gritted her teeth and slowly walked along the ridge, the red snow crunching underfoot. With one hand clenched tightly around the shaft of her spear, pistol holstered at her thigh, she fished through her coat pocket, hoping and praying that she would still be greeted with the cold touch of carved metal. As her eyes shot back open and the dam broke, she felt relief at the touch of the Illusion pendant still deposited in her pocket, a token of her brief betrayal of her people, a reminder for what she needed to redeem herself.

And a beacon that could save at least one person.

Mother, she thought, not breaking her sight from the image of her mother writhing in the war-torn snow, surrounded by her brothers- and sisters-in-arms. *I'm coming.*

"Sehhh...Sen..." Tez's voice just barely carried over the squalls.

Sen stopped, turning her head over shoulder, and saw her sister rising unsteadily to her feet, one foot slipping out from beneath.

Planted in the snow, pelted by the furious snow, Tez reached out her hand as though pleading for Sen to remain.

"I can save her," Sen said, unsure if she could be heard over the storm. "I *have* to save her." She offered a placating gesture with her hand, beckoning Tez to stay put, and immediately turned on her heel and sprinted as best as she could through the accumulated piles of snow, kicking up heavy tufts of white and red with each strenuous step.

Bodies littered the pathway, traitors and loyalists alike. The surviving Wolfsigns along the ridge watched her manic approach, all of them still hunkered down with arrows half-nocked, faces frozen in shock just as they collected ice in their bloodstained locks of hair.

Faintly, a rumbling crack echoed over the howl of the wind, enough to rouse the attention of the surviving parties. Sen's lungs protested as she forced herself to move faster, unsure of the cause of the noise, but unwilling to stand pat to find out. She shoved gawking hunters out of the way, shouted for others to clear a path for her, surely bearing every image of a madwoman. She cared little for the watchful eyes, regardless of whether they belonged to Tribe or Invader.

The ridge sloped downwards as the valley's mouth came into closer view, the Land still screaming heavy squalls down upon them in its anguish. Through the dense barrier, Sen could just barely see the attention of those in the valley shift to the west, away from the sight of her. A louder crack beyond the tree line startled her, causing her to lose her footing. Her ankle rolled, her legs falling out from under her. She landed ass-first against the slick packed snow, a jolt running through her as her body slid and rolled down the slope.

Sen grunted in pain, her vision spotty as she stopped rolling. She pushed herself to a knee, grateful she did not inadvertently gut herself with her own spear. As the dizziness wore off, she patted the outside of her coat, feeling the packed snow that had filled her pocket, along with the Illusion pendant that still thankfully remained inside. Using her spear as a crutch, she howled as she rose back to her feet, a fire running through her ankle, though not so intense that she could not put weight upon it. The pain didn't matter. Nothing would matter if she couldn't make it to her mother.

Despite the agony, Sen forced a run, feeble as it was as she limped through the snow, some of it already piling as high as her calves. With each step, she hissed in pain. Each hiss became angrier, almost feral, as though only the rage could carry her forward.

Turned backs were all that she saw in front of her. Loud thumps echoed in the woods ahead. Snowbirds fled in droves, braving the storm. Crashes followed snaps followed creaking wood. Dread coursed through Sen, just as the Wolfsigns ahead nocked their arrows, the Invaders aiming their Deatharms. The wall of Tribespeople surrounding the fallen Bearsigns grew so close. She cared little for what was approaching. Damn the pain in her ankle, damn the danger, damn whatever approached.

Voices rose indistinctly over the next blast of howling snow. The Wolfsigns diverted their attention from the woods, redirected their nocked arrows toward the host of Invaders. For their part, the Invaders' attention was evenly dispersed between the noise growing ever louder in the forest and the arrows threatening to rain upon them. Orders were bellowed over the wind, the stretching of bowstrings near enough to grate in Sen's ears. The distant thumping grew more rhythmic, falling into a steady meter. Screams echoed over the wind, the roar of battle threatening to return. The Tribal wall was but paces away.

The fire in Sen's ankle burned and burned and burned, but she pushed through it until she was three steps away, two steps, one. She reached out toward a kneeling Wolfsign, Arrow Tribe from the look of her. "Out of the way!" she screamed. But it wasn't enough.

Luck surged through her as the sound of the Invaders' Deatharms cracked the sky, the sound of bullets whizzing past her ears. The plucking of bowstrings answered the call in unison, feathered tufts breaking the path of the heavy snow.

And a thunderous snarling roar silenced all—the Invaders, the Tribes, the very wind itself. The arboreal barrier broke in an explosion of snow and gargantuan splinters. The Wolfsigns nearest to Sen fanned out, knocking her off balance, sending her rolling backwards through the snow away from the impending fray. When she stopped, all she could see past the dense snow squalls was a mountainous blur of dark grey fur blitzing through the air.

Aritz had never seen a beast so massive.

His heart skipped a beat as an enormous wolf perched itself atop the canyon ridge, bearing fangs the length of an Acrarian broadsword. Its eyes appeared to glow against the heavy snow, a glimmer of malicious amber breaking the storm.

The men about him froze in place, all loath to raise their weapons and attack. He flashed a sneer at them all, wordless though all intent of the expression blazing in his gaze.

Wide, cowardly eyes, a sea of them, all met his, the wordless silence speaking all it needed to. Despite him, despite the authority Aritz held over these cravens, they denied him all the same.

The wolf leaned back on its haunches and leapt, descending back to the earth in a wide crescent arc, snow billowing off its grey fur like a cascading waterfall of ice. Its front paws landed squarely atop two lads at the mouth of the valley—two who had elected not to stand their ground against the charging bear who now lay dead at his own feet. The two cowards had no chance. The wolf's weight crushed them, blood and bone spurting underfoot in an instant, even as the beast itself made no noise upon impact.

Aritz snarled, calmly reloading his pistol, and walked over to the ursine corpse before him. The blade bequeathed to him by Kama still jutted out from the bear's skull, a makeshift sheath for the wicked weapon. But in this moment, he was willing to use all the tools at his disposal and offer his repentance to the Savior at a later date. This departed beast was the Savior's will, and Aritz would take up his Lord's blade no matter how many times he was asked.

He gripped the blade's hilt tightly and sharply pulled, the steel scraping against dense, reinforced bone. The blade, once a glimmering silver, left the beast's body a deep crimson, tainted by the taste of heathen blood. Turning on his heel, he held the blade toward the wolf, who silently bared its teeth, its fur standing straight and rigid as icicles, its front paws digging into the ice and stone below, ready to strike. Digging his palm into the blade's hilt, Aritz drew a deep breath, flashing his own teeth, ready to challenge another pretender god. "One god has been felled by my hand already today," he said softly, somehow assured that the wolf would hear him. "Dare you to test your own luck, beast?"

As though in response, the wolf shot to the side, swinging its enormous head, headbutting a pair of his men with enough force that they met a bloody end against the valley walls. A tuft of hot breath puffed from its snout as it stalked from side to side at the valley's mouth, offering no means of passage for Aritz or his men.

The only way out was through.

"Charge." Aritz's voice was near to gravel, the rasp of the day's orders vibrating the length of his throat.

A meek yelp of protest squeaked in his ear. "But-but sir! We can't—"

Aritz turned on his heel and grabbed the naysayer by the collar. His eyes narrowed, anger flaring through him as he met the man's eyes. Lieutenant Pock-Face. Who else would give voice to such cowardly insubordination?

Pock-Face's lips quivered, but he quickly offered a salute. "We need to fall back, sir! The beast will give us no quarter!"

Holding the blade to the lieutenant's throat, Aritz snarled as though he were the beast. "You will have more to fear of me than of that creature should you disobey my orders again, Lieutenant. I gave an order, and you will obey that order. Do you understand?"

The lieutenant offered only a squeak as some sort of foul smell exuded from him.

"Fouling yourself is not an answer, Lieutenant. Do. You. Understand?" Aritz could feel himself growing red in the face.

Pock-Face tenderly nodded, careful of the steel at his throat. "Yes, sir," he said.

Good enough, Aritz thought. Withdrawing the blade, he shoved Pock-Face backwards, watching the rigid posture the lieutenant was suddenly forced to adopt. Sneering, Aritz looked back toward the wolf, the beast still pacing along the valley's opening. He took two steps forward, holding the blade outward, drawing in a breath. With eyes narrowed in defense of the howling wind, Aritz bellowed, "Finish what we started and fell that beast!"

Rifles locked in place as a host of soldiers rushed forward, screaming at the wolf as some measure to exhibit their undying courage. Aritz stood and watched them, fully aware that they were all rushing to their demise, but caring little, so long as he was the one to deliver the killing blow to that monster.

The wolf roared in acceptance of the challenge, pouncing at the charging contingent, its fangs moving faster than the soldiers could fire their own weapons. Steel teeth tore into the front lines, men and women alike disappearing in a mist of blood, bodies thrown apart in pieces, limbs removed from their respective hosts and raining down on the battlefield unceremoniously. Even as the song of rifles and pistols chorused against the storm, the bullets did little more than bounce off the beast's flesh, much as they did to the charging bear.

From behind the wolf, the glint of arrowheads broke through the snow squalls and fell upon Aritz's soldiers, felling them before the beast even had a chance at them. A surge of anxiety passed through him as he watched noble Acrarians—the truest followers of the Savior's will—fall so unceremoniously to these vile creatures. If the bear's assault was indicative of the savages' violent rage, then that of the wolf was some measure of their cunning capacity to kill.

Aritz caressed the cold steel of Kama's blade, the bear's blood running thick along its length, and drew a deep breath, soaking in the strength it had so recently instilled within him.

He awaited the flow, closing himself off to the anguished screams of his soldiers meeting their end at the jaws of this supposed god. Reinforcements passed him by as he remained at the rear guard, patiently awaiting his moment to strike, baiting the wolf to charge him like the dumb beast it was. But arrows continued to rain down, blood continued to spray, lives continued to be returned to the Savior's embrace.

And the flow of strength did not course through him.

Furiously, he looked around him, watching the countless soldiers rushing to their inevitable demise, knowing full well the jaws of death that awaited them. He watched plumes of smoke erupt from their rifles as they unsuccessfully attempted to pierce the beast's devilish and invulnerable hide. Some drew their own blades in an attempt to carve into the wolf's flesh, but met nothing but their own ends before they were even within striking distance. One by one they all passed Aritz by.

But he could not find Kama among the bunch. Her vibrant red hair should have stood out against all, and yet that beacon did not appear. It was a beacon he sorely needed. A beacon of answers. For there was only one among them who could inform him why this devilish tool no longer worked, and she decided suddenly to desert him.

He snarled, pacing slowly toward the wolf, his face pelted with heavy squalls as they mixed with the mists of departed Acrarian life. Shoving one soldier after another from his path, he held his pistol steady, praying for aim to fire true, and pulled the trigger.

The flight of the bullet was short, the winds pushing it from the intended target of the wolf's skull, instead leading it to be casually swatted away by its tail as though it were shooing a troublesome fly.

Even as the Acrarian assault continued to rain down upon it, the wolf ceased its own offensive, save for kicking away those who found their way inside its guard. As bullets and steel bounced off its thick hide, its jaws dripping red with Acrarian blood, the beast appeared focused in Aritz's direction, its amber gaze cutting once more through the storm. It slowly paced toward him, its head lowered, but its eyes not breaking from him.

Soldiers meekly parted from its path, a parting of the blue Acrarian waves, even as they feebly continued their assault only to be pelted by the raining arrows. In a rush, Aritz loaded his pistol and fired another quick shot at the wolf, but the effort did little more than agitate it further. The beast's pace quickened, snow crunching underfoot, desperate pleas echoing about him in a round, one scream following another as men and women were knocked aside, blood spraying, shots firing, arrows descending, and lupine footsteps growing louder and louder and quicker and quicker.

Aritz met the challenge, holstering his pistol and charging forward with blade extended, ready to pounce in his own measure. He drew another deep breath, hoping desperately for the surge of strength to return, finding none of it remaining, his feet leaping forward in a mighty bound, meeting that of the wolf as they flew toward each other, one assured to meet their end at the end of the arc. *O Savior, mighty and true,* he prayed, *may Your guiding hand see fit to—*

A snarl broke him from his prayer, his arm jerked, and in a blur, he was tumbling through a crowd of soldiers who gratefully broke his fall, even if the effort broke them. Dazed, Aritz pushed himself back to his feet, his vision spotty as the immediate effects of whiplash overtook him. A set of hands held him up, but he shoved them away, grimacing and growling all the while. The muscles in his arm protested as he rose his hand again, eager to draw the blade once more.

But his hand was empty.

He slapped the side of his head, quelling some of the dizziness, and gritted his teeth as the wolf turned its gaze back toward him.

In its mouth was his blade.

The size of the steel was almost comically small relative to the rest of the beast's head, bearing a resemblance to little more than a dinner knife, but the wolf did not seem keen to let it go. It almost seemed ready to *use* it.

Before Aritz could comprehend that possibility, the wolf charged again, swinging its jaws towards him, the arc of the blade just passing over Aritz's head as he ducked underneath the strike, the steel kiss instead opening the throats of the two soldiers who had held him upright. Aritz rolled as quickly as he could from the striking beast, searching for his pistol, but his arm protesting the sudden movement. A tuft of gray fur thwacked him in the face, the wolf's ice-encrusted tail searing his skin with burning ice, blood pouring out from the gashes it drew.

Another set of arms shoved him backwards as a host of soldiers lined up to guard him against the wolf's continued assault. The lupine god spun around on its heels, the path of its turning head sending the tip of the blade through a series of throats and skulls, blood spraying the snow and ice below like paint spatter. Bodies tumbled together, collapsing in on one another, the wolf glowering upon them all with spite and malice, all the world's evils instilled in this one beast, this beast these savages worshiped as a god.

Aritz dove for a deposited rifle, aiming and firing just as he withdrew his own flintlock pistol and performed the same. As the bullets predictably bounced off the wolf's body, a successive hail of arrows pierced the earth, puncturing stone and flesh alike, Aritz's arms scored by their edges as they grazed through his overcoat. He grunted in pain, sucking in a sharp breath, and steeled himself as the wolf dove for him, the blade just passing him by as he ducked underneath the beast's enormous frame. Still clinging to the rifle, its ammunition spent, he swung the weapon as he would a war hammer, just like the legendary Sir Satarias of the Second Acrarian Civil War of decades before, hoping to knock the wolf off-balance.

He may as well have been hammering a wall. The force of impact jolted the rifle loose from Aritz's grip, the weapon flying into the surrounding crowd, and yet the wolf was hardly impeded by the attack. It kicked its front legs back as though it were digging, Aritz evading its claws even as chunks of reddened snow and ice assaulted him. He rolled out from under the beast, but before he could even begin to think what next to do, he was lifted off his feet, sent hurdling through the air toward the mountains' southern slopes, the icy impact of the wolf's heavy tail sending a torrent of pain through Aritz's spine.

Though his landing was cushioned by the depth of the fallen snow, the pain did not forget him. Blood still poured down the gash in his cheeks from the initial attack by the beast's tail. His limbs felt twice as heavy, a fire burning through his spine. Hapless soldiers continued their futile assault on the beast whilst evading volleys of arrows, and all of them met the same end. Aritz bunched his fists, damning the pain in so doing, and as reinforcements filed in beside him, he growled and uttered words he never believed he ever would.

"Retreat."

A soldier to his right craned her head toward him, eyes wide with shock—though Aritz could see a modicum of relief in them as well. "Did I hear you correctly, sir?"

Aritz snarled, not even dignifying it with a response. He just turned and walked away.

After a moment's pause, he heard the cries for retreat echoing behind him, a flurry of movement thundering behind him as Acrarian soldiers—the greatest warriors in the entirety of the Homeland, the arm to wield the hammer of the Kingdom—ran in fearful solace toward the south, some leaving their discarded weapons behind, all bearing wounds ranging from superficial to horrid. If Aritz was not in as much pain as he was…he felt as though he would run along with them.

But instead, he hazarded a last glance over his shoulder, at the bloodthirsty beast who had felled his men with such ease. It gave no chase. It merely spat out the blade and sat amidst the carnage, staring angrily at Aritz.

When it tilted its head back and howled into the storm, Aritz let loose a shudder, disgust and relief passing over him in equal measure. He had never experienced such defeat.

But he still had his life.

A billow of red hair caught his attention as he drew closer to the mountain path, where the hastily constructed caravans began their treacherous descent to the war camp. Aritz growled and narrowed his gaze at Kama as she leaned casually against the rock wall, enclosing herself from the fury of the storm.

Aritz rushed her, pinning her to the wall by the strength of his forearm, but she showed no fear nor regret in her gaze. If anything, there was simply amusement. "I should hang you as a deserter," he threatened, his voice reduced to a gravely nothing.

Kama smirked, tilting her head. "It was a tactical retreat, Aritz. One you should have taken when the wolf showed its head."

He looked back toward the valley, where one god died but another still lived. "Your blade failed me."

"I would say it did exactly what it was meant to do. You are a god-slayer now, Aritz."

"And yet still one roams this earth."

"Two, actually," Kama said, looking at her nails with disinterest. "That blade's power diminished the moment you drove it through the bear's skull."

"And you did not see fit to inform me of this fact?"

"I informed you of exactly what you needed to know. But fear not. This is but the beginning. I still have but more tools to offer the Sword of the Savior." She flashed a grin and forced Aritz's arm off of her, shielding herself from the snow squalls as she descended the slope.

Aritz growled, clenching his fists. "Mislead me again and the Savior's Sword may fall upon you."

Kama continued to grin as she looked over her shoulder. "You are not the first to threaten me thusly, and yet here I still breathe. Now, come along."

His gaze widened at being ordered to follow like a pet. But the dogs of war had been loosed, and he would require all within his power to pen them again. He wiped away the flowing blood from his face, flicking the smeared red upon his hands down toward the marred snow, and descended the mountain slope, the weight of defeat disgusting him to his core.

The Arrow Tribe screamed their distinctive victory cries as the Invaders retreated down the mountains, the victorious proclamations echoing amidst the other Tribes' warriors in short order. For Sen, it was a relief to have the momentary respite while the Invaders, somehow impossibly, departed to lick their wounds.

But it was also relieving to know she could finally shove her way through the wall of Wolfsigns and into the throng of collapsed Bearsigns. The entire ordeal lasted but minutes, it seemed; the Wolf's sheer ferocity, coupled with the arrow volleys, was more than enough to drive the Invaders back. But they were also an incredibly long handful of minutes while Sen waited for that protective wall to break apart, to reveal the rows upon rows of felled warriors within.

Against the backdrop of celebratory screams, Sen parsed through the frozen faces of the Bearsign warriors. Many of them were faces she did not know, whether from other Tribes or merely one from her own Tribe with whom she never interacted or encountered. It was disheartening to look upon: the very strength and backbone of the Tribes felled in an instant. Alive, but not there. They may as well have joined the departed souls in the Otherworld, for this seemed a much crueler fate.

Slowly, she stepped over the fallen bodies, careful not to step on anyone, despite there being stretches where the warriors had simply collapsed in on each other. It was a haunting sight, to see them still draw breath and yet appear so far gone.

Her mother had been so easy to spot from atop the ridge, but down here, she may as well have been attempting to find a needle in a haystack. The frozen expressions all looked the same after a while, the rasped and pained breaths instilling in Sen a desire to abandon the search entirely and accept the inevitable.

No, she assured herself. *It worked for Tez, and it will work for Mother. I have to find her.* She patted her pocket, relieved that the Illusion pendant still rested within its contents.

Step by step, she scanned the various faces, finally finding faces she recognized. The great Keeper guardian An Rhan, his weight supported only by his spear still planted in the ground. The Lake Chief Tenazt, once ferocious despite his advanced age, his face now exhibiting a serene calm betrayed by the gaping hole in his throat; and beside him, his counterpart Yhaan, or what remained of the giant man after his face appeared bashed in. She even spotted Hollow nearby, his face matching his name as it appeared a bullet passed through it. Part of her wanted to spit on his corpse. *Hard to kill, my ass,* she thought. *Just a bullet to the brain will do it. Isn't that right, Ziia?*

So distracted she was by her temporary comrade that she tripped over a nearby body, hissing in further pain as her mangled ankle got caught in the crevices of two departed warriors. When she pulled herself free, cursing under her breath, she realized that one of the bodies belonged to Fann. Sen rose to her feet and looked down at him, the feelings welling within her entirely too complicated. He had once been such a close friend to her...and then saw fit to make her life absolute hell. That he was in equally dire straits as Koelhe felt like well-deserved retribution...but it still pained her to see him in such a state.

Kneeling down, she slapped him in the face three successive times, hoping that some external stimulus would restore some of his mental faculties. When nothing happened beyond mindless groans, she slapped his face again and again, each time doing little to remedy the situation until finally she had to stop herself, realizing that it was becoming less about reviving her former friend, and simply more about the act of slapping him.

Sen stood back up, clenching her eyes shut, grimacing in disbelief, until finally she heard to her left a distinctive groan, a voice she would always remember until the end of her days. There was no stopping the tears, nor did she have any attempt to stop them. All she could do was follow the sound, her legs quivering with every step, her ankle screaming with agony, until she finally fell to her knees beside her mother's body, spear still in the hand of the mighty warrior, but face frozen in the same shock as everyone else.

Her hands trembling, Sen reached into her pocket and withdrew the Illusion pendant, bringing the ornament to her lips with a tender kiss. She whispered a soft prayer to the Wolf and the Owl and whichever gods may still have been listening to her and looped the chain around Dennalhir's neck. Sen pressed the ornament into her mother's chest, the tremors traveling up her arms as she pushed harder and harder.

But no matter how hard she pressed, no matter how much she tried to force it...Dennalhir's expression did not change. It was too late. Beneath the red warrior paint of the Bearsign, the great Dennalhir, matriarch of the Stone Tribe, was gone.

"Please..." Sen murmured under her breath, her tears nearly freezing to her face from the force of the storm. "Please, Mother. Please..."

Her pleas were lost behind her heavy sobs. She reluctantly pulled her hands away from the pendant, its effect lost entirely on her mother, and buried her face into her hands, the snow piling high atop her. She felt a hand on her shoulder, and she didn't need to remove her face from her palms to know it was Tez.

They said nothing, for there was nothing that could be said. They just held each other, the storm howling around them, their tears turning to ice, and as the victorious exaltations continued around her, Sen could not help but wonder what was there to celebrate when they had just lost so much in an instant.

CHAPTER TWO

Sorrows

The Year 1556 Anno Salvatoris
15 Years After the Invasion

Over the course of the day following the battle, a vague memory of normalcy cast itself over the True Heart of the Land. It was quiet. It was calm. It was peaceful.

But Sen could see the façade for what it was. A mask collectively worn not only by the Tribes but also by the very world around them.

Nature mourned, but it knew not how to properly show it. Gentle flurries of snow cascaded down to the earth as though the skies were weeping, blanketing the scars of death that still lingered underneath. The once pristine hallows of this sacred plane, of this divine enclave most holy, had never been witness to such horridness. It was a place of worship, of communion. Where the bridge connecting the mortal world and the realm of the gods was constructed, never to be destroyed.

But suddenly, the True Heart felt a little less sacred, a little less holy, not only to Sen, but clearly to all those who survived the battle, as well. Words were unnecessary, but following the Invaders' retreat, they were also scarce. And in the wake of the Bear's defeat and death, no words could be relayed that could possibly deter any waves of fear hovering over the valley, threatening to crest and crash at any given moment. The air about the survivors spoke in the same manner: if a god could be felled so easily, what hope did any of them have?

Sen sat atop the ridge overlooking the valley, near to where she had positioned herself before the world cried havoc around her. For the better part of the last hour, she was entranced by the action happening below, her spear resting listlessly against her forehead, the pistol discarded in the packed snow beside her.

"ONE! TWO! THREE! PUSH!" called a voice below, one of the Fens from the Arrow Tribe, most likely, though Sen had not yet discerned the difference between Osenta and Poven.

At the call, a collective grunt and groan echoed through the canyon as the group once again gave a mighty push to the Bear's lifeless corpse. A path of red snow trailed in their wake, the smear that had stained the ground below the god's opened throat and skull cutting a swath through the freshly fallen white.

Since the Invaders' retreat the day before, efforts were immediately underway to return the Land's fallen protectors to the earth while also provided for the Bearsigns whose minds were destroyed by the slaying of the Bear. Existing tents and dwellings were repurposed to house those fractured souls, and one by one, the Bearsign warriors were carried inside.

For Sen, it felt...strange to be on the helping end of the task. Granted, she had a mother to tend to, an emblem of courage who had been reduced to nothing. But she also felt immediately responsible for it happening. *I had the opportunity*, she had thought. *I had the chance to...stop her. To stop all of them. And I didn't.*

No one had raised it as an issue. No one had raised anything in the way of concern, misgivings, or transgressions. All that mattered was to remove these Bearsigns—mindless as they were, but still cruelly alive nonetheless—from the bitter cold. Whatever happened after that could be discussed later, once everyone had a chance to breathe.

Once everyone had a chance to reflect on how they still kept their own lives.

And though the field was cleared of the unfortunate ones with minds in disrepair, there was still a large matter to consider. What to do with the Bear. There was no precedent set for burying a god's perished body. But it was universally agreed upon that the Bear could not remain motionless in the valley. It had to go elsewhere.

It was Fen-Osenta who suggested they bring the god to its rightful place upon its shrine, and there was no argument to the contrary. Sen had been unsure whether the shakiness in the Fen's voice was due to his own disbelief at the topic, or if he was still in shock at his brother Detu's death during the battle. She could only assume it was a task that would enable him not to think of the loss for a little while. That was something she understood all too well lately.

How many were continuing to push the Bear's corpse was beyond Sen's ken, but it seemed as though whenever someone stepped away or collapsed from exhaustion, another immediately jumped in to take their place. But the process had been slow and laborious regardless of the number; in the hour that she had observed the act from above, they had still only made it roughly two-thirds of the way through the valley, their efforts impeded by the god's sheer mass in addition to the heavy, compacted snow beneath and ahead of them.

Sen closed her eyes as the sound of crunching snow and screamed efforts surrounded her. She ground her spear's shaft in her hands, the wood beginning to splinter and drive shards into her palms. With every successive push, her eyes clenched tighter, another thunderclap clouding her mind, her shadow once again the source, but no longer were the death wails simply of her family, of her people. The pleas grew more bestial, more animalistic, until at least they were not the familiar words of a close relation, but the dynastic roar of power and strength. A roar drowned out by a successive thunderclap. Sen winced as a shiver ran through her which had little to do with the mountain chills.

Her hands shook as she slowly opened her eyes back open, her gaze trailing toward the makeshift medical tents. *Every single life in those tents, their blood stains my hands,* she thought. *Every* single *one of them. I would offer my life a thousand times over for them if it were in my power to do so. If my life was ever worth that much to bring them all back.*

"Hold," the commanding voice called from below, whichever Fen it belonged to.

From the corner of her eye, Sen could see a skulking mass of gray slowly approaching the group. The Wolf had hardly moved from its perch since the Invaders' retreat. It had kept a watchful eye to the south, ready to strike the moment the Invaders mounted their counterattack. The god of the hunt was acting every bit the predator, the leader of the pack, protecting its subjects while mourning its closest kin just the same.

But now, as it silently strode toward the Bear's corpse, a gleam of recognition appeared to glint in its amber eyes, its head bowing as though in a nod. A hush fell over the group as the Wolf sniffed at the Bear's opened skull and throat, a soft growl echoing off the canyon walls enough for Sen to hear it. It opened its wide jaw and grasped onto the scruff of the Bear's neck, locking eyes with the large group before it began to push all its weight towards its hindquarters, as though it was prepared to engage in a game of tug-of-war.

The intent was not lost upon the group. The shouts for readiness were immediate, and though the effort was still monumental, with the Wolf's help, they gradually grew ever closer to the Bear's shrine. *At least, now, they'll make it before nightfall,* Sen observed.

Her eyes did not break from the sight. For all the effort the Wolf was putting into assisting, it had only struck Sen then that the god was mourning just the same for its own fallen brethren. She was under the assumption that remembrances for the deceased were reserved strictly for the land of mortals, but in the Wolf, she knew even gods felt pain, sadness, loss. It knew, it understood. And Sen's heart broke for it just the same. She could only imagine the means by which the Owl mourned; no one had seen it since it fled during the heat of the battle, but she held on to the hope that the avian god would return in short order.

The crunching of compacted snow behind her roused her attention. Turning her head, Sen saw Tez approaching, spear still in hand, her posture and balance much steadier now that she had grown acclimated to the sensation of Brin's pendant. Her older sister knelt beside her, clutching her shoulder, just like their father used to do. The recollection sent a chill through Sen's spine.

You were taken from us only so recently, and yet it already feels like half a lifetime ago.

Forcing a smile as best as she could, Sen put a hand atop her sister's, giving it a brief squeeze. "Are you managing all right?" she asked, gesturing with her eyes toward the new pendant adorning her neck.

As though by instinct, Tez reached for the pendant, wrapping a hand around the ornament. "I...don't know," she said, her words hesitant for her uncertainty rather than an inability to form them. "It feels as though a...part of me is missing. Like there's still something within me that was ripped out and apart."

Sen bit at her lower lip, apprehensive. She looked from Tez to the sight of the Bear being dragged by the Wolf to its altar and back to her sister, her eyes fixated on the glistening metal laying slack at Tez's chest. Her heart felt heavy. "I...I just wish I could have—"

Tez held a hand up, shaking her head. "I know what you're going to say, so please. Don't." She closed her eyes, drawing in a deep breath, her hand shakily clinging to Brin's pendant again. "Please don't blame yourself. I...I couldn't bear it if you placed all of this on yourself."

The words did little to lift the weight from her. Sen could hardly find it within herself to even look her sister in the eyes, puffy and bruised though they were from her broken nose. "Do you remember," she asked, "the day I left to try and rescue Brin? And I said that, regardless of whether or not I *am* cursed, it doesn't mean I can't make things right or do good for the Tribe?"

Tez remained silent, but nodded, regardless.

"Look at what's come of it all since then." Sen gestured widely toward the snow-covered fields of the True Heart, to the white once again glistening serenely. "How many did we return to the earth? How many fell to the Bear's slaying? I said that making things right started with rescuing Brin. Well, I failed at that—and look at what has been left in my wake." She flinched away as Tez outstretched a comforting hand, biting back a well of fresh tears.

Tez sighed, remorse heavy upon her breath. "Do you believe that none of this would have happened had you remained in the village all the while?" She planted her spear between them, the shaft cutting a dividing line. "You may very well have been among those beneath the earth had you stayed. The world would have kept spinning, and we would still be fighting here to our last. You can't earnestly believe that you're to blame for all of this."

A sharp breeze rolled through, sending a tremor up the length of Sen's body. She huddled herself within her coat for warmth as best as she could, her lips quivering into a frown. "Ever since that night...when Father was murdered. It just seems...something—or someone—is punishing me. Or ensuring that the consequences of my mistakes are suffered by all." Tears broke the dam, and her cheeks already felt the threat of ice forming. "I could have *done* something about them, Tez. About the Children of the Black Moon. Instead, I thought my only course was to join them. I thought in their midst was the only place I belonged. Every single moment I spent in their presence, I was spitting upon Father and Brin's memory."

Giving Brin's pendant another tug, Tez looked down at the memento, her eyes glistening from the weighted burden. "And yet our brother's Memories will remain pristine in here."

Sen was quick to shake her head. "And I would ask you'd keep them as such. You don't need to see where I failed him—and the many times over I did so."

"You might have failed, but do you think you're the first to do so?" Sen finally allowed herself to match her sister's gaze in response to her words. "Gods, Sen, I've failed plenty of times. At times, I've certainly not known how to rise above my failures. But we fail, we learn, we survive, we move on. And no matter the depths of your failures, the strong always find their way back to the surface. You're strong, little sister. I've seen it. And I'll pull you back up to the godsdamned surface myself if I must."

The words shook Sen. She knew not how to respond. A grimace passed over her lips, a tremble in her hand, a twitch at every distant echoed effort that continued to rumble in her ears. Her mind returned to the depths of the Forest, her every step steeped in death at the Invader onslaught. The dancing shadows laughing at her. The cold kiss of the flintlock's barrel against her forehead. How close she had been to falling forever below the surface, never again to rise from its murky dark. The realm of ghosts was once so near and welcoming, but now felt as an avoidance of a longer punishment she still deserved.

"Sen?" Tez's voice grounded her again, pronounced worry gleaming in her bruised eyes. "Are you still with me?"

Sen's lip quivered, her breath shaking, but she managed a nod just the same.

Tez flashed a gentle smile, her braid swaying in the gentle mountain breeze. "Good," she said, holding out her hand to Sen as she rose back to a knee. "Come. We should check in on Mother."

The reminder was painful enough. Sen couldn't say for certain how long she hovered over her mother's motionless form the day before. It seemed a horrid dream then, and still she was trying to wake from it. But with reluctance, she allowed herself to be pulled back to her feet by Tez, opting to humor the nightmare well enough until she at last was roused from her bed and returned to the days when none of this existed even in the realm of possibility.

No matter how hard she tried to wake herself, though, Sen knew there was no escape from this reality. Each successive step in the crunching snow below, her feet numb from the biting cold, only reinforced that there was nothing to wake from.

Her sister wrapped a comforting arm around her as her sorrows only remained eminent. Sen barely had the words to respond, but she was thankful just the same—for the comfort, and for the warmth.

A controlled chaos was visible in the area surrounding the healers' tents. Owlsigns were traipsing from one tent to the next, exhaustion deep-set in each of their faces. It was a bit more subdued than it had been the day before, but only relatively so. For the sheer volume of Learneds hovering around each entryway, it was near impossible to find one's way in without shoving three people out of the way.

Shove they did, and Tez led Sen through the web of makeshift beds until they reached their mother's side. It was remarkably warmer inside than out, even for a dwelling whose door was nothing more than a flapping snow leopard pelt. Candlelight and incense provided a subtle heat and pleasant smell, respectively, enough to take Sen's mind off the concealed horrors outside, if only to thusly remember the more pronounced within.

It was a welcoming sight to see Ket tending to Dennalhir. Sen still had yet to ask Tez for the entire story of how she had grown so acquainted with this healer from the Lake Tribe, but there were greater matters to worry about first than the origins of a fling. At the very least, Sen was grateful to have learned their name. Tez had placed her trust in them, and that was more than enough for Sen.

Tez approached Ket gently, softly touching her hand to theirs, a hesitant smile creasing her lips. "How's she doing, Ket?" she asked.

Ket allowed their fingers to intertwine with Tez's and Sen couldn't help but roll her eyes at the sight. *So coy, as though you didn't keep the entire mountain range awake two nights ago,* she thought.

The prolonged silence said more than enough. Ket blankly gestured toward Dennalhir and all the other Bearsigns present in the room. "Much the same as you see with the rest of them," they said. "When we saw this happen with Barrah, I thought I had seen the worst of it. But all this...gods, Tez, what do we even do?"

Tez gulped. "I wish I knew. I really do." She removed her hand from Ket's and stood closer to Dennalhir, leaning over her mother with a fear and apprehension that Sen had never quite seen in her sister before. Tez bit at her lower lip, her head shaking in rhythmic disbelief. "Sen," she called her over shoulder, not fully turning. "Was there...anything you learned? Anything that could...help all of them?"

Sen frowned, rubbing her hands along her arms to quell both the chill and the anxiety. She approached her mother's bed. The state Dennalhir was in absolutely defied reason. This was not how she was to meet her end, clinging listlessly to a life ripped away from her by forces beyond her control. She was always a woman who controlled her own destiny, her own fate, and yet, here she was, condemned to the same squalor as her brethren.

Flashing a glance at the chain along her sister's neck, Sen closed her eyes and shook her head. "I have no solution, Tez. When that steel opened the Bear's skull, it was a knife driven through the mind of every single Bearsign. There's nothing we can do."

"But," Tez put her thumb through the chain of Brin's pendant, holding it out for her sister to see. "You did *this*. You saved *me*. Can you really not—"

"It was far too late, Tez," Sen snapped, a flaring sadness roaring through her. "I tried to get to her as quickly as I could, you know that. But I didn't have enough time. That you were just beside me as it happened was a stroke of—"

She froze. The word stilled itself upon her tongue.

Tez rose her eyebrows expectantly. "Luck?"

Sen grimaced, nodding with reluctance. *It sure as hell doesn't feel like Luck,* she thought. *What great fortune has fallen upon us.*

"But how did you know it would work?" Ket asked, craning their head into Sen's periphery. "If there was any way to—"

"I didn't."

Ket stopped with their mouth agape. "Pardon?"

Sen closed her eyes, drawing in a deep breath. "I took a chance. Out of desperation. I have so few people left now. I couldn't lose her." She turned toward Tez with hesitation. "I couldn't lose you. And I can't lose Mother." She gestured toward Dennalhir, to the husk who had raised them both. "But you saw me yesterday. There was nothing more I could do than what I already tried. There's nothing any of us can do but...prevent it from happening again."

"You fear the worst." Ket's words were not a question, but a statement of fact.

A long pause gripped Sen, the words tight in her throat, before she had the strength to say, "I cannot fear what I know to be an inevitability. It's only a matter of how long we can stand against the inevitable."

"It's that Kamataa woman," Tez muttered. "Isn't it?"

Sen couldn't help but feel anger at the name. *Aritz a Mata may be the face of the Invaders,* she thought, *but Kamataa is a puppetmaster carrying them all along her strings.* She bunched her fists along the side of her mother's bed, the pain setting in more and more the longer she looked at Dennalhir. The glazed eyes, the rasping breath, the sheer expression of shock and silent agony frozen upon her face. She would never stop feeling herself responsible.

Her father. Her mother. Her brother. Her Narva. Their fates all tied to her hand, and she had not the knife sharp enough to cut loose the threads. And how many of those knots were cast by Kamataa, herself? Sen shuddered to consider it.

As anxiety welled within, her chest heavy as her heart thumped faster and faster, Sen clenched her eyes shut and turned away. "Sorry. I just...I need some air." *Some cold, stagnant air.*

Before any protests could be voiced, Sen shoved her way through the crowded confines of the healing station, past a bed carrying Fann's moaning body, through a throng of Keeper Owlsigns impeding her path, until at last she pushed past the leopard pelt opening and felt the biting chill rush through her lungs. Little was there to keep her from collapsing in the snow, the shocking freeze invigorating her through the exhaustion.

She just didn't expect so many to already be huddled about her by the time her face hit the snow below.

A hand guided her back to her knees, not so gentle as an embrace but not so forceful as a command, either. Her face was already numb from the ground, but she managed a wince as she took in Ko Zaran's weathered expression. The Keeper elder brushed snow off Sen's shoulders and hoisted her back to her feet without care for protest. Sen felt inclined to protest, too, but bit back her tongue.

It had been quite some time since she ventured this close to the old Owlsign. She cast him hardly a second glance when he conducted Brin's Trial—half a lifetime ago though that felt—before she retreated instead to Ko Seln's tavern. The only time worth noting beyond that was her own "Trial" four years past, when he did nothing but stare upon her in fear and shock as though she were a disease and a menace.

Half right, at any rate, she thought.

But now, Ko Zaran merely regarded Sen with hesitant acceptance, backing away from her just as soon as he finished helping her to her feet, yet still remaining at a perfect conversational distance, his old fingers twitching against each other.

Surrounding him, a number of faces—familiar and unfamiliar—stared at Sen, eyes sharp yet hollow, heavy yet empty, hopeful yet unforgiving. She recognized faces such as Ne Shanne, who had facilitated her sham Trial four years ago; Ne Arsah, with whom she had shared drinks with when last she had been in the Heart; and, Fen-Poven, apparently taking a break from hauling the Bear back to its altar. Even Sharrabha was present, her kinship with the Keepers coming well in handy these last few days. Sen was grateful to find her alive. She hadn't yet seen Tawa since the battle, but she had heard tell of him tending to the wounded and felt it best not to disturb his process.

Sen's throat dried as she took in all of their faces, her heart racing to match the intensity. Instinctively, she felt her fists clenching as though a fight was imminent, but everyone appeared far too forlorn for further conflict.

"Sennalhat," Ko Zaran finally said, his voice grand and proper, the words rasping against a tired and torn throat. "Daughter of Fannalhen and Dennalhir."

A silence prolonged, and all Sen could do was force a smile and nod. "At your service," she said listlessly.

Ko Zaran nodded in kind, looking slowly to each of the present Owlsigns and Wolfsigns, as though the words were rehearsed and he was misremembering the following lines. "The threat of the Invaders is unlike anything we have experienced," he said. "Their might is unprecedented. Their ability to sway our very people to their cause is unimaginable. From the strength of our mightiest warriors sundered, they may well be unstoppable." The elder stopped, bunching his heavy robe tighter around his chest in defense against a sudden sharp wind. "You marched alongside them, privy to their methods. Viewed and handled their Deatharms firsthand. Broke bread with them, stood among their ranks."

The pit in Sen's stomach grew only wider and deeper. "You speak too much, Ko Zaran, when you could simply say I betrayed our people."

Sharrabha stepped forward, shaking her head with a kind warmth. "But you *returned*, Sen," she assured. "I won't pretend to understand the reasons, but everything you experienced brought you back here. Back to your people."

"And if there are any among us who can speak to the capabilities of our enemy..." spoke Fen-Poven, his face sunken in grief, the wound of his brother's passing rumbling in his voice.

Sen flashed a reluctant half-smile. "It would be me." She closed her eyes, drawing in a deep breath, the cold thin air biting at her lungs. *How have we reached a point where my greatest shame is our greatest hope?*

Ko Zaran gestured forward, holding his hands out in a placated manner. "If there is *anything* at all you might share in preparation for the days to come...I would plead that you offer it."

The wind whistled through the nearby trees, knocking piled snowdrops loose from weakened branches. A chill nipped at the back of Sen's neck as she slowly regarded each of the expectant faces before her until finally, she nodded. She spoke of everything she knew of the Invaders—or, the Acrarians, as she addressed them. She detailed their weaponry, their training and battle strategies, the City they had built upon the lands of the Haunted, the slave camps they constructed where they harbored and destroyed the lives of countless Tribespeople. Everything she could speak in great depth, she did, and for that which she knew little, she shared little.

"...and their leader, a man named Aritz a Mata," Sen growled, her fist bunching just at the utterance of his name. "He who killed my father, who kidnapped my brother. He is the architect of all of this. A horrible man. A monster. A demon."

As she paused, Fen-Poven cracked his knuckles, his gray locks fluttering loosely behind him in the breeze. "Then we remove the demon's head, and the rest shall follow."

Sen truly wanted to believe that to be the case. She solemnly shook her head. "For all the terror he has wrought upon our people...I fear that there is only worse behind him."

"Eh?" Fen-Poven raised an eyebrow. The confusion was reciprocated by the rest of the gathering.

Digging in her heels, Sen shuffled snow about underfoot, her teeth grinding. "The Children of the Black Moon," she said, spite billowing from her tongue. "All the horrors you would try to pin on me simply for being Eclipse-born...they are the root of them all. They infiltrated the Acrarian army using stolen Illusion pendants, infiltrated our own people with their agents, all to see the Tribes crumble to nothing. And their leader, Kamataa, is the true scourge worthy of the spite handed to those born during the Eclipse."

"But why?" Ko Zaran asked, his brow furrowed with consternation. "What would cause one of our own to..."

"Live for four centuries while being told you are a blight upon our people and you'll feel inclined to prove them correctly," Sen snapped sharply. "I very nearly believed it myself. But for all the drive Aritz commands to destroy all memory of our people, Kamataa has the means to do so."

Sharrabha stifled a gasp. "Sen, you don't mean…"

Sen clenched her eyes shut and snarled as she turned back toward the medical tent where her mother and countless other Bearsigns lay broken. She marched toward Ko Zaran, gripping the old man's pendant, tugging it tightly for all to see. "These are our Boons, and yet they are also our curse. The longer we possess these trinkets, the more inseparable our connections to the gods become. Until we reach a point where our minds cannot handle being apart from them."

Ne Shanne tucked her head into view, her arms folded across her chest. "Then you mean to say that when the Bear was slain…"

Immediately, Sen pointed a sharp finger toward the medical tent. "*That* was the result, yes."

A stunned silence gripped the group. Sen loosened her grasp on Ko Zaran's pendant, allowing it to fall back to his chest. Everyone began looking upon their own pendants with apprehension, as though each of them wondered whether they had consigned themselves to their own deaths simply by completing their Trials. Sen wandered over toward the ridge, where the Bear's corpse had nearly reached its altar. She planted her hands on her hips, her heart heavy.

"Sen." Sharrabha's voice held a calm air, but there was enough abrasion to her tone for Sen to hear the huntress was frightened. "If that's the case, then…"

Sen did not have the heart to turn back around yet. All she could do was slightly turn her head over her shoulder. "All of us could be felled in one swoop, just as the Bearsigns were, yes." She looked up to the sky, the gentle snow continuing to be nothing more than a façade held up by the mourning heavens. It was a false innocence masking the grievous sins underneath.

"Then…what do we do? What *can* we do?" Sen had only ever known Sharrabha to be confident, self-assured. To hear her take on such a panicked tone was disheartening.

Turning on her heel, Sen could do little else but chuckle. "'Do?' We fight and we hope to survive, Sharrabha." She held up three fingers. "Between the battle yesterday and the battle in the Stone Tribe village, we have felled three of the Children of the Black Moon. And yet, four still remain." *And I cannot account for Cin's whereabouts*, she thought to herself.

The Wolf's grunts and whimpers echoed enough to catch Sen's ear. She looked over to see the god nudging at its fallen comrade with its snout, mourning in its own way, sitting proudly beside the corpse of its brethren, attention drawn again to the southern horizon.

"When they return," Sen said coolly, "we know who their targets will be, and they will not allow any of us to stand in their way." Faintly, she could hear someone muttering vague nothings in prayer. "Spare your prayers, for the Wolf and the Owl don't have the time to hear them. If anything...*we* may have to answer *their* prayers."

Aritz had certainly not anticipated returning to this squalid village so quickly. Even a day later, retreating with his tail tucked between his legs hardly sat well with him. Were it within him, he would immediately march back to that clearing and place a bullet in that beast's skull.

If only his bones did not protest with each subsequent movement.

He holed himself up in the largest hut he could find, one he recognized from his prior venture here. The stench of the tribal chief he had killed still lingered in this place, mixing with a wafting smell of burned incense and stomach-churning stew. The savages had not even bothered to empty their meal before it spoiled.

But a bed was a bed, and he had no qualms over resting in what little comfort could be afforded in these disgusting dwellings.

Whenever he closed his eyes, he still saw that giant wolf cutting swaths through his men as though it were nothing. How it wielded his blade so deftly. *The very idea that beast possessed the intelligence to do so is ridiculous!* he thought. But the very memory of it was enough to send a shudder through his body as he stared up at the stone ceiling, his hands propped behind his head against a feather-filled pillowcase.

Aritz had always felt powerful. As a boy in Acraria, he never wanted for anything and was taught never to settle for weakness. Power was always within his grasp, and rarely had he ever had to strain his arm in trying to reach for it.

This land, so easily it had landed in his lap. All he ever needed to do was take a step forward. He could force the savages to remain deep within the mountains while he built his own empire in these verdant moors where the Savior could more easily keep a watchful and assuring eye upon them all. But the prize in the mountains was too rich to pass up. And the task bequeathed to him by an Envoy of the Savior could scarcely be discarded. The Savior wished for him to fell the three beasts the savages worshiped as gods, and that was fully what he intended to do.

And for all the power he had held in his life, never had he felt as powerful as he did when he slayed that vicious bear, only for it to be thrown so carelessly away in an instant.

I am a god-slayer. None can take that from me.

He needed only the strength to do it again. The pains stood only as a sharp reminder of it, especially as his face continued to throb from the healing slash beneath his eye.

Outdoors, the cacophony of pained moans and calls for medical attention overwhelmed the ordinary rousing of frivolity inherent in most of Aritz's camps. At the first utterance of a call for drinks, Aritz felt nothing but disdain. *One does not drink to failure,* he thought. *Those who drink to failure are long since buried beneath the ground.* It was almost to his relief that many of his soldiers were too injured or infirmed to indulge. It permitted him a more ample space to rest and collect his thoughts.

Slowly, his thoughts drifted away to the promise of a new day, his eyes drooping close...

And footsteps echoed underfoot as a pair of soldiers entered the hut.

Aritz loosed an exasperated sigh. "I believe I ordered that none were to disturb me," he called, not bothering to lift his tired head from the pillow.

"Yes, and given what I must offer you, I elected to ignore that order," responded a familiar female voice.

A well of anger toward Kama still resided within Aritz for the failure in the mountains—not to mention her desertion—but he still rose to a seated position regardless. The tight skin on his face tugged painfully as he sneered at the red-haired soldier, the heathen with the locks of fire. Beside Kama stood another of his soldiers, one he did not recognize by face. Her brow was furrowed in a scowl, her arms crossed, eyes a piercing blue, long brown hair draped and untied over her shoulders.

"What is it, Kama?" Aritz asked, wincing as the words ached his muscles. "Rest with the remainder of the soldiers. A strategy can be laid on the morrow."

Kama chuckled, fluttering back a tuft of red hair from her eyes. "I've had plenty of time to rest. We needn't wait for all the wounds to be thoroughly licked."

Grunting in acknowledgment, Aritz rolled his eyes and pushed himself back to his feet. He nudged toward the other soldier with his head. "And her? Another of your...compatriots?"

Flouring her hand broadly, Kama grasped her companion's shoulder. "Think of her merely as another extension of our goodwill toward you. You may call her Sha'a."

I will only call her "Soldier." I've not a use for her name.

Sha'a took a half-step forward and bowed her head slightly. "A pleasure, General."

Aritz raised his brow with curiosity. "And why have you brought her to me, Kama?" he asked. "I find myself hardly in the mood for introductions among your cadre."

A smile creased Kama's lips, but it did little to reach her eyes. "My 'cadre' has fought, bled, and died for you just the same as the rest of your soldiers. If it not for them, your forces would have done naught but walk into an ambush and I am inclined to believe we would not presently be conversing were that not the case."

"Speak plainly, woman. I've not the patience."

Kama bowed with exaggerated grace, the insincere smile still gleaming upon her face. She walked into the bedchamber, hands clasped behind her back, maintaining a healthy distance between herself and Aritz. "We experienced but a taste of the victory I have sought for years upon years. A triumph so decadently sweet upon my tongue. I know you long for that taste as well, do you not?"

Aritz folded his arms across his chest, opting only to respond with a suspicious glare.

"Hmph," she grunted, continuing on. "Very well. You are a man of means, aren't you, Aritz? You do not allow defeat to deter you. You take what is yours, fight for what you desire. You stood your ground against two ferocious gods and slayed one by your own hand. One defeat in the face of odds stacked against your favor is not enough to impede you, is it not?"

"The *point*, Kama," Aritz demanded, his wound searing as he snarled once more. "I care little for empty platitudes."

"What if I told you that wolf could fall with little more than a touch? Would you seize that opportunity for yourself?"

Aritz rolled his eyes. "If I wanted to pet dogs, I would return to my manor. I fail to see what a touch could do what a bullet could not."

"Hmm, quite so," Kama responded, a candid joyfulness coloring her words. "But as the saying goes: seeing is believing. And so I shall ask again—would you seize that opportunity for yourself?"

Scoffing, Aritz shuffled in place, examining the simple architecture of this squalid hut. *I am sleeping in the bed of a man I once felled, in dwellings ill-fitting of any devoted servant of the Savior, and am promised that a beast can be killed with naught but a flick of the finger. Savior's breath, how has my company become so devolved?*

Kama appeared to detect his apprehension. "Tell me, Aritz. Who among your soldiers is particular cause for irritation?"

"I beg your pardon?" Aritz felt genuine curiosity for the blunt question. *I stand amidst bones piled high, stripped from my men. Lives have been lost due to their own inadequacies. I feel irritation toward them all.*

The woman smiled once more, something that approached genuine. "You enjoy the platitudes of those beneath you, though you are loath to admit it.

But you do not suffer the adulation of weak men. Surely, there is one who fits that description."

Allowing himself a long moment of consideration, Aritz shook his head and made for the doorway. "Fine, then. I shall indulge whatever point is to be made here."

Sha'a was quick to move, keeping a wide breadth away from Aritz as though avoiding him entirely.

Strange, Aritz thought. He poked his head out into the cold northern air and spotted a soldier wandering nearby. "You there!" he called.

The lad quickly stood to attention, offering the Acrarian salute as though by reflex. "Sir! At your service."

Aritz hesitated a second, gnawing at his lower lip, until finally he called, "Fetch me the lieutenant, post-haste!"

"Which one, sir?"

"The pock-marked one!"

Without further instruction, the soldier scampered off, nearly in a dead sprint. He departed with some degree of confidence. Aritz interpreted that to mean he knew exactly where Pock-Face was.

Ten minutes passed as Aritz wandered the central room, one he judged to be some sort of meeting chamber from the firepit in the middle and the surrounding seating arrangements. Rapid, muddy footsteps clapped outside as the lad from before dashed indoors, his lungs heaving.

"Apologies, sir, for the delay. I—I've—brought Lieu—tenant Ettor as you—as you asked."

Aritz waved a hand, half in thanks, half in disregard. "That will be all, son. Dismissed."

The soldier saluted and immediately returned to whatever wandering he had been up to before, and in his place appeared Lieutenant Pock-Face, his own breath heavy and his gait unsteady. He smelled like piss, though Aritz could not determine if it was due to the foul drink in this village or if it was the man's own bodily fluids.

"Sir!" Pock-Face saluted, despite his wobbling posture. "I am told you requested my presence."

Aritz crossed his arms and examined the lieutenant, rolling his eyes that he had to request his arrival in the first place. "Kama," he called over his shoulder, his voice echoing off the cavernous stone walls of the hut.

Kama and Sha'a appeared in an instant, almost too eager for Aritz's liking. The lieutenant exchanged a sneer with Kama, clearly not forgetting her insubordination from a couple days past. Wordlessly, Pock-Face turned his head from Aritz to Kama, as though believing of some abhorrent, unseemly behavior.

I would sooner render myself a eunuch than defile myself in such a manner, Aritz thought.

The silence prolonged as Sha'a slowly approached Pock-Face, his confusion—and likely drunken stupor—preventing him from questioning what the woman was doing to begin with. Sha'a exhibited not a hint of hesitation as she drew closer to the lieutenant, reached out, grasped his shoulder as though comforting him.

Aritz barely had time to blink before the man collapsed in a heap, his body gone limp, not even a gasp or a whimper escaping from the lieutenant's lips. Instinctively, he reached for his pistol, his hand finding the grip as it remained holstered along his thigh.

"Now, now, that shan't be necessary," Kama assured, walking slowly between Aritz and Sha'a.

Feeling his eyes widen at the sight, Aritz was dumbstruck. "Did...did she...?"

"As I said, seeing is believing." Kama approached him, that sly smile remaining strewn about her face. She grasped his wrist, dragging his hand away from his pistol. "You are not a man to permit any obstacle to stand in your way. And a good general uses all the tools at his disposal to rout the enemy. Therefore, I ask once again: will you seize the opportunity for yourself?"

A moment's hesitation gripped Aritz as he could not break his gaze from Pock-Face's dead form. His mouth remained agape as he slowly chanced a glance toward Sha'a, the woman remaining ever calm and collected as though the act did little to faze her. A serene calm in the face of danger. One that would be altogether too important in the days to come. He turned back toward Kama, his eyes matching hers.

"Yes."

Every step brought with it only further agony. The splinters would remove themselves in time. If only the bones would heal half as quick.

It had been easy for Cin to evade the panicked Tribal masses after the battle. A dead god will do that. *Just wish I could've seen it.*

How long he had stayed in the snowbound forest, he couldn't say. The Bear's mighty swing had knocked the lights out of him. He had never felt such an intense surge of Luck before as when he was soaring between dense trees, narrowly avoiding having his head taken clean off.

The Moon shone brightly overhead as he slowly descended the mountainside, taking care to avoid the main pathways. He craned his neck skyward, wincing for his stiff muscles, and grunted with apprehension at his liege. "Intent on keeping me alive, aren't you?"

He received no response.

An inadvertent gasp of pain escaped Cin's lips as a divot was deeper than he realized. It was getting far too dark to continue, but he needed to press on. *Surely, they search for me still.* He couldn't help but stare once again at the Moon. "What next, my Lady?" he muttered. "Where does this road take us from here?"

"If it is questions you have, then perhaps they should have been voiced long ago."

Cin stopped dead in his tracks, slipping on a patch of slick ice. His feet fell out from underneath, sending him tumbling down a slight but rocky slope. Jabs of jagged stone tore at his clothing, a sharp sear coursing his side as warm lifeblood seeped from an open wound. His momentum carried him toward a pile of packed snow, and he was more than content to lie there for a while yet.

It had been some time since the lost had spoken with him. Too long, in fact. He had lost track entirely. Even after leaving the Tribe of his birth, his Haunted blood could not escape him, and neither could the voices of the dead. A curse passed on to the descendants of the perpetrators of the Pale Night of four centuries past, a blight instilled by a vengeful Moon for the indiscriminate murder of her children. The irony never left Cin that he remained so cursed, despite carrying the blood of both the Moon and the Haunted within him.

But as he reluctantly pushed himself back up to a seated position, he cared not for the voice's intent. They could hardly serve him anymore. Nothing more than a fly buzzing in his ear, failing to find its way out.

"Are you truly so inclined to burn it all to cinders?" the voice asked. *"Or do your doubts guide you to a path long since abandoned?"*

Cin rolled his eyes. "Quiet," he said. He was all too familiar with this voice. It had warned him all those years ago to leave the Tribe's confines while he still had the chance. In some respects, he was grateful for it; if not for the warning, he would surely have fallen victim to the Acrarians' assault. Luck guided him that day. But in the years since, the voice, that remnant of his ancestors from ages past, had been little more than an annoyance, always finding its way to the forefront of his ears, overpowering the other voices of the lost so desperately clinging for purchase.

"I am all too familiar with this path you currently walk, Cin. I have seen the devastation to which it leads before."

"And the history of the Dusk Tribe was thenceforth drowned in flame," Cin responded, flicking a hand of dismissal toward his invisible companion. "The embers rise yet again. You know as well as I the inevitability of fate, Zarrow."

Zarrow's voice scoffed. If it still had a body, Cin imagined it would have been shaking its head. *"There are branches to every path, Cin. I regretted for the rest of my days my inability to find the branch necessary to prevent the Pale Night from occurring. Instead, I performed heinous acts, even if they were not of my own volition. That need not be the same of you."*

Cin shook his head, sucking in a breath as he put a pile of packed snow against his open wound in an attempt to dull the pain. "I am allowing the river to carry me along wherever it will take me."

"And if you may find your way to shore beforehand?"

"Then the strength of the current waned too much to be natural."

The voice silenced, but Cin still felt its presence. It felt as though Zarrow was hovering over him, watching his every move, the night playing host to fallen ghosts. "Say what you came to say, Zarrow."

The heavy sensation subsided, instead growing lighter to Cin's side, a companion residing against the treacherous rockface. *"I learned that night there are forces beyond our understanding,"* Zarrow said sullenly. *"We committed...grave atrocities, and those of us who did not, merely failed to stop it. I do not think it coincidence that the Eclipse did not return again for close to four centuries afterward. I understand the consequences of hatred. And I would not wish it upon you."*

Cin sat in silence, feeling nothing but the pain still scoring his flesh. "What more do I have than this?" He stared down at his palm, his hand quivering from the discomfort in his arm. "This is all I've known. We are angels of retribution, the voice of all our brethren slain by misunderstanding hands." But even as he said the words, they did not feel natural. They did not feel true.

"Are the words yours? Or do they belong to Kamataa?" Zarrow's voice was blunt. *"The hands that felled our brethren are long since passed. Your fight is only with an army of ghosts. Do not allow them to haunt you further."*

An involuntary chuckle rumbled in Cin's throat. "Rich, coming from you," he muttered.

Zarrow's presence vanished before offering a rebuttal of any sort, the heavy incorporeal weight lifting from Cin's shoulders in an instant.

Cin sighed, tucking his Acrarian coat as snugly against his body as he could manage in defense against the cold. Unsteadily, he rose back to his feet, aware of the dangers inherent in traversing these rocky slopes in the dark, but intent on finding some means of shelter until day broke again.

And yet, all inclinations returned his gaze back to the Moon, Her light shining radiantly in the clear night sky. "Do You desire for us to be Your angels?" he asked. "Surely, You desire retribution." He sighed again, shaking his head at the vast expanse of treacherous darkness ahead. "I simply do not know for whom."

Barely a further word was exchanged in the time between when Aritz accepted Kamataa's help and when she opted to regroup with Vanta.

Kamataa had noticed an air of reluctance in the General. Or perhaps apprehension. It surprised her, honestly. *He has been the cause of so much death already,* she thought. *Why does it matter the manner in which it happens?*

Regardless, the thought was little more than fleeting as she traversed with Sha'a the remains of the Stone Tribe village, now an area of recuperation for the Acrarians. To her eyes, it was a beautiful thing. Men and women sung songs for victory in the night air, drunken fools caroused the pathways, and a man patrolled the streets with one of those new contraptions that captured "photographs." She was still rather fuzzy on the specifics of that.

She found Vanta in an empty hut at the end of the lane, far from the frivolity and cries for help. The convenience of the village's size meant for ample space to continue hiding in plain sight, regardless of Aritz's understanding of who she truly was. It was a perfect size for them, likely having housed a small family beforehand. A small fire was already roaring.

Vanta had long since dispelled her Illusion, her dark hair coming to a stop just past her ears, framing her chin. Kamataa followed suit, and Sha'a after her. After so long disguised as these foreigners, it felt good to be within her own skin once again.

"Any news of Cin?" Kamataa asked, huddling herself around the warmth of the flame.

With a frown, Vanta shook her head, massaging her bare arms against the cold's bite. "His good fortune won't allow him to pass just yet. He'll surely return soon enough."

Kamataa nodded, though not with any degree of certainty. The last few days had already seen her lose Ziia, Hollow, and Zara. She was not afforded the time to properly mourn them, nor could she make the time if Cin was added to that list. All she could do was murmur into the dancing flames, awaiting what was next to come, and hope that Cin's Luck had not yet run short.

"So, then," Vanta continued. "Did he accept?"

Sha'a chuckled, staying a small distance away from the flames. "In truth, I believe he was relieved to be rid of Lieutenant Ettor. He was willing to accept anything after that."

They all laughed, even if Kamataa could not feel the joy in it. "He would take any guidance and frame it under the guise of divine intervention, the foolish man. For all his ambition, he remains quite the gullible sort."

"I am still impressed you convinced him you were an 'Envoy' of his god," Sha'a said with a smirk. "It's fascinating, how easily their hearts are swayed."

Kamataa managed a soft smile at that. "Humanity will justify any action if they claim it to be for their faith. So long as it continues to be for our benefit, then I am content to be whatever 'the Savior' wishes me to be." She rolled her eyes at the term.

Vanta leaned back on her elbows, lounging against the heat. "What shall the 'Envoy' request of us this evening, then?"

Rising back to her feet, Kamataa gestured with her fingers for her companions to follow suit. She watched Sha'a and Vanta line up before her, arms crossed behind their backs. The flames crackled beside her, firewood popping into charred splinters. "I'm ordinarily loath to put ourselves in the line of fire...but we will require the Touch in the battle to come. A concentrated amount of it, at that."

"Whatever we need to do, we shall," Vanta said assuredly.

"Envoy," Sha'a added, a grin on her face.

Returning the grin, Kamataa held her hand out. "Your blades, if you will."

Sha'a and Vanta both winced as though on instinct, but they complied, regardless, drawing their hunting knives from the sheaths at their backsides, and carefully handing them to Kamataa. Their hands remained far from Kamataa's; one inadvertent touch and the plan would be for naught.

Kamataa nodded and gripped the hilts, one in each hand, the steel glinting in the dancing firelight. She drew a deep breath, her face a blank canvas. "For Ziia," she said.

"For Hollow," added Vanta.

"For Zara," added Sha'a.

"For us all," Kamataa finished.

And she drove the blades into the meat of their shoulders.

MEMORY

PRISM

THE YEAR 1531 ANNO SALVATORIS
10 YEARS BEFORE THE SETTLING

Pristine clouds passed overhead against a vibrant sky ceding its ocean blues for an ethereal golden orange. The crisp alpine air of the Acrarian summer evening caressed Aritz's nostrils, setting his mind at ease as he sprawled out in the soft grass before his family's estate, his eyes unbreaking from the mountaintops cutting into the eastern horizon.

It provided enough serenity for him to mute the soft din of guards patrolling the grounds and servants passing him by. Appreciative though he was, Aritz could not quite escape the overbearing feeling of his father's eye watching him vicariously through his staff. *I needn't be watched so,* he had wanted to tell the guards. *The grass will not hurt me, nor the sky fall upon me. Exciting though that may be.*

Aritz stretched his limbs, vocalizing with satisfaction. He hadn't realized how long he had been laying about out here. His intent was to take in the fresh air on another beautiful and perfect day after his tutors had left after his studies were completed. But minutes had turned to hours and suddenly the afternoon was gone.

Hardly a bother, though. Poor form it is to waste a lazy day indoors, so Father says.

He sat up, dusting off blades of verdant green grass from his plain white top and azure satin trousers. The faintest shade of a stain colored his sleeves near the shoulders. One of the servants would remedy that, surely.

A commotion drew his attention past the line of hedges to his right. Voices were distant, yet still excitable—more than enough to break the monotonous rhythm of clinking sword belts and heavy boots. Aritz rose to his feet, brushing away any remaining blades from his legs, and sauntered toward the greenery, which flanked a stone-cut pathway leading into the main parlor of the estate. Propping his arms atop the shrubs—though his short stature required him to stand on his toes to do so—he kept his gaze focused on the approaching din, the voices growing more distinct and comprehensible. Something about fine finds and excellent deals and other merchant talk he never quite understood.

A host of people came into view, guards draped in armor bearing the Mata colors and sigil marching in single file in two parallel rows, a third row sandwiched between them. Many of the faces were obscured from his sight, but Aritz could judge from the finery and gaudy clothing that they belonged to the mercantile class, likely hailing from the Northern Marches due to the presence of silk in their attire. Boisterous conversations and hearty laughter were shared amongst the group, and none more prominent than from the voice at the head of the party, heralded by a tall, imposing form carrying gravitas and regality.

His father had returned home.

Lord Nofre a Mata turned the corner, his face red with mirth, a shade matching the auburn his hair once was, though it was now reduced to peppers of black and gray. His attire and posture spoke of the command and station he held. A fine blue jacket with a gold silk fringe trailed down past his waistline and covered a casual white undershirt, unbuttoned below his collarbone and exposing curls of graying chest hair. Brown leather boots were cuffed and worn up to just below the knees, his tan trousers threaded with fine satins from beyond the Kingdom's borders. At his hip lay a royal saber, sheathed in a scabbard embedded with sapphire gemstones that glinted in the setting sun's light; it was a blade not fit for combat, but rather for a proclamation of status. Not that Nofre needed the visual aid to exemplify his high standing, for his composure and stride did all the acting necessary. He offered not a single glance behind him—it was ill-fitting a man of his renown. A Lord of the Acrarian Kingdom did not turn to a man at his back; his words and gaze were to look ahead, not at what had been. And the merchants seemed cognizant and appreciative of that fact, content simply to be in his presence.

Aritz could not help but smile at the sight. With a hop in his step, he descended from the row of hedges and shuffled halfway into the main path, slyly poking his head out from behind the shrubs. He stifled a chuckle as he noticed his father catching sight of him.

Nofre suppressed a grin and adjusted his cuff links before holding an arm out as a signal for his entourage to stop. He approached Aritz with a glimmer in his eyes, reaching his hand around the end of the hedges to tussle his son's auburn locks.

Feigning a wince as he dipped away from Nofre's tangling grip, Aritz allowed himself a brief laugh and clasped his father's hand with both of his own. "How was your trip, Father?"

Lord Nofre patted his free hand atop his son's and withdrew himself from the grip. "Prosperous and profitable as ever, my son. I've every intention of taking along you and your brothers on a future endeavor—if naught else but to see the Marches for yourselves."

"I would like that. The three weeks without you are dreadfully boring."

A grunted chuckle passed his father's lips. "Your tutors ought to be keeping you too occupied to face boredom."

Aritz shrugged. "I choose boredom." He craned his head around his father to get a closer look at the merchants. "What have you come back with this time?"

Nofre patted his head once more. "You are far too curious for a boy of ten, my boy."

"Curiosity pays its weight in gold. That's what you've always said." Aritz put his hands on his hips, adopting an assertive stance. "And if I'm leading our House one day, I must know to where my curiosities should lie. Right?"

Seeming to concede the point, Nofre raised an eyebrow, a rumble sounding through his throat. "So long as you can take advantage of your counterpart's own curiosity. What is commonplace to us is a luxury to them. Do you know what this ring cost me?" He pointed to the silver band on his left pinky finger, a beautifully smithed piece inset with a green gem. "A few bundles of saffron and peppercorns. Know the value of what you trade…and embellish it." He flashed his teeth in a wide grin. "You may just add to the wealth of our estate."

Aritz could feel his eyes light up with astonishment.

With a quick tug, Nofre pulled the ring off his finger and enclosed it in his son's hand. "As a reminder." He winked.

Opening his hand, Aritz eagerly put the ring on each of his fingers, though was quick to find his digits too thin to properly adorn it. He knew he would have to be careful not to lose it. Despite that, he felt powerful wearing it just the same. "Thank you, Father," he said, warmth in his heart at the gift and the lesson. He glanced back at the merchants, who still waited patiently for their summons, like hounds trained to heel. "But what else is there? Anything good?"

Nofre shook his head, waving his hand in dismissal. "In due time, Aritz. Our guests will present their offerings to us over supper. And speaking of which, hadn't you best get changed? Those grass stains are unseemly in the presence of our company." The tone of his father's voice changed ever so slightly, but it was enough. It was subtle, but his words took on a more abrasive edge when giving even the most tenuous of commands.

With heat rising in his face, Aritz peeked at the faded green coloring of his shirtsleeve and nodded. "Yes, of course, Father. Right away." He scurried along inside, followed immediately by a sharp whistle signaling a rhythmic march of heavy boots and a sonorous melody of clattering sword belts.

To call it a veritable feast was an understatement. Aritz felt full before the second course was even completed.

He peered along the length of the table, trying not to lean or slouch for fear of reprisal from his mother, even though his gut felt fit to burst. Innumerable chairs lined each side of the table, the chamber cavernous yet not at all overbearing in its size. Cabinets were filled with the finest dinnerware that Nofre had collected in his travels. The wooden walls were carved expertly by the finest craftsmen in the Kingdom, while wondrous pieces of artwork commissioned by the great Messer Camora filled in the gaps between carvings. Nofre's guests attacked their food as though it was the first meal they had ever eaten. Plates and bowls were filled to the brim with cured meats, paella, gazpacho, albondigas, bacalao, and so much more than Aritz could comprehend. He himself had already filled up enough on empanadas and croquettes during the first course. How many courses still remained was entirely beyond him. All he knew was that a deep sleep was imminent; only the raucous chorus of northern merchants kept him at an inattentive wakefulness.

Utensils and glassware clinked against the pervasive din as conversations overlapped one another, hands reaching in and out, bringing new plates in just as old ones were taken away. These feasts were always a blur to Aritz, but despite his lack of participation in the proceedings, appearances were, as ever, everything. He dressed as expected: a dark blue velvet dinner jacket buttoned tightly with a white cravat puffing out from underneath, his auburn locks slicked back and tied taut just above his hair line, a puff of powder adorning his face. All as high society demanded.

In the two chairs to Aritz's right sat his brothers, Lorente and Alsonso, aged eight and seven, respectively. Somehow, they had both remained enamored with the food continuing to pile before them; no eruptions of the stomach seemed imminent as of yet. At the head of the table, immediately adjacent to Aritz, sat his parents. His mother, Aldorisa, slowly picked at the offerings of paella still at her plate; she had always related to Aritz the importance of pacing oneself at a large feast, but the act and reasoning for doing so was still lost on him. Beside her, Nofre was deep in conversation with the man directly across from Aritz, the merchant captain who had returned alongside Nofre as part of the arriving retinue. Aritz had heard his name spoken earlier in the evening as Pandrea.

"And so I had little choice but to say no," Pandrea said with a droll, ineffectual accent. The food haze had cleared Aritz's mind enough for him to focus on individual conversations once again. "What manner of tradesman would I be were I to part from such value in exchange for but a stable of mules? As though we have a scarcity in the Marches! Have they not seen our sigil?" He laughed heartily, his red cheeks puffing with every breath, tears streaming from his glimmering hazel eyes. He almost looked short of air altogether.

It must be a good joke, Aritz thought, scratching his head in confusion.

His father seemed to think so, at any rate. Lord Nofre slapped his knee and patted Pandrea's arm with amusement, the whole of his body gripped in the throes of laughter. "You're all asses in the Marches, the lot of you—and in more ways than one!" He tilted his head back and cackled, the volume managing to echo off the walls despite the number of people present in the chamber.

Aldorisa shook her head with bemusement, muttering something under her breath. A slight grin stretched her lips, but Aritz took it to be less than genuine. The smile did not come close to reaching her icy blue eyes, and rather than meeting her husband's remark with mirth, she merely tucked a curly brown lock of hair behind her ear with disinterest. Aritz had never known his mother to be a woman of many words, but she spoke plenty through the movement of her brow, and he could tell she did not find the jape in good taste.

Not that it seemed to matter at all to Pandrea, who met Nofre's remark with equivalent levity. "We must give thanks to those qualities, for we would have never successfully liaised with you otherwise! Imagine had we ceased at the first negotiation!"

"Why, I would still be richer for my spices and your food would taste only of soil! I believe I would get along just fine." Nofre's laughter had begun to subside, his grin slowly receding.

Pandrea met the calm with a hand to his chest, exposing the shining gemstones adorning his fingers. "Ah, but a man of your station would be remiss without such proclamations of your own standing, would you not? I trust you have found our jewelers to be the finest in the Kingdom and beyond, no?" The words colored his eyes with what appeared to be genuine hope and a feeling of camaraderie.

Nofre gestured a hand toward Pandrea and offered an acquiescing nod. "Your gemstone mines are surely the most illustrious in the world."

"And my House of Ponsa all the more fortunate to have laid our claim to it, writ in ink and blood."

Aritz did not want to consider what the merchant meant by "blood."

"But it is to my greatest happiness," Pandrea continued, "that my House has been graced by our many years of partnership with the House of Mata. Lord Nofre, I have nothing but gratitude for what I believe to be not only a mutually prosperous business accord, but also a dear friendship."

With a slight bow in his chair, so far as the table before him would allow, Nofre flashed a smile. "The privilege is mine, my friend. I wish only for it to continue in the years to come."

The merchant reached an arm up, the silken weaves of his jacket pulling taut, and snapped his fingers twice in quick succession. Aritz spied movement off in the corner of the chamber, a door opening, and indistinguishable commotion ruminating in the hallway.

Pandrea looked over his shoulder until one of his men reentered the dining room. As he turned back to Nofre, he flashed his teeth in a wide smile. "Then permit me to offer a gift as a testament to our continuing partnership. I ask for nothing in return." He remained silent for a moment and then slyly leaned over as though in preparation for a grave secret. "Though, if you wish to share the recipe for this paella, I would be remiss to decline."

Both men laughed heartily, Nofre slapping his counterpart with force along his shoulder.

From behind Pandrea emerged a northerner draped in far less garish attire than his liege, his robe woven of simpler and more muted fabrics, his features much more gaunt than some of the others Aritz had spied in the merchant's close circle since his arrival. The man was holding an ornate box cast and carved in white gold and shimmering blue gemstones. He stood between Nofre and Pandrea and offered the box to the latter with a deep bow, offering not a word besides.

Pandrea grasped firmly the box with both hands. "My thanks, Jair. You are dismissed."

Jair departed without further confirmation.

Slowly, the merchant opened the box, its contents faced toward him, a glint from the chandelier hanging overhead casting a flash of light over his face. "My friend, I offer this to you and your family as both thanks for our successful partnership, and as hope for our continuing friendship." He turned the box around, revealing a wonderfully ornate necklace inset with stunning crystalline jewels, polished and cut to the degree they were nearly transparent. Light reflected off them in a prismatic array, all the world's colors present in each stone.

Aritz's breath caught in his chest at the sight. Though it was not his place to speak, regardless, he was beyond words.

The same could be said for his father. Nofre's eyes lit up just as the gemstones did. His smile embodied a sense of disbelief that Aritz had never once seen on his father's face. There was shock and awe only barely hidden behind a thin veil in grave threat of falling to the floor. It seemed all Nofre could do was laugh.

"Savior's breath, man," he said through hardly suppressed laughter. He stayed his hand, though it was clear he had every intention of reaching out to grasp the necklace. "Are these...?"

Pandrea nodded with a knowing look in his eyes. "The reflective stones are fine quality diamonds—no expense spared for you, my Lord. Inset beside each one are the richest rock crystal quartzes we have mined. All refined and polished to befit a man and House of your station. I hope you treasure it dearly."

Nofre was approaching giddiness. "Without question, my friend. Without question." He reached toward the box and pulled it toward himself, examining the necklace with the awe and wonder Aritz faintly recalled him showing toward Alsonso on the day he was born. If he was not mistaken, he could have sworn he saw a tear trickling down his father's cheek.

As Aritz watched his lord father chuckle to himself at the sight, Aldorisa leaned over, placing a gentle hand against her husband's arm. Her eyes lit up just the same, though hardly with the same intensity flaring within Nofre's.

"Is it not the most beautiful thing you have seen, my love?" Nofre asked, flashing an exuberant smile.

Aldorisa offered a gentle nod and a warm grin. "Tis a truly captivating sight, dear." She turned her attention to Pandrea, placing a hand to her chest in thanks. "Pandrea, I must speak in place of my husband to say we are humbled and honored to receive such an illustrious gift. The hospitality of House Mata is extended to you and yours, on this day, and all days to come."

At the proclamation, tankards and goblets were raised to the air, splashes of wines and liquors flying every which way. Aritz felt at least three different sources of liquid land upon him, though from whom, he could not be certain. Not that he was unused to it. Such was the custom in the Acrarian High Houses: upon receipt of noble gifts, it was tradition for the Lord to gape in stunned awe while the Lady offered her profuse thanks on behalf of the House, after which drinks flowed both in and out of their respective cups.

Or, that was at least how it proceeded in the House of Mata. Aritz had known no other way.

But regardless, of all the wondrous boons granted to his father across the years, this one was by far the most captivating, the first to truly take hold of Aritz's attention. It possessed a beauty he had never before been gripped by. And when the box was closed and his father passed it along to an attendant to stow in the safety of their bedchamber, Aritz only a deeper longing to gaze upon it further, a sorrow of such sweetness at an untimely parting.

Uproarious commotion passed over him in waves as the feast resumed in earnest, course after course placed before him and taken away in their untouched state. For all that gripped Aritz's attention was the prismatic glimmer of a priceless ornament.

The evening passed, the morning came, and Aritz did not sleep a wink. Too much excitement, too much to think on. And there was hardly anything for him to keep his mind occupied today. No tutoring and his parents were off at engagements with the merchants from the Marches from morning to late afternoon.

Which meant only that their bedchambers would be unoccupied for the day.

He knew the morning routine. He knew the regular guard, Ynigo. He exchanged pleasantries with him upon waking. If there was any time for him to get a closer look at that necklace, it would be now. He had no greater opportunity than what was currently presented to him.

He dressed in his standard casualwear—an untucked white button-up shirt and plain tan trousers—and emerged from his bedchambers without even tussling his unruly hair into some semblance of order.

Before scurrying to his parents' chambers, though, he turned the corner and rapped a knuckle along the door to his brothers' rooms. His younger kin opened their doors almost simultaneously, Lorente still in his sleepwear while Alsonso rubbed at his eyes with clear grogginess in the motion.

"Aritz?" Lorente said inquisitively, exhaustion still rampant in his voice. "What is it? It's barely past sunup."

"Are our tutors here already?" Alsonso asked, apparently unaware of the day.

Aritz flashed a wide smile, hands planted firmly on his hips. "No tutors to-day, remember? Come on, follow me." He nudged his head forward, directing them toward their parents' chambers at the end of the hallway.

"Aritz, wait." Confusion was plastered across Lorente's face, intermingling with a clear sense of dismay. "Could you at least tell us what's going on?"

Barely stifling an excited chuckle, Aritz turned on his heel and waved his hands to his brothers, beckoning them to come forward. "Brothers, come now. Don't tell me you haven't been thinking about it all night, as well."

"Thinking about what?" Alsonso asked, still rubbing at his eyes and wiping away the dry flakes between his eyelids.

"That necklace! The one Pandrea gave Mother and Father last night. Don't you want to see it up close?"

"It's Mother and Father's," Lorente protested, never more apparent that he simply wanted to return to bed.

"No, it's *ours* as well, remember?" Aritz could feel the glee rising in his voice, and he cared little for hiding it. "Pandrea gifted it to not just Mother and Father, but our House. That means *us*, too!"

Lorente was quick to shake his head. "I'm sure we'll see it another time. I don't want Father to get mad at us."

"Remember the last time?" Alsonso added. "He got so angry that he—"

Aritz raised a hand, stopping his youngest brother before he could say more. "Trust me, both of you. I talked to Ynigo earlier. Mother and Father are off with the merchants all day, and he's the only one watching the door. It'll be *fine*. And come on, you saw how beautiful it was, didn't you? Don't you want to hold it, just for a little bit?"

His brothers seemed to consider the words, Alsonso fishing his hands into his trouser pockets and Lorente crossing his arms pensively. Aritz looked at each of them with excitement budding in his heart, hoping his smile would instill in them the same vigor that was currently coursing through him.

Slowly, Lorente conceded a nod. "It was really pretty, yeah. I wouldn't mind taking a closer look at it. What about you, Alsonso?"

Easily swayed as always, Alsonso sighed and nodded his head in turn. "As long as you're sure it's okay, Aritz."

"*Trust me.* Everything will be fine." Aritz felt relief at his brothers' acquiescence. "Now be quick about it and dress yourselves. I don't want to wait another minute!" He paced in place as Lorente and Alsonso retreated to their bedrooms to change, clicking his heels together in anticipation. The hallway remained silent but for the subtle rummaging of discarded and replaced clothing and Aritz humming softly to himself. His ears perked as one door opened after the next, a joyful smile stretching across his lips as his brothers appeared ready to take on the day.

Alsonso still rubbed at his eyes as his shaggy hair fell messily to his brow. He seemed to force a smile upon glancing at his older brothers and, without a word, shuffled his bare feet down the carpeted floors of the hallway.

Aritz widely gestured his arm to Lorente, motioning him to follow along, the smile still wide upon his lips.

Lorente waved a hand aside, meeting the smile with hardly a shred of genuineness, though he was likely still exhausted, judging from the dark bags hanging heavily below his eyes. He filed in beside Alsonso, shoving him gently with his shoulder, an act immediately reciprocated by the youngest brother.

Whistling a tuneless melody to himself, Aritz put his hands in his pockets, absently fiddling with the contents inside, and trailed his brothers, their parents' chambers growing ever closer.

Before him, Lorente and Alsonso were having a terse, inaudible conversation amongst themselves, the wide corridors offering no assistance in bouncing their voices off the portrait-lined walls. Aritz could not deny a modicum of curiosity at their words, but the sneer upon Lorente's face and the offended scrunch of Alsonso's told him all the story he needed. Typical brotherly bickering, as was typical of them.

The guard, Ynigo, eyed them with curiosity as they approached, his hand resting atop the pommel of his sword as it always did. He tutted his lips and opened his mouth as though to protest, but no words emerged.

A hesitant noise loosed from Alsonso's lips; it appeared he was attempting to have an explanation burst forth, but all that sounded was a stream of stutters.

Let me spare us all the pain, little brother, Aritz thought. He pushed hard against the small of Alsono's lower back, nearly thrusting him through their parents' door. "Just go inside, brother. It's alright."

Alsonso turned with confusion, his brow furrowed, but he was quick to relent and open the door, the wood giving a slight creak for the effort, and rushed inside. Even this old house was slow to awake upon the morn.

For his part, Lorente simply shook his head and followed along, nodding to the doorman on his way in. "Good morning, Ynigo."

Ynigo returned the nod. "Good morning, Master Lorente."

Aritz watched his brothers roam about through the vast expanse of their parents' chambers—he had to assume it to be the first time for either of them—and fished his hands back through his pockets, again feeling the contents within. He offered a wordless acknowledgment to Ynigo and entered in turn, swiftly closing the door behind him.

As though the act of crossing the threshold awakened something within him, Alsonso scurried about the room, like a beast seeking the trail of its escaped prey. A fervor gripped his gaze as he looked this way and that, an anxious panic evident upon his face. "Where is it, Aritz? We should be quick!"

Dismissing his youngest brother's worry with a flick of the hand, Aritz peered to the corner of the room, the familiar shape of the gift box catching his eye beside his mother's vanity mirror. "Relax, brother," he said, barely hiding the shade of annoyance in his tone. "Would you think a necklace would be found anywhere but among Mother's other jewels?" He inclined his head toward the vanity and urged his brothers to follow.

"He might be right, Aritz," Lorente said, his voice shaking ever so slightly. "I…I—"

"Calm yourselves, both of you," Aritz muttered. He hardly thought the reality of being alone in their parents' chambers would instill such fright so quickly. "A few minutes, and not a second more. Yes?" He turned his head, raising his brow to his brothers.

Frowns were apparent on both their faces, but they nodded wordlessly regardless.

"Good." A sharp smile turned Aritz's lips. "Not another word of worry from here on."

The jewelry box loomed ahead, ever so inviting, the allure of the beautiful treasure within all too enticing to ignore. It was as though a hypnotic melody had gripped him, much like the creatures in the mythology of the Erosian peoples from the southeastern Seas; the story went that these aquatic demons would lure sailors out to sea with an enchanting melody, only to slaughter them while their guards were turned.

Aritz never understood the point of the story. It had never frightened him, and the silent melody cast by the jewelry box would not herald his doom. He would not allow it.

As he gripped the sides of the box and lifted it open, his heart caught in his chest once again, his eyes fluttering at the gorgeous sight of the crystalline quartzes and prismatic diamonds embedded in the necklace's body. He tucked his fingers beneath the chains and carefully hoisted it up, the weight carrying a far greater heft than he had initially assumed. Everything about the necklace, from the resplendent shine of the gemstones to the remarkable craftsmanship of the silver lining of the ornament, screamed regality. It was a gift fit for royalty, and here he was, holding it for himself.

With an excited smile directed at his brothers, awe frozen upon their own faces in turn, Aritz carried the necklace over to the looking glass with an abundance of caution, taking careful measure of each step, wanting not to trip with such a valuable piece still in his hands. He held it up against his chest, admiring the reflection, and then clasped it about his neck, the sudden shift in weight nearly dragging him down. Readjusting his posture, he rested his right hand just below the necklace, puffing his chin out, turning one cheek over the next. And no matter the pose, no matter the angle, no matter the appearance...

Aritz loved what he was seeing.

The possibilities flew through his mind. A crown atop his head, florid and pronounced regalia draped about him, a wealth of servants at his beck and call, a flood of loving subjects heeding his every word. He wanted it all. He hoped to attain it all one day. The future was bright. Anything he could ever hope to want would always be within his grasp. And it would not be long until merchants from the Marches would bequeath gifts such as these directly to *himself*. He sighed contentedly. *If only those days would hurry up.*

With a turn of the heel, Aritz faced his brothers, the heft of the necklace throwing him off-balance; despite the near embarrassment, he took it in stride and gestured his arms wide. "What do you think?" he asked them. "Do I fit the part?"

Lorente's lips were pursed, his feet seemingly eager to jolt forward before the rest of his body did so. "It's amazing," he exclaimed. "I didn't think it could look more impressive than it already did, but seeing someone wear it is just..."

Aritz could feel the excitement exuding off his brother. It was his turn to play the part of the enchanting melody, luring the unknowing in. "Just think, brothers," he said, cautiously wrapping a hand around the pendant as he unfastened it from his neck. "One day, I will stand in Father's shoes and receive gifts such as these in great numbers. And when that time comes, I'll make sure there's one of these for each of us. Surely, this will not be the only one Pandrea ever makes." The chain fell slack in his hand and his hand drooped against the weight of the ornament's gemstones. "Now, would you both like to try it on as well?"

His feet finally seizing the desired opportunity, Lorente rushed ahead, reaching his hand forward perhaps a bit too eagerly; the pendant nearly fell between their grips, but Lorente was quick to recover. He held the necklace up to eye level, his hands shaking, the chain jingling in his grasp.

It did not take long for Aritz to realize his brother was nearly hypnotized by its beauty, much as he was.

The trance was broken only when Alsonso reached a hand around Lorente's shoulder and tugged hard on the chain. "Give it here!" he shouted. "I want to see it!"

With a snarl on his face, Lorente slapped his younger brother's hand away. "You'll have your turn, Alsonso! I'm looking at it now!"

Alsonso flashed his teeth and grasped at the necklace again. "No, you're gonna take too long! I want my turn first!"

"You're the youngest, so you go last. Those are the rules!"

The two brothers grabbed either end of the chain, each trying feebly to pull it one way or the other, spittle flying from their mouths as they snarled at one another, heels digging into the area rugs and knocking them out of place.

The weaves of the chain slowly came undone with each successive tug, Aritz watching with eyes wide as neither Lorente nor Alsonso gave the other an inch.

But all the inches of ground in the world mattered little when the chain snapped, the pendant fell, and the sickening shatter of crystal echoed in the hollow room.

Aritz felt his heart sink.

His brothers stood frozen in shock, their gazes unbreaking from each other, mouths agape as though to pass the blame unto one another, but the words remained unspoken, unwarranted against the silent screams of the shards upon the floor.

Tears were already cascading down Lorente's cheeks. He sank to his knees, furiously gathering the crystal shards in his hands, paying no heed to the blood streaming from his cut palms, and paying even less heed to his blood marring the pristine shine of the quartz. "Come on, help me, both of you! We need to put it back together!"

Alsonso dove to the ground and acted in much the same manner, sweeping his hand along the rug in a wide swath to corral the pieces of quartz, even though many of them were too small to gather. They may as well have been collecting grains of sand.

"Aritz!" Lorente shouted. "Don't just stand there! Help us!"

The sight of his brothers panicking on the ground, attempting in desperation to put back together a work of art crafted by the best jewelsmiths in the world, was enough to freeze Aritz in place. There was nothing that could be done. He accepted that the moment the necklace fell to the ground.

The futility was only punctuated by the sound of footsteps approaching from outside the door.

The hair on Aritz's neck stood sharply.

Lorente and Alsonso jerked their heads in the direction of the door. Alsonso pressed his bleeding palm to his mouth to muffle a frightened scream.

"All is well, I trust, Ynigo?" a muted voice rumbled from outside.

"I did not expect you back so soon, my Lord."

"Did you forget? Pandrea requested we reschedule for this afternoon. I was more than happy to oblige."

"We're so dead!" Lorente sharply whispered through gritted teeth, blood still dripping from his slashed palms. "What do we do, Aritz?!"

Aritz knelt to the ground, holding his hands out in placation. "It's okay, Lorente. Calm down. It'll all be okay." He curled his lips upward. "The blame falls on me. I will tell Father as such."

Hardly a moment remained for reassurance when the door creaked open, the heavy footsteps of their father ceasing with a startled gasp.

"Boys, what are you doing in here?" Nofre asked, slowly walking toward them. "Lorente, Alsonso, are you both bleeding? What happe—"

Aritz was never one to believe in magic, but even he couldn't deny the sudden change in the presence of the room. The heat rose as though flames were summoned from nothing, and when he gazed upon his father's beet-red face, he would not have been surprised if a furious pyre was soon to erupt from his nose and ears.

"What is the meaning of this?!" Nofre bellowed, pointing a shaking finger to the shards upon the floor. "What have you boys *done*?! That was a *priceless* gem—am I now to turn to Pandrea and request it be replaced because you have foolishly *destroyed* it?!" He clenched his hands into fists, his rage densely palpable; it seemed to exude from every one of his pores. "Which of you is responsible for this? Tell me *now!*"

Lorente and Alsonso fearfully turned toward Aritz.

In response, Aritz rose to his feet, locked gazes with the bestial ferocity gripping his father's eyes. "It was the two of them. They were trying to fight one another for it until the chain snapped and sent it shattering on the floor."

His brothers stammered out a panicked, wordless protest, fear gripping them as sweat poured down their faces, their hands trembling. Already was there a wet spot spreading in Alsonso's trousers.

And Aritz stood firm, not wavering in his accusation.

"If I may, my Lord." Ynigo stood beneath the threshold of the door, a frown set upon his face. "I can confirm Aritz speaks truthfully. I heard Lorente and Alsonso squabbling over something in here. I knew not of what until I heard the sound of the necklace breaking. Forgive me for not stopping them."

Nofre seemed to consider the words for a long, uncomfortable moment, his focus shifting from Aritz to Lorente and Alsonso, but the fury did not once depart his face.

"Aritz," he growled, the bones in his fingers grinding as he clenched his fists tighter and tighter. "Leave."

Aritz did not need to be told twice. He scurried past his protesting brothers, listening not to their panicked cries as their father bore down upon them. Ynigo grimaced and shook his head before turning back to his post.

The first blow was an almost sickening sound, the sound of hard bone on soft tissue. The pained cries of his brothers fighting against the effortful grunts of his father made for a hellish chorus, far removed from the enchanting melody that had drawn him to the necklace in the first place. But that trance was broken the moment the crystals shattered upon the floor.

And even as the hammer of his father's fists fell again upon his brothers' fragile bodies, Aritz could not help but smile.

He stopped to close the door, muting the horrors within from the outside world, and flashed a glance at Ynigo. Nodding to the guard, Aritz fished through his pocket, finding the coin he had been fiddling with earlier, and flicked it to Ynigo. Words were not needed when payment was more than enough.

Whatever today brings, Aritz thought, *I know now it will not be as monotonous as yesterday.*

And as he walked down the empty hallway, away from his father's savage roars and his brothers' enfeebled cries, Aritz chuckled.

CHAPTER THREE

All That Remains

The air remained heavy, even long after her captive audience departed to their other tasks.

Despite the numbing cold of the Heart's frigid winds, Sen could not find it within herself to retreat to the inviting warmth of the Tribes' makeshift homes and hearths. She had hoped the burden weighing upon her would have been lessened once it had been shared amongst her people. But, if anything, it only grew greater on her shoulders, as though it would drive her through the earth and bury her beneath if but an extra pound were to be placed on her.

The reality of it all was too much for any of them to bear. She knew it. She knew that the impending return of the Invaders, the imminent revenge of Kamataa, none of it would instill in them hope. Hope was for a time before a god was felled by mortal hands. The days following, and the days to come, exuded only a pervasive air of dread.

Sen had watched it from atop the ridge, her perch from which she could observe the detached manner in which the Tribes prepared themselves for the coming doom, the way they shuffled their feet through the piles of fresh-fallen snow blanketing the dark stains underneath. Strategic planning was voiced via broken and unenthused words, eyes drawn to the Bear's unmoving body and the Wolf's attentive and imposing form watching over it, a wordless acceptance and expectation of what yet awaited them no matter how thorough their counteroffensive would be.

The well of emotions within Sen was overflowing. Anger as she gazed upon the remains of a dead god. Sadness as she watched the mourners gathered about the ursine deity, the Wolf among them. Fear at the dense snow impeding the view of the southern approach, a barrier of mist promising the arrival of an insurmountable foe. Distrust toward herself for all she had failed to prevent in her brief time walking among the enemy. Unease as she closed her eyes and wondered how many more moments she had left to share with her remaining family and friends.

The sun hung low. It brought a tear to her eye. *I don't want to close my eyes and have that be the final time I see Tez.* A shudder coursed through her at the thought. She knew not what to do, not an inkling of what to say to anyone. She hardly believed herself wise enough to figure it out for herself—just as she was willing to seek out those who were.

I need to find Tawa.

Her bones protested as she lifted her boots out from the snow, the sensation of oppressive cold finally returning to her. As she trudged through the calf-deep piles, Sen dug her hands into her coat pockets, desperately attempting to find some bastion of warmth. She was used to the northern chills, but nothing compared to this.

A medical hut loomed along the southern walls. Sen knew Tawa had primarily stationed himself there prior to the battle, and she had no reason to think he would not still be there. He had been the only one willing to tend to Koelhe's catatonic state—though whether he was truly "willing" was a matter of debate. Surely now, there were even more to attend to. Sen knew not his capabilities to heal, but healing was altogether irrelevant at this point, and she at least was immensely familiar with his inclinations to care. *I could use plenty of that, at any rate.*

A surge of warmth mercifully greeted her as she reached the hut, the dancing flames within casting an inviting beacon of heat in defense against the biting winds emerging from the aching woods beyond. She rushed inside and furiously patted the accumulated snow from her coat and trousers, kicking loose the buildup stuck between the treads of her boots. The medical tent was quiet, save for the crackling of firewood and the rushed footsteps clacking from the adjacent room. A hesitant step forward was all Sen managed before she caught sight of the broken Bearsigns lined in parallel rows on either side of the room. They numbered a fraction of those in the tents on the other side of the valley, but the sight was no less disheartening. She knew none of them, but the shock-addled faces sung the same aria that had chorused too many times already since the battle.

It was enough for Sen to want to turn around and traipse back through the snow. Until she spied Tawa standing beneath the threshold separating the two rooms. She hadn't seen him since before the battle—not face-to-face, anyway. But she knew he had survived the hell of the day. When last she spoke with him, he had wandered off to parts unknown with a hand covering his tear-stained face, surely steeling himself for vengeance against those who killed his dear son Narva. Sen's beloved Narva.

The last handful of days did not appear kind to him. Tawa looked as though he hadn't slept a wink. Bags were heavy beneath his eyes, which were near-bloodshot from exhaustion. The yellow markings of the Owlsign had faded almost entirely from his face. A few fresh cuts and bruises littered his cheeks and his exposed arms, and his shirt sported a collection of puncture holes and slashes. It seemed he was on the receiving end of both the Invaders' strikes and those of Kamataa's traitors hiding amongst their people.

Weathered though he appeared, Tawa still managed a soft smile, even if it was clear from his eyes he was surprised to see her. "Sen," he said, gesturing to her with an open hand. "Come in, get out of the cold. I do not wish to see you catch illness."

Sen brushed the sides of her arms for warmth and approached the fire, sighing with relief as the dancing flames radiated before her. She grabbed Tawa's extended hand, clasping it between both of hers. "Under the circumstances, I think illness would be the least of my worries."

"Illness breeds greater troubles," he reminded her, but his eyes seemed focused instead on the Bearsigns. "Though I suppose there are afflictions even we cannot prevent."

Would that I could have when I had the chance, she thought, grimacing. *And yet, here we are now, whimpering mindlessly before a waning flame.*

However long she remained silent did not register with her, but Tawa seemed to take notice. "What is it, Sen? What troubles you?"

Chuckling, Sen pulled her hands back and gestured broadly about herself. "Besides the obvious, Tawa? Are you saying you're *not* troubled?" She stared at the mindless gathering, her fist instinctively clenching the longer she stared at the Bearsigns, the anger reaching her limbs before it extended the rest of the way to her mind. "Have you even left this hut since the battle?"

Tawa sighed. He stepped forward with his hands placed on his hips, his eyes downcast. He didn't need to speak the words for Sen to know the depths of the grief. "I find that busying my hands is the best thing I can do for myself right now."

"You don't need to do so alone, Tawa." Sen bit at her bottom lip, struggling to look at him even as his focus was cast toward the flames. "There's…nothing we can do for them. Unless you've learned how to raise the dead. If you are, that could have come in handy a few times lately."

Despite it all, Tawa still managed to laugh. "I fear any pursuit of that would leave us much the same as the Haunted. Miss him though I do, I would rather not have your father egging me on from beneath the earth."

Part of her wanted to ask if he would pursue it for Narva, but she ultimately thought against it.

"Though, with things as they are now," he continued, "who's to say how much longer we are for the Otherworld? We may soon be laughing with him yet again."

"You don't need to be alone in your grief, Tawa," Sen said, taking a half-step toward him. "We…*I* could certainly use you right about now."

A grimace passed Tawa's face. He folded his hands behind his back, puffing his chin out toward the fire. His lip quivered, but it seemed he was trying his utmost to hold it all together. "I…I am not a strong man, Sen. I know we have all suffered tremendously in these recent days and weeks. Some may find comfort and solace in the company of others to quell their grief. But…I cannot find myself to seek that same comfort. The words of strange company are hardly a boon to me."

"Am I strange company?" Sen asked, feeling the inquisitiveness burst from her eyes.

Tawa's frown set even deeper into his face. "Of course not, Sen. But one by one, the company I seek has disappeared. I lost my wife when my son was born. Your father pulled me from the darkest depths of my grief, and Narva only lifted me higher. Before I could blink, I lost both of them. Countless of those whom I considered friends were lost on the night of Koelhe's uprising, either felled by traitors or joined with traitors. Countless more on this battlefield, either struck through by a Tribesperson's weapon or an Invader's; or left mindless by the Bear's felling. One by one, they all vanish, until I am left with no more close companions than I can count upon one hand. And when the number dwindles to nothing, when I cannot tally a single person upon my fingers, what more can I do...than keep my hands busy?"

The finality, and the acceptance of it, sent a shudder through Sen. An all-too-familiar shudder. "You're stronger than you give yourself credit for, Tawa. I...I..." She clenched her eyes shut, grimacing at what she was about to say. "In normal times, I would not have lasted half as long as you have. I...almost didn't even make it past the Forest."

"Many do not make it past the Forest," Tawa said bluntly. "The Sun Tribe are indicative enough of—"

"No, Tawa. That's...not what I meant."

Tawa's eyes widened in recognition as he turned to face her. He opened his mouth as though to say something, but the words appeared lost on his tongue. There were no words he *could* say; they both knew they would not take back what nearly happened.

When she closed her eyes, Sen could still feel the kiss of the barrel against her forehead, her finger dancing around the trigger. She had been so close to pulling it. She had *wanted* to pull it. The laughing shadows that continued to haunt her entreated her to do so. The final hesitation was all that saved her, even as her finger successfully found its way to the trigger.

Finding the strength to look Tawa in the eyes was immensely difficult, but she managed to do so, if only barely. She expected disappointment, but gratefully found the compassion that she had always readily anticipated seeing upon his face. "I don't know what stopped me," she said. "And I don't know why I didn't try again. I guess I simply...busied myself much the same as you're doing. A...different kind of busy, granted. A much more heinous busy.

But I'm still here. And even though it doesn't feel like it at all to me right now...there's always something to fight for. It can't be for nothing. We'll stand as we stand, and if we fall, we'll do so on our feet rather than our knees."

Somehow, for some reason, Tawa laughed at her final comment.

Sen raised an eyebrow. "What? What did I say?"

Quickly, Tawa shook his head. "I apologize, Sen. I did not mean to. Just...I remember Tez mentioning your mother having said that...the night of Koel-he's coup. I sometimes forget...just how much of your parents is in you and your sister. And Brin as well, for that matter."

She didn't know how to react to that. It was a confusing feeling of grief mixing with gratitude.

"And though I do not know what the coming days will bring," Tawa continued, "I am thankful you still walk among us. I will walk toward our end with my head held high and a spear in my hand, knowing that you are still among those walking beside me."

A swirl of emotion swelled within Sen until there was little to be done to prevent the tears from falling. She brusquely wiped at her eyes, her hands trembling, the thought of that day in the Forest irreparably heavy upon her. "For however many steps we have left," she finally agreed. "For my parents, for my brother...for Narva."

Tawa reached out and placed a hand on her shoulder, just like her father used to do in the days that seemed half a lifetime ago. "For all whom we have lost."

"With spears and bows in our hands until we meet our ends."

"But may our ends come long after those of the Invaders."

It felt a false hope, but Sen could not protest. She only nodded. *So long as our rest is peaceful and theirs agonizing, that will be enough.*

Tawa offered a firm squeeze of her shoulder before turning and heading back to the adjacent room he had previously emerged from. He loosed a heavy sigh as he shook his head, his hands placed firmly on his hips. Only the corner of his face was visible, but Sen could see some combination of frustration and relief upon it. "It is amazing, the way things change in the blink of an eye. Not so long ago, I am certain you would have delighted at this sight. But now?" He blew a puff of air, wispy tufts from his mouth dissipating against the firelight. "Now..."

Sen followed after him, intrigued as to what grabbed his attention. There were only two bodies in this room, their faces obscured initially by Tawa's body, but it was not long for her to gasp in equal measure.

Koelhe lay upon the ground, eyes transfixed to the ceiling, a rasped groan grinding against her throat in an almost droning chorus. Sen had not seen the state of her when she initially returned to the Stone Tribe village, nor did she seek her out upon the journey through the mountains and subsequent preparations in the True Heart. This woman haunted her dreams; she was such an easy target for Sen's hatred and anger, a justification for everything she was so briefly willing to do whilst among the Children of the Black Moon. But now? Seeing her reduced to...this? She had not the words for it.

Beside mother lay son, as Fann was prostrated in much the same state. He was far more battle-worn than Koelhe, his flesh marred by fresh wounds and dried blood, the bandages wrapped about his shoulder stained in a blackened red, his prior injuries likely reopened during the battle.

One whose mind was rent the moment his god was slain. The other who faced the somber realities she had so deftly ignored. And yet, the outcome appeared ever the same.

"Would you have felt catharsis at this sight?" Tawa asked, half-turning his head over his shoulder, a keenly sharp glare in his eyes. "Before...all of this, at any rate."

Sen stepped alongside Tawa, her clenched fists trembling. It didn't take much for her to break out in a cold sweat. When she closed her eyes, she could hear their mocking voices urging her toward each of her basest de-sires, anguished screams vanishing at the sound of a Deatharm taking them between the eyes. So much of her pain, her anger, her misery...everything traveled back to these two sad bastards.

She bit at her lower lip and drew a deep breath through her nostrils. "They deserved worse," she muttered, gravel finding its way into her voice. "But they also did not deserve *this*."

"I would be loath to wish this upon anyone," Tawa agreed. "Despite everything, despite all they have done, despite all the blood that lays soaked beneath their feet..."

Sen shook her head. "The consequences will never be theirs to know. Where is the fairness in that for us?"

"The most heinous among us never suffer what they have wrought, and so it is for us to gather and repair what remains."

"And is that what you're doing here, Tawa?" Sen asked, gesturing to Koelhe and Fann, her nose scrunching at a sudden waft of foulness reaching her nose. "Tending to their sundered minds and...cleaning up once they've shit themselves?"

Tawa frowned and stared down at his flexing fingers. "I cannot allow myself to be what little they thought of me. When we reduce ourselves to the depths our enemies sink, we render ourselves no better than them."

A response was ill-formed in her head, and so Sen said nothing, offering nothing more than a grimace.

"But," Tawa continued, still glancing at his hands, "it would be a lie if I were to say it is anything more than that. Truly, my hands simply need to remain busy. My conscience grows no heavier at this sorry sight, but likewise, my heart is filled with anger."

"I don't think I've known anything but anger when looking at either of them," Sen said, that same fire burning within her as it always did. "I just didn't think I would ever feel a shred of remorse for them, though. It was not long ago that I would have gladly danced upon their graves, damn whoever would cry foul for it. Not only would they have done the same to me, but they also had every intention of sending me to an early one."

A weak, shocked gasp escaped Fann's mouth as though the last hope of air was being driven from his lungs. Instead, he kept breathing as a river of drool trailed down the cheek of his misshapen face.

"Gods help me, but I wish I could feel joy for this," Sen growled, her flame continuing to flare inside her. "Simplicity is relative, but I wish for those simpler days before those runaways arrived in our village. Were things still the same as then, I would gladly watch over them as they wither away."

Tawa merely regarded her in silence. The twinge in his face did not offer any shred of disagreement.

"But I have nothing left to feel toward them." As the words left her lips, the lingering shadows lifted from her. The haunting laughter in her ears quelled, the shrill shrieks dissipating until nothing remained and the echoes faded like the final crackle of burning coals. Though a weight still bore down upon her, she felt some of it disappear just the same. "What they deserved was for simpler times. What they deserved was before a madman plundered and stole our land, killed one of our gods. What they deserved was before a psychopathic witch whispered in that madman's ears, leading him to the slaughter he eagerly seeks. What they deserved...was not this. Were it within the power granted to me by the Moon, I would restore them to sanity just so they could see what remains in their wake, what could have been prevented had they not ripped everything out from under us. But I was never that Lucky. I am a child of fortune, for all the misfortune it has brought. And how unfortunate it is that I cannot find catharsis at the sight of either of them. Nor to any of the others who looked upon me with grave disdain whose minds have been irreparably destroyed. Despite it all...we are still Tribe. And we are Tribes' last remaining voices." Grinding her teeth, she snarled at Tawa, her nails digging sharply into her palms, near enough to drawing blood. "So may our voices haunt the Invaders until their dying days."

The ghost of a smile stretched across Tawa's tired lips. "I could not have said it better, Sen." He turned, his gaze seemingly focused past the rows of the incapacitated in the adjacent room. He reached for his coat, long since discarded upon the floor, and made for the doorway. "Come. It appears nightfall is upon us. The stars are sure to be bright."

Though startled by Tawa's sudden change in priorities, Sen bundled herself back in her coat as best as she could and followed, the bite of the mountainous cold near to torture after enjoying the warmth of home and hearth. As her feet crunched through the packed snow, she looked left and right until she found Tawa settling himself along the edge of the ridge, his head craned skyward, all tension seemingly gone as he relaxed against his elbows, ignoring whatever chill was surely running through him. Sen stumbled through the unsteady landing until she caught up with Tawa and threw herself to the ground, preferring to allow the ice to assault her all at once rather than easing herself into the cold.

"I suppose I misjudged," Tawa admitted with a chuckle, gesturing broadly to the night sky. "Far too many clouds to view the full body of stars."

Sen offered him a pitying, but amused, glare. "It hasn't exactly stopped snowing since we've been here, Tawa. You might do well to step outside more often."

Tawa nodded but said little else. The gentle snow flurries cascaded down and glistened upon his weathered forehead, the cold biting at his skin with each flake. Despite a visible grimace, he appeared ill-inclined to cease staring at the nocturnal clouds. "This takes me back," he said. "To those 'simpler times' you spoke of."

Folding her legs up into a fetal position for warmth, Sen inclined her head toward Tawa. "Oh?"

"I spent many evenings like this. With Narva. Simply...staring at the stars above and wondering what stories each of them would tell. What mystical magic is housed within them."

Magic, huh? Sen thought. She stared up at the snow clouds, wondering if every star was like the Moon, if power was dictated by what the stars saw fit to grant people.

"Many people would listen in on our conversations, and I am certain they all thought us little more than wishful fools. Magic is merely a word to describe the feats of man which defy description. I would be surprised if the Invaders did not see our communion with the gods—and the Boons we are fortunate to receive from them—and decry it all simply as 'magic.' It is simply within our nature to fear what we cannot describe rather than make an effort to understand. You know this better than most, I am sure."

"I fear that the few who *would* understand are quite intent on rendering our unwillingness to learn irrelevant," Sen said with the shadow of a smile. *The few who remain of that few.*

Slowly, Tawa nodded. "I would not say the Eclipseborn are the only ones who understand the Eclipseborn. When I was young, before I had a son to raise, I often made treks to the Heart to learn from the Keepers—much to my late wife's chagrin." A soft, amused chuckle escaped his lips. "I had only heard the tall tales from my father and my father's father, but surely there was more to it than the generations of fables. The records of the Eclipseborn were often incomplete, as though pages were ripped from memory. But I learned much from Ko Endra and many of the other Owlsigns. There is much curiosity among the Keepers, and though they also fear what they do not comprehend, there is at least effort to unravel the mysteries. I was always enamored with that. To this day, I still gaze upon the night sky and wonder how much more there is for us to discover. For you are proof of that celestial magic. Whatever exists within their bodies...it exists within you, Sen."

Sen couldn't help but grimace at that. The hidden stars lost their allure, and all she could ponder was what was soon to return from the south. "But maybe we're right to fear what we can't grasp. The power of the stars should be unattainable, and those of us who are given the Moon's gifts are seen as unnatural. Kamataa is only proof of that. The only path the stars above carve is one rife with vengeance."

"By that logic, would you claim that the path of the Owl is one rife with treachery?"

The bluntness of the question took Sen aback. "N-no, of course not, Tawa, but—"

Tawa held a hand up, bidding her to stop. "The Signs under which we are born may dictate our proclivities and aptitudes, but they do not predetermine the paths we walk. We have infinite paths from which to choose, and just as Koelhe walked her own path, I followed along my own. All that remains the same between is that the Owl granted us a piece of its power. Do not think yourself lesser simply because the other Eclipseborn have walked along the same path. You will find branches and tributaries just the same so long as you look for them."

Sen dug her bare hand through the snow almost as a reflex until the cold numbed all feeling. "And still, I felt powerless to do anything to stop them. Every time I look over this valley, I see everything I could have stopped. And yet I did nothing."

"But that hardly means you are the same as Kamataa or any of the rest of them." Tawa reached out again, firmly placing both hands on Sen's shoulders. "Whatever led you to join with them, whatever happened in that City, whatever happened on your journey south to rescue your brother, all of it brought you back to where you needed to be. You are still *here*, and that will be enough. Ignore all those who would say otherwise."

Nocturnal critters chirped and cawed as Sen pondered the words, shivers traveling up and down her spine with each snowflake that landed upon exposed skin. "I just..." She blew out a deep breath, clenching her eyes shut. "I can't help but wonder if...if he could see what I've done, what I allowed myself to become part of, what I got myself involved in...if he could see all of that, would Narva think the same of me?"

"Of course, he would," Tawa said without hesitation. "There was not a day gone by where he did not see you for the person you truly are. Nor has there been for me. There may be those who remain distrusting, but that is the reality of the situation. Do not let it change who and what *you* know you are. Your actions will always speak louder than their words."

Sen smiled, hesitant though it was. "Thank you, Tawa," she managed to say. *But no matter how many times I hear it...I don't know that I can bring myself to believe it.*

Tawa gripped her by the elbows and hoisted her back up to her feet, dusting off the accumulated snow from her coat. "I can tell you are still thinking too much on it."

"A mind reader, as always." Sen couldn't help but laugh.

"Do not think I have not picked up on your tells after all these years." He flashed a calm smile that could have warmed her if it wasn't so godsdamned cold out. "Think tomorrow. Sleep now."

She nodded. "I'll do my best."

Tawa made his way back toward his makeshift dwelling, back among the stench of mindless defecation and stale drool. He turned his head over his shoulder, the snow still crunching underfoot, and said, "Tomorrow is but another day in the fight for our lives. Who knows if this is our final night to rest?"

The thought did little to help Sen, but there was no denying Tawa's logic. As she watched him retreat inside, she trudged her own way back to her temporary home, unsure if rest would come, but at the very least certain the warmth of a fire would be invigorating.

Tawa had left her with much to think on, and it could not wait for tomorrow. There was still a branch in her path to discover.

CHAPTER FOUR

The Shadow of the Gods

The Year 1556 Anno Salvatoris

15 Years After the Invasion

The spear had always felt an extension of her, and yet, it now felt so foreign to her.

There was no steady ground to be found beneath Tez's weary feet, an issue beyond the slippery landing resulting from the packed snow and ice. Each landing felt unassured, uncertain. Her arms ached from the weight of her weapon in a way they never had before. Her chest strained as each thrust and swing required an exertion of effort entirely unknown to her.

She spun on her heel, the field behind her as empty as it possibly could be in this death-stained enclosure. Privacy was a matter of perspective, but her perception still had yet to recover to what it once was.

Gritting her teeth as she swung, swung, thrust, a heavy fog still lingered in the back of Tez's head. Each successive step of her routine felt further and further away, as though she was years out of practice. The memories of the Endurance that had long coursed through her still throbbed, a phantom limb permanently adhered to her soul. She felt the Bear's death like none other who still had their wits about them. A pain pervaded in her blood, a part of her ripped asunder over and over.

The spear was only a reminder. What was once an extension of her body was little more than a memory, a memento weighing as heavily upon her as the well of her brother's recollections hanging slack from her neck. She could not dare to look upon them. Intrusive would hardly have been the word for it. But to the pendant itself, to the life it held within, she could only feel indebted.

Ironic, she thought, her arms protesting as each subsequent section of her routine only further weakened her. *For all the times Brin needed protection, here he is, protecting me.*

Tez planted the butt end of the spear in the snow, twirled about it, swung a vicious low sweep with her left leg. The momentum slid her off balance, her steel flailing wildly as she tried and failed to drive it into the ice before her. Instead, she fell to her knees, the weapon clacking unceremoniously against the ice, and she was left with naught else to do but spit her frustration into the snow, cursing underneath her breath. *So this is what I'm reduced to. The last Bearsign. The Invaders are certain to cower at the sight of me.*

She snarled, the weight of her exhaustion piling atop her as she rolled to her spear, thrusting it as she threw herself forward. Her right boot caught itself in an unyielding pile of snow and ice, the muscles in her leg screaming from the overextension, and she crumbled without struggle. Tez's left knee buckled, a sharp pain surging through it from the awkward landing, and she was grateful at least for the soft powder in which she landed. The gratitude was fleeting, however, and immediately gave was to frustration, the growl in her throat all that remained in her of the Bear's power and Boon.

"Godsdamn it!" she shouted, hurling her spear toward the nearby rockface, the tip planting in the ice for three seconds before the weapon toppled over. Righting her contorted body, Tez pushed herself up to a seated position, her knees crying out as she folded herself inward, clutching her legs for what comfort she could manage. A snow squall burst through the forest's clearing and pelted the side of her head as though sympathizing with the anger stewing within. She bunched her fingers through her knotted hair, her braid long since undone, her eyes clenching and widening as her breaths grew rasped and ragged. Everything ached.

She was content to wallow until the crunch of approaching footsteps drew her attention.

Sharrabha and Ket approached her warily, their expressions each telling their own story.

The furrow to Sharrabha's stern brow spoke of fear, anger, the desire to avenge those who fell to the Invaders' tricks. Tez had to remind herself that it was not just those of the Stone Tribe for whom Sharrabha grieved, but also her close companions among the Keepers.

Meanwhile, Ket's eyes sang an aria of worry. The sharp features of their cheeks and chin were framed by the heavy hood cloaking them, covering their shorn hair entirely from the wailing snow, which mercifully was beginning to quell.

Tez looked up at them both, her lips quivering, her fingers red and raw from the cold. Her teeth clattered as the silence prolonged, no one in any rush to say anything.

It told Tez all she needed to know.

"How much time do we have?" she asked.

Sharrabha closed her eyes, a dense puff of air billowing from her nostrils as she sighed. "Dawn, most likely." The Packmind rune on her pendant glinted just bright enough to glow through her heavy coat. "Judging from what's been relayed amongst the group from the Sensors, and based on the Invaders' location and pace...we might even get as lucky as mid-morning. But not much longer than that."

Tez closed her eyes, picturing the furious might of the Invaders' return. *I don't even want to imagine what fury and ambition is driving them to return. All I know is there is no doubt in my mind that they do not fear the Wolf. Gods help us.* She clenched her fists and attempted to warm them with her breath, to little avail. "And our numbers?" she croaked. The desperation in her voice was not lost upon her.

"Compared to what we were before the first battle?" Ket's voice reeked of defeat, but it was clear they at least attempted to mask it with half-hearted assurance. "Half-strength. Those who can handle a spear or bow, will. Anyone with a beating heart and functioning mind sees has little option otherwise." They left the words hanging, but Tez could see the implied recognition in their face. Ket may have been able to mask their voice, but their face was another story entirely.

There were no words to say. How could there be *any* words to say? "What do we even do?" Tez muttered, the wind doing its utmost to howl over her words.

Sharrabha could only shake her head. "Fight. Survive. Until our quivers run empty and our steel ground dull. They can bleed us dry as much as they wish, but they've yet to taste the fury of a pack of cornered wolves. If we fall to our last, it will be at their great loss."

The silent yet heavy steps of the Wolf sounded in the distance, the lupine god still prowling the altar where its departed kin still lay dead, its golden eyes still ever alert to the valley's approach where the Invaders would soon re-emerge.

Tez could hardly feel anything in her heart but pity and fear. Her gaze shifted between Sharrabha and the Wolf, and she had to wonder if the rage in the huntress's voice was the manifested anger of her god taken form.

"We need you, Tez," Sharrabha pleaded, her fists bunching, her teeth glinting against the snow. "None remain who are more adept with the spear than you. I'd wager to say that even before the Bear fell, you were among the best. I don't think any among us would want to follow anyone into battle more than they would you. We would gladly fight to our last behind you."

Despite the gravity of the situation, Tez couldn't stop the grin from creasing her lips. "You've been spending too much time with the Lake Tribe the last few days." Her gaze turned to Ket's gentle smile, the softness of their face setting her heart at ease, even if her lungs still burned with exhaustion. She closed her eyes, Sharrabha's proclamation echoing in her mind. *I don't feel like the arms master you say I am anymore, Sharrabha. I'm just a shell of what I was. A dead god's shadow and nothing more.*

That's what she wanted to say. That's what she wanted to admit. But what came out of her mouth was, "I will gladly lead the charge."

There was no shade of pleasure on Sharrabha's face, but at the very least, there was what appeared to be relief. She half-turned, her head craning toward the row of tents by the gods' altar. "We should convene with the strategists, then. As soon as we can."

Tez nodded, but she felt no inclination to rise back to her feet, to return to the throbbing aches that still coursed through her. She could already feel the swelling in her ankle from twisting it in the snowbank. Hopefully nothing more than a sprain, if she was lucky. "Give me a moment, Sharrabha," she called over the wind. "I just need a moment."

An acknowledging smile passed over Sharrabha's lips and the huntress was off, one hand burrowed deep in a heavy pocket and the other resting atop her quiver of arrows.

One can only imagine how quickly the first arrow will fly from her bow, Tez thought.

The monotonous sea of white gripped Tez's attention for long enough to distract her from Ket's approach. She didn't even register their presence until she felt their warm arms wrapped about her shoulders.

Ket's grip was such that it seemed they would never let go. It was a small gesture, but it was one that evaporated any lingering shreds of aches in Tez's body, if only for a little while.

Slowly, Tez touched her hands to Ket's, linking her fingers with theirs. Words failed her. Only her tears could speak. A weight rested against her neck as Ket's heavy hood burrowed against her exposed skin.

"Are you ready for this?" Ket asked. Their voice indicated they already knew the answer.

Instinctively, Tez shook her head. "You couldn't understand what it was like being brought back from the brink as I was. When the Bear was slain, I felt...I felt everything rip apart, only for it to be shoddily stitched back together. But the threads are poorly tied, some wound too loosely, some too tight. I feel gaps where there weren't before, and even though I can see to the other side, I just cannot clear those gaps." She bit at her lower lip, wincing at the admission. "I am the final Bearsign standing, but I'm hardly the one you would have followed into battle before. That Tez died on the battlefield, and...I don't even recognize the one sitting before you now."

She expected Ket to let go, to walk away. She was the furthest thing from what the Lake Tribe respected and admired. But instead, she felt the grip tighten, her arms uselessly pinned against her sides as she remained wholly ensnared by Ket.

"That Tez is still very much alive," Ket said, the assurance in their voice far more genuine than it had been before. "You are much more than your strength and prowess, Tez. You always were. I knew that from the moment we met. You are fiercely loyal, protective. You challenged two of the strongest men in the Land without batting an eye because you valued unity in the face of uncertainty above all else. I would not follow you simply for your skill with a spear. I would stand with you for the strength of your will, the ferocity of your heart. Nothing will take that away from you." They reached a hand up and touched Tez's cheek, turning her toward them. "I have no reservations reminding you of that, no matter how many times it takes, no matter how long it takes."

Tez gulped and pushed down an anxious breath. "You know, we may not have more than a day left. You'll have to push yourself hard."

"I'm nothing if not persistent."

They leaned into one another, their lips touching, the passion enough for but one tender moment before the reality of the moment returned.

"Are *you* ready for this?" Tez asked, her eyes wide with concern as she pulled herself away from Ket's lips.

The Lake healer stifled a nervous chuckle, their hands shaking against Tez's neck, their eyes welling with shimmering pools threatening to freeze over against the mountain's breath. "You do know how to set the mood, Tez of the Stone Tribe."

Tez managed a sheepish laugh. "I'm sorry," she said, her eyes downcast. "You'll just...tomorrow you'll have to—" A firm finger to the lips halted her words.

"I know full well what I will have to do tomorrow." Ket's gaze was stern in a way Tez had not seen before. "But I'm intent on not thinking about it until I must. So just shut up and kiss me while we still have the opportunity."

Tez gladly obliged.

"Are you confident you've chosen correctly?"

"Be quiet and get out of my head."

Cin rested out of view of the marching Acrarian army, his aching body wedged between the natural rock formations he had been using as a makeshift shelter. His bones still protested with each subsequent movement; with each passing moment, he was thankful he had thought to draw in Restoration while being flung through the woods before he passed out and the Bear was slain. It surely mitigated what would have been a proper mess.

But he was in no condition to fight. His participation in the battle to come would hardly change the outcome. One way or the other.

It was more than enough for him to catch sight of the Acrarian convoy, noticeably thinned from their initial strike, but carrying all the same poise and confidence. The last thing Cin had remembered before sinking into unconsciousness was the earth-shattering roar of the Bear in full charge. That they seemed hardly undeterred from returning to the scene impressed Cin in no small amount. Or, at the least, such could be said of Aritz a Mata, his face gleaming with the prospect of a second chance. Cin could hardly blame him; he hadn't known him to ever need one.

But what he did not expect to see was Kamataa marching right alongside Aritz, Vanta and Sha'a following closely behind them. The vibrant red locks of Kamataa's Acrarian disguise were a beacon in the waning daylight made all the more eye-catching by the golden rays of the setting sun. *Just what are you planning?* he wondered. *What is your gambit now?*

Turning on his side, damning the discomfort of stiff bones against cold stone, Cin narrowed his gaze at the approaching army, taking in every face, every emotion. Skin battle-worn, apparel threadbare, hands shaking and unsteady, but weaponry at the ready.

He grunted, though whether it was with approval or disbelief, he wasn't quite sure himself. There was no chatter among them, no idle conversations. Only a sense of apparent resignation toward the fact that they had just escaped with their lives mere days ago. How many of them would be lucky a second time?

Luck is not all it's cracked up to be, Cin thought. *You all can trust me on that.*

"Do you envy them?"

Zarrow's voice grated at the back of his head. He winced and clenched his eyes shut, unsure if the discomfort was from the voice of the lost or the positioning of his body. "I believe I told you to get out of my head," Cin whispered sharply, cautious not to draw undue attention to himself from the

Acrarians on the valley trail below. His pilfered Tribal pendants clattered against his chest, though not loud enough to echo.

"Their end seems all but predetermined, wouldn't you agree?" Zarrow said, clearly taking no heed to Cin's demands. *"Perhaps they all know they are but mere steppingstones for Aritz a Mata to reach what he desires. They have never had a choice but to be tools. But your story has not yet been written. You have not yet decided where to let the river carry you."*

"I told you; I am content with where fate's flows have taken me." An inadvertent snarl scrunched Cin's nose as he kept a weary eye on the Acrarian march. Zarrow's presence hovered above him, the weightlessness of the Otherworldly visitor bearing down heavily upon his mind, itching at him, the sensation of one reaching their hand out just close enough not to touch, but arrogant and amused enough to remain there. "I do not envy marching into certain death."

"Yet you seemed altogether willing naught but days ago."

"And now I walk the path the Moon has set out for me."

"Is this *the path She has set for you?"*

"Yes," Cin barked, his fists bunching against the smooth cold beneath him. "Just as your path is the seeking of an eternal rest that may never come."

"Few are we of the Dusk Tribe. Should the Acrarians persist, there may no longer be any remaining to haunt." Zarrow's voice paused, tutting his incorporeal lips. *"Though perhaps, could it be that is all you seek? An end to the curse of our Tribe?"*

"They are no Tribe to me. They never have been." He gritted his teeth, craning his head around the rock formation to watch Kamataa's vibrant hair disappear around the corner. "What remains of my Tribe is here, marching toward a welcomed end. You must be jealous, Zarrow. *They* will at least be offered the long rest you wish for."

Zarrow was quiet for a moment, but Cin could only imagine him pacing back and forth in the Otherworld. *"My fate is not quite the curse you think it to be, Cin. The Moon may have cursed us amongst the living, but we who have passed on are afforded much more...perspective than we had in our prior days. Loath as I am to agree with my father..."*

"Your father?" Cin turned his head and raised his brow, despite there being no one behind him.

"*It's unimportant,*" Zarrow said dismissively. "*But do not be so callous as to throw away what remains of your people—your* true *people—in pursuit of hollow replacements and vacant shadows.*"

"I throw away nothing." Cin gritted his teeth, threw a fist at the empty air he assumed Zarrow was occupying. "I *pursue* nothing. The only home I've known is among my fellow Eclipseborn. They are as close to kin as I care to have. I would stand before the Otherworld itself for them, which is far more than I can say for the extinct peoples who birthed me."

The sensation of the lost's presence was always strange to Cin. He couldn't necessarily feel the "emotions" of those with whom he communicated from beyond the pale. But the weight bearing down on him simply felt..."different" in response to changes in demeanor. Happiness would feel distinct from anger, anger would feel distinct from sadness.

But what he felt from Zarrow now was unlike anything else he had experienced. It seemed almost akin to disappointment. Resignation. Perhaps even frustration. The interior of Cin's mind was a stone-lain path, and he could feel Zarrow kicking rocks down the lane as though giving up on the discussion.

"What?" Cin asked bluntly. "You have something to say, so say it."

He heard Zarrow sigh, almost forlornly. "*You would face death itself for these Children of the Black Moon, you say. Would they do the same for you?*"

Gravel scraped against Cin's throat as he grumbled. "What are you implying?"

"*I have watched our people for long enough—unable to intervene beyond advising from the land of the dead—to know when one has embarked upon a fool's errand. My days saw the greatest foolish mistake of all, and I did nothing to stop it.*" Zarrow's presence pulsed a feeling of regret. "*Do not follow them into the same madness that our people have suffered for centuries.*"

Cin threw his hairs up into the air in frustration. "What is your *point*?" he hissed, his voice nearly breaking the plane of a whisper. He sharply turned his head to ensure none of the marchers heard him, but the tail end of the convoy was about to turn the corner.

"*My point,*" Zarrow said, pulsing condescension, "*is you should be more privy to where you place your loyalties. You would lay down your life for your fellow*

Eclipseborn, but would they of you? They have not made any attempt to find you since the battle."

Words failed Cin. He opened his mouth, but nothing came out beyond a resigned sigh. He had no answer.

"*It would appear you already know.*"

"Surely, they assumed me dead."

"*Assumptions upon assumptions, Cin.*" Zarrow's tone was rife with admonishment. "*Is that why you warned the Tribes of the Acrarian return?*"

With a growl, Cin gripped at the Packmind bangle hanging from his neck, one of an assortment of still-functional pendants in his possession. Its glimmer had long since dimmed, but the moment he saw the Acrarians' approach, some hours ago, he passed the knowledge along without hesitation.

But all the same, he ripped the chain from his neck and tossed the pendant aside, the ornament clacking against a nearby rock, a crack forming in the face alongside the carved Packmind rune.

A pulse of curiosity surged from Zarrow. "*Does it trouble you so? That you gave the Tribes that much longer to prepare?*"

Cin closed his eyes, the imagery of Zarrow's retelling of the Pale Night still so vivid in his mind. "It matters not," he asserted, the weight of the pendants around his neck suddenly feeling incredibly heavy. "A few more hours of preparation will hardly make a difference. Their end is come, and we will at last avenge the horrors of four centuries past. The Moon will shine brightly upon us once again."

Another pulse of resignation. "*I will ask again,*" Zarrow said. "*Are you confident you've chosen correctly? Your words and your actions are in contradiction.*"

"I do not need a lecture on contradiction from someone whose words protested the Pale Night, but whose actions allowed it to happen, regardless. The Moon shall herald a new dawn; that is all anyone need concern themselves with." Cin gritted his teeth at the sight of the cracked Packmind pendant, an arm's reach away from him. "Now leave me be, Zarrow. I have made my position clear."

Zarrow grunted. "*You have not.*" And then he was gone.

Cin allowed the silence to scream through his makeshift enclosure. It was all the vocalization he could permit himself. He ran his fingers through his hair, resisting the urge to pull it out by the roots, until he brought a fist down onto the cold stone beneath him, hammering at it until his knuckles came away bloodied. He held his hand up, trembling from the pain, quivering with anger, shaking with doubt. Blood dripped down his wrist and to his elbow as he stared fiercely ahead into the emptiness before him.

"Tell me, my Lady," he rasped, his voice a meek scrape against his throat. A tear fell down his cheek, his hand throbbing as he finally recognized the pain. "Is this...not what You want? Do You not wish for retribution? We were to be Your anger, Your pain taken flesh. Please, tell me. Have I...have I fallen astray? Or is Zarrow correct? Will the current simply carry me to the depths of madness?" He tried to make a fist of his hand, but the rawness of his fresh wounds only allowed for it to half-close. "Or is the madness merely a price to pay for Your favor?"

He expected no answer. Echoes bounced against the enclosure and encircled him until all he could hear was his voice crying, "madness." He buried his face in his bloodied hands, the slick warmth strangely comforting against the smooth cold of the mountains.

Do you interpret the disease plaguing our Land as My will? Do you see this as seeking My favor?

The sudden voice startled Cin. Quickly, he looked in one direction and the next. There was no sensation to indicate one of the lost had begun to communicate with him. It was a voice altogether unfamiliar to him, yet the commanding presence it instilled in him made all doubts and queries seem meaningless. Crawling out from his enclosure and into the unforgiving chill of the Heart's early evening, Cin's initial instinct was to crane his gaze skyward.

The Moon had already begun to glow. It seemed too early for it, but She was subject to Her own whims.

Still shaking, Cin sunk to his knees. "M-my Lady," he said, bowing his head. "What...may I ask, what do you mean?"

The Moon remained still as though in silent contemplation. She seemed to let it hang between before Cin before finally responding. The disease with whom you have allied yourself. Do you believe them to be agents unto Me?

"D...disease? Do you mean...the Acrarians?"

Another silence. Cin could picture Her nodding.

Tell me. It was by My will that your people were punished for slaughtering My children. Do you now think yourself above such punishment that you would put to rout this Land's denizens?

"But, my Lady!" Cin put his forehead to the earth, wincing against the jagged rocks and biting cold. "These are the descendants of those who carried out the Pale Night!"

All of them?

"N...n-no, my Lady, but—"

I do not seek indiscriminate bloodshed for crimes long since passed. I wish only for My children to live in harmony amongst the Signbirthed. You only become what they decry you to be should you continue this path.

Cin felt his mouth fall agape with shock. "But...Kamataa! All this time, she—"

All this time, she has blinded herself with the thought of revenge. She speaks not for Me. She abandoned the right to My voice long, long ago.

He hardly knew what to say. All he could do was stare in disbelief at the Moon's vibrant glow, shocked tears streaming down his face. "Then...what...what am I to do?" Cin's bloodied hands trembled once more. "Please, my Lady. I..."

I have made My will known. The Moon's voice was one of disappointment. But it is not My place to determine how you interpret it. Her light flickered and dimmed as though it were the last embers of a fire log being quenched. A silhouetted bird flew northbound past Her light, vanishing into the encroaching nighttime, the size of its shadow playing tricks with Cin's eyes for the sheer enormity of it. And everything simply felt...still.

The snow and ice underfoot were long stained in red before Cin found it within him to rise back to his feet. He looked to the north with a resigned sigh. It was far too late to safely follow after the Acrarians in this dim light.

Another night in the rock shelter would have to do, for what little sleep he believed he would get.

But as Cin lay himself down against the cold stone, all he could do was quiver. In part due to the cold. In part due to the intensity of the Moon's admonishments.

Most of all, though, it was due to the uncertainty. The river before him was finally beginning to branch.

Dawn broke, and the snow had mercifully ceased. Clouds glowed in pink arrays as the sun breached their covering, bathing the True Heart of the Land in its rays for the first time in what seemed to be days.

Some may have deemed it a beacon of hope. To Sen, however, it provided only greater shadows to be cast over the thinned numbers of able-bodied and adept warriors.

The valley was quiet as they all gathered in their loose formations. None dared to speak. Words felt unnecessary. The feeling of dread sang in loud enough volumes. There was no need to add their voices to the haunting chorus. Wolfsigns lined up along the ridges overlooking the valley, their arrows trained to the south, to where the wave of Invaders would crest in horrid volumes. The verdant trees creaked and cracked as the Wolf slowly prowled through their depths, its form discernable only by the large shadow looming. On either side of Sen, Owlsigns handled spears and bows with unease and uncertainty, some of them likely wielding either for the first time. She had to remind herself that although the Stone Tribe was keen to train its scholars in the way of weaponry should the need have arisen, the custom did not apply universally. But despite her people's more widespread lessons, the Owlsigns she could see from the Stone Tribe still appeared timid in the face of what was to come.

The only exception was Tawa. His brow was furrowed, his teeth snarling at an enemy not yet arrived, anger painting his face in red as though he had been a Bearsign all along. Sen had heard from Tez the prowess with which

Tawa handled himself on the night of Koelhe's coup. If there was any among this crowd she need *not* worry about, it was him.

As she dragged the end of her spear through the snow, leaving a thin trail in her wake, Sen filed in beside her sister and exchanged a wordless nod with her. Her eyes drifted toward the back of the crowd where she spotted Ket, the steel of a spear tip wavering above her. Sen grimaced at the sight, not just for the desperation the Tribes found themselves in, but also for her sister.

Tez's eyes were heavy, cracks of red breaking the white plane, dark bags coloring her face in tandem with the lingering bruises resulting from her broken nose.

I don't think anyone slept a wink last night, Sen thought. *But Tez looks as though she slept even less than that.* All day yesterday, she had heard her sister's frustrated grunts and screams while training. Despite the posture with which Tez held her weapon, Sen knew she was not the same warrior she had been just days ago. But it still made her the best one of this bunch, regardless of diminished skills.

The Tribal formations took a more defined shape the longer the waiting tarried. Sen repeatedly regripped the shaft of her spear, switching from one hand to the other, flexing her fingers along its length to stave off the cold. As though by compulsion, she checked the number of bullets remaining in the pistol she kept strapped to her thigh, hoping a fresh batch would spawn in its chamber in the minutes since she last looked, but it remained the same every time.

Only one. I need to make it count. Simply a matter of whether it should be saved for Aritz or Kamataa.

The seconds stretched into minutes, and the minutes built atop each other, one after the next. A blustering wind carried with it a cold bite and snowy powder from the trees. Sen's joints were locking from the freezing temperatures, her feet numb in the packed white beneath her despite the insulation in her boots.

Prayers were murmured from behind. A handful of coughs. Someone sniffling the dripping snot from their nose. More prayers. The trees cracking and snapping. A low growl cutting through the soundless void, the Wolf ready to pounce at the impetus of provocation. Bowstrings winding and creaking. A shrill whistle from the wind.

And a clattering to the south. Footsteps pounding on uneven stone in even cadence. A rhythmic march punctuated by orders echoing in an incomprehensible tongue.

Sen couldn't yet see them. But they were coming. They were close.

The Invaders had returned.

A frustrated puffed sigh sounded to Sen's left, Sharrabha emerging from her periphery. It was to Sen's surprise that the huntress was not yet upon the ridge.

"Astonishing," Sharrabha muttered with disbelief. She took a handful of steps forward, removing arrows from her quiver and positioning them between her fingers like vicious claws. "They are now familiar with the terrain, but they do not fear what awaits them from above. They approach just the same."

"Do not discount their capacity to kill, Sharrabha," Sen warned, a flatness to her tone that superseded any disbelief she would possibly have. "The Wood Tribe had all the advantage in the world, and they're nothing more than a ruin now. Be ready for anything." She sucked in a deep breath, her arms shaking, her mind flashing back to the proceedings of a few days prior. "And protect the Wolf at all costs." *And the Owl, wherever it may have flown off to.* "At *all* costs."

Sharrabha nodded and rushed up the hill, sliding into formation beside several of the archers from the Arrow Tribe, Fen-Poven among them, already eliciting some sort of invigorating speech, the contents of which Sen could not quite hear over the wind.

The opposite ridge exhibited much the same, a mélange of Wolfsigns and Owlsigns alike, bows trained upon the breach where the Invaders would soon emerge. Much like his brother, Fen-Osenta's voice bellowed over the shrieks of nature, his indistinct words answered with broad cheers and clacking of arrows against the frames of bows.

Heaviness gripped Sen's chest, the air in her lungs growing thinner, her heart pounding, her head swirling. From the corner of her eye, she saw her sister, her lip quivering; Tawa, spear already held in position; faces familiar and foreign, all cognizant of the fact that they were the last defense of the Tribes, the sole remaining voices to sing the histories of a people facing insurmountable odds, a final chorus for songbirds.

One by one, spears were held level, feet digging into the snow, desperate for even landing. Sen's legs twitched, ready to jump forward at any given moment. Tremors and shivers and tears assaulted her all at once. Everything rode upon this moment. Everything the Tribes were, everything they represented...it would be decided here and now.

And the moment arrived with a thunderclap, a billow of smoke, and blood painting the white canvas of the True Heart.

Sen pushed off her back leg and charged.

The sea raged through the valley, and with it arrived the fury of the Savior.

Aritz stood firm as his soldiers charged out from behind him, encircling him, matching their war cries to the roar of their rifles. The stench of gunpowder stung his nostrils, the smoke obscuring his vision. But through the gray clouds billowing before him, still could he see bodies falling unceremoniously from atop the ridge, meeting their ends in a bloody pulp.

Arrows rained down just the same, quills finding home in the flesh of his soldiers' necks and thighs, the snowbound pathway singing a rhythmic thump with each arrowhead that missed its intended target. Rows of red fletchings littered the valley, whether bound to the earth or stuck deep in a bleeding body.

It was a chorus of disorder, far from the measured formations Aritz had witnessed a few days prior. Only chaos ruled this day, his soldiers gone rogue in vain attempts to clear the way for him, the savage archers eager to punch holes in any who would dare approach their heathen domain.

Aritz's heart thumped with the rhythm of war. Excitement at this last desperate defensive from the savages, and the vengeful hell they would soon be sent to. Each one felled was another step toward that goal. By the Savior's will, it would be done.

And the Savior basks upon us His bright light in recognition of this day, he thought as he craned his gaze toward the sky, watching the sun break through the dense layer of snow clouds. Outstretching his hands, Aritz felt the warmth and radiance of the Savior's glow filling him with all the strength and power he would need. He drew a deep breath.

And felt a surge of apprehension, a weight upon his chest. Surely due to the company still flanking him, yet to leave his side.

Kama flashed a wide grin toward him, two of her...colleagues standing at either side of her. Aritz was still inclined to steer clear of the one who had killed Pock-Face was little more than a touch. She had not exhibited any inclinations of harm toward him, thankfully, but seeing such horror only gave Aritz a further drive to wipe these savages from the glory of the Savior's light. *Even if their wicked magic is to my advantage.*

"Are you ready, Aritz?" Kama asked, her tone melodic and brimming with exuberance. She chuckled, not even an evident attempt at suppressing it.

"This had better work," Aritz muttered, cracking his knuckles as he reached down for his pistol. His skin protested at the cold bite of the handle, but he drew in a sharp breath through clenched teeth and cocked the hammer back. "I will not suffer another failure at your hands."

Outstretching her pale fingers, Kama merely shook her head, the glint in her eyes speaking only ill intent. "These are not hands checkered with failure. All I have done has been to lead you to this moment. Now, seize it."

"Do not deign to claim this victory for yourself. I allow none to lead me." Aritz puffed out a hot breath from his nostrils and began his approach toward the valley, his brow furrowed at the array of death already displayed ahead.

Kama filed in beside him again, her cadre close behind. "Leader or no, I still urge you to stay by our side. Lest you do not wish for your moment of glory to arrive...Godslayer."

Aritz bared his teeth in a snarl, a cold snap of wind biting at his neck. "I see no beast yet, witch."

"Oh, the beast shall arrive in due course. But first..." She cast her gaze to the northern reaches, a charging wall of spears closing in on them, the deafening roar of rifle fire overtaken by the desperate cries of a heathen party already lost. "Our hosts have come to greet us, and it would be rude of us not to accept their invitation. Unsheathe yourself, Sword of the Savior!" Her long curly hair bounced after her as she took off, her companions following suit, their battle cries threatening to sunder the very earth upon which they ran.

With a scoff, Aritz spat on that hallowed ground, christening it anew with a godslayer's breath, washing clean the stench of accursed blood from all the Savior's light touched. "Very well," he spoke under his breath. "Unsheathe I shall." He raised his pistol upward and fired, caring little to glance at his aim. The gurgled response and hollow thumps as flesh met hard stone was all the confirmation he needed that he met his mark. "May the edge of the Savior's Sword never dull."

The gap between armies closed step by step, the Invaders no longer paying heed to the archers from above and instead lining up with great alarm to focus upon the spears bearing down upon them.

Sen's legs cried out with each successive step, the underfoot landing poor, her boots slipping on ice every handful of paces. She would not allow her momentum to send her to the ground. Whatever it would take, she would stay on her feet. She growled, she screamed, she roared. For everything, for everyone.

Narva. Her parents. Brin. The shadows that had haunted her coalesced into one voice, one horrid visage draped in red curls and cackling all manner of wickedness. The shades of those long gone stood with her, carrying her, propelling her forward. As though reaching through from the Otherworld, she felt a presence with her. Multiple presences with her. No words were spoken, but they all screamed in sync with her own bellows, strode forth with their own spears in hand, carrying that last vestige of hope for the Tribes upon their shoulders.

Their strength and will flowed through Sen, and as the sensation of Luck surged, the wind pelting the side of her face with flecks of ice, the air rippling as a bullet passed by her ear, she lifted herself off her feet, spear held high, and came down at terminal velocity, pinning a hapless Invader to the unforgiving ground by the weight of her spear.

In an instant, the Owlsigns and Wolfsigns at her heel followed suit, and the valley descended into a cacophonous chaos of scraping steel and sundering thunderclaps. Bodies engulfed and encircled Sen, the available space around her entranced in an arrhythmic dance of death. Stone Owlsigns batted away the Invader rifles by the strength of their spears, holding the strength of the Deatharms back while hunters of the Arrow Tribe wove in and out of the fray, hamstringing the enemies in the same motion as slitting their throats. Wild swings of the unexperienced caught friend and foe alike, knocking Tribal warriors down while giving Invaders another chance to fire, but also catching extremities by sheer force of fortune rather than skill.

The Invaders were ill-equipped for this type of warfare. None of them carried bladed melee weapons, and as they found themselves in between bullets, they resorted to using their rifles and pistols as bludgeoning clubs, an improvisation that proved just as deadly as it would have been had they simply fired the weapons.

Sen ducked beneath a vicious swing, an auburn-haired, fresh face on the other end of it. On a successive swing, she reached out, tugging on the unloaded rifle until she found herself inside the Invader's guard. He aimed a hard headbutt, catching her in the shoulder. Sen snarled in pain and kneed him in the thigh as he desperately tried to pry the rifle loose in a tug-of-war distracting enough for him not to notice the spear goring him. A rush of blood warmed Sen's legs as she ripped her spear loose and wove her way to her next opponent, some poor bastard whose throat was suddenly far less opened than it had been moments prior.

Dropping to a knee, Sen drew a sharp breath, feeling another surge of Luck pass through her as a bullet clattered off the nearby valley walls. She followed the trail of smoke to its source and lunged forward, opening a blonde-haired man up at the groin. She had only a second to withdraw her weapon before a painful force sent her flying, the spear coming loose from her grasp as she rolled in the stones and ice. A burly Invader stood five paces away and was quickly closing the gap. He brought the butt end of his rifle down but met only the ground where Sen's head had just departed. Sen rolled to the side, slick blood dripped from her chin and onto the snow below. Her spear was out of reach. She stayed on a knee, her hand reaching to her tailbone where a hunter's knife remained sheathed. Awaiting an opportunity to pounce, her breath grew ragged, panicked, the thunderclaps roaring louder and louder.

Her vision went black.

For only a moment.

But it was enough of a hesitation for the Invader to press his advantage. He swung with all his strength, and Sen had not the time to move out of the way before she caught the brunt of the impact in her ribs. She wheezed a weak breath, hacking through pain as something stabbed at her from within. It had to be a rib fracture at least.

Another bullet passed by her head as she forced herself back to her feet, lunging at her assailant with hunting knife drawn. The Invader caught Sen by the wrist, twisting it until the blade fell from her grasp, the pain shooting up the length of her arm. Dropping his rifle, the man grabbed the knife before it reached the ground, fumbling it as he attempted to secure a firm grip on the hilt.

An arrow robbed him of the opportunity, a fletching jutting out from his eye before Sen could even blink. He fell to the ground, nearly taking Sen with him, sending her off-balance and stumbling to her knees, the sharp pain in her ribs forcing her to hiss in pain. A shrill whistle from above caught her attention, and in the spare moment afforded her by a host of her kin encircling her, Sen followed the whistle to find Sharrabha nodding at her, loosing a flurry of arrows without so much as a second glance.

Sen reciprocated the nod, hissing in another pained breath as she bent down to pick up her spear. In the shadow of the valley, she could see no faces she recognized, only a homogenous mass of bloodied visages and faltering forms. She flexed her shoulders, growling at her cracked ribs. Her chest heaved as she collected herself, watching the violence before her, remembering all the faces robbed of the chance to defend their people here. Spittle sputtered from her dried mouth while she awaited her next opportunity to rejoin the fray. Her fingers wrapped tightly around the shaft of her spear, its length held level to the ground, weight favoring her front leg.

Blood splashed to her left as the Lake Wolfsign in front of her collapsed to the ground, her forehead punctuated with a gaping hole. Sen didn't even hear the rifle fire. It all blended together amidst the cacophonous thunderclaps and vicious roars, battling against the whipping winds and creaking woods.

But damn the noise. Her opportunity had arrived. Pushing off her front leg, Sen surged forward, a rush of Luck flaring within as she swung her spear, metal swatting away metal as a bullet was flung wide. The momentum spun her around into a roll, an agonizing roll, but one that led her spear into an Invader's throat.

Bodies piled from friend and foe alike, but none among them the faces she sought above all else.

He had to give the savages credit, at least. They fought for what they felt was theirs. Misguided though they were. And despite the overwhelming odds facing them, they refused to surrender, despite their filthy presence being counter to the Savior's will.

Aritz was more than happy to send them to their wretched afterlife, whatever heathen hell they would find themselves to be.

The damned archers were horribly persistent. It was only as soon as Aritz fired and reloaded that another would emerge to take their place. *Just how many of them are hiding up there?* he wondered. *I find myself running short of men to shield me from their arrows.*

The recoil of his shots flowed through his arm, his elbow twisting as a means to absorb it. Each reloading period meant a different soldier to duck behind, all of whom were happy to oblige. For those who were not as thrilled to do so, they were free to perish in misery.

The air was gripped by a melody of gunfire, music to Aritz's ears. He was the conductor, his soldiers the instrumentalists, and the savages an audience entirely too captivated to offer any meaningful contributions to the orchestra. He was lost to the rhythm, one movement flowing to the next, his arms taking on life of their own in a routine of aim, shoot, reload, aim, shoot, reload. The cold wind tore at his sweat-slicked face, but he cared not. The heat of battle was more than enough to warm him.

Per the instructions he reluctantly followed, he kept a close distance to Kama and her companions. Kama was a wildfire in motion, her long red locks a blur as she turned this way and that, never letting a moment pass where she was not pressing her next strike. In a flash, she would drop to a knee and fire her rifle, only to spin on her heel and introduce an assailant to their own spear. She was a fury, a whirlwind, an angel of destruction. A *fallen* angel, to Aritz's eyes. *No true angel would kill with such tenacity and excitement.* The grin creasing Kama's lips only made the sight all the more unsettling.

The same could be said for her companions. Short bursts of laughter, wide smiles, violence in excess. Both women exhibited it all in spades. And what made it worse was that...ability they both possessed. Enemies were falling with little more than a grasp of the shoulder. Were they to merely do that, Aritz was certain the savages would fall in droves. But these two witches seemed content to prolong the suffering, land a shot to an opponent's stomach, bludgeon them with the butt of their rifles, anything and everything that would instill a desire for release. And only then would they grant them that.

Aritz could not help but snarl, but he knew he was hardly in the position to decline destructive assistance. There was no time to question it. Arrows still rained down upon him, barricading him from the radiance of the Savior's light. The threads of his coat were loosened by arrowheads skimming past, the flesh of his arm scored against the rippling air, but he continued to feel protection from on high. He would not fall here. The plan was laid out for him, and he was certain the Savior did not determine this horrid place to be his end.

"Push forward!" he shouted, spotting diminishing numbers in the northeastern corner of the valley. "On!" His pistol matched the roar and screamed toward another collective atop the ridge, taking a woman in the throat just as her fingers left her bowstrings, sending the arrow wide into the crowd to the north.

The soldiers before him pressed their advantage, driving the heathens on their heels. Acrid smoke billowed out in bursts as order finally returned to the Acrarian formations. Defined marching lines began to reform, a wall of some ten to fifteen rows protecting him from harm on the ground. The side rows flanking him set their attention upward, the archers growing more frantic and panicked in their movements, wholly aware of the death awaiting them, but too stubborn to accept the inevitability.

Momentum carried Aritz and his soldiers forward, inch by inch, the cheers growing more and more electric as they found themselves closer and closer to the clearing beyond the valley. The advantage was slowly becoming their own, and this orchestra of war was building to an invigorating crescendo.

But the focus of the conductor was broken as Aritz felt a sharp pain in the meat of his arm, his balance thrown until he collapsed to a knee, soldiers instinctually surrounding him. He sucked in a breath as he spotted a long shaft protruding from his bicep, the flesh tender from the horrid sensation pulsing in a wide radius. He spat on the ground and yelled, "Pull it out!" to any who would hear.

The lad to his immediate right, likely no more than twenty years, immediately dropped his rifle and knelt beside his general, pressing his palm against Aritz's arm for leverage. "Apologies, sir," the boy said, making note of the grimace in response. "I'll be quick. One, two, three!"

The bolt slid out with a horrendous sensation, a fire radiating through Aritz's arm. "Savior's goddamned *breath!*" he growled, his hand quivering, blood already sluicing from the open wound. He didn't even bother to bind it; he simply rose back to his feet with pistol in hand. He had half a mind to admonish the lad, who still stood dumbfounded with the bloodied arrow in his hand.

The opportunity didn't present itself. Iron burst out from his forehead before a single word could be uttered, his body crumbling to nothing onto the ice below. Successive rifle fire from apparently grieving greenhorns rid Aritz of the worry that area of the ridge would cause him.

The pain renewed Aritz's focus. That a savage would force him to bleed his own blood was ridiculous. *A Sword does not bleed. A Sword* shall *not bleed!* A deep growl rumbled in his dry throat as he screamed for the front lines to press harder, the wind carrying the orders in contest with the loud ringing in his left ear of cracking and snapping wood.

The rain of arrows from the left ceased, despite the chorus of gunfire and scored flesh continuing to harmonize. A viscous warmth covered his hand as blood continued to drip down his arm. Each shove forward left a red imprint of his hand on the backside of whoever fought in front of him. With every subsequent inch, he could see the fear glinting in the savages' eyes. Their strength was waning, their drive to fight dissipating, until it seemed they all collectively stopped, diverting their attention to the upper ridge.

To Aritz's surprise, so, too, did his own soldiers.

"What is the meaning of this?" he bellowed, the din of battle vanishing enough for his voice to carry over all. "Press forward!"

Beside him, Kama cleared her throat.

When the devil did you get there?

She nudged her head upward. "Has your edge yet dulled? The Savior is in need of His Sword."

Aritz squinted his eyes but followed where all attention had been redirected. His heart plummeted into his stomach, the memories of the shame of retreat still fresh upon his mind.

And the beast atop the ridge was at the center of it all. The lupine god stood tall, overlooking the bloodied valley, its wide and wild fangs bared, the ground rumbling in concert with its deep, low growl.

No sooner did multiple orders to fire echo through the valley that the wolf lurched onto its hind legs and pounced into the heart of the fray.

Aritz raised his pistol and fired.

Tez's muscles burned in a way she had never experienced before. With each passing thrust or jab, her arms felt heavier, her energy sapped. It took all the strength she had simply to remain standing, her legs wobbling from beneath her.

She had never been more grateful to see divine intervention at work. The Wolf's arrival segmented the advancing Invader forces, creating a clear line between the few who had breached into a decidedly Tribal territory and those who were to face the wrath of a furious and vengeful deity. She watched bodies being hurled into the air, the god unperturbed by the flurry of Deatharms strikes. Invaders fell to the ground in hapless heaps, blood spurting and splashing as skulls were opened on the unforgiving ground. Stray limbs flew about the crowd, weaponry and clothing alike descending along with them.

Though there was still a plentitude of Invaders on this side of the Wolf, the advantage had still returned to the Tribes. Tez was all too eager to seize the opportunity.

Clumsily, she wove between a pair of Wolfsigns, their deft hands cutting open a path for her to strike the next Invader beyond. Her spear found a home in the woman's belly, the river opening and branching into separated streams around the length of the weapon. The Invader's eyes glossed over as she fell, and Tez could not keep from collapsing along with her.

The cold ground was comforting. Too comforting.

Get up, you fool! she screamed to herself. *On your feet, Tez!* But though her mind commanded it, her body would not obey. Exhaustion limited her to a crawl. She could do little more than drag herself to the Invader she had just felled, gripping tightly to the shaft of her spear for leverage. Spurts of blood cascaded down upon her from above as stray arrows opened throats. Slowly, she managed to return to a knee, her hands wrapped firmly around her weapon as she heaved.

The dead woman's stomach would not let go. Or Tez had not the strength to pry it free. *Damn it, damn it, damn it!* Holding the corpse in place with her foot, she slowly wiggled it free, her mind too much of a fog to take heed of her surroundings. The air rippled by her head as a pained gasp sounded behind her. The impact of flesh stuck with quills echoed in her ears. Tez's vision swirled before her the greater she exerted herself, until at last the spear came loose, knocking her flat on her back, lightheadedness and dizziness all she now knew.

A tear escaped her eye as her body failed her. All motivation and ability to return to her feet was gone. The cries of battle continued to sing around her. Steel slicing through soft flesh. Blood spilling onto an innocent earth. The click of a Deatharm cocking into place, ever so near to her. She closed her eyes, accepting its arrival. *What good am I, now? This...was all I was.*

A protesting shout from a familiar voice drew her attention, followed quickly by the whip of steel streaming through the air, the impact against flesh, the gurgled breath of a throat drawing in its last. A firm hand grasped Tez's arm and heaved her back up to her unsteady feet. She was still blinded with dizziness, the world spinning. The thin mountain air was making her nauseous. There was a threat of vomit, but Tez forced it back down to her stomach and rested her weary forehead against the shoulder of her savior.

"Stay with me, Tez!" cried the voice, comfort in the tone despite the horrors surrounding them.

"K...Ket?" Tez's eyes fluttered, her balance leaving her once more, her spear promising to drag her back into the snow. "I...I can't..."

The ghost of a slap rung against Tez's cheek and before she knew it, the spout of a waterskin was shoved in her mouth. Pristine and pure ice water dampened her raw throat. The world stood more firmly in place, the blurs and spots in her vision slowly fading away until she could at last make sense of the shape of Ket's face. There were fresh cuts opened from brow to cheek and blood spattered all over their coat, but they seemed otherwise in good condition. Tez grasped tightly onto either side of them for stability and allowed a smile to crease her lips. "You didn't have to slap me so hard."

Ket grinned but just as quickly dove to the side, an Invader pressing his charge with a vicious swing of his unloaded Deatharm. Ket drove their spear forward in a wide arc, the path opening the man up by the belly, organs spilling out in a steaming pile beneath him as he fell. Rising back to quivering feet, Ket ran past Tez without another word and aimed an unrefined jab at the next nearest opponent, still successful in striking their target.

Though she felt like a drunkard with her weakened legs, Tez charged in equal measure, unwilling to be outdone. She filed in beside Ket, covering their blind spot, a rush of Invaders appearing from nowhere. One fired their Deatharm, the shot sailing wide, clacking off the rock face of the valley wall. Tez reached behind her and grasped the hunting knife at her waist, flinging it at the unlucky Invader and introducing his eye and brain to it. Catching his companion in his moment of shock, she lunged forward, the spear tip grazing her opponent's hand, knocking loose the hold he had on his weapon. Blood poured out from the back of his hand in a steady volume as he ducked his shoulder down and charged at Tez. There was no time for her to react and he was quickly inside her guard, his arms wrapped around her waist. Feebly,

Tez attempted to bring her knee into his throat, but the angle was poor and she had no momentum with which to drive any force. Within moments, she was back on the ground and a fist was reopening the wound on her broken nose while a hand clasped around her throat.

She clawed at the man's wrist but could not pry his fingers free of her throat. Spots clouded her vision until she felt like she was underwater, the air constricting in her lungs, the stark white clouds above glowing more profoundly in an opulent light.

A gush of fresh warmth splashed over her face, and the world suddenly felt heavy again. The obstruction on her throat was gone and she began hacking, spurts of blood loosing from her throat and out her nostrils. When she opened her eyes, Ket was slowly pushing the Invader soldier off of her, the man's head remaining atop his neck. Tez scurried back to her feet, spear on the ground beside her, hands on knees as her lungs cried out in agony, her chest heaving its lost breaths. "Okay...that's two I owe you," she said through pained breaths.

There was only enough time to register Ket's grin before Tez spotted the two Invaders approaching behind them. They locked their Deatharms into place, only moments away from pulling the triggers. Tez's eyes flared open and she picked up her spear and dashed past Ket, prying loose their spear on the way by, and lunged forward toward the Invaders. Their widened eyes spoke of shock as Tez fell upon them with twin spears, running them both through the chest, their weapons scattering into the midst of the chaos beyond. There was enough adrenaline still running through her to pry the spears loose and toss one back to Ket, an arc of blood trailing after it in the air.

"And...we're even," Tez chuckled as her legs failed her.

Ket quickly lurched forward and wrapped their arms around Tez's waist, dragging her to the rear guard, away from the main fracas.

"No, no, I can...I can still—" Tez's words were slurring together.

"You can rest and permit us to handle this!" Ket shouted, their tone heeding no acceptance to the contrary.

Wanting so desperately to protest, Tez reached out to Ket, who merely swatted away her hand and charged back into the fray. She could only close her eyes and shake her head, wondering how it was possible that she could fall this low, reduced to one who rested at the rear lines, watching others bleed and die while her body could do nothing to prevent it.

Her ears rang with the cries of death and fear against the might of the Wolf. *But if only my cries were among theirs.*

The Wolf snarled, and so Kamataa felt it fitting to snarl in return. She bared her teeth to the beast, its fangs stained red, blood dripping from its snout, its fur already matted with signs of battle.

A flurry of gunfire pelted the Wolf, the bullets doing little more than bouncing off its sturdy hide and further agitating the god. With a snort, a puff of air burst from the beast's nose and it pounced forward, snapping at the nearest Acrarian with its mighty jaws, piercing the man's chest and throat in an instant.

The poor bastard never stood a chance.

Whipping its head back and forth, the Wolf assaulted nearby soldiers with their dead comrade's corpse, blood streaming every which way in dark rivers. Two brave idiots, probably intent on becoming the stuff of Acrarian folklore, charged at the god, their rifles raised like clubs, foregoing entirely the prospect of shooting the beast. The first soldier fell within the arc of the Wolf's shaking head; the force of the blow sent him soaring into the nearest valley wall. All that remained of him was a pulp of crushed bones and viscous brain matter. The second was at least smart enough to duck underneath the lupine god's head. He was *not*, however, smart enough to remember his rifle was loaded. The moment the Wolf turned back to face him, he turned loose a mighty swing, meeting the beast's unyielding skull. The impact set his rifle off, and the next thing he knew, he was bleeding out in the valley, his stomach pouring blood.

Kamataa rolled to the side as the Wolf finally let go of the long-dead soldier, his life raining over her as he was sent flying. She ran a hand over her face, feeling the blood smearing across her eyes and nose, her tongue wincing from the tang of it. She deposited her pistol into the holster wrapped about her thigh and reached for the short blade she kept at her waist. Her hand rested upon the hilt, fingers rapping against its length, eager with anticipation, ready to draw the blood of the divine. *I have long been thought of as little more than a wicked beast.* She smiled. *It simply but means I am the most well-equipped to* slay *a wicked beast!*

The Wolf swatted at the row of soldiers before it, their rifles doing naught but billow smoke to obscure the god's eyes. A swath was cut through them by its claws, polished and honed to a sheen greater than any spear could manage. Entrails spilled out on the cold earth, the air rife with the stench of dying acts, a cacophony of deafening gunfire replaced with the desperate pleas and cries of grown adults wishing for their parents to nurse them to health.

Your pleas shall always fall upon deaf ears. I consider myself quite the authority on that.

As Kamataa awaited her time to strike, arrows continued to rain down from above, majestic arcs interspersed with high velocity shots. Those who were fortunate enough to evade the beast's horrid jaws or blade-like talons were still met with the grave misfortune of acting as the pincushion for Tribal arrows. Kamataa danced out of the way of the raining quills, the ground pelted with carved steel and stiff fletchings. The beast's jaws drew ever closer to her, near enough for her to catch the stench of its breath, stale with death. Rows upon rows of the Acrarian soldiers met their end either bravely or stupidly, the valley quickly becoming littered more with corpses than with the nauseating snow.

Turning a sharp glance over her shoulder, Kamataa spied Sha'a and Vanta keeping a vigil around Aritz, readying and firing pistols toward the archers while resting their weak arms along the hilts of their blades. Their smiles had not left them this entire skirmish, and the glow in their eyes only became more vibrant the more Tribespeople fell to their strikes. Behind them, Aritz continued to bark orders, deny help, force others to suffer mortal blows for him. His right sleeve was soaked through with dark blood, his arm hanging limply, his complexion growing pale in the cold. But there was a rage in his glare that Kamataa was all too familiar with, the rage that blinded men to all else but what they sought to destroy.

And what Aritz sought was destroying his army, one by one.

Who am I to deprive the great Aritz a Mata of his quarry, after all? Kamataa thought, chuckling to herself as death continued to roar around her. She held more firmly to the hilt of her blade, licking her lips, tasting the fresh blood that continued to stream down her face unimpeded.

The Wolf lurched into the air, the ground shaking as it returned, men and women alike thrown off-balance as its claws found hapless victims, slicing through them like a hot knife through butter. Each clamp of the jaw around another soldier's neck or torso elicited a frothing snarl, its spittle no longer anything more than the blood of those unfortunate enough to be in the way. A deep growl sundered the earth in these tight quarters, pebbles and stones shaken loose from the valley walls as it prowled closer, its disinterest in this cannon fodder apparent. It was clear it knew the head of the army.

And Kamataa took that as her time to strike.

"Sha'a! Vanta!" she called, drawing her blade from its sheath, the steel screaming against the scabbard, glimmering in the morning sunlight.

Her remaining kin tossed their pistols aside, the need for them long past, and pulled their knives from their respective sheaths. Red stains marked the spots where the blades had been sunk into their shoulders. It was clear upon both Sha'a and Vanta's faces that the wounds were still tender.

But the way the light dances *off the steel now!* Kamataa exaggerated a gasp as she watched Sha'a and Vanta charge forward, weaving in and out of the way of the Acrarian soldiers. Her heart leaped with anticipation, her hands shaking with excitement. She had never felt such a thrill in her long, long life. Positioning all her weight on her front leg, Kamataa leaned forward, flashing her teeth at the approaching god. "Careful, wolfy," she warned. "You're soon to learn that *our* bite is far. More. *Deadly.*" She sharply turned her head over her shoulder, back toward the rear guard. "*Aritz!*"

The general shot an angry glare back toward her, an arrow taking the throat of the man beside him.

"Ready yourself!" she yelled. "The time is at hand!" She did not wait for his response.

She shot herself forward toward the Wolf, Sha'a and Vanta not far behind, and brandished her steel at the beast's right front foot. The Wolf stomped its paw down at the spot where she had just vacated, slashing at its heel but doing little more than trimming away excess fur. The god's eyes flared at her, a fire burning that sang of anger and malice. It clamped its jaws at Kamataa but she backed away from the snap, swatting at its fangs with her blade, the edge screeching against its razor-sharp teeth. Another succession of chomps followed her—*one, two, three!* But Kamataa evaded each lurch, her chest pounding and feet slipping. The beast was growing frustrated; that much was immediately apparent. It seemed wholly intent on sinking its teeth into Kamataa's throat.

That's good. Keep your eyes on me. A shame you think so much like a beast. The realm of strategy is lost upon you. After all...I am nothing more than a trickster and a fiend leading tricksters and fiends.

"Now!"

The Wolf snapped its head back toward the rear guard in just enough time to watch Sha'a and Vanta sink their blades in its chest. Right up to the hilt.

The roar of the Wolf stunned the Tribes into near silence. Sen's redirected her focus toward the god's imposing form, gray fur stained and matted red with blood. Withdrawing her spear from the dead Invader she stuck it in, she once again felt her heart sink, her chest pound, lungs constricting for want of air.

She could not see well enough past the rows of Invaders still separating her from the Wolf. All she could know for certain was...it was in agony. *Something* was happening. "Kamataa," she growled. "What have you done?"

Luck surged through her as an Invader's bullet soared past. She spun on her heel and caught the Acrarian square in the throat when he was ill-advised enough to charge. As she kicked him off the steel, Sen shot her eyes to the top of the ridge. "*Sharrabha!*" she screamed. "*What do you see?*"

An expression of pure shock was apparent on the huntress's face. Not even just shock. *Fear.* Her bow quivered in her hand, arrows dropping to the ground below her. Unsteadily, she reached her free arm up to her Wolfsign pendant, grasping it with what looked to be an acceptance and expectation of what was soon to come.

"*Sharrabha!*" Sen repeated, tears welling in her eyes. The clang of steel and blunt impacts still sounded about her, but she could not tear her gaze away from the huntress, from one of the last remnants of her father's council.

Sharrabha released the pendant, letting it fall back to her chest, and drew an arrow to her bowstring, her aim wavering in a way Sen had never seen from her before. The huntress craned her head and stood on her toes, evidently trying to devise some plan of attack, but the hesitation spoke volumes in a way words could not.

Sen's first instinct was to run up the ridge, take in the sight for herself. But countless bodies, alive and dead, separated her from the inclined path, countless more advancing from the opposite direction. She called out to Sharrabha again, fully aware of the desperation settling into her voice.

"It's..." Resignation was rife upon Sharrabha's tongue. Her tone exuded the same cadence as her hesitant body language. "The Children! Those...death walkers! They're..."

"*Don't let them touch the Wolf!*" Sen screamed, her voice raw and cracking and panicked. "*Stop them!*"

"It's too late, Sen! They're already..." A disgusted growl echoed over the valley as Sharrabha broke off, wiping her arm across her eyes. All along the ridge, archers tried to line up their shots, but none loosed their arrows. "Damn it!" Sharrabha shouted. "They positioned themselves too well; I can't hit them without hitting the Wolf!"

The archers on the opposite ridge seemed to face the same dilemma. Tentative arrows were fired, but none contained the ferocity befitting a Wolfsign. Not even the Fens readied themselves with any notable confidence.

In a panic, Sen kept glancing from one ridge to the next, hoping, *praying* that someone would stop Sha'a and Vanta.

But the moment did not arrive.

The Wolf's roars became growls became whimpers became low mewls.

And as Sen looked up at Sharrabha with tears in her eyes, she quickly realized the huntress was glancing upon her in much the same fashion.

"Aritz! *Now!*"

His head swirling and his arm ablaze, Aritz stared as the witches slowly encumbered the foul beast with little more than a knife and their hands. His heart thumped and thumped and thumped, unsure if the distrust and unease were winning out over the exhilaration, or vice versa.

But as the wolf god wavered upon its feet, the vicious and devilish ferocity fading from its bestial eyes, Aritz felt the gaze and power of the Savior succeeding over the wickedness of these heathen savages. All he needed now was a seizure of the opportunity.

Kama stood in wait, her eyes affixed to Aritz as she pointed her blade at the wolf. There was clear expectation in her gaze, the fulfillment of a promise, one he was loath to reject but reluctant to accept in the manner it was offered.

The Savior need not stress over how his Sword strikes, so long as it strikes true. O Lord, pray forgive my follies in seeing Your will done.

Aritz held his pistol level. "Men! Form up!"

"I'm...proud of you, Sen. All of us are," Sharrabha said, her tone accepting the finality of these moments. "Never forget that."

Sen stifled a gasp, biting at her index finger in defense of the nerves. "No...Sharrabha, please, no."

"Your father and mother...never gave up on you. They believed in you...and their faith was well-deserved."

Rifles clicked into place. Aritz felt the itch in his finger.

"Ready!" he shouted.

Foreign voices echoed over the valley. Everything before Sen was a watery blur. She could feel the desperation in everyone surrounding her, in those who continued to fight despite the inevitable soon to arrive. Wolfsigns slashed and jabbed and thrust, knowing full well that each attack could be their last. Invaders fell, Invaders laughed, Invaders cried.

And all Sen could do was reach out toward Sharrabha, the distance between them as far as it always had been, but the weight no less impactful.

"Goodbye, Sen…" Sharrabha said, her voice only barely carrying over the din.

The whimpers of the beast had faded near to nothing, the two witches tentatively keeping their hands fastened to the wolf's flesh, their eyes focused entirely on the firing squad headed by Aritz.

"Aim!"

"I will look forward to seeing you in the Otherworld, however soon or faraway that day may be." Sharrabha wiped away a stream of tears from her cheeks and closed her eyes.

Sen broke into a run.

"Fire!"

The recoil surged through Aritz's elbow. All he could see was smoke.

"Sharrabha!"

As Sen sprinted toward the ridge wall, the roar of gunfire thundered across the hollow battlefield. The ground shook in response to a resounding thud, a quake kicking up flurries of bloodied snow.

In an instant, bodies began to fall atop the ridge. The story repeated itself in much the same manner as when the Bearsigns were collectively lost. The hunters on the ground collapsed into the snow, their eyes glazing over, some sharing haunting final glances with Sen before their bodies gave out. She had to duck and weave out of the way of several whose mental faculties sundered, stunned shock frozen upon the faces of each of them.

Not breaking her gaze from Sharrabha, Sen could do nothing but allow her heart to be shredded once again as she watched the greatest huntress she had ever known waver on her feet, her eyes rolling into the back of her head, and fall forward, her momentum sending her off the edge of the ridge, headfirst toward the ground below. Her legs burning with exertion, Sen forced herself ever forward, harder than she had ever run before, faster than that wretched night when she had lost both Brin and Narva, in an attempt to catch Sharrabha or brace her fall.

But she knew her Luck would not carry her that far that quickly. It merely only sunk in when Sharrabha's head split open against the unforgiving earth, Sen herself still some ten to fifteen paces away from making a difference.

The horror only further sunk in the more Wolfsigns followed suit—hunters from all Tribes, the Arrow Tribe's Fens, none were safe from the Wolf's slaying. And as more and more collapsed and fell off the edge of the ridges to their certain demise, the sight of an entire third of the Tribe's people becoming mentally broken somehow became even more harrowing the second time around.

If the sudden déjà vu perturbed the Invaders, they did little to show it. Hesitation was apparent on some of the nearest faces as Wolfsigns crumbled about them. Others exhibited some degree of gratitude at the blades homing in on them simply fell to the earth. Further along in the valley, plumes of smoke burst forth as their rifles roared in static rhythm in the direction of the ridge, the defensive team up top reduced to inexperienced Owlsigns who lacked the proficiency with the weapon.

Sen skidded to a stop, ice and snow kicking up around her ankles. She held her spear level in one hand, standing side-face against the renewed confidence of the Invader forces. More and more Wolfsigns fell around her, a shattered few who lacked the longevity of connection to the Wolf shared by the elder crowd, a more torturous fate as they awaited the inevitable to grip them. Unsteady fear shone in their eyes as Sen locked gazes with them, bows and blades quivering in their hands as their legs gave out from underneath.

Her first instinct was to catch the one nearest to her as he fell, a young man from the Lake Tribe probably not much older than Brin. His blood- and sweat-slicked hair fell in front of his tear-strewn eyes, his hand shaking as he reached up toward Sen. "I—I—I—don't want...I d-d-don't want t-t-to...go..." His weight shifted in Sen's arms and he rolled to the side, tongue lolling from his mouth as the affliction caused by the Wolf's death at last gripped him.

All Sen could do was stare at her empty arms, befuddled and horrified at the sight. Luck was flaring up her limbs and through her shoulders, shot after shot missing her, ice and snow erupting from the impact of the bullets gone by. She gritted her teeth, slowly turning her head toward the approaching Invaders. As she reached for her spear, she watched as the Owlsigns, the final line of defense for the Tribes and the True Heart of the Land, readied their weapons, gripping their spears and nocking their arrows to the best of their ability. Sen spanned her gaze across the battlefield, observing this forced and reluctant bravery grip the typical non-combatants of the Tribes. She saw Tawa leveling his spear at a nearby attacker. Ket, desperately weaving their way out of a succession of swings from an Invader rifle. Ko Zaran and Ko Endra, two men who could not be further apart in the Keeper hierarchy, bellowing for all their worth as they ran Invaders through on their spears.

And Tez...broken yet still standing, sweat streaming down her exhausted face. She slowly paced this haunted valley, this catacomb of horrors, walking over the shattered bodies of Wolfsigns cast to the in-between of this mortal plane and the Otherworld. A grumble turned into a growl turned into a scream as she launched herself off a prone body and into the otherwise preoccupied form of an inattentive Invader, blood bursting from the soldier's throat, every single motion of hers an incarnate fury.

A fury shared entirely with Sen. The surge of Luck was now a persistent sensation, no longer a radiating throb and instead a constant burning as Sen slowly walked closer and closer to the Invader offensive, the barrage of gunfire little more than wind at her ears. Her pace quickened, her spear readied, the air rippling about her as her walk became a sprint and her raw throat screeched with what was remaining within her for a battle cry. Her vision went white hot as she felt the impact coursing through the length of her arms as her weapon sliced through an Invader's chest as though it was nothing. The fire in her ribs was little more than an afterthought as she pushed the dying Invader into the column of soldiers behind him, Sen's spear finding its way into the ribcage of the next soldier.

As her next assailant approached, she abandoned the spear, finding it not worth the effort to withdraw, and pulled her knife from its sheath, ducking beneath the swing of a rifle and a powerful right hook as she sliced open the Invader at the wrist, digging straight into a vein. Blood squirted out in a torrent and she pressed his guard, driving the steel into his chubby throat.

Something crashed into her head with enough impact to knock her off her feet. Sen hissed in pain as she landed on and slid against her fractured ribs. She propped herself to all fours until a heavy kick to the stomach lifted her in the air, stealing the air from her lungs. Agony surged through her and it was all she could do not to vomit as a result.

An Invader pushed her onto her back by the weight of his foot and kneeled to punch her with a gloved fist. She turned away the first punch by the waning strength of her hands, only to feel the brunt of the next against her cheek. The tang of blood filled her mouth. In desperation, she kicked out and managed to clip the Invader's kneecap, knocking his leg out from under him. Sen rolled, allowing the soldier to land face-first into the ice and stone, bunched the man's hair tightly in her fist, and brought his face down repeatedly onto the ground. She knew not when to stop, only that he had stopped moving long before she did.

And it was only when she did, that she felt the valley shift about her. A cold wind blew in from the tree line, one that felt unlike any wind she had experienced before. It brought with it a chill...but she did not feel cold. It was almost ethereal in nature. And as the wind continued to trail through the valley, a dense mist emerged from the woods, almost a cloud made sentient. Sen watched it encircle the altar upon which the gods had lay, flanking it like a snake devouring its own tail, until it burst from its holding and blanketed the chasm in its opaque embrace.

She could hear protests in a foreign tongue, confusion evident from the tone, but Sen did not fear this mist. She felt somewhat...comforted by it. And given the fact that none of the Owlsigns were crying out in fear, she could only assume they found peace in its covering as well.

RUN, SENNALHAT.

Sen's heart jumped at the sudden voice. She turned in a circle, finding no one about her. "Who's there?" she barked.

RUN!

She had never heard this voice before, but she was immediately taken by its commanding, firm intonation. She saw no reason to disobey it. If this was to be how she'd survive the day...it was an out she would reluctantly take. Finding her blade a short distance away and grabbing a discarded spear from the ground, Sen set off in a dead sprint, slashing at any unwavering form she found in the mist. Warm blood streamed across her arms as she slashed and thrust indiscriminately, the advantage all her own to fell as many Invaders she could as she traversed the mist.

When she felt a tuft of fur graze her arm, she knew she was close to the entrance to the valley, staving off the tears of mourning for the Wolf and all her fallen comrades until the path to escape was cleared. Steady and clacking footsteps echoed in her ears, ones she could be certain as belonging to Tribespeople. Whoever this voice was, it was clear she was not alone in being addressed.

The density of bodies waned the further along in the mist she ran until finally, her vision was restored and the entirety of the island was visible to her from atop the mountain ranges of the Heart. She briefly allowed herself a rest to catch her breath. And to wait for more to emerge from the mist. She was thankful to not be alone for long as Owlsign after Owlsign burst from the wispy barrier, faces she recognized and faces she didn't. Keepers she had encountered, members of her own Tribe, Ket...

...And Tez. It set Sen's heart at ease to see her sister emerge unharmed.

But it was no time to feel gratitude. Sen knew they could suffer no hesitation. They were granted this opportunity by forces beyond their control.

All Sen could do was run for her life.

The burst of mist at the trail's peak was more than enough to draw Cin out from his enclosure. Resting a tired arm against the entryway, he furrowed his brow and shook his head, perplexed at the sudden cessation of audible combat. "What has happened up there?" he wondered aloud.

A breeze passed down the mountain trail and encircled him, the air seeming to take on a life of its own. He held out his hands and could *feel* the air taken corporeal form, a lurid density to it beyond his own understanding. Words would not come to him.

"Something happened within that mist. Or...some*one*." Cin ran his fingers through his hair, knotted strands catching and wrapping against his knuckles. He allowed the collected air to drop and pass him by, returning itself to the natural wisps of the world. "Zarrow? Have you ever seen anything like this?"

The ghostly presence was just that: a ghost. Cin was met only with silence, save for the mysterious wind.

"Assumed as much," he scoffed, placing a weary hand against his chest, grasping at the collection of pendants dangling from his neck. He felt no energy within the Wolfsign pendants he kept on his person. "Guess that's that, then. One to go." Pumping his fist, Cin wanted to feel exhilaration at another god felled. It was what the Children of the Black Moon had worked toward all these years. What *he* had worked toward.

But the Moon's admonishment still hung heavily upon his mind. He thought this was what She would have wanted. But now he knew not what to think at all. All he could do was watch the mist envelope the mountain's peak and pray it was the doing of the Moon Herself. "That would make matters so much easier."

Cin was turning to walk away from the view when a rush of footsteps echoed down the length of the mountain path. He kneeled behind the rock walls of his enclosure and peered his eyes around the corner, squinting as faraway dots became defined bodies. With curiosity piqued, he watched with anticipation as the bodies drew ever closer, the speed at which they approached instilling a desire to reach for his weapon.

The faces became more defined, the voices familiar, the words in a tongue he had heard all his life. The intrigue he felt quickly gave way to confusion as he eyed a particularly recognizable face at the head of the pack.

"...*Sennalhat*?" he wondered aloud. He was almost aghast.

With numerous Owlsigns closely following her, Sennalhat's face spoke entirely of exhaustion and defeat, but Cin could see it in her eyes that a determination to rid herself of this place was superseding all delusions of stopping. He had not seen this energy from her and could not help but inquire internally where that was the entire time she traveled along with him and the other Children.

The Tribespeople rounded the corner of the trail, many struggling to keep up with Sennalhat's pace, one woman in particular—Stone Tribe from the look of her—near to a crawl as though she had never run a day in her life. But even as they vanished from sight, Cin kept his eyes affixed to the southbound trail, his chest aflutter with emotions he could not define.

"Have they...abandoned the gods? Have the Acrarians won?" From what he knew of the Keepers specifically, it was better to die in service to the gods than abandon them, and there were certainly Keepers among that retreating cadre. "I don't understand this."

I TOLD YOU, CIN. I HAVE MADE MY WILL KNOWN. The dense air surrounded Cin once again, the familiar commanding voice of the Moon returning.

Cin turned on his heel, kneeling to the ground as though by instinct. He knew not where to look; the sun was still bright in the sky. It couldn't have been any time past mid-morning. "My Lady. The Tribes, they..."

THEY RETREAT, YES. THEY ARE FORTUNATE TO ESCAPE THE HORRORS YOU HAVE HELPED TO SET UPON THEM. MY WILL IS DONE. YOU NEED NOT INTERPRET IT ANY LONGER.

Furrowing his brow, Cin scampered in place, throwing his arms out at his side. "My Lady! What do you mean? Please, tell me!"

There was only silence. The wind left him and an avian shadow flew overhead. Cin was left only to his thoughts, just as he had been these last few days. What they would reveal to him was simply something he'd have to ponder.

Whether the answers would reveal themselves to him in the north or the south was something he had yet to decide.

After what seemed an eternity, the strange mist finally cleared. Aritz had never felt a stranger sensation before in his life. Whatever wickedness existed in those murky threads had held him tight, unwilling to loose him from their shadowy grip. He clenched his eyes shut and reopened them, his vision readjusting to what was now little more than an empty valley.

The savages were gone. Those who were still in charge of their wretched minds, at any rate. The chasm was littered with bodies both dead and alive, but mindless just the same. He turned in place, matching gazes with several of his soldiers locked in the same sense of astonishment. His arm felt weak, his right hand more blood than skin, and his head was enveloped in as much of a fog as it had been before this mist had appeared.

On unsteady legs, Aritz holstered his pistol and slowly made his way toward Kama and her companions, the three of them huddled around the corpse of the dead wolf. Though he had seen it once before already, disbelief was all he could feel at crippling the savages simply by slaying their gods. It was a foulness he wished never to be a part of, and yet it had brought him that much closer to claiming this island under the Savior's banner.

As he approached Kama and her witches, the Acrarian soldiers began to cheer, irrespective of Aritz's own views on the matter. Chants proclaiming a tremendous victory erupted in the air, many linking arms or embracing, others falling to their knees in solemn prayer, offering thanks and begging forgiveness to the Savior for all they achieved during this battle.

I know not how to feel, he thought. *This is a victory of much greater certainty than what we faced mere days ago. But have I the right to celebrate with such alacrity when I employed wicked magic to do so? Blessed Savior, what am I to do?*

A wide smile stretched across Kama's face, her arms outstretched. "Congratulations, *General*," she said, emphasizing Aritz's title and rank almost as a sneer. "You have officially laid claim to the impenetrable holy ground of the Tribes. Sullen glances are of ill favor when achieving such a monumental victory."

Aritz briefly raised his eyebrows in acknowledgment, his eyes cast upon the giant beast before him. "We are not yet finished. There are still yet savages roaming about upon the Savior's rightful land."

Kama brushed her hand aside, offering a barely concealed chuckle. "Those who remain are little more than scholars, many of whom had never held a weapon until this battle."

"And those same 'scholars' are armed just the same. I will not suffer their presence upon my land any further."

"*Your* land?" Kama scoffed. She crossed her arms and raised a curious eyebrow. "A moment ago, you called this your Savior's land. Which is it, Aritz?"

Aritz snarled. "It is of little consequence to you."

A snap and a flash from behind drew a wince. One of the soldiers had brought one of those…photographic machines with him, much to Aritz's own confusion. It captured images to print on pieces of paper. The concept was entirely foreign to Aritz, and to put to print the picture of countless war dead—even if one of them was an alleged god—seemed tasteless. Aritz only allowed it because the lad said no words otherwise. Less muttering for him to have to listen to.

"I *would* have you explain to me this, however," Aritz said, turning back to Kama, a frown settling upon his face. "What *was* that mist? Surely, it is something *you* would understand." He cared little to veil the implication of what his words meant.

In response, Kama merely flashed her teeth, exchanging a knowing, amused glance with her companions. "Well, Aritz, I must say it is of little consequence to *you*."

Aritz took a stern step forward. "That mist incapacitated my army and allowed the heathens to escape with their lives. It is of the *utmost* consequence to me, and I will accept no other explanations to the contrary. Do you understand?"

Kama crossed her arms, tutting her lips. "You need not worry of it, Aritz. This holy ground is removed of its gods. They cannot play their tricks on you now."

"But there are three gods, are there not? What has become of the third?"

She dismissed the concern again with another sidelong brush of the hand. "In due time. It is of the least measure of concern to you, and to us. The Tribes are on their final legs. You needn't wait much longer."

With a grunt, Aritz shouldered his way past Kama and glanced out at the valley. A pervasive din of hollow groans and moans echoed within the chasm, bodies slight in motion but bereft of any of the faculties that made them the facsimiles of humans they were. He felt Kama's presence slide next to him. He did little to suppress his disapproving growl.

"*So,*" Kama said, prolonging the word. "What will you do with them?"

Aritz looked at her with confusion and gestured broadly with his hand in confirmation to the direction of her question. When she nodded, Aritz asked, "They are not dead, correct?"

Shaking her head, Kama adopted an air of confident satisfaction, something gleaming in her eyes as though she were reminiscing. "No, Aritz, the dead do not tend to make noise. They are merely mindless. But I suppose you could say they are still pliable."

"Hmph," Aritz offered in acknowledgment. "More bodies for more work. Tis easier when they do not question orders."

Kama looked at him with pronounced silence before chuckling to herself. "A shame. Here I saw you to be a man of ambition and vision."

"Speak plainly, Kama. I've no patience for riddles."

She bowed in an exaggerated fashion. "But *of course*, General. Allow me to ask you a question."

"No."

"The Kingdom of Acraria is one of the most technologically advanced nations in your homeland, is it not?"

Aritz sighed, seeing no point in not humoring her. "Aye, and what of it?"

Kama smiled. "Surely, the trails of progress do not suddenly stop. Advancements in technology are beyond my ken, personally, but I know this land. I know its people. And I know what its people can do for *you*."

Raising his brow, Aritz turned his attention fully toward the woman. "What are you suggesting?"

The fire-haired woman threw her hands to the side, the grin growing ever wider. "Tell me this: are you willing to pave the way for the greatest technological advancements the Kingdom has ever seen?"

Slowly, Aritz nodded his head. "Yes."

"Good," Kama said, her voice reaching a new low register, an obscene satisfaction coloring her tongue. "Then what are you willing to do in order to walk down that pathway?"

INTERLUDE

Sound and Fury

The Year 1581 Anno Salvatoris
40 Years After the Settling

"That which you so ardently profess as the 'Harvest' is a grave circumstance for which I hold no remorse, nor shall I ever."

Aritz sneered through his teeth as the words left his lips, the hair on the back of his neck dampening from the sweat dripping down against the rising heat in his chamber. The sea breeze still wafted in through the window, but its intensity was waning, the aroma of saltwater dissipating, leaving behind only the pervasive odor of must and dust. His nostrils twinged, the residue of the crushed shards of his hard-earned trophies scattering throughout the room, wafting about in a stream of shattered memories.

But he stood firm regardless, even as the nose of his pistol was near to caressing his own nose, the assailant wearing Kama's face still glaring at him with the fires of hell burning in her pupils. His palms were damp, still clasped together, his forearms burning up beneath the heavy fabrics of his lordly robe. *I must not appear weak. I must not appear frail. I am the Founder, and I shall not be deterred by such wickedness.*

"For to feel remorse," he continued, "the incident in question would need to have happened as you state it did. And to feel remorse for creatures of your station, a station far below my own, is beyond such need. A man need not mourn so for a beast. I am not the butcher you attempt to paint me as—nor am I the butcher you play while you wear my face. I am but a humble shepherd, guiding my flock to be cleansed in the wondrous light of the Savior.

Is that such an atrocity with which to vilify me? Or is piety merely a path to devilry amongst your people?"

The woman closed her eyes for the flash of a second, grinning with what could only be described as sordid amusement. She stared at Aritz with clear disbelief on her face, her mouth agape as though lost for words, her arm wavering but the pistol remaining steady. "This is simply a lie you have recited to yourself over and over, isn't it?" she asked, raising her brow, the ghosts of her vibrant red hair swaying with the limited draft. "You repeat the lie over and again, you demand the same of others, and no longer can you discern the truth from the lies. You've become a victim to your own falsehoods." She gave Aritz a pitying look.

It was enough for Aritz to laugh, his moist palm snaking to his stomach as his gut bounced with the amusement. "Do you find me such a fool that I would mistake truths for lies, stories for histories? Savior's breath, woman, for one who claims to have 'learned much about me' these last twenty-five years, you certainly know *little* about me." He turned his back to her, confident she would not have the gall to pull the trigger on him. The further he walked from her, the more it became apparent he was correct. His eyes found the illustrations of his war map, his trusted companion during those early years of Ferranda, the source of his obsession and exhilaration on those long, stagnant days lacking promise and progress. The contours of inadvertent punch-holes and slashes from pens grooved against his fingers as he ran them against the length of the map. It brought a smile to his face.

"I am nothing if not comforted by that which I accomplished in these lands," he said, satisfaction coloring his voice as he spied his assailant from the corner of his eye, still as a statue. "When a people are overwrought by the threat of those with wicked intent, it is customary to remove the threat. When a weed rears its head in the middle of a beautiful garden, you have no course but to rip it out by the stem. You may hate me for it as much as you like, you may paint me the devil, you may label me a 'Lightscourge' or whatever nonsense your heathen people say of me, but I am a man of means protecting and enriching the lives of those beneath me. The weight of burden is only for me to carry upon my back, but my back has never felt stronger."

The woman looked defeated. The pistol fell to her side, her arms thrown out sidelong with confusion. "You speak in nothings," she hissed. "All you have confirmed is that you fashion yourself a god as justification for ordering the slaughter of thousands upon thousands. It is not for you to decide who shall live and who shall die, not should it fall upon *anyone*, be they man or god!"

"*That* is nothing more than the meager claim of one beneath the right to decide such things." Aritz slammed his fist on the old war map, scattering the remaining extant pieces from the days of conquest. Wooden pieces scattered on the floor, collecting amidst the granules of heavy dust. "You do *not* receive holy orders from on high and think yourself to be one possessive of greater morality than your god. You carry out His orders without question and without faltering!"

"And *now* you revert to hiding behind the supposed colored words of your precious Savior to condone your crimes." The woman closed the gap between herself and Aritz, the floorboards crunching beneath her heel. "Perhaps you are correct, though. I may not know the true Aritz a Mata after all. For so long I deemed you a monster, but you've simply removed another mask to show the face of a petty man eager to place the blame upon another for you can do no wrong yourself. Any who would claim otherwise are just those who want to see you fall, isn't that right? You're the self-crowned image of perfection, aren't you? A gift to grace this earth, bestowed upon us all by your dear Savior, and yet your words of worship are nothing more than performative, the guise of a man who has never in earnest worshiped a day in his life. But do go on: tell me how the Harvests were a holy order, that the slaughter of innocent people to feed your bloodlust was the will of a god!"

Aritz shot an accusing finger at the woman, the heat rising in his face. He could feel the veins bulging in his neck. "Still your tongue! You cannot speak to the wickedness of another's god when yours are beasts who bloodied countless of my soldiers!"

"In defense of our rightful land!"

"*No land is your rightful land!*" Aritz bellowed, his throat raw with the effort. "You fouled upon this precious ground for far too long in grave disregard for the Savior's light! You allowed your wills to be tainted by the pull of animals who persuaded you into believing them divine. But no divinity would permit themselves to fall to mortal hands. *I* proved your gods to be false, and therefore, it is by *my* right to determine your right to life upon *my* land!"

"Is it *your* land, or is it your *god's* land?" The disbelief upon her face was visibly shifting back to amusement, as though she felt wholly in control of the conversation. "You cannot claim both to be true!"

Again, Aritz slammed the war map, sending more pieces scattering to the floor. "It is the Savior's land, and by extension as His Sword, it is *my* land! Ferranda is *mine*! And I will entertain no claims to the contrary! From the night His Envoy appeared before me, I knew it to be true. There was a reason for which I happened upon this land. The threads laid before me were clear all along. I mourn only that I took too long to follow them. But He was patient in determining the right time to send His Envoy to me. What further proof need you?"

In response, the woman only laughed.

"Do you find the harsh truth too amusing?"

She shook her head dismissively. "Humor me this answer, Aritz. Has this 'Envoy' appeared before you since?"

Aritz rolled his eyes. "I fail to see the significance in that question."

"You fail to see much of many things, but answer the question, regardless."

His hand raw and bloodied from the splintered war map, matching the open wounds on his opposite hand from brutally assaulting his own desk earlier, he shook his head and said, "No, I have not."

A smile creased the woman's lips. "And were you not in the presence of Kamataa, one who you know to have been able to change her form at will?"

Aritz scoffed. "What of it?"

"Then let that be all the confirmation I need."

"What confirmation?"

"Merely that all you profess to be, as a 'Sword' carrying out the will of your Savior, is naught but a front hiding you for what you truly are: a man so thoroughly consumed by his hateful views that a woman masking herself as a holy messenger is enough to convince you of your own delusions. A fool you truly are, Aritz a Mata. A hateful, violent fool, but a fool, nonetheless."

Aritz remained undeterred. He glared at the phantom with all the hatefulness she claimed him to be consumed by. "And yet I am still the fool who is standing atop my quarry." His voice sunk low, gravel grating against his raw throat. "I do not accept the words and claims of a murderer. My wife and children were slain by your hand. Snakes are incapable of truthful words. But if I am not wielding the Sword of the Savior, then I will still gladly speak His words. For I am His retribution incarnate, and it is I who served it upon your primitive and savage people."

The pistol twitched in the woman's hands. That heathen intent and instinct was immediately apparent in her eyes. *Good, good. Give in to what you truly are. You need not hide from it. It is soon to return one way or another.*

She flashed her teeth in a snarl. "But to what end did you slaughter thousands in the name of 'retribution?' For what purpose was it to feed us to your blood machine? For progress? Was that all people were to you? Fuel for a fire? I suppose I needn't remind you that your kindling failed to light. Innovation has been greeted only by stagnation these last twenty-five years. But you would still call it 'retribution,' regardless, wouldn't you?"

Aritz felt a deep laugh building in the back of his throat. "And *that* is what you so adamantly call your Harvest, is it not?"

"I would call it whatever it needs to be called. But the facts remain the facts."

"But what if the 'facts' are predicated upon lies, instead?"

"Your lies count for nothing when I am fully aware of what I have seen with my own eyes."

"But who can stomach such wretched 'truths,' when there are stories that are much more palatable? What you hope to uncover would simply tear these good people of Ferranda apart. For all your squabbling about the treatment of your 'innocent' people, you surely seem quite disinclined for the innocents among *mine*."

The woman sneered, her fingers rapping against the handle of the pistol, her thumb clicking the hammer back and forth.

"But you care little for them, don't you? What a shame. Your feelings are little more than dirt upon my heels. It matters not at all, regardless. Your people are long gone, your culture dust on the wind, carried away to who knows and who cares where. And if they were 'fuel for my blood machine,' as you say, the good people of Ferranda are happy to revel in everything I have built for them; how it was done is of little consequence to them."

She looked ready to pounce at him.

I'll never give her the opportunity. Aritz looked a final time at the southern reaches of the war map, where Ferrand City now stood tall and proud. He placed a fond hand atop its borders. "You may sing the mournful aria of the Harvests all you want, woman. But it does not change the fact that those stories are nothing but falsehoods. Categorically."

CHAPTER FIVE

Vanity

The mountains were long behind her, and the hell within chose not to follow.

As Sen finally permitted herself to collapse upon the ground, her legs had long since forgotten the painful sensation coursing through them. Fire surged through her breast, originating from the jagged edges of her fractured rib. Soft soil padded her landing, the granules of dirt still coated with the stench of death. Despite that, their cool touch was delightful against her exposed skin, her heavy coat having been abandoned some time ago as the brisk air of the mountains receded to the more comforting environs of the plains and grassy dunes south of the Stone Tribe village.

It was not long ago that Sen would have anticipated her presence in the Forest as being one to promise safety. But as it was now, it was a hollow bastion for the last remnants of a Tribal resistance. The pastel colors overhead no longer carried the dense dread she had once feared, when she and Narva traversed the woods' dangerous depths in a futile attempt to rescue her brother. Those likely to have wished harm upon her were surely nothing but corpses upon the ground, victims of an assault she had neither the power nor the courage to prevent.

Shames upon shames awaited her, and yet Sen found it not within her to mourn for those crushed underfoot. Relief was all she could allow herself to feel. Relief at her miraculous survival, despite the overwhelming odds. Relief at separating herself from the horrors casting a dark shadow upon a once holy and impenetrable ground. And relief at the numbers of her kin still with her, a number that seemed inconceivable just a day ago, but now the representative of the faintest glimmer of hope.

Sen rolled to her back and propped herself up against a nearby tree, its bark sticky with dried sap and old blood. The numbness in her legs vanished until the pervasive reminder of aches and pains assaulted her, her hand instinctively reaching for her tender side and the throbbing pain radiating from there. She glanced at the not-insignificant number of Tribespeople resting, collapsing, and weeping amidst the falling leaves and tainted soil. Gentle Owlsigns not accustomed to being thrust into such desperate violence. Her sister, no longer the ardent warrior, but merely a survivor just the same as the rest of them. All of them carrying scars, old and new, yet all cognizant of the great fortune they were granted to still lay claim to their own lives—and to the sanctity of their intact minds.

The Moon does not grant Her luck simply to me today, Sen thought.

But despite the feelings of gratitude toward seeing so many of her people still remaining, the sinking feeling in Sen's chest was quick to return as the absence of that many *more* stood out as not being present within this surviving party. She felt an involuntary quiver of her lips as the lingering silence danced about, the unspoken solemnity recognizing the two-thirds of people who did not return from the True Heart of the Land.

Sen ran her palm over her mouth, clamping her teeth down against a finger, nearly hard enough to draw blood. Her eyes clenched shut, wanting to not to permit the welling tears to stream down her cheeks. There had been enough tears shed these last few days. She wanted to be done with them, just as she also wanted to shed a tear for each life lost in those desperate battles, for each mind irreparably ruptured and sundered at the felling of two gods. The impossible had happened within those bloody depths—deities falling to mortals, and yet their own escape from the same fate remained possible.

The weight of it all crashed upon Sen with a shudder, and she buried her face in her hands, feeling nothing but the pure sensation of helplessness. Tears leaked through the slits of her fingers and cut swaths through the bloodstains painting her skin. Her choked sobs contributed to the day's somber music, joining hands with those who sang in equal measure. What she felt was not lost upon anyone. There was nothing else *to* feel but the crippling assault of forlorn emptiness.

A hand pressing against her shoulder startled her to attention. Sen glanced up, her eyelids heavy from the emotion and exhaustion, and saw Tawa towering above her, his own eyes red and glistening from the tears. Words choked in her throat as she clasped her hand to his, forcing a smile and pleading for him to sit beside her, patting her free hand on the soil to her right.

With a wordless nod, Tawa complied, consideration and compassion glowing on his face. They both looked ahead at the Owlsigns filtering in through the arboreal border, many collapsing in a heap at the first sign of sanctuary. As more and more collected in the woods, the mutual terror and disbelief sounded, the echoes of weeping bouncing off the trees. Countless held tightly to their nearest neighbor, many of whom Sen had to assume they were interacting with one another for the first time. Nonverbal exchanges seemed to be the only thing anyone was capable of, the purpose of words a mystery when comforting embraces were much more effective.

No one was without a partner, so far as Sen could tell. She saw people of the Sun Tribe arm in arm with those of the Wood Tribe, scholars of both sides of the Lake Tribe setting aside their differences in the name of companionship, longtime enemies turned friends in an instant. Because none of those petty squabbles truly mattered anymore. *And had that realization come sooner,* Sen thought, *we could have been far more prepared for the Invaders' arrival. Instead, it was just war amongst ourselves. And on that note...*

She squinted her eyes in examination of the various Owlsigns in the woods, the waning golden sunlight bleeding through the clearing toward the northern plains. She locked eyes with Tez, her sister appearing far more weathered than she ever had. There was comfort, at least, in seeing Ket beside her, their fingers intertwined even as they stared ahead with shock apparent in their gazes. Not far from them was Grafhar, the mute Linguist who had worked in her father's employ what felt like so long ago. Sen hadn't even noticed his presence in the mountains, but she was grateful to see him alive, nonetheless. Faces she had passed by but a few times—the tavern keeper, Ko Seln; the great elder, Ko Zaran; even the Linguist, Dantalhat, who had translated the night Aritz a Mata arrived to kill Sen's father and kidnap her brother—blended into the tapestry of survival, despondent at the circumstances uniting them together.

But despite these numerous names and faces, Sen did not see Koelhe among their rank. *How unfortunate it was that she cannot see the pain she has left in her wake. Catatonic or not, I wish only the worst upon her for all of this.* She bunched her fist into the dirt below, her aching knuckles straining as soil collected beneath her cracked fingernails. She did not miss Koelhe's presence by any stretch of the imagination, but the fact remained that the consequences should have been hers to face. *Left in a mindless state, unable to do anything but shit herself and wait for someone to feed her? She got off easy compared to the rest of us.*

An air of unease held the survivors in its grip. Sen hardly knew where to begin assessing their remaining numbers. All she knew for certain was that when they retreated to the True Heart in defense of the gods, the Tribes numbered in the thousands. Now? She'd hazard to guess it was down to the hundreds. The *low* hundreds, at that.

She released her clasp on Tawa's hand and glanced at him, hoping he would have *some* answer to illuminate the way forward. He was the smartest person Sen had ever known, the most measured and even-tempered. But as she looked upon his face, she knew immediately that in his mind dwelt the same thoughts as everyone else. Still, she could not help but ask, "Tawa...what do we even do, now?"

The prolonged silence was all the answer she needed. All the *confirmation* any of them had at their disposal. When Tawa turned to face her, Sen saw in his expression an uncertainty she had never known him to possess. Tawa had *always* known what to do, regardless of the inherent challenge. He was blunt and honest, but always in a kind manner. But as his lips turned in a frown, Sen could only feel an acceptance that they had not survived so much as they delayed the inevitable of what was soon to come. *That* was the only certainty.

"I wish I knew what to do," Tawa admitted, his voice shaking as he folded his hands before him. His eyes were downcast as though offering a prayer in hopes of forgiveness. "And loath as I am to say it...what hope have we now?"

Tears were welling in his eyes, his hands shaking at the reality and gravity of it all. "I am sorry, Sen."

A quiver gripped Sen, a small part of her wanting still to cling on to what little threads of hope remained. She turned her head toward her sister, near enough where she knew her voice would carry. "Tez," she called, the beckoning drawing the attention of several nearby who had evidently been content with the mournful silence.

Even at this distance, the severity of the red lines cracking Tez's eyes was clear. She looked absolutely defeated, more so than most in this crowd. She didn't say a word in response to Sen's voice.

Sen upturned her hands at her sides, gesturing in a placating fashion, shrugging when words did not immediately come to her. "Do you…have any ideas? Any strategy for what we can do next?"

A hush gripped the crowd, the soft echoes of weeping dissipating as they anticipated an answer, a shred of guidance in this unassured time. None among them were warriors…save for Tez. Though none said it, it was clear the surrounding Owlsigns were expectant of Tez to know exactly how they could fight their way out of this.

But as Tez grew more visibly aware of those expectations, a tremble overtook her, nerves that she had never once outwardly exhibited. Sen's heart plummeted as she watched her sister curl into herself, hiding her face behind folded knees, her body heaving as the once proud warrior she was regressed into a defeated shell. Ket wrapped their arms around Tez, whispering something into her ear, words that Sen could only assume were assuring words of comfort, but could not be picked up by the strands of wind that ventured into these woodland depths.

Guilt attacked Sen for even questioning Tez about a plan in her current state, but she knew they could not be content with remaining an exiled people in hiding for much longer. Someone had to have *some* semblance of a plan, good or bad, so long as it was *something*.

Unsteadily, she rose to her feet, all attention falling upon her. It was not lost upon her, the mistrust still apparent on the faces of some. She could not blame them for that. Regardless of whether it was resultant of her desertion to the Invaders—irrespective of their understanding of the brief enthrallment she felt toward the Children of the Black Moon—or if it was because of lingering resentment for her being Eclipseborn, Sen couldn't care less. She had been at the center of all of this through no want or fault of her own. At some point, she knew she would have to learn to embrace it.

"I do not profess to be a leader of any sort," she said, her voice shaking. "I've been the root of more trouble and misfortune than I care to admit or acknowledge. I've been part of misdeeds that I will always come to regret for the rest of my days, however few or many those days come to number. But I do *not* want to regret awaiting the inevitable if there was *any* hope of emerging victorious in the face of it." She paused, holding her right hand steady as it began to tremble from the nerves. "I don't expect any of you to have a plan that will lead us through to that hope. All I ask is that we devise *something*. I don't know what. But doing something is far better than hiding until the worst returns to claim the rest of us." She clasped her hands together. "I beg of you—*all* of you. Don't allow this to be the end of our people."

Deaf ears were the only things to greet her plea. Eyes averted away from her with defeat and embarrassment painted in even, disparate strokes. A murmured din arose from the earth, none addressing Sen's words and all focused instead on individual conversations as though Sen did not exist at all. Glances stole their way toward Sen's direction in brief bursts, numerous people seeming to check if she was still standing before them, awaiting their replies.

The tremors in Sen's hands quelled as she balled them into fists. Frustration welled within her as she ground her teeth, digging her worn-out boots into the soil below. "That's it, then, is it?" she posited to them all, her lip quivering. "You're all content to lie down and die, am I wrong? All those who fell against the Invaders, *this* is how we honor their memory? By giving in? By giving up? There's a reason we made it out of there alive—I *know* there is. And it's *not* to shake in our boots and wait for the end! Why can't you all—" She thrust her hand out to the side, but her stern fist was grasped firmly.

Tawa sat on the other end of her arm, his eyes downcast as he lowered her arm gently. He did not even bother to rise to his feet. "Sen. Look at these people. Look at what we have been reduced to."

She jerked her arm out of Tawa's grasp. "Do you not think I know that, Tawa?" she snapped. "We stand little chance. If the Invaders can kill two of our gods, then how do we stand against that might? I understand that. But then I stop and think about my parents, and about Brin, and about..." She stopped, slowly turning her head toward Tez, her head still buried in the crest of her arms. Sen clenched her eyes shut, her nails cutting swaths in the flesh of her palms. "When I think about *Narva*. All of them fell to the Invaders. I accept that I may very well do so myself. But I've run from this for long enough. Pitied myself for not stopping it for long enough. You told me that my actions will always speak louder than the words of others. Well, I'm ready to put that into practice until I can finally believe it myself."

Wisps of wind continued to pester the dense overhanging tree branches, the branches creaking and groaning as avian wings flapped from above, despite the absence of birdsong in the air. Tawa thoughtfully stroked his stubbled chin with his hand, covering his mouth and whatever soundless words he may have been voicing. Though the proclamation had originally been his own, it didn't even appear that he himself believed them. Doubt colored his eyes, just as it did those of all the Owlsigns present.

Fear was their pervasive assailant, and it was proving to be the more abled combatant.

Sen closed her eyes, the imagery of waves of Bearsigns and Wolfsigns collapsing in an instant flashing in her mind over and over. The roar of the Invaders' weapons was met with a collective *snap* as though necks were twisted around at the felling of the gods. Laughter rained from above, shadows swarming out from the clouds in a threatening mist, snaking their way toward Sen with clear malicious intent. The ever-familiar face threaded into the shadows' midst melted away, falling away from the body and grasping and pinning Sen's wrists by the strength of dark tendrils. An unseen force pulled her head back by the length of her braid, forcing her eyes to stay open at the sight of the Tribes' greatest warriors falling again, and again, and again, until none remained but herself within a scarred plain unforgiving and unwelcoming of her presence.

When next she blinked, the full brunt of the Invaders stood before her, and the taunting laughter echoed in her ears, pointed and shrill.

The wave of gunfire roared before her, and she fell backwards with a jerk.

When she opened her eyes again, she was back in the Forest, hundreds of curious eyes watching her with either gentle regard or dismissive annoyance. Tawa hovered over her, wrapping one arm around her and placing the other gently upon her shoulder. Sen massaged her temple, the shadows' hold over her still throbbing. Her heart pounded, rhythmically beating in discordant harmony as the falsely inattentive murmurs of the crowd became those of concern.

"Look at her," a faint voice said.

Sen parsed through the gathering for the source, her sense of sight still wavering, but found it to belong to a male Keeper with whom she was unfamiliar.

"She stands before us, claiming to be the best of us, and yet, she is hardly in control of her own wits." The man rose to a knee, his long dark locks of hair greasy and dampened by the glistening sweat of his chest and brow. "Is it *she* who shall guide us against the Invaders?"

The exaggerated noise of someone hawking and spitting sounded next. A Sun Tribesman stood to his feet, gashes still fresh upon his exposed right arm. "I hear no volunteering from *you*, Keeper. At least the Stone Tribe girl has not given up!"

"Of course she hasn't!" shouted the Keeper. "The Eclipseborn has never had anything to lose!"

"Watch your tongue, now!" exclaimed a nearby Lake woman, her shorn hair falling in front of her eyes in unruly strands. "Eclipseborn or no, she still helped prepare us for the Invader offensive."

"Tell me, then! Tell me how her involvement saved us!" Another Sun Tribesman shot to his feet, some five or six paces away from his compatriot. "Did we misplace our warriors? I don't see them anywhere!"

"Quiet, all of you!" Tawa bellowed, his voice bouncing off the dense bark of the Forest's trees. He removed his hands from Sen's shoulders and began to close the gap between the contesting Tribespeople.

"So quick to defend her, aren't you, Stone man?" responded the Sun Tribesman, nearly barreling over the rows of seated individuals before him.

"Do you willfully blind yourself to her mistakes, or are you content with following her to your deaths? Be my guest if so, surely!"

Sen groaned as arguments overlapped with one another, the noises pounding at her skull. She ran her fingers through her knotted hair, leaves and feathers dancing down to the earth from above, the air a cacophony of strawman's arguments and fearful pleas for togetherness. It was the most spirit she had seen from the survivors, at the very least, but she had wished such a return would have been the result of a drive to stand against the Invaders, not stand against each other. The angry voices assaulted her just as did the shadows' shrill laughter, the roar of gunfire, the waning war cries of deceased gods. She looked amongst the crowd, many having risen to their feet, some grasping at shirt collars, others shoving each other this way and that, and others still remaining seated. Tez counted among that number, though she had at least lifted her head at some point to watch the proceedings.

"We saw what became of the Bearsigns and Wolfsigns!" shouted the Keeper who had initiated the argument. "The Invaders know by now that they need only slay the Owl to defeat us! We're but one errant shot away from becoming lost entirely!"

"Then we ensure they do not get the opportunity!" Tawa responded, his tone fiery.

"Brilliant idea! If only we could account for its whereabouts!"

"Is that not *your* job to track its comings and goings, Keeper?" answered the Lake Tribe woman, her eyes rolling.

"I'm not sure that you were aware, but we've all spent much of this time simply trying to survive!" The Keeper seemed exasperated, his fingers running through his damp hair in a panic. "We know only that the Owl still lives."

"And for all we know, the Invaders could hold it in their grasps as we speak!" shouted a voice of unknown origin.

"The Invaders would not be so callous as to hold a god hostage when they know spilling its blood would spell the end for us," Tawa said bluntly. "The Almighty Owl remains free, though where is not for me to say."

The belligerent Sun Tribesman threw his hands in the air. "For all we know, then, it could very well have abandoned us. Turned tail and flew far away the moment it realized it could be killed by mortal hands!"

Sen slammed her fist on the ground. "The Owl would not abandon us!" she yelled.

"Oh, really?" the man retorted, shoving various people aside in a vain attempt to approach her. "And what would you know of the gods' propensities, Eclipseborn? The Owl must have seen you among our rank and determined us expendable. So long as it still lives, it surely cares little for our own suffering! We'll die in its name, and it won't shed a tear from upon its hidden perch! It matters little what we can do now—we fight for a phantom pulling us by its threads!"

Something skirted through the air with a blur, and in an instant, the Sun Tribesman was on the ground, collapsing with a resounding thud. He made no further noise beyond a meek and dazed groan.

Sen jumped to her feet, her hand fumbling for her spear while her other hand reached for the pistol strapped to her thigh. *Still only one bullet remaining...but if needs must, then needs must.* Her eyes traced a mental path of whatever passed by, following its trails up toward the murky shadows encasing the treetops. Many others followed suit, ignoring whatever pain the Sun Tribesman may have been in.

With unsteady arms, Sen raised her spear toward the trees, her heart thumping in her ears. "Who's there?" she shouted. "Show yourself!"

A discordant hum resonated, sending vibrations through the air. Shocked gasps gripped the crowd, some knocked off-balance by the sheer force shaking them.

"What is this...?" a voice murmured loud enough for Sen to hear. She looked to her left to see a Stone Tribeswoman with whom she was unfamiliar kneeling and picking something off the ground near to where the belligerent Sun Tribesman fell. "Is this...a feather?"

The air rippled at the question, a flurry of loose feathers descending from high above. YOU ALL FOCUS TOO MUCH UPON WHAT YOU *CAN* DO, WHEN WHAT YOU SHOULD HAVE BEEN ASKING IS WHAT YOU *MUST* DO.

Sen felt her breath catch in her throat. "That voice…" *It's so familiar. But…how?*

Leaves and branches rustled above as spears and bows were aimed upward, despite the hands holding them displaying more fear than desire for battle. A violent *snap* sent forth a flurry of wood chips and splinters and an enormous avian form burst out in front of it all. Its wings spread wide as it descended, its talons reaching eagerly for the ground below. It bore all the majesty that Sen expected of it, but had not been privy to when she initially encountered it deep in the True Heart of the Land. When its feet met the earth, all the survivors fell to a knee as though by reverent instinct.

"Almighty Owl," Sen whispered, her head turned down. The acknowledgment was voiced by most of the crowd in unison with her.

The Owl withdrew its wings as it surveyed the group. It craned its head, its wide eyes wells over observation, a curious trill vibrating from its throat. DO YOU THINK ME SO VAIN THAT I WOULD ABANDON YOU ALL AT THE FIRST SIGN OF TROUBLE? YOU ARE ALL MY STRENGTHS INCARNATE; OURS IS NOT THE WAY OF WARFARE. IT IS WISE TO KNOW WHEN TO RETREAT AND WHEN TO FIGHT, IS IT NOT?

"It…it speaks?!" exclaimed a voice from the back. Sen couldn't say for certain to whom it belonged.

"Of course, it speaks, you idiot!" responded a second unknown voice. "Think of the Boons! Knowledge, Memory…Language! It probably knows every tongue in the world!"

An amused laugh escaped the Owl's beak. It did not acknowledge the assertion, nor did it seem inclined to deny it.

Recognition and recollection hit Sen all at once. The familiarity, that despite only hearing it speak two words beforehand, the firm intonation maintained in its speech now was more than enough confirmation for her. "That voice in the mist…" she murmured, catching the Owl's attention. "That was you, wasn't it?"

The Owl nodded without hesitation. IT WAS MY WILL MADE KNOWN. I WOULD NOT ALLOW YOU ALL TO FALL THERE. AND THERE IS MUCH MORE STILL TO BE DONE.

Sen rose to her feet, drawing a sharp gasp from several of the Owlsigns surrounding her. She felt a sharp tug at her shirt by Tawa, but she disregarded him. "What was that mist? What...what do you intend for us?"

"Sen!" Tawa hissed. "It is not our place to ask such things!"

BE AT EASE, TAWANDHAR, the Owl said assuredly. I DO NOT CLAIM OFFENSE TO HER QUESTION. AND IT IS HARDLY FOR ME TO DEMAND ANYTHING OF AN ECLIPSEBORN.

Sen drew in a nervous breath at the label.

CALM YOURSELF, SENNALHAT. I DO NOT BEGRUDGE YOU THE CIRCUMSTANCES OF YOUR BIRTH. NOR DID THE BEAR OR THE WOLF. WHAT YOU ENDURED IS ONLY THE RESULT OF THE FALLACY OF THE IGNORANCE OF MAN. THE SUFFERING YOU ENDURED WAS...UNFAIR.

A succession of tears streamed down Sen's cheek. First, one of elation and relief. But then, one of frustration and anger. "If you knew that all along, then why did you not—"

ADVISE OTHERWISE? The Owl shook its head, loose feathers descending from its giant form. IT IS NOT UPON ME TO INTERFERE IN THE WHIMS OF MAN. I AM MERELY A GUIDE AND AN OBSERVER UNTIL THE CIRCUMSTANCES DEMAND OTHERWISE.

An involuntary tremor gripped Sen's fists. *All those years of being treated as an outcast could have been avoided if...* She snarled, closing the gap between her and the god. "And those circumstances did not arise until just recently, then?"

I BELIEVE YOU ALREADY KNOW THE ANSWER TO THIS QUESTION, SENNALHAT. THE BEAR AND THE WOLF FELL DUE TO THESE SAME CIRCUMSTANCES.

Sen bit at her lower lip. "Surely, then, these...circumstances are not over. You called forth that mist—somehow—to aid our escape. But it is not clear to me why—or how you did so in the first place."

The Owl stood firm, eyeing Sen with its wide, curious gaze. DO NOT UNDERESTIMATE THE STRENGTH OF THE BOONS WE THREE DEITIES HAD GRANTED YOU ALL. IT CRANED ITS HEAD TOWARD ALL THE GATHERED OWLSIGNS. ILLUSIONS NEED NOT EXTEND ONLY TO THE BODY. ONE MUST SIMPLY POSSESS THE KNOWLEDGE TO EXPAND WHAT ONE CAN

CREATE WITHIN THEMSELVES. BUT THERE IS LITTLE TIME TO DIVULGE ON SUCH MATTERS. YOU ARE CORRECT IN YOUR ASSERTION, SENNAL-HAT. I AM IN NEED OF YOU STILL. I AM IN NEED OF *ALL* OF YOU. I CANNOT STRIKE BACK AT THE DISEASE PLAGUING OUR LAND WITHOUT YOUR HELP.

"Strike back?" questioned Tawa. With clear caution, he rose to his feet and filed in beside Sen. "My apologies, Almighty Owl, but you should know as well as I that we are not warriors. We have not the acumen to attack with the strength-at-arms you would require of us. We are only scholars; the only fighter among us...is..."

Sen sighed as she noticed Tawa's inadvertent choice of words. A frown settled upon the man's face. Glancing over her shoulder, Sen caught sight of Tez, her sister's expression still rife with despondence. There was no hiding the displeasure in Tez's eyes. *What chance do we have to strike back, when the only one worth a damn with a spear is nothing but a shell of herself?*

The Owl trilled. THERE ARE BUT MANY WAYS TO WAGE WAR, TAWAND-HAR. A MAN OF YOUR KNOWLEDGE SHOULD BE AWARE OF THIS, YES? IT MAY BE AN ARM WHICH CASTS THE FIRST BLOW, BUT IT IS THE MIND AND THE VOICE WHICH ENABLES IT TO STOP. The god's plumage began to glow, motes of light glimmering about its form. AND IT IS THE KNOWLEDGEABLE MIND THAT KNOWS HOW BEST TO STRIKE AN ENEMY'S WEAKNESS. THE INVADERS MAY HAVE DISCOVERED OUR GREATEST VULNERABILITY, BUT I AM EQUALLY CERTAIN OF THE WEAKNESS OF ONE GENERAL ARITZ A MATA.

A burst of light surged from the Owl's form, twisting and reshaping until it shrank severely in size, its imposing height vanishing and reappearing in a shape all too familiar to Sen. She could not help but gasp in shock.

VANITY.

The words were the Owl's. But the body and voice belonged to Aritz a Mata.

MEMORY

MARKS

The feeling of a heavier pocket, punctuated by the melody of metallic jingling, was always music to Aritz's ears. A day was much better spent with a coin toiled and earned.

Sunrays filtered in through the vast windows in the family treasury, its top-floor positioning a more-than-adequate deterrent from thieves and robbers inclined to scale the estate walls, and its view of the mountains and valleys far in the distant Acrarian countryside was perpetually stunning, almost too beautiful to be real and not a vibrant painting.

It always brought a smile to Aritz's face, and his eyes near to a tear. But for all the enticement of nature's wondrous vistas, the distinctive smell of gold was far more beckoning. The manor guards paid little mind to his presence on this floor, and if they did, it was hardly their place to speak out against their Lord's eldest son. He heard the leathers of their boots meet the floor behind him in muted footsteps as he surveyed the countryside, hands folded behind his back, and finally broke away from the sight.

When the guards turned the corner, Aritz set into motion, scurrying toward the treasury door and swiftly opening it, skidding into its depths. The walls were lined with coffers constructed of fine oak, stained and polished to a beautiful glow in the morning sunlight. Aritz caught his breath for a moment, his heart thumping with excitement. He held still, ensuring the hush outside the door was of a more elongated sort, and rushed to the nearest coffer. As he lifted it open, the rays of light bounced off the glittering shimmer of gold pieces, his eyes wincing reflexively. He flexed his fingers and scooped a light handful—enough to satisfy his needs, but not so much to draw attention to sudden bulges or clattering in his pockets. With caution, he closed the coffer back up, distributed the coin evenly through his pockets, and pranced out the door.

The guards had not returned from their patrol when he re-assumed his position by the windows, a contented smile stretching across his lips. It was still some minutes more before their footsteps resounded in his ears.

Mornings had often been spent thusly of late. He needed some manner of entertainment before the tutors arrived to instruct him in lordly and worldly matters. Traipsing about the gardens had long since lost its charm. His parents were otherwise too occupied more frequently than not. His brothers avoided him with particularly pronounced fear these last few years, exchanging words with him only at gatherings requisite of their presence. Words, but hardly a glance. Servants were dreadfully boring and served primarily as a reminder of the divide between his high status and their low. He was not permitted to travel on his own beyond the estate's holdings.

Amusement had to be made for himself. Even if it was simply one coin at a time. But all good things would inevitably meet their end, and his morning routine was interrupted, as it always was, by the clunking footsteps of an entourage far too numerous to be another guard patrol.

"Master Aritz," a male voice called from behind.

Aritz turned, cautious not to create too much excess noise from his pockets, and adopted his warmest smile. Ynigo had come to fetch him, his stern frown ever the familiar sight. "Is it that time already, Ynigo?"

Ynigo nodded, puffing his chest out with authority. "'Tis mid-morning already, yes. Come along, you must change before your tutors arrive."

For Aritz, it was always a rather humorous display to watch Ynigo act with attempts of assumed dominance. But in absence of the Lord and Lady of the house, the line of authoritative succession apparently passed to their doorman. Regardless, Aritz acquiesced with a nod, and followed after Ynigo without protest, as he always did.

Never had Ynigo questioned the reasoning for Aritz's presence on the treasury floor—nor was it his place to ask—and today was no different. The descent to the first floor was traveled in silence save for the echoing footsteps bouncing off the carved marble of the stairways. The retinue surrounding Ynigo did not even acknowledge Aritz and seemed to serve only as a human wall preventing Aritz's escape to parts unknown. *As though there is anywhere here for me to roam in secrecy.*

The long hallway housing his and his family's bedchambers loomed before him, a beacon heralding the end of the morning's merriment. He sighed as the household guards dispersed with nary a word, fanning out in all directions from the gardens to the retaining pool to the kitchens. For his part, Ynigo at least turned to face the young Master, if only to wordlessly incline his head in the direction of Aritz's bedchamber.

Aritz waved a hand in dismissive acknowledgment, flashing an attempt at an earnest smile at the dedicated doorman and went about his way.

"The maidservants have laid out the day's outfit for you, Master Aritz," Ynigo called, the measure of command in his tone seemingly more adamant now that Aritz was not facing him. "Do take attention to dress promptly and make your way to the library posthaste."

"Promptly and posthaste," Aritz muttered under his breath. "Oh, and with all due attention, of course. Thank you, Ynigo." He was certain the doorman could not hear him, and the lack of follow-up was the confirmation he needed.

As he entered his bedchamber, Aritz quickly discarded his morning robe and tossed it on the floor before remembering the handful of coins he stashed in its interior pocket. He instinctively slid to where it landed and fished through it, happily finding the sensation of cold metal brushing against his fingers. He pulled free the gold pieces and walked over to his stash, a small compartment he fashioned into the rear of his dresser, and deposited the day's collection into the ever-growing personal treasury.

At the age of fourteen, he hardly had a need for the coin. His options of travel were horridly limited, and he wanted for nothing in this wonderfully charmed life of his. Material wealth was something he needn't worry over. There was not a single thing he had needed to exchange even a simple copper for, and he hardly anticipated such a day arriving any time soon. But to have this stash of his own…it felt right. This was *his*, his earnings that he had toiled over, studied the monotonous proclivities and routines of the upstairs guards who lacked the backbone to protest to his presence. Truly, it was difficult work. He earned it all.

Sometimes, it simply felt good to be earning his weight. Soon enough, his personal collection would *literally* be his weight.

He stowed away the compartment, hiding it behind a row of overcoats and trousers hanging overhead, and listlessly made his way toward the clothing laid out for him along his bed. Shades of the Mata variant of the Acrarian blue colored the apparel: an uncomfortable, narrow-cut leather jerkin to be worn underneath a fur-lined cloak, flowing and vibrant. His trousers appeared mercifully loose-fitting, tapered at the calf to exhibit his gold-buckled shoes and midnight-blue stockings. With a shake of the head, he lazily removed the remnants of his morningwear and replaced it with the day's formal vestments. Appearances were everything, after all. And he could not be seen as being underdressed in view of the help.

Once completed, Aritz rolled his shoulder, stiffened by the tight confines of his jerkin, and made his way back to the hallway, ready to begin the long trek across the estate to the library. Truly, it was a misery to waste such a beautiful day in such a long transit. He longed for the day when his tutors would come to *him*, not the other way around. But such was his meager lot in life.

The manor bustled with activity as maidservants roamed the expanse of the estate carrying various sundries, foods, and materials to parts beyond Aritz's knowledge or caring. Every day was much the same; none of it was for his attention, and thus, it was far beyond him to acknowledge it. All it meant for him was the persistent pattering of hurried footsteps echoing through the cavernous hallways, orders given to pass some such over to so-and-so in order for them to place it in its rightful place somewhere. One day, he knew he'd have to care about these matters, but such days were hindered by the supposed necessities of learning of the exploits of Acrarian heroes whom he would never meet.

So lost in thought was he that he nearly barreled into a servant carrying a small wooden chest. The man, no older than his early twenties, stumbled and slid to a knee, a wince coloring his freckled and wide-eyed face. The threads of his trousers gave, and a scraped knee was laid bare for all to see. A flash of frustration flared in his eyes as he sharply turned his head, only barely holding on to the chest, its contents still safely housed within, but anger evaporated to embarrassment when he bowed his head toward Aritz, a dark red shading his face.

"M-Master Aritz! I must apologize, I did not see you approach!"

Aritz brushed a hand aside with dismissal. "You needn't worry about me. Come now, back to your feet." He did not extend an assisting hand.

The servant nodded and unsteadily rose to his feet, a crimson red staining the white marble underfoot. He began to stammer through some continuation of words, but stopped when he realized Aritz's immediate inattentiveness. He turned and skirted off to the adjacent dining hall, the typical meeting place for hosting engagements, left the wooden chest atop the large wooden table, and hurried off, disallowing of his eyes to meet with Aritz's once again.

It was enough to stop Aritz in his tracks. *The library is ever so far away, and I've grown tired. Perhaps I shall rest my weary legs in the dining hall.* Cutting in front of another clumsy servant, the wet contents of their cleaning bucket spilling entirely over them in a feeble attempt to divert away from Aritz's person, the young Lord brushed his hand along the intricately carved chest, its frame engraved with golden vines hiding a proud bear in celebration of the Mata family sigil. He undid the clasp with his thumb and forefinger and lifted it open, his eyes bursting open at its contents.

Inside was an impossible collection of royal marks, somewhere between one- and two-hundred in total. A royal mark was the most powerful currency in the Kingdom; one mark was worth a thousand gold pieces. So much for something so insignificant in size. Already could Aritz feel the twitch in his fingers. Before he knew it, his hands were wrapped about the leather drawstring closing the marks' pouch tightly, and suddenly a mysterious mass bulged from the space between his right rib and his cloak. The jerkin pulled even tighter at his skin than it did already.

Positioning his arm firmly against his side, Aritz shuffled back to his bedroom, shoving lackless and inattentive maidservants out of the way, sending dirty water and dirtier clothing in every direction. By the time he returned to his bedchamber, his chest was on fire, his heart near to bursting, and a smile wide upon his face. He rushed back toward his hidden stash of coin and pulled the royal marks' pouch out from underneath his jerkin, running his fingers through the coins one more time, the sensation somehow all the more invigorating than gold coins, and pushed it into the compartment as best as he could.

When he ran back to his door, Ynigo was standing in wait, his fist raised as though in preparation to knock. He lowered the hand and brushed the front of his servant robe. "Master Aritz," he said, clearing his throat. "Your tutors are still awaiting your arrival."

Aritz bowed deeply, feigning an apologetic appearance as best as he could. "I am sorry, Ynigo. I was on my way but had forgotten…something and needed to return. I am on my way now." He hammed up his present breathlessness, feeling the coating of sweat on his forehead added to the plausibility of his claim. He smiled at Ynigo and patted an appreciative hand along the man's waist, his finger catching briefly in the crest of the doorman's pocket. "My gratitude for your attentiveness. If you'll excuse me, now."

He did not wait for Ynigo's response, and ran down the hall, his cloak flapping behind him, the messes of several clumsy maidservants peppering the walkways. Aritz was cautious not to lurch forth in a dead sprint to avoid suspicion, but kept a steady pace to maintain the lie well enough.

The library at last loomed ahead, its shelves filled to the brim with books he had never once opened and had hardly the inclination to. Behind a desk sat the disapproving face of the day's tutor, a middle-aged woman named…something. Aritz was sure she had a name; he simply never cared to learn it.

"You are late, Master Aritz," the tutor spoke, barely hiding her irritation. A stack of papers rested to her left, and scribblings on the chalkboard behind her promised only monotony for today's lectures.

Aritz bowed in apology and slid into his seat. "I am deeply sorry, ma'am. The morning got away from me, I fear."

She scowled. "Be thankful, then, that your lessons will not."

He groaned with frustration, the morning rush diminishing to a painful crawl.

The day's lectures were a complete blur, and Aritz recalled none of them. When next he regained cognitive consciousness, he was being told to ready himself for another banquet.

It was the third such banquet this month. After a while, they all seemed to blend together. But it also meant the best of the cooks would arrive and cook in enormous quantities, so it was hardly for Aritz to complain.

A maidservant had outlaid a rich blue petticoat for him, a leather tunic, a simple cravat, and puffy trousers that traveled only to the knee. They were comfortable, but he always found them to look ridiculous. Appearances and lordly station, such a horrid effort at times.

At sundown, he sat himself at his normal seat, the corner of the head of the table, his parents situated at the head, his brothers fearfully to his right. Aritz knew not the occasion, but he did take note of the lack of excitement upon his father's face. Normally, with these extravagant banquets, Lord Nofre was exuberant and boisterous, but tonight, an evident exhaustion was deep-set upon his face, annoyance glimmering in his eyes.

The chairs across from Aritz stayed empty for a time while initial courses were distributed amongst those who had arrived on time. Aritz nibbled at an assortment of fresh fruits and leafy greens before leaning toward his mother with curiosity. "What is tonight's occasion?" he asked in a murmur.

Aldorisa mimicked her son's lean, flashing a bemused smile toward him. "A new theater troupe is meant to dine with us this evening. Your father has been considering acting as patron to them." Her breath was already heavy with the smell of wine.

Aritz scrunched his nose. "Are they any good?"

His mother stared at him blankly. "They're a theater troupe, Aritz."

Acraria was not necessarily abreast with prominent stage actors. Most of note originated from the isles in and around the Silk Sea to the southeast. Patrons of the Acrarian sort were primarily paying to dispense them elsewhere and have little else to do with them. Suddenly, Nofre's flummoxed expression made all the more sense.

Aritz craned his head toward his brothers, flashing them a smile. "Did you hear that? *Actors.* Have you seen this troupe before?"

Lorente picked at his greens with his fork, chewing listlessly and doing his best to pay his elder brother no mind, even if his stolen glances and shaking hands indicated otherwise. Alsonso at least looked in Aritz's direction and shook his head, but he spoke no words otherwise.

Raising an eyebrow, Aritz maintained his grin. "I asked you both a question."

"No, Aritz," Lorente finally said with a sigh, though he still only stared at his plate, which was only growing emptier and scraped of its pristine shine as he scraped his fork against it. "Haven't seen them. And I don't really want to."

"What about *being* an actor? Would you ever want to do that? You must think of other avenues as second- and third-born sons, after all."

Lorente grunted. "You are much more the actor than we," he muttered under his breath.

Aritz leaned in close, placing a hand on his brother's shoulder, feeling it tense under his grasp. "What was that, now?"

"*Boys,*" their father called, his tone displeased. "That is enough. Our guests are due to arrive any time now."

Bowing in his seat, Aritz offered his smile toward Nofre. "Of course, my apologies, Father."

The dense tension still lingered in the air as string instruments played a muted melody in the corner of the room, one Aritz had heard a thousand times but could not place the title or original composer even if there was a blade held to his throat.

Three courses came and went, full plates were offered to empty chairs, and Aritz watched as his father ate less and less with each passing moment. Nofre rested his cheek against a propped hand, rapping his fingers against his gemstone-embedded armrest and smacking his lips together with clear and persistent consternation. He held his hand high and snapped his fingers, summoning one of the many guards patrolling the dining hall.

"Yes, my Lord?" the guard asked.

"Find this troupe *immediately*," Nofre said, menace seeping into every word. "This indignity shan't be suffered a moment longer."

"At once, my Lord."

The guard turned on his heel with hand rested upon the pommel of his sword and made for the door when a sudden commotion echoed through the adjacent halls. Choral harmonies fought against the melodious tunes of the chamber's cellos and violins in discordant parallels, voices growing louder and more prominent with each passing second until at last, they burst through the doors with a flourish, nearly knocking the guard flat on his ass. *What a horrible guard,* Aritz thought.

At the head of the arriving crowd was a man with flowing curled locks of brown, his face cleared of any and all promises of facial hair. Behind him, numerous musicians filtered through, carrying lutes and flutes and hurdy-gurdies, all joining in a round and singing professions of something or other in a language with which Aritz was unfamiliar.

He leaned back toward his mother. "I thought you said they were a theater troupe."

Aldorisa swayed in her seat as she looked at Aritz. She just *exuded* the smell of red wine by this point. "Musical theater?" she offered, seeming unsure. She held out her wine glass in a shaking hand, demanding more. The glass's renewed contents were gone just as soon as they arrived.

These bards were a pitch or two off-key, so Aritz could not blame her one bit. *It would be nice to be offered the same luxury.* The leader of the troupe danced and harmonized around the approaching guards, approaching the table, at Nofre at the head of it, without shame or fear, a broad smile gleaming off his face. He was fashioned in flowing silk, an overcoating trailing past his knees and fluttering freely, jewels and rings shimmering along his neck and fingers to symbolize that, perhaps, he and his troupe had little need of this patronizing sum.

With flamboyant exaggeration, the man bowed before Nofre, his long hair falling forward past his shoulders. "Lord Nofre," he announced with a pronounced southern Acrarian accent. "A tremendous pleasure to be in your presence."

Not a shred of amusement was visible upon Lord Nofre's face. Aritz watched with great interest as his father slowly lifted his bemused head off his propped fist, the annoyance and disinterest evident in his eyes quickly shifting to an anger scrunching his nostrils. He rose to his feet, fingers flexing as he undid his cuff links. "It is ill form to leave a potential patron of my station waiting. A *grave* insult. I trust you are aware of this."

The troupe leader flourished his hands behind him, signaling the bards to cease their melodies. He tucked his hair behind his ears, and in an instant, the boisterous showman vanished, replaced instead by a stern businessman. "And my apologies are only grave in kind, my Lord. I confess my delay was due in large part to securing an adequate offering befitting your station."

Nofre raised his eyebrow. "Your 'services' are meant to be your offering, and it is for those that I pay. Are you perplexed at the concept of patronage, son?"

"Oh, no, no, not at all, my Lord!" The man clasped his hand to his chest. "Your great generosity in supporting our ventures needs a reward just the same. Our talents are hardly equivalent to your patronage." He gestured toward the window. "You may confirm with your stablemaster, but I bequeath unto you five Iabran Lowland horses for you and each of your family members. I am certain a man of your means is well aware of the value of these noble steeds, though it is to my understanding you do not have even one in your possession. May that change today."

Pursing his lips, Nofre nodded, his anger mellowing. "In that, you would be correct. That is a rare breed, and no small expense on your part, I am sure."

"No expense is too great for you, my Lord."

Nofre grunted. "Hmm, yes. Well, you have my gratitude...*ahm...*" He gestured with his hand, twirling it toward the troupe leader.

The man bowed once more. "I am called Savastian, my Lord, and *this—*" He swung his arm back, nearly hitting a guard in the head, and directed the gathering's attention to the troupe. "—is my troupe, the Sons of Ilsten."

"Ilsten?" Nofre repeated, raising an eyebrow.

Savastian smiled. "His is a name known far and wide to those of a theatrical inclination, my Lord. He was a bard of great renown some three hundred years ago to the north in Gododdinia and performed for seven monarchs. His songs were said to be both invigorating and prophetic."

"Well," Nofre said, evidently disinterested in the history lesson. "May this offering of my own set you upon the same path as your namesake and idol."

It was not lost upon Aritz the unspoken intonations of his father's words: *And may the path carry you far away from my ears.* The hidden meaning passed entirely over Savastian's head, however. The troupe leader only continued to smile widely.

As Lord Nofre waved someone over with his fingers, Aritz caught from the corner of his eye a familiar sight. The servant from earlier in the day—the one who tripped in front of him and skinned his knee, walked up beside his Lord father and held out a wooden chest inlaid with gold etchings. The very same one that Aritz had rummaged through before his lectures.

Hmph. Oh dear. He made certain to exhibit no emotion upon his face whatsoever.

Nofre braced the chest in his arms, looking down briefly at what was assuredly a lighter weight than he was expecting, and slid it along the wooden table in front of Savastian. "Within, you will find two-hundred royal marks. I trust that shall be more than enough to support you for all your days to come."

Savastian's eyes nearly bulged out of his head. The momentary twitch seemed to signal a suppressed urge to dive into the small chest and bathe in the exorbitant amount as poorly as possible, but he regained his composure and sense of decorum rather quickly. "My Lord, this is a tremendous honor. I speak on behalf of the Sons of Ilsten when I say we cannot *begin* to express how grateful we are for your patronage."

"May it serve you well in all your travels, both here and *abroad*." Extra emphasis was placed on the final word.

With eager eyes, Savastian nodded once more to Lord Nofre and opened the chest at the Mata patriarch's urging. "Forgive me for my excitement, my Lord. I just have never seen—" He looked down, and his face sank nearly off his face. His eyes flicked between the contents of the wooden chest and Nofre's expectant gaze, his mouth agape all the while. "—an empty chest? Is..."

"*Empty?*" Lord Nofre shoved the bard out of the way and hovered over the coffer long since drained of its wealth. A blazing fire was already flaring in his gaze, his face darkening to a deep red.

"Is...the value of the chest equivalent to—"

"No, you fool!" the Lord bellowed. His heavy hand gripped Savastian's shoulder and tossed him aside, his frantic face seeking out his nearest guards. "You!" A sharp finger summoned the sentry who had fallen to the ground at the arrival of the Sons of Ilsten. "Gather every man and *find that coin!* I will not suffer such thievery under my nose!"

The guard ran off, pulling a peer along with him by the arm.

Aritz folded his hands at his waist beneath the table, twiddling his thumbs, hiding as best as he could how much his heart was racing. *Well, that's unfortunate. They really shouldn't have left such a tremendous sum in broad view. Truly, this is the fault of that servant.*

Beside him, his brothers quivered in fear at the return of their father's wrath. They had trembled at shows of anger for years now, sweat and tears intermingling as Lorente and Alsonso both bore the appearance of those who wished only to vanish into thin air.

Lady Aldorisa, for her part, simply sloshed about the wine in her glass, long since abandoning opening the nose and instead going straight for the stomach. She looked upon her husband's rage with notable disinterest, the occasions never impacting her personally, and the knowledge it would soon pass was surely on her mind.

"Search every room of this manse from top to bottom!" Nofre bellowed as more guards filtered into the dining hall. "Find the thief and *bring them to me!* The pilfering hand shall be no more once I have my say!"

Aritz knew not whether to stay or depart, a notion seemingly shared amongst the rest of his family. *Well, the brothers are too paralyzed with fear to depart, at any rate.*

Savastian extended his placating hands toward Lord Nofre, a pleading groan molded unto his face. "Lord Nofre, please, I beg you not to sow distrust simply for my benefit."

Before Aritz could blink, he heard the sickening crunch of a heavy fist shattering facial bones. The troupe leader collapsed to the floor in a heap, an arc of dark blood trailing after him.

"Do you think yourself above my household security, bard?" Nofre screamed, flexing his fingers from the impact. Blood coated his knuckles, but Aritz did not believe it to be his father's own. "This matter is *beyond* you! Do not think to offer me dissuading words again, else they be the last words you shall ever utter. Do we have an understanding?"

Aritz could not see Savastian on the floor, but the pained mumbling seemed to indicate an uncertainty to respond for fear of reprisal and retaliation.

Time stretched on and on, punctuated by tense and sharp silence. Aritz chewed at his bottom lip as he watched his father pace back and forth, his hands clasped behind his back, the scowl in his brow appearing to be permanently affixed with little hope it would ever disappear again. *How could I blame him?* he pondered. *Two hundred royal marks gone missing is no small matter. Tis a shame the inevitable outcome.* He rested an elbow on his armrest, chewing at the nail of this thumb while his mother further imbibed herself and his brothers further wet themselves. *Calm yourselves, little brothers. You both know yourselves to be innocent of this. Punishment comes only to the guilty.*

The door opened, and a guard rushed over to Lord Nofre, whispering softly enough into his ear that his voice did not quite reach Aritz. However, the glances in Aritz's direction seemed indicative enough of the evening's eventualities. Nofre's brow furrowed and his nostrils scrunched, glaring at his guard with what appeared to be equal parts confusion and disbelief. Anger had not made its return, though it likely had never departed in the first place.

"Aritz," he said, walking toward the door without a passing glance. "With me."

With a brusque nod, Aritz rose to his feet, offering sparse regard for his mother and brothers. "Right away, Father," he responded, quickening his pace to fall into step with Nofre.

The pair walked in silence as they navigated the vast corridors of the Mata estate until the hallway housing the family bedchambers came into view.

Household sentries flanked them, swords at their hips, escape near to an impossibility. Ahead, outside the threshold of his bedroom, Aritz noted the presence of Ynigo, his vigil over these hallways as diligent as ever.

Guards circulated about the door to Aritz's bedroom, parting to either side of the corridor as Nofre and Aritz made their way through. Turning into the chamber, Aritz made note of the wretched state of things; his mattress had been overturned, his drawers thrown about the floor, clothing scattered as though the maidservants had not arrived in months.

Imitating his most lordly voice, Aritz stepped past his father and shouted, "What is the meaning of this? You do not think *me* a thief, do you?" He motioned to say more but was halted by the sudden presence of his father's hand on his shoulder. Nofre's firm grasp turned him to the corner, where a familiar sight caught his eye.

The pouch holding the two-hundred royal marks.

"Have you anything to say of this, Aritz?" There was a sharp ice to his father's tone that, if Aritz was as weak-willed as his brothers, would have dragged him into the deepest bowels of fear.

Instead, it was easier to feign ignorance. "What is it?" he asked.

With a sigh, Lord Nofre shouldered past and grabbed the pouch from the soldier holding it. He loosened the drawstring and opened it, allowing the shine and smell of the royal marks assault Aritz's senses.

"A large cache of gold pieces was found in your dresser, Young Master," said the guard, little humor in his voice. Perhaps even a little pain at the accusation.

Aritz raised an eyebrow. "And you assume *I* am responsible for its presence?" He focused on his father, ensuring to maintain an expression of pure bewilderment. "Father, for what purpose would I hold coin for myself? I have no need of it. I have not the communion with the lower classes that you do. The realm of commerce is beyond me, and I want for absolutely nothing. The presence of this coin—and the bards' endowment—in my chambers is as much a mystery to me as it is to you."

Lord Nofre's scowl deepened as he regarded his eldest son in silent regard for a long while. A collective breath was held amongst the present guards as they awaited a decree or a punishment to be passed down. But instead, the

Mata patriarch said softly in that same icy tone, "You have no knowledge of this, then?"

"Father," Aritz said, clasping a hand to his chest, the cravat loosening from his neck. "I understand the consequences of theft—and the graver ramifications of speaking falsely to you. The punishment for thievery would be both wasted upon me, and entirely unjust, for I am not the party responsible."

"And who," his father pondered, "do you propose *is* responsible, Aritz?"

Aritz bit his lower lip and shook his head, holding his hands out at his sides. "I know not. It is beyond me the reasoning for stowing tremendous personal sums in *my* chambers, of all places. I do not wish to sow deeper distrust amongst your rank and file, but...surely there are a select few who know *precisely* of our comings and goings."

The slow nod of Lord Nofre's head was a welcomed sign. "Ynigo!" he shouted.

The doorman sauntered into the bedchamber, his hands clasped within the wide fabric of his sleeves. "My Lord?"

Nofre motioned with a quick, curling finger. "Empty your pockets. Quickly, now."

Puzzlement creased Ynigo's brow. "Ah...y-yes, of course, my Lord." He reached into his pockets, gripping the lining with firm fists, when a sudden hesitation gripped him. Just as he was about to turn loose the contents of his robe, he stopped, sucking a hissed breath in through his teeth.

The pause was not lost upon Nofre. He inclined his head toward his trusted doorman. "*Now*, Ynigo."

Aritz could see the moment Ynigo's heart ripped in half as the clatter of coin echoed upon the floor. Six royal marks bounced on the hardwood, one coin spinning in place on its side before finally resting, its wobbling resounding through the silent chamber.

Something flared in Ynigo's eyes as he glanced at Aritz. Betrayal, perhaps. *Pray do not take it personally, Ynigo*, he thought. *It would have been foolish of me not to have a contingency plan in place. You were just in the wrong place at the right time.*

The quiet was broken by Nofre's deep, grating growl. "To the gaols with him. Now."

Two guards slipped gauntleted arms beneath Ynigo's shoulders and dragged him away, the doorman's feet trailing and scraping against the cold wooden flooring, his heels carving a swath in his wake. He did not scream for mercy; he did not plead for reconsideration. He only stared with an anger in his eyes, one that attempted—and failed—to supersede the fear widely evident upon his face.

A hush fell over the room. At Lord Nofre's wordless urging—the slightest of nods masking the gravest of disappointment—the guards filtered out into the corridor, leaving father and son alone to themselves.

"It gave me no pleasure in accusing you, Aritz," Nofre said solemnly, yet sternly.

"Nor I in being accused, Father," Aritz responded, in as minimally chastising a fashion as he felt he could get away with. "But it gives me even less pleasure in knowing Ynigo, of all people, stole from our family."

Nofre shook his head, clearly bewildered. "It makes little sense. But tis always those you suspect the least." He held his son's gaze, his eyes likened to icy daggers. "*Never* forget that."

Aritz nodded. "I shall never."

His father reciprocated the nod. "Good." And he walked out, murmuring to a nearby attendant to send for a maidservant to fix up his son's chambers with the greatest of haste.

I wonder if Lorente and Alsonso are to receive the same preferential treatment. He chuckled to himself.

As days passed, Aritz could not help but ponder the state Ynigo was surely in. If he would ever escape the wrath of the gaolers, and his father who commanded them. It was not for him to see, regardless, but one silent evening, he was certain he could hear the faint echo of agonic screams traveling through the corridors like a ghost upon the wind.

It was enough to lull him to sleep.

CHAPTER SIX

Puppet's Blood

Centuries ago, when Kamataa rummaged through the libraries of the Keepers and learned the secrets they kept hidden from the Tribes, she could not even have dreamed of setting foot within the sacred confines of the True Heart of the Land. Though she knew it to be a real place, its untouched and pristine visage seemed more the derivations of myth. A holy land protected by Keepers of the highest order, a haven for the gods taken flesh.

Reality, however, was often the victor when faced with the tall tales transcribed in myths. And the reality was that no one land shall hold forever. Havens were meant to crumble. And under the light of all that falls, the sacred shall inevitably fall to the profane.

Blood still marred the trampled snow and valley walls; not even the wistful flurries descending from overhead could conceal it all. Pulp and entrails alike, and the soldiers from whom they originated, were discarded and ignored, ill-fitting of the proper rites to bid them fond farewell into the embrace of the Savior. Such was the decree of General Aritz, at any rate. *I cannot help but be curious as to his reasoning: either a soldier fallen to the Tribes is unworthy of his Savior's light, or this is a dreadful place to honor shattered remains. Somehow, I believe both to be true.*

The commotion ahead of Acrarian soldiers drew Kamataa's attention as she patrolled through this valley of death. There were no rounds or guard duty to speak of; no one expected the remnants of the Tribes to return to this place. As far as they were concerned, they had won. At great cost, yes, but it was victory, nonetheless. Already out of their minds was the mist that had frozen them in place, permitting the survivors to escape. In their minds, there was no reason to believe it would return.

Kamataa knew better, though she was also of the inclination that the mist, and the Owl along with it, was not likely to make a reappearance so soon. There was no reason for them to assault this defiled bastion other than wounded pride. At least in that, Kamataa could empathize with them.

After the battle, she had needed time to herself, regardless of what short-sighted tasks Aritz had set his soldiers about. She promised him guidance and walking this Acrarian escapade into a brighter future. But the time for fulfilling such assurances was yet to come. It would be some time still before the Acrarians made their way back south, away from this frozen hellscape of biting cold and sacred ghosts.

And it was better for her to ruminate on the proceedings of the last few days, something she had hardly the time and inclination to do before she had watched become true what the scholars of this land deemed to be pure fantasy. *If only they knew the limits of their wisdom.*

She had requested of Sha'a and Vanta this moment of solitude, and they gladly complied. She was far beyond the need to have someone watch over her shoulder under the guise of protection, when all she needed to do was watch the clouds roll by for an indeterminate length of time and ponder on everything she had lost in the pursuit of everything she sought to destroy. It was, again, the reality of it all. That she would bid farewell to several of her kin without being afforded the opportunity to say goodbye was inevitable. But it stung in a way she had been ill-prepared for, even after a lifetime of relentless and perpetual stings.

As Kamataa surveyed the southern horizon, it was impossible not to feel the weighted absence of Ziia beside her. All those days and nights of gazing ahead exactly like so, watching the world proceed below as they stalked from above as the giants they should have been in defense against the ants threatening to crawl over them. But those moments were dashed in an instant from the moment Sennalhat saw fit to smatter the contents of Ziia's head against the length of her family's walls.

Sooner or later, she had thought, *your Luck will run out, Sennalhat. And I look forward to passing down your judgment when it does.*

Meting out such retribution was not an endeavor for Kamataa to embark upon alone, loath as she was to admit it. There was a part of her that yearned to leave the travails of the Acrarians behind; they had achieved more or less what they set out to do. She needn't play their games any longer. To her, they were a tool to an end so nearly within reach.

But Kamataa could say with authority that the Moon did not glance upon Her traitors with any shred of kindness, and Sennalhat's betrayal of the Children of the Black Moon was an offense of the gravest order. Kamataa had endured enough to feel confident in a role of executor for all Eclipseborn whom had been unjustly slain.

But a quick death was far better than what Sennalhat deserved. There was still much and more Kamataa felt she could do. *And if I must continue along with this Acrarian rabble to do so, then so it shall be.*

By the time she returned to the Acrarian encampment, her boots stained and soaked with snow and blood alike, a deathly hush had fallen over the soldiers. There was none of the frivolity and joy that had arisen from the successes over the Wood Tribe in the Forest. The stores of ale taken from the Stone Tribe village were consumed not with merriment, but with deep mourning—and likely disgust, as well. Somber shock was strewn upon the faces of each of the men and women who had survived the bloodshed of the past few days. If there was but a single word uttered, it was not for Kamataa to hear. Only the sloshing and gulping of consumption rung in her ears, mixed intermittently with a stifled sob or two.

None paid her any mind as she surveyed the crowd, scanning the faces to parse out Aritz. *In all likelihood, he's probably keeping himself warm inside somewhere,* she thought with a scoff. She knew it was not within him to sit among his soldiers. Such connection was beneath him. With this in mind, Kamataa patrolled around the perimeter of the drinking crowd, nodding to Sha'a and Vanta as she spied them quietly mingling, though she was unsure if the lurid feelings of grief and shock were emoted by them in earnest or if they were simply doing their part to blend in. There was a row of huts in the far corners of the clearing under the covering of the tree line. The first few she peeked her head into housed only the mindless drone of shattered minds and the horrid stench of fouled bedrolls. A sight she genuinely reveled in.

It took only a few more huts before Kamataa could locate Aritz. The Acrarian General sat on the floor, his arms wrapped around his knees as he gazed into the lit fire, keeping a close proximity to the blaze for warmth against these harsh elements. On his face was not the pronounced grief and mourning shared amongst his soldiers. Rather, he remained wholly focused, his brow furrowed as though seeking answers in the dancing flames. A flick of his eyes seemed to indicate his acknowledgment of Kamataa's presence, though he made no motion toward her otherwise. She took the opportunity to ingratiate herself to the hut's warmth.

"Does your Savior speak to you through the flames, Aritz?" she asked with a hint of smug satisfaction in her tone.

Aritz scoffed. "I would caution you not to speak so dismissively of my god, given what I did to yours." The crackling embers illuminated his eyes, their reflections a window into his perpetually angry soul.

Quite so, and with not even a hint of assistance. She brushed a hand aside with dismissal as she sat across from him, his head only just towering above the peak of the fire. "They were never *my* gods. I relished in their slaying just as much as you did."

He shook his head. "Truly, you savages are beyond my understanding."

"We're not so dissimilar from one another."

"Forgive me if I still have my doubts, given what I have seen you to be capable of."

"I, myself? No." She flashed a grin. "My own proclivities are altogether similar to yours. All that separates us is our points of origin. We want the same thing. You needn't assume otherwise."

With a wordless grunt, Aritz resumed his surveying of the flames. He blew into his hands and rubbed them together in a futile attempt to fight off the pervasive mountain cold. "Do you truly wish the same as me, Kama?" he asked. "What *is* it you seek?"

Kamataa tutted with her lips and wetter her thumb to smear away a spot of dried blood from her hand. "I should think my actions to this point have been indicative enough, Aritz. You seek the destruction of the Tribes for your own reason. I seek the same for *my* own. That is all either of us need concern ourselves with."

"And Acraria?" Aritz looked up, his gaze burrowing into Kamataa, his face illuminated in that fiery-orange glow. "Of what import to you is the technological advancement of my homeland?"

"To me, personally? Very little." There was no harm in honesty. "But the pursuit of it shall be beneficial for the both of us, of that I can assure you."

"How so?" Aritz rose to his feet, his arm still falling slack from the arrow he had taken to the shoulder. He was much steadier on his feet now that the bleeding had been staunched and his wound bandaged, but the bloodstains on his hand had not yet been washed away. "You spoke of a pathway toward the greatest technological advancements the Kingdom has ever seen, but you elaborated no further. I am a man of means, Kama. There is little I would not do to serve Their Highnesses, and lesser still the lengths I would go in service of the Savior. If you know of any—"

"Spare me the dedicated servant spiel, Aritz. We both know you speak out of your ass."

Aritz froze with mouth agape, his eyes flaring at the accusation. But for all he could have done in that moment, there was the briefest of hesitations, a twitch in his lip as he closed his mouth, a flash of the teeth, that seemed to indicate an acknowledgment of Kamataa's assessment as the cold truth.

Though reluctant to leave the comfort of the warm fire behind, Kamataa stood, greeting the harsh, frigid air once again. She puffed her chin out and folded her hands behind her back. "Do not decry me as judging you for thinking of yourself and your aims first, for I would not dream of it. You take what you feel is yours. You let little stand in your way. Anything that chooses to find itself without legs to stand upon. I hold no resentment for that fact, but rather, I respect it. So do not speak to me of the liege lords and ladies whom you claim to serve, or the god you supposedly act in great fear and subjugation of. Such proclamations are easy to decipher as false when you have heard the words time and time again yourself."

"You would speak from experience, then." Aritz narrowed his eyes and nodded to her, crossing his arms to maintain his warmth, despite a forced appearance to the contrary.

Kamataa grinned. "And so I would speak from experience. The sooner you can admit your only fealty is to yourself, the sooner you can have no restrictions to hold you back." She turned toward the entrance to the hut, glancing out toward the snowy landscape beyond the threshold. "So, are you ready to advance the power of the Kingdom—unimpeded?"

Aritz grumbled something beneath his breath, and said, "You still have not elaborated on how exactly you propose to do so."

Turning with a flourish, Kamataa held her arm out at her side, the embers dancing around her hand. "The city you have built to the south is a technological marvel, for having risen from nothing in fifteen years. The Kingdom has benefited greatly from its pursuit of knowledge, and the mechanisms your people have created have made future production all the easier. I have been in your people's factory, seen its inner workings firsthand, and have been nothing short of impressed at the achievement of it all. Yes, I am aware this may be commonplace for you in your homeland, but think of we native to this land, having not the capacity to comprehend the benefits of 'industrializing,' for we never had cause or reason to pursue it."

"Yes, yes, get to the point," Aritz said, rolling his eyes.

With a curt smile, Kamataa continued. "There comes a point where certain advancements have reached their limit. I have lived long enough to know this to be the truth." She caught Aritz opening his mouth as though to question her last point, but she pressed on before he had the opportunity to do so. "There is only so much you can accomplish in your present state. The Acrarian Kingdom is on the verge of something great in these lands, greater than what you have already achieved. But there is so much *more* that could be done. Blood, sweat, and tears are the cornerstones of progress. And in this land, this previously...undeveloped land, you and your people have poured ample amounts of sweat and tears into turning it into what you've achieved in the south...but not nearly enough blood, I would say."

Aritz raised an eyebrow, offering a perplexed scoff at the last claim. "And what is *that* meant to imply, Kama? Ought I have lopped off the hands of my workers to color this dream I apparently never had? Was it our folly to not bleed all over the machinery in the hopes they would perform better?"

Kamataa allowed the question to stew for a moment, the silence punctuating her intention.

Realization immediately sunk into Aritz's face. "Savior's breath, that *is* what you intend, is it not? Here I thought you were speaking in metaphors, and yet you have instead emerged from the stories of monsters my wetnurse would read to me as a child." He made for the exit, shaking his head.

With a jolt, Kamataa raised her arm out straight, impeding Aritz's approach to the exit. "There are no stories of the macabre here, Aritz. Only bold realities. I understand your reluctance. I am sure it seems the make of the fairy tales of your youth. But trust that I have an understanding of matters beyond your ken, just as you have your own understanding of that which lies beyond mine. You needn't commit to the idea right this moment, but at the very least, permit me to explain further." She lowered her arm, letting it fall to her hip.

With gritted teeth, Aritz closed his eyes and puffed out a heavy breath of air from his nostrils. Shaking his head, he gestured a cold hand to her. "Enlighten me, then. I am building a nation of my own in this land. I should be privy to all its mysteries, regardless of their wickedness."

"You decry it as wicked simply because you do not yet understand it. Now, follow me. I will need to demonstrate something for you."

An immediate shiver coursed through Kamataa as she stepped back into the mountainous chill. The snow crunched underfoot as she trudged through the packed drifts of trampled ice. A second set of noise echoed behind her, indicating Aritz would at least humor her for her explanation.

The nearest hut was as good an option as any to elaborate on her point. A long-doused fire pit sat in the middle of the room, the lingering embers glowing in the charred remains of kindling offering a memory of warmth that did little to invoke it. A small number of Tribespeople lined the walls, most of them Bearsigns from their burly appearances, all bundled in makeshift bedrolls and blankets, shivering from the air's hard bite, though their broken minds could hardly comprehend it.

Aritz's presence loomed heavily behind her. Kamataa could hear him utter something between a remorseful sigh and a disgusted grumble. She smiled to herself, silently regarding the various forms suffering on the ground, analyzing the runes upon their pendants which no longer held the capacity to glimmer.

"Is there a reason you've brought me here?" Aritz asked, his voice rife with annoyance and distaste.

Kamataa held a finger up as she kneeled beside a muscle-bound man, early thirties by the look of him, burl and brawn lining his heavy arms. She pulled the ornament of his pendant up toward her, nodding as she ran her thumb along the carved rune. "This one will do," she whispered.

"Pardon?"

She turned her head over her shoulder, still flashing her teeth with anticipation. "There is a power which runs through the bodies and minds of all the Tribespeople. I am sure you know this already. You have seen it. It runs deeper than themselves, and not even the felling of their gods is enough to rid us of their power."

Aritz furrowed his brow with vexed confusion. "Explain. Do you mean killing those beasts served no purpose?"

The absurdity of the question was enough to make her laugh. She gestured broadly to the mindless husks on the floor. "Look around you, Aritz. Clearly, your actions spoke loudly. But many parts compose the larger whole. You would not claim your grand orchestra has vanished simply because the conductor perished, would you? These husks are much the same: listless notes longing to be guided by a steady hand. Marionettes still holding to their strings, awaiting their puppet master to dance them along." Kamataa narrowed her eyes. "Do you understand?"

Her question was met only with silence as the Acrarian General crossed his arms, distrust still coloring his face.

"Hmph," she scoffed. "Allow me to speak more plainly, then. I posited to you that you and your people have not spent enough blood to see your dreams for a grand Acraria realized, yes?"

Slowly, Aritz nodded. "And I still fail to see the intent of your words. What purpose do *these*—" He swung his arms about the room, gesturing to the Bearsign bodies. "—serve? I speak not in riddles, and I expect the same of you."

Kamataa laughed softly and shook her head. "None of this has been a riddle, Aritz. Strange though it may be, these husks serve a greater purpose than you give them credit for."

Aritz regarded her with an ice-cold glare, punching daggers into her chest that did little to loose the air from her lungs. "You mean to say their blood."

"There is a power in the blood of the Tribes beyond what you allow yourself to understand." She sneered at him in an attempt to indicate it was all too obvious. "Their gods may be gone from this world, but their power still remains. All we need to do is take control of their strings. Power resides in the hand of he who holds them. And if your fealty is truly to yourself, and none other, should you not seize this opportunity, puppet master?"

Hesitation flashed upon the Acrarian's face, a twitch of the eye, a flare of the nostril. He crossed his arms, fingers tapping along his elbows, his gaze peppered with uncertainty.

Kamataa raised her brow and motioned him to approach with a flick of her head. "Come, look at this." She waited as Aritz rolled his eyes and shuffled in step beside her, kneeling before the Bearsign's body. Pointing at the rune inscribed on the man's pendant, she asked, "Do you see this? *This* is what the Tribes call a 'Boon.' I won't bore you with the specifics of it all—nor do I expect you to care a whit—but all you need to know is these talents are granted to the Tribespeople by *those* gods you killed." She pointed out the door, in the vague direction of where she believed the corpses of the Bear and Wolf to be.

Aritz held out a hand, pointing to the marking. "Then what does this 'Boon' mean?"

Either he's playing along, or he is showing genuine interest. It matters little to me, regardless. "This is an indicator of 'Strength.' An augmentation of physical prowess. If in the battles against the Tribespeople, you ever felt greater force from a blow than you thought possible from another man, it was likely they were granted this Boon."

The look on Aritz's face indicated he was about to cry foul.

"You may call it sorcery as much as you wish," Kamataa said before he even got the chance. "But it changes little. There is no witchcraft or wickedness at play here. Only the realities to which you have been exposed over these past days and nights. And all around this room—" She gyrated her finger in a broad circle. "—are people imbued with not only Strength, but Endurance, and Restoration. Refuse to accept these truths all you want, but the facts care not for what you believe."

"What does it matter, though?" Aritz shrugged his shoulders. "Their gods are dead."

"As I said, the power remains. Or it *should* remain, at any rate."

"I was under the impression that you were operating with a larger degree of certainty than the word 'should' allows."

"I would argue the word allows for plenty of leeway." Kamataa flashed a smirk, reaching to the hilt of the blade resting against her waist. She drew it from its sheath, the steel scraping against its leather holdings. "And besides, would you not think this to be a release for them?"

"A release?" Aritz glanced at the groaning and incoherent man. "You mean to kill them, then."

"A few drops of blood will help no one, Aritz," she replied, as though it should have been obvious to him. "But look at him. Look at *all* of them." She allowed the request to linger, waiting for Aritz to scan the room on his own. He did not. "What life would these husks even live from here on? Even if you wish to let them toil for your purposes, they are hardly in a condition to do so now. The reality of it is, they're suffering. Detest them as you will, I am sure you would agree they do not deserve to wallow in such a manner, even if they are worshipers and practitioners of a wicked faith. Would you not appear the pious and righteous man, were you to release them from this pain in service to a greater cause?"

A soft chuckle escaped Aritz's lips. "I believe we established I am hardly a man of faith."

"Appearances are everything, no?" Kamataa raised an eyebrow. When the question prompted no answer, she pointed the tip of her blade to the man's chest. The steel did not waver in her grip, nor did she hesitate as Aritz observed her every move. "A source of power may vanish from this world, but its effects will linger as long as possible. Bit by bit, inch by inch, it is a bond forever linked by the threads of memory. And those threads..." She drove the blade into the man's chest, hearing the inane mutterings turn to choked and wet breaths as blood pooled and spilled from his gaping mouth. "...shall be yours to hold."

The steel was buried inside the Bearsign up to the hilt, dark red rivers pooling and staining the cloth of his battle-worn shirt.

Confusion colored Aritz's face as he looked at Kamataa with what looked to be morbid curiosity. His was an expression housing a million questions but knowing not the words with which to ask them.

After a pregnant pause, Kamataa ripped the blade free of the man's chest cavity, a red fountain erupting in a violent burst. She paid little mind to the backsplash covering her arm and examined what once was steel of a shimmering sheen, now instead coated in a thick veneer of blacks and reds and bits of flesh and bone. From within her pocket, she pulled a thin needle, one used for engraving purposes—such as ceremonies to christen ornaments with their intended Boons. Steadying both her hands but working as fast as she could before the blade dried, she carved the shape of the Strength rune into the steel of the blade, allowing the crimson pools to seep into it. A festering wound of a different kind. She pressed her hand against the marking and closed her eyes, willing the man's blood to become one with the steel that claimed him.

She let out a long breath. "There."

Aritz blinked thrice, left his mouth agape, and then threw his hands out at his side. "There, what?"

With a smile, Kamataa twirled the blade in her hand, a spatter of blood trailing in a circular arc, until her hand met the hilt. She held the hilt out toward Aritz, just as she did in the days prior to the first battle in the Heart, and inclined her head to it. "Try it."

Subtle hesitation seemed to grip Aritz once more, but he clasped his hand around the hilt and hefted the knife closer to himself, though clearly keeping it at enough of a distance in avoidance of the fresh blood. "Try what, precisely?"

Kamataa held her hands out placatingly. "What do you feel? Do you find it...similar to the blade with which you slayed the Bear?"

The Acrarian focused his attention on the weapon, his movements slow and deliberate.

"It likely will not be the same intensity as before. Remember: this would be but a remnant of the Bear's power, not the full extent of it," Kamataa added.

The silence carried on for moments that stretched into seconds. Several handfuls passed by, the stench of blood and death beginning to assault Kamataa's nostrils in conjoining with the already pervasive smell of fouled bedrolls. She watched quietly as Aritz continued to consider the weapon, turning it one way and the next, tightening and loosening his grip on the hilt, offering a succession of thrusts and slashes.

Minutes passed before he finally looked back at Kamataa and slowly nodded his head, his movements still rife with uncertainty, but a glint of promise glowing in his eyes. Realization seemed to sink in shortly afterward.

"If we can enhance a simple weapon by using your method..." Aritz murmured.

Kamataa rose to her feet and held her arms out, gesturing to the rows of the incapacitated before her. "We have plenty of room for creativity, Aritz. As I said already, Strength is hardly the only Boon at our disposal. You have seen the auspices permitted by a Strength-imbued blade before. Now, think of your manufacturing machinery coated with the power of Endurance, never falling victim to breakdowns or necessitating repairs. Think what you could do with a machine bestowed with Restoration: a self-replenishing device that will limit the amount of materials you would require to run it and produce with it." She grabbed Aritz by the shoulders and lifted him back to his feet. "We are on the *cusp* of greatness here. The products of labor would be astounding, unlike *anything* the world will have seen."

Aritz still had not removed his eyes from the blood-coated blade in his hands, but finally relented and dropped it to his side. "It seems still...uncertain. There is a *wealth* of machinery in our factory. Surely, this would not be sufficient to power all of them. And what of my workers? Already, they have—"

A dismissive hand silenced Aritz's misgivings, and Kamataa offered a comforting grin. "The workers in the city's camps are likely in much the same state as those you see here. We would simply have the same conversation later that we are having now." She took a step toward the exit, planting her hands on her hips as she gazed upon the western horizon peeking out from behind the trees. "But, in my view, you are in a no-lose situation if we pursue this, Aritz. On the one hand, if we are successful, you would be seen as a scion of innovation, the figurehead of the Kingdom's great industrial age. You would be hailed throughout history as one of the most prolific minds this age will have ever seen."

A long, hummed grunt seemed to indicate Aritz's consideration on the matter. "And if we are *not* successful?" he asked.

Kamataa chuckled. "Then all you've done is eliminate a wicked and dangerous people from the watchful glow of your Savior's light, and isn't that what you want the faithful public to believe you had done, anyway?"

"You may be right," he relented, nodding slowly.

A gust of wind howled from outside, the only song emanating from an otherwise hauntingly quiet landscape. Aritz let the notion hang in the air between them, the blade hanging listlessly in his hand, his body language speaking of reluctance, yet of an accepting nature. He threaded himself between the waning fire and the mindless rows, and stood beside Kamataa.

"I'll instruct my soldiers to ready the wagons. We're returning with more cargo than I had anticipated."

Kamataa bobbed her head in an approving nod. *Temptation is quite the motivator for glory.*

The Acrarian stepped into the cold and snow, an involuntary shudder gripping him the moment he returned to air free of stagnation. The waning light passed him by, the golden light of the setting sun instead illuminating what snow flurries still strove to descend upon a tainted earth. Aritz made his way toward the makeshift tavern, where his soldiers continued to drink in sullen sorrow and silence, when he stopped and craned his head toward the gods' altars.

The Bear's corpse still remained, unperturbed since the fire and fury of the last battle, beyond the congealed blood that matted its dark fur.

Aritz turned back and faced Kamataa, nodding to himself as he narrowed his gaze toward her. "And what of the beast? Is this...'power' still lingering within it, as well?"

And glory serves only to blind. Kamataa smirked. "We won't know until we find out."

CHAPTER SEVEN

GAMBIT

A hush fell over the Forest so profound that not even the wind dared to whistle through the creases of the dense arboreal barrier. The trees, and the branches atop them, chose not to creak and rustle. It felt as a moment suspended in time, the very fabric of nature itself stunned into silence.

Sen brought a hand to her agape mouth, the attempts to mask her shock utterly pointless when stacked against the mutual reactions of those present. Her legs shook, all manner of strength threatening to vanish from underneath her. Neither a murmur nor a whisper rumbled from behind her. All were gripped by the same unbelievable visage.

There was an unseen radiance in the form the Owl assumed that served only to instill discomfort in Sen. Aritz a Mata, the man who killed her father, who kidnapped her brother, who was responsible for the Invasion in the first place...the prominence with which the Acrarian stood before her was wholly unsettling. Nothing in his presence and posture pronounced that instinct to destroy that Sen associated with him, even as the haunting scowl and self-satisfied grin remained affixed to his face. The knowledge that it was the Owl behind the mask was comforting, but it was a comfort which invited only conflict into Sen's heart.

The Owl took two steps forward in its disguise, its watchful eyes still examining the crowd with the same pensive ponderance as before, something that felt entirely counter to everything Sen had known of Aritz. A scattering of footsteps broke the prolonged silence as Tribespeople instinctively made to run in the presence of the Acrarian General, even knowing it was merely an Illusion.

Sen could hardly blame them. In seeing the Owl's initial steps, she wanted nothing more than to charge the false visage with spear leveled and the weight of her offensive heavy with the memory of her family. At the least, it was fortunate enough she was far too entranced by the Illusion to even move. Even as she made to raise her hand in anger, it was pushed down by Tawa, his own face exhibiting a conflict of fear and anger.

The god approached ever closer, its steps cautious and deliberate as though pronouncing its unfamiliarity with a human form. *But if it can do this any time it wants...is it unfamiliar? Has the Owl walked among us this whole time?*

Stifled cries were bitten back as Aritz's form drew nearer. "This...this isn't possible," someone finally said. Sen turned to see the voice belonged to Ko Seln, the erstwhile tavern keeper. The disbelief was a far cry from the evident annoyance inherent in her last encounter with him, what seemed ages ago. "How is..."

IT HAS BEEN ESTABLISHED ALREADY, KO SELN, the Owl said, its words still carried by Aritz's voice, now immediately fluent in the Tribal Words. IT IS FROM ME YOUR BOONS EXIST. IS IT STILL TO YOUR SURPRISE THAT I AM HERE, AS WHAT YOU SEE BEFORE YOU?

The tavern keeper stuttered a wordless response, running his fingers through his tangled dark locks of hair. "But why, though? Why this disguise? Why now?"

"Isn't it obvious?" shouted a belligerent voice. Sen couldn't find the mouth from which the words originated, but she knew the voice to be the argumentative Sun Tribesman from earlier. "That bastard Invader has been the Owl the whole time! It's been killing us off one by one, and now it's come to finish—"

A heavy crash of bone on flesh silenced the man. "Shaddup, you idiot!" cried another man. "Are you that daft?"

The Sun Tribesman didn't respond. His form was invisible from Sen's vantage point, but she could only assume the punch knocked him uncon-scious.

WERE I THE INVADER ALL ALONG, I WOULD NOT HAVE WASTED FIF-
TEEN YEARS TO SEAL YOUR FATES, the Owl said plainly. IT WOULD NOT
HAVE TAKEN A SECOND THOUGHT TO DO SO. The stern and blunt tone of
the words served dispelled the notion of the Owl acting behind the guise. It
now matched Aritz perfectly.

Sen shuddered.

The Owl flexed its shoulders, a motion which likely would have broadened
its wings had they been present, but the intent was not lost upon anyone.
Phantom wings could very well have sprouted from its back. DO NOT MIS-
TAKE ME. IF IT WERE WITHIN MY POWER TO PREVENT THE INVASION, I
WOULD HAVE DONE SO. WE CANNOT REGAIN WHAT THE FLOW OF TIME
HAS STOLEN FROM US. WE CAN ONLY SEIZE WHAT LAYS IN THE FUTURE
YET TO COME.

Tawa stepped forward, his brow furrowed as he dropped to a knee. "But,
almighty Owl. I—"

RISE, TAWANDHAR. I SHALL SUFFER NONE OF YOU BOWING BEFORE
THE FORM OF THE ENEMY.

Flummoxed by the command, Tawa blinked and shook his head, reluctantly rising back to his feet. "I...do not understand, almighty Owl," he said.
"Why this form?"

The Owl raised an eyebrow, hiding it behind a veil of curly auburn hair. I
HAVE DEEMED IT NECESSARY. TO OBSERVE THE INVADER HAS BEEN TO
MASTER HIS MANNERISMS, HIS TONE, HIS POSTURE. ALL OF IT HAS BEEN
TO PORTRAY THE PERFECT MIMIC. HIS OWN PHANTOM, AS IT WERE.

Sen threw her hands out at her side, closing the gap between her and the
god's disguised visage. "For what purpose, though? Do you intend to march
us back up the mountains and confuse the hell out of the Invaders?"

Turning its head, its attention diverted to the Forest's depths, the Owl
trilled, its throat seeming to vibrate in a manner ill-fitting a human form. IT
IS NOT THEY ON THE MOUNTAIN WHOSE FAITH SHALL BE TESTED.

"What the hell does that mean?" Sen said, leaning forward with eyes
widened.

"Sen!" Tawa hissed sharply.

The rebuke went unheeded. Sen hardly paid Tawa any mind as she patiently awaited the god's next confusing words.

Its attention remained solely affixed to the south, to the bloodied ghosts who surely roamed the woods, wishing desperately for vengeance upon their mortal foe.

Unless they're privy to the goings-on of the world of the living, they'd be confused as hell were they to see this, Sen thought.

THE LANDS SOUTH OF THE FOREST HAVE REMAINED FIRMLY WITHIN THE GRASP OF THE INVADERS THESE LAST FIFTEEN YEARS, NEVER TO BE THREATENED BY OUR LIMITED MIGHT RELATIVE TO THEIRS.

"We would have had a chance had Fannalhen grown a pair and marched south with—"

Another resounding punch echoed through the Forest. Apparently, the Sun Tribesman had regained consciousness. Sen would later have to seek out the kind soul who did a service to the rest of the group. Deep down, she now knew it would have made little difference the number of people who marched south, and she was hardly in the mood to suffer slander against her father.

BUT IF THERE WAS EVER A TIME TO RETURN OUR PEOPLE TO THOSE STOLEN LANDS, the Owl continued, the commotion evidently not bothering it whatsoever, THAT TIME WOULD BE NOW.

Sen inclined her head, narrowing her gaze to the Illusioned god. "What are you suggesting?" she asked.

The Owl turned back toward her, the ice in Aritz's gaze freezing her in place. SENNALHAT. YOU SPENT AMPLE TIME IN THIS "CITY" WITH THE ENEMY, DID YOU NOT?

The bluntness of the question threw her off-guard. Her brain sputtered as she struggled to devise the words necessary, but she at last managed to say, "I wouldn't...call it an 'ample' amount of time, but..."

THE LENGTH OF TIME IS IRRELEVANT. The god shook its head, the auburn curls hiding its eyes as a rare breeze found its way past the dense arboreal barrier. AND DO NOT THINK I ADMONISH YOU FOR YOUR CHOICE TO DO SO. YOU DID WHAT YOU HAD TO, WHAT YOU FELT WAS RIGHT AT THE TIME.

Her heart caught in her chest, the passage of air through her throat choked off for a brief moment. *I don't need to be reminded. What I felt was right was horribly wrong.*

When it realized Sen would voice no response, the Owl nodded and continued. ANSWER AT LEAST *THIS* FOR ME: WHEN THE INVADERS' NORTHWARD MARCH BEGAN, HOW MANY OF THE CITY'S FIGHTING FORCE JOINED?

Sen shrugged her shoulders. "I think you've seen just how many fought, killed, and died."

BUT HOW MANY *REMAIN* IN THE CITY?

"I don't..." Sen paused, considering the question. She pursed her lips, nodding at where the Owl's line of thought was leading. "Not that many, so far as I could tell. Probably no more than was necessary to keep watch on the slave camp. But everything happened so fast for me that I can't quite say for certain."

BUT THAT IS MORE THAN GOOD ENOUGH TO GO ON. THANK YOU.

Raising an eyebrow, Sen cast a sidelong glance at the Owl as it turned its back to her, facing the dark depths of the Forest with what appeared to be great interest. She stepped toward it, evading Tawa's cautionary grasp with a turn of her shoulder. "Will you tell us what you plan to do? What you wish *us* to do. You said you are still in need of all of us."

AND THOSE SENTIMENTS HAVE NOT CHANGED. THE INVADERS LAID CLAIM TO OUR STRONGEST LINE OF DEFENSE, SO WE SHALL DO THE SAME TO THEM. It turned on its heel, watching the Tribespeople from the corner of its eye, a glint of fire in its gaze so eerily reminiscent of the true Aritz a Mata, but with a distinct glow that was all its own. WE WILL TAKE THE CITY AND BRING ITS PEOPLE TO THEIR KNEES, PAY BACK IN BLOOD THE SAME TOLL THEY EXPENSED UPON US. THERE IS NO GREATER TIME THAN NOW.

The words could not find their way to Sen's lips. She ran a hand across her mouth, considering the plan, but unsure how to react to it.

YOU HESITATE, the Owl said plainly. ARE THE INVADERS' NON-COMBATANTS ABOVE REPROACH, OR SHOULD WE NOT HOLD THEM TO THE SAME LOW STANDARD TO WHICH THEY HELD US? YOU HAVE WALKED

THIS CITY'S STREETS, SENNALHAT. YOU HAVE SEEN THEIR PEOPLE LIV-
ING WITHOUT CARE OR REGARD FOR THE DARK TRUTH OF THEIR CITY'S
CREATION. DO THEY NOT DESERVE PUNISHMENT JUST THE SAME?

Sen recalled a similar conversation she had with Narva during their failed
attempt to rescue Brin. She remembered having those same thoughts, wondering whether they were worse or better than the Acrarian soldiers merely
for the act of not raising their hands in intended violence.

THIS IS MY WILL. I WILL NOT HESITATE TO OFFER THE RETRIBUTION
NECESSARY. AND UNDER THIS GUISE, it gestured to its Illusioned form,
THEY WILL BE TOO FRIGHTENED TO STRIKE BACK. THESE INVADERS
FEAR ARITZ A MATA AS THOUGH HE WERE A VENGEFUL GOD. WERE
THEY TO BE FORCED INTO OPEN COMBAT WITH HIM, THEY WOULD
SOONER FALL ON THEIR OWN SWORDS THAN RAISE A HAND TO HIM. BUT
THEY HAVE NOT BORNE WITNESS TO A *TRUE* VENGEFUL GOD. I SHALL
GRANT THEM THAT. YOU *ALL* SHALL GRANT THEM THAT.

Tawa grumbled beneath his breath, crossing his arms with great consternation upon his face. "Surely, though, you are aware we are ill-equipped and
ill-trained for such tasks. Ours are not the aptitudes fit for conquest and
seizure."

The Owl shook its head. THERE ARE MANY PATHS TO CONQUEST. YOU
ALL ARE DISCIPLES OF WISDOM. YOU ARE THE INTELLECT, THE MEM-
ORY, THE LANGUAGE, THE VERY SCRIPTURE OF OUR CULTURE ITSELF.
THERE IS A STRENGTH BEYOND BRAWN WITH WHICH YOU ARE ALL
MASTERS. DO NOT THINK YOURSELVES USELESS SIMPLY BECAUSE THE
BATTLEFIELD IS NOT YOUR PLACE. AND REMEMBER THIS: WE ARE NOT
ALONE OUT HERE. THERE ARE MANY WHO STILL REMAIN INSIDE THE
CITY. MANY WHO ARE STILL WELL WITHIN THEIR FACULTIES, WHO WILL
RELISH THE OPPORTUNITY WE SHALL PRESENT TO THEM.

The memory of the slave camp flashed in Sen's eyes, the horrid sight of
lifeless and soulless eyes staring blankly upon her. Faces all but given up,
hope nothing but a failed endeavor. She couldn't even begin to imagine the
panic created by the Bear and Wolf's slaying among those still in grips with
their minds. All that could have been on that night when she failed to rescue

Brin, all that could have been different had she tried to free them all right then and there.

It would be horribly late, she thought, *but freeing them from their shackles would…at least set* some *of this to rights.* She clenched her fists, her arms shaking for the force of the act. Flashing a glance toward Tawa, Sen nodded, her lip quivering. Words were necessary, but they did not come. Even in the silence, though, the understanding seemed to be there. Sadness and guilt seeped into his heavy eyes, matching what Sen felt in her chest.

Putting to steel the non-combatants of the City—for she could not ascribe to them the label of "innocent"—did not quite sit well with her. But spurning loose the captured Tribespeople from their inhumane pen? It needed to be done. *If bloodshed necessitates it, then so be it.*

She stepped forward, meeting the Owl halfway. "What is your plan? Speak plainly." She heard a sharp hiss of breath to her left at the bluntness of her words, but the time had passed for oblique discussions.

As the god turned, its eyes appeared distant and observant, much more those of the divine than the man it feigned to be. But it seemed the Owl also recognized the time for evasion was over. The expression upon its face was enough to suggest it regarded Sen with what looked to be a degree of respect. THE INVADERS WILL BE UNEXPECTANT OF THE RETURN OF ARITZ A MATA. WE WILL USE THAT TO OUR ADVANTAGE. It inclined its attention past Sen, to the large gathering of Tribespeople behind her. Raising its voice, it said, FOR THE ILLUSIONISTS AMONG YOU, I URGE YOU TO TAKE AN INVADER'S FORM. THE REST OF YOU SHALL ACT AS PRISONERS, NEW ADDITIONS TO THEIR FORCE OF "UNPAID LABOR." IF THEIR NUMBERS ARE AS MINIMAL AS SENNALHAT SUGGESTS, WE SHALL DISPATCH THEM UNAWARES AND SET YOUR BRETHREN FREE UPON THE UNSUSPECTING. SENNALHAT, IS THERE A CENTRAL POINT OF CONTROL IN THIS CITY?

Sen frowned as she considered the question, but nodded her assent. "You named a target to strike as Aritz's vanity. What better place to capture and situate ourselves than his manor? It's the largest construction in the entirety of the City."

AND THEIR MORALE SHALL BE STRUCK THUSLY. The Owl mused the tactic, a ghost of a grin creasing its lips. THEN THAT SHALL BE OUR FINAL

GOAL. WE SHALL MEET AT THIS MANOR'S DOORSTEP TO STRIKE AT THE HEART OF THE BEAST.

Pensive murmuring echoed through the Forest as the Tribespeople pondered the plan. Sen could not pick up the individual conversations, but from what she could tell of their tones, none were raising any objections of note. If anything, the slim hope of turning loose brethren long thought lost was enough of a motivator to proceed with the plan.

Tawa crossed his arms and scanned the crowd, consternation upon his tired face as he listened intently to the overlapping discussions. Ever so slightly, he craned his head toward the Owl, smacking his lips. "My concern still remains, however," he said. "Though we survived the battles in the True Heart, that was largely due to Your intervention. Even against a small number, we may well become overwhelmed."

The Owl focused its attention on Sen, its eyes trailing downward toward her leg. THE INVADERS HAVE SHOWN US ALL THE WAY OF BATTLE IS CHANGING. SENNALHAT. It pointed a finger to Sen's thigh, and the pistol holstered against it. WOULD THE INVADERS HAVE KEPT A CACHE OF THESE...WEAPONS IN THE CITY?

Sen reached down, caressing her hand against the handle of her pistol. She thought about the single bullet still remaining, and the target she intended it for. Of the thunderous roar of the Deatharms' deadly chorus, laying claim to those who dared to stand against it. Distant cries still echoed in her mind at merely the thought of the noise. But to put the weapons in the hands of her people, somehow, she felt a strange comfort in that.

Slowly, she nodded her head. "I don't know how many were left behind, but I would assume more than enough to arm those patrolling the City." She managed a slight smile.

THEN WE SHALL TURN THE INVADERS' TECHNOLOGY AGAINST THEM AND RECLAIM WHAT IS OURS. The Owl turned on its heel and set off into the depths of the Forest, heedless of any followers, disinterested in any daring remnants of the Wood Tribe. COME. WE MUST MAKE THE GREATEST OF HASTE IF WE ARE TO CLAIM THE CITY BEFORE THE INVADERS RETURN IN EARNEST. THERE IS MUCH GROUND TO COVER YET, AND NIGHTFALL LOOMS.

An unspoken caution gripped the Tribespeople, many of them seeming uncertain at the veracity of this plan. But as the hollow seconds stretched, and the Owl absconded deeper into the Forest's depths, small pockets of Owlsigns set their feet to motion and followed after their god. The surviving Keepers appeared keen to follow first, and wave after wave of Tribespeople followed suit shortly thereafter.

Sen could not ignore the plummeting sensation holding her chest, the nerves and apprehensions at revisiting the scene of her greatest failure. Her hands shook, her legs quivering, but she managed to put one foot forward, and then the next, and before she knew it, she was one with the herd, shepherded by a god in whom she had never placed her faith, as near to a literal wolf in sheep's clothing as could be in the wake of the actual lupine Deity's felling.

Her heart pounded with rapid rhythm, heat rising within her. She could not escape the pervasive presence of the shadows looming within the Forest. All that was within her power to do was close her eyes and blindly reach for Tawa's shoulder to guide her. Even as she willingly placed herself in her own darkness, she somehow felt safer than she would have had she kept her eyes open. She had no intention of opening them again until they left the Forest.

One by one, the crowd dispersed, a strange and unsettling sight of Tribespeople following in the footsteps of Aritz a Mata. Tez watched each of them depart as she remained seated against a tall oak tree, her legs curled up to her chest, her body still gripped in the throes of exhaustion. She could not immediately bring herself to follow them, not even when her sister departed, Tawa by her side.

Before she knew it, only Ket remained with her, their hand holding firmly to Tez's.

The sound of soft footsteps sinking into well-trodden mud faded into the depths of the Forest, leaving Tez and Ket behind with only the rustling of windblown leaves to keep them company. Tez furrowed her brow, watching the final few disappear into the shadows, and grunted with concern.

"Something is troubling you," Ket said plainly. It wasn't a question, but a stern assessment of what was immediately obvious.

Tez nodded. "The Owl has shown its prowess with, at the very least, two of the Boons attributed to it: Illusion and Language. Obviously, the other three are well within its grasp."

"Right," Ket agreed, nodding their head with a raised brow. "What does that matter? We would expect the same of the Bear and Wolf, were they alive and traveling alongside us."

Weaving her way out of Ket's grip, Tez unsteadily pushed herself back to her feet, propping herself against the tree for support. Her legs still felt weak and wholly drained of energy, but she still had the strength remaining to stand. "I have no doubt it is fully capable with Knowledge and Memory, as well, but...that final Boon is giving me pause."

Ket stood beside her. "Foresight."

Tez grunted again. "There's something it's not telling us. It seems all too confident this plan will succeed...but what comes after?" She bit at her lip. "I don't like this."

A long sigh escaped Ket's nostrils. "Nor do I." They closed their eyes tight, muttering something beneath their breath. "Is there an alternative, though? Or is this simply...a tiny step along a longer path?"

"I don't know." Tez felt the strain in the words. Hope was immensely elusive and illusive. "What little hope there is...I don't think we have a choice but to grab what we can of it right now. But I can't escape the feeling that we are just pieces on a board to the Owl. It's a game I don't wish to play."

"I'm less concerned with the game itself, and more with how long we are to play."

"I suppose..." Tez ground her teeth as she listlessly followed the entrenched footsteps, "there is but one way to find out. I only pray the Owl knows how this game is played."

MEMORY

The Natural Order of Things

The promise of the future was eminently bright, but the mood of the day could not have been cast in more muted tones.

The tutors had not arrived for Aritz today. Nor had they yesterday, or in the last week, or the last month. It could have been even longer than that; he was simply far too content to keep track of their absences. If it weren't for the imminent storm clouds looming over the horizon, he would have spent the day in the Mata estate's gardens, watching the day pass him by, and he would have been happier for it.

But alas, he could not dwell too much on nature's inconveniences. There was more than enough cause to celebrate on this day, and more so for tomorrow. He was to turn eighteen on the morrow, and with it, he would come into his inheritance. All that needed doing was a formal meeting with his father.

He looked out his bedroom window, surveying the rolling expanses he would one day lord over. A smile found its way to his lips, unable to be suppressed. *It's nothing but a vast emptiness; little more than grass rolling unto itself, endlessly until interrupted by the mountains. And yet, it will soon be* my *vast emptiness.*

A servant had yet to arrive to lay out his clothes for his meeting with his father. No one had even knocked on the door. It was midday, and he was still in his morning robe. As comfortable as it was, it would hardly do for a lordly heir on this most important of days.

With a grunt, Aritz spun on his heel, the smile vanishing, his eyes glowering toward the door. His curly auburn locks impeded his vision as he swung around, the length becoming unwieldy. He was not accustomed to tying it back, but it was growing to be a necessity in the wake of barbers refusing to see him in recent weeks and months. Reaching for a hair tie, he fumbled with securing his fringe so it would no longer block his eyes and walked out to the hallway.

It was a surprise to hear it so quiet. Patrolling footsteps were echoing less and less over the last couple of years. For what reason, it was hardly for Aritz to say. He was not one to mind it, for it meant a quieter and less bothersome day for him, but there were times where the absence of adequate maidservants—or a maidservant of any quality, for that matter—was a deep inconvenience. Today was one such day.

Aritz smacked his lips as he scanned the length of the hallway, hands on his hips, and shook his head with discontent at finding and hearing no one. "Useless, the lot of them," he muttered beneath his breath. "And I had just grown accustomed to my newest servant, as well." He shrugged, hardly inclined to allow this inconvenience to mar the course of his day, and made his way down the corridor toward his brothers' rooms.

He reached Lorente's room first, the ornate wooden carving of the door showing cracks in the center. *I will have to see to it that more adequate carpenters are brought in to re-do this shoddy handiwork.* Clearing his throat, he pounded on his brother's door, the impact echoing through the hollow halls with a thunderous roar. The crack in Lorente's door grew only longer, an indentation in the wood becoming more prominent. "Brother!" Aritz called, his voice bouncing off the wooden frame. "Are you decent? I have need of you!"

His greeting was met only with silence. Whether Lorente was in or not was beyond his knowing. As far as Aritz was aware, Lorente was still meeting with his tutors, and he could very well have been in the middle of a lesson.

Alsonso, however, did not meet with tutors any longer. Something about a learning disability or some such. At any rate, Aritz knew his youngest brother would be present. He saw little point in knocking and permitted himself in.

A startled gasp punctuated Aritz's entrance as Alsonso nearly fell to the floor at his brother's arrival. Why he was standing in the middle of his bedchamber, Aritz could not say, but his youngest brother had always been an odd sort. In recent days, he had some swelling and bruising around his left eye, but he was beginning to look his normal self again, even with a bit of residual puffiness. Alsonso put a hand to his chest, gripping the tuft of his morning robe, heaving a startled breath. "Would it kill you to knock, Aritz?"

Aritz threw his arms out at his side and flashed a smile to his brother that he knew did not quite reach his eyes. "Surely, you heard me knocking on Lorente's door a moment ago. That should have been signal enough to my arrival."

Alsonso sneered and walked to the other side of the room, widening the gap between him and his eldest brother. "I could have been changing."

"And you think I have not seen your pasty arse, Al? You've nothing to hide from me, for I've seen it all." Aritz paused and raised his brow toward him, enough to draw a squirm from Alsonso. "Though it being midday, I would hardly consider you to be in a hurry to change into your day clothes, and thus your point is irrelevant."

"What do you *want*, Aritz?" Alsonso's tone was brusque and edged, far more bite than Aritz had ever known his brother to bare.

"Far be it for me to enjoy the company of my brother, as it were." Aritz bowed, motioning his arm with great exaggeration. "But alas, I do have urgent matters to which I must attend today, but I do not believe our maid-servants have visited us today."

"Lorente and I were visited already. We have different maidservants, remember?"

Aritz put a hand to his chin in thought. "Do we, now?"

Slowly, Alsonso nodded his head. "It has been that way for some time now."

"Then, pray tell, could you advise as to whether you have seen or heard *my* servant rummaging about?"

"Which one?"

Aritz shrugged. "My newest one."

"Yes, but what is their name?"

"Am I *expected* to learn a servant's name?"

"Would you presume that *I* learn them for you? Your servants up and quit so frequently that it is hardly worth my time to learn who is who."

"I don't suppose you infer that to be *my* fault, do you, brother mine?" Aritz slowly approached Alsonso, cracking his knuckles, grinning widely as his brother backed away until pressed to the corner adjacent to the window. "If they think serving the future Lord of this House is beneath them, then perhaps their wellbeing is hardly *my* concern. They should consider it an honor, would you not agree?"

Alsonso shook in the corner, averting his eyes, gnawing at his lower lip. "Father hasn't named you his heir," he muttered, only barely audible.

"*Hah*, not yet," Aritz said with a scoff, rolling his eyes at his brother. "But tis only a formality. Tomorrow shall mark my eighteenth year, and Father will name me his heir in earnest." With hands on his hips, he half-turned, glancing out to the rolling fields to the west, a stunning view. Alsonso was even lucky to have a spot of sunshine on his side of the corridor. "And besides, if it is not I who Father names his heir, then whom? *You*?" He laughed, hand gripping the fringe of his morning robe with raucous exaggeration. "Do not worry yourself with the welfare of our House, little brother. The burden shall be mine to bear."

Words escaped Alsonso's mouth, but in far too low a volume for Aritz to discern.

"What was that?" Aritz leaned in closer, a flare burning in his eyes as he beamed at his brother's form, still slinking away from him. "If you've something to say, you needn't hesitate. I am, and shall ever be, a Lord of and for the people, after all."

His lip quivering, Alsonso shot a furious glance at Aritz. "The burden will be *ours* to bear with *you* as Lord of this House." As the words left his mouth, he shuffled back as though on instinct, futile though it was with a wall and a window immediately behind him.

A sharp silence punctuated the air between them. Aritz straightened himself out, cracking his knuckles as he considered the words. "Is that right?" he pondered, listlessly strolling forward to the window. With pronounced deliberation, he craned the windows open, permitting the rich breeze to waft inside, even as thunder roared in the distance as it rolled in from the east. Allowing the quiet to hold them for a while longer, Aritz lost himself in the scenery, the promise and hope that it would all soon be his.

But a stifled whimper drew his attention back to the reality at hand, a reality marred by the pervasive and familiar odor of urine. He looked to his side and noticed Alsonso huddled in a fetal position where the corners of his wall met, cracks of red breaking the whites of his eyes, his hands folded between his thighs in a vain attempt to dam up his still-flowing stream. Aritz dropped to a knee, meeting his quivering brother at eye level, and said softly, "Tis a shame those who are burdened shall have no say in the matter. *Isn't it?*"

He lurched forth and gripped Alsonso by the fringe of his robe, snarling and gritting his teeth as he lifted his brother off the floor.

"Oh God, oh God, please, *NO!*" Alsonso screamed, his eyes bulging out of their sockets, hands feebly swatting at Aritz's stronger grip. "Savior above, please, Aritz, I'm sorry, I'm sorry, please don't, please *DON'T!*" His feet scrambled underneath him, scurrying in place. He twisted and turned his body, the threads of his silk robe tearing in Aritz's grasp. The left shoulder came loose and Alsonso fell to his side, gasping in a shocked breath, tears flooding from his eyes, shuffling backward with his bared arm outstretched. His chest heaved up and down, quicker and quicker as he realized the space running out behind him.

Aritz stood tall above his brother, still grasping the billowing remains of Alsonso's silken sleeve. With disinterest, he flicked it out the window, watching from the corner of his eye as it drifted along in the gentle breeze, descending to the gardens below like a falling leaf. He smacked his lips, rapping his fingers against his arm, and stood in stark silence as he listened to the inane, panicked ramblings of what likely passed for pleas for mercy.

And then he laughed.

And laughed.

And *laughed.*

Aritz doubled over with amusement, wiping away a tear as he felt the heat rising and an ache in his head forming. "Oh-ho-ho, dear brother, did you—" He broke off, unable to continue without breaking into further laughter.

"You didn't think...you didn't think I would actually cast you out the window, did you?" He bared his teeth widely, uplifting his head to let loose another uproar. His chest was beginning to hurt. The laughter at last subsided. "Ah, that was good. I hadn't had a good chuckle like that in ages. Come now, back to your feet, hup-hup."

With eyes still glaring wide, Alsonso did nothing but tremble in the corner, near to sitting in a lake of his own making. His teeth rattled as he shook his head.

"I said, *to your feet!*"

Alsonso shot to his feet, barking back a whimper like a wounded pup. The crotch of his trousers was entirely damp, and dark stains were beginning to trail down his left leg. *Savior's breath, has he even pissed at all today?* He reached behind him for the wall and shuffled along its length, not breaking eye contact with Aritz as he made for the door.

"Where are you off to, then?" Aritz asked, arms outstretched as he followed along after his brother. "Are you trying to leave? We are in *your* bedchamber. If either of us were to leave, it should be I, no?"

As though on instinct, Alsonso nodded his head profusely, tears and sweat—and hopefully not urine—flying every which way in the motion.

Aritz smiled and bowed with grace to his younger brother and motioned toward the door. As he reached the threshold, a relieved sigh rang in his ear. No sooner had the sigh disappeared on the intaking breeze that Aritz turned on his heel and rushed Alsonso, planting an outstretched arm against the wall beside his head, drawing another stifled scream.

"Just remember, little brother," Aritz whispered, near to touching noses with the whimpering whelp. "Do not think yourself burdened, for the burden is mine alone. After all, burdens are heavy, and I fear I shall not catch you should you bear too much upon your shoulders." His eyes flashed back to the open window. He need not look at his brother to know his point was illustrated well enough.

With a push, Aritz put all momentum back on his heels and walked back to the door. "Oh, and call for your servant again, Alsonso. This attire—" He gestured to his morning robe. "—simply shall not do for my meeting with Father today. It has taken on a rank odor." He sniffed twice, grunting at the lingering scent in the air. "And do keep that window open. I fear it has grown a bit musty in here."

He was grateful to have had a servant dole out his formalwear for him, even if it did take the woman until mid-afternoon to arrive. Words were not needed in order to voice his displeasure. Aritz merely sat in the chair in his chamber, one leg crossed over the other, head resting atop a propped-up hand with visible distaste, and the woman, though bereft of words herself, bore the appearance of one eminently repentant. She had run out of the room the moment she laid Aritz's clothes along the bed for him, not even granting him the decency to approve or reject the selection.

She was damned lucky I chose to approve it. How do *Lorente and Alsonso deal with such grave incompetence?*

Hardly had he the time to fasten his cuff links and perfect himself in the looking-glass before he realized he needed to meet with his father within the hour. An informal formalwear would have to suffice. His shirt was lined in rich silk, cut in vibrant blues and golds. Comfortable satin comprised his trousers, tapered just above the ankle to expose his skin. Socks were not necessary today; it was much too warm for them, and his leather buckled shoes would ensure on their own his feet would be slickened in a layer of sweat. Thrown atop it all was a dove-tailed jacket, falling past his waist at its shortest length and to the back of his knees at its longest. Emblazoned upon the breast was the Mata sigil, a mighty and fearless bear, accentuating the broad shoulders in a show of strength.

Aritz cut a swath through the listless routes of the estate's working staff, all of whom left a wide berth for him to pass. In his periphery, he could spy averted glances and distrustful glares, all the while their idle conversations ceased to a volume below a whisper. The click-clacking of Aritz's shoes against the marble flooring echoed through the entirety of the manor; of that, he was certain.

The great hall was his destination. It had been some time since Aritz was present at a gathering. Likewise, it had been some time since his father had hosted anyone. He could not help but wonder if an epidemic of reclusion was roaring through the estate, given the disappearances of his maidservants and his father's limited visibility. Even family dinners were growing fewer and farther between.

He paid it no mind. There would be a tremendous gathering on the morrow, and Aritz could not wait for it.

As the great hall loomed ahead, Aritz could not help but feel a fluttering in his chest, a sensation wholly unfamiliar to him. Apprehension? Nervousness? *My, what a strange feeling. Surely, I am not anxious of what is to come.* This meeting was merely a formality. The outcome was predestined. It was merely the natural order of things.

Drawing in a deep breath as he reached the doors to the great hall, Aritz steadied himself, flexing his fingers and cracking his neck, and pushed his way through, heedless of the guards situated on the other side.

The footman was the first whom Aritz locked eyes with, a pudgy man with a hairline long since receded and a chin long since vanished into the depths of his folds. He cleared his throat, and proceeded to yell, "*Presenting, the young master Aritz a—*"

"My father knows who I am," Aritz interrupted, shouldering the footman out of his way. *Dumb bastard.*

Pillars flanked the length of the hall, all the same marble as the flooring outside in mimicry of the architecture of the isles in the Silk Sea. A hand-woven carpet was rolled out from the door to the far edge of the chamber, handwoven with great care by the most prolific artisans in the eastern reaches, threads of dark red cut with remarkable silver fringes.

At the other end of the hall, atop a pedestal of matching twin ornate chairs carved in rich oak and lined in resplendent gold, sat his father. Lord Nofre reclined in his chair, fingers rapping against the cushioned fabric of his armrests. His eyes did not break from Aritz's approach, nor did he vanquish the silence with even so much as a greeting. He merely sat in wait, his expression a blank slate devoid of emotion.

Casting a wide smile as he reached the pedestal, Aritz propped a leg atop the first step and inclined his head with gracious respect. "Father," he said in greeting. "Pray forgive my tardiness. I must find a new maidservant with the greatest of haste. I had to make use of my brothers' servant—is that not absurd?"

Nofre raised his brow as a deep grunt gurgled in his throat. "It has not even been the passing of a month and you are in need once again of a new maidservant?" His eyes were sunken, exhaustion quite apparent. He looked as though he had not slept in weeks. Age was catching up to him, even as he had yet to see his fortieth year.

Aritz shrugged and shook his head. "I had mentioned the same to Alsonso earlier today. Tis not my problem if they believe the work to be far too beneath them to even show up when required. A shame, truly."

"It is not an issue I have found with your brothers. Why, I believe Floriana has served them both well for several years now."

"Lorente and Alsonso lack the heart necessary to voice their displeasures, I fear. I requested this Floriana's services today in absence of my own, and I daresay I was hardly impressed with her work. Do my brothers not deserve better than that?"

"Hmm," Nofre grunted. "I'll see to it they are given the service they deserve."

Aritz offered a deep bow. "I am certain they will be most appreciative of the gesture." Planting his hands on his hips, he turned in place, surveying the confines of the great hall with contented satisfaction. "Ah, but forgive me, there is a time for airing our grievances of the help, but it is not why we meet today, is it not?"

A ghost of a smile creased Nofre's lips. "No, of course not."

"May I sit?" Aritz asked, gesturing to the empty seat beside his father.

A quiet moment stretched to a handful of seconds as Lord Nofre looked upon the chair. "You are aware this is your mother's seat."

Not waiting any further for permission, Aritz ascended the short steps and sat himself beside his lord father. "Oh, but of course. But if I am to sit this chair one day—whether this one or the one beside me—I wish to grow accustomed to this view." He reclined, holding his arm out straight to cut a wide arc over the perimeter of the great hall, picturing a host of reverent constituents looking upon him with great anticipation, rather than the empty confines currently housing only a handful of inattentive guards and an overzealous footman. "The quiet moments such as these are few and far between, I am sure, so I feel there is no better time than now to appreciate the silence."

Rhythmic tapping moved in sync with Nofre's considering nods as he rapped his front two fingers against the armrest, his eyes not quite meeting his son's. Something strange glinted in his eyes, something Aritz could not quite place. Not anger, not sadness. If anything, it appeared to be a pang of...regret?

Whatever lurked within the man's heart, Nofre outwardly betrayed nothing. Still not completely facing Aritz, he spoke, in a voice almost too meek to be his own, "Quite presumptuous today, aren't you?"

Raising an eyebrow, Aritz offered a chuckled retort and said, "Presumptuous? Well, yes. Is this not what we were to speak on today?"

Nofre leaned back in his chair, inclining his head upward, sighing as he clenched his eyes closed. "I know not what you expected of me when you requested this conference."

Aritz laughed, though hesitant in the act. "You jest, Father. Surely you are aware of what tomorrow brings, yes?"

"I am not oblivious, my son. I know you are to turn eighteen tomorrow."

Rising back to his feet, Aritz rolled his hand out and exposed an empty palm, as though wishing for his sought-after response to be placed upon it. "Which means tomorrow..." He paused, waiting for his father to finish the sentence. Instead, he was met with further silence as Nofre continued to maintain his meditative quietude, eyes still clasped shut. "...I am at last eligible to be named your heir." He leaned forward, making no secret of wanting that confirmation.

A rumble echoed in Lord Nofre's throat as he tutted his lips and shook his head. His head drooped down, his fingers clasped together as he propped his elbows against the armrests. "That will not happen."

With mouth agape, Aritz narrowed his eyes at his father, far too flummoxed to devise any retaliatory words. He felt the heat rising within him, droplets of angry sweat fastening his shirt to his chest. For silent moments akin to an eternity, he waited for Lord Nofre to, at the least, turn and face him, to stand behind the dagger of his words. But instead, he stared solemnly ahead, the slightest of grins creasing his lips as though satisfied by the admission. Satisfied by his betrayal. "I beg your pardon?"

"You may beg," Nofre said, gravel in his voice, "but it shall not be granted." His eyes no longer bore the stain of one soaked with shame. Rather, it appeared a weight was lifted, a sense of ease returning to him.

Flaring his eyes between his father and the useless guards at the door, Aritz threw his hands out, his fingers drawing more the imagery of talons ready to strike. "I do not find this a humorous jest, Father."

"Nor should you. Tis not a jest."

"Then you are far more a fool than I ever believed you to be."

"The only fool among us is *you*, Aritz."

Aritz scoffed, taken aback. He paced to the other side of the pedestal, widening the gap between him and his father, nearly falling off the edge in his irate fervor. "And who would you deign to name in my place? Lorente? Alsonso?"

"They would be greater suited to the task, the both of them." Still, his father would not look at him.

"On what basis? They are cowards both!"

"Lorente is a gallant knight-in-waiting and Alsonso a keen intellectual mind." Nofre rose to his feet and at last turned toward him. "They have done well for themselves for all the years of cruelty and torment they faced at your hands."

Aritz's eyes widened at the accusation. "You make me out to be some sort of monster."

"Do not think me blind and deaf to your actions over the years." Lord Nofre clasped his hands behind his back, puffing out his chest and chin in some signal of his assumed authority. "Word travels, lines are connected, and I would be remiss to allow our family legacy to be tainted further by one so vain, arrogant, and brutish as yourself."

Through it all, Aritz could not help but laugh. "Brutish? My hands bear not the blood which stains yours. I have seen your anger, your violent rage, your own brutality. If you fear *I* would taint the Mata name, you must be ill-aware of the damage you have done yourself." He gestured to the emptiness gripping the great hall. "After all, it has been some time since you last hosted a fete or gala, has it not? Mayhap disgrace has already colored our halls."

"Aye, it has. Words *do* escape these halls, Aritz. The comings and goings of merchants and passersby permit fleeting gossip and traveling accounts. There is a fear that has taken hold of our servants which did not exist in years past." Nofre paused and glanced at the guards and footman at the other end of the great hall. "I admit the faults of my temper, but I also treat these people with fairness and dignity. They are beneath us in status, but they should never feel as though they are beneath us in humanity. They would lay down their lives for me, and I for them." His eyes shot back to Aritz, bearing knives in their icy hold. "But they would sooner trample you underfoot, just as you would them."

Bemused, Aritz shook his head, disbelieving of the words he was hearing. "You've grown soft, old man. This is not the man I thought you were."

"And you are not as clever as you believe yourself to be." Slowly, Nofre approached his son, each step punctuating the next jab. "Something was amiss when you tricked us all into putting Ynigo to the gaoler's knife. Even in the moment, I was ill-convinced. I put up my own blinders, wanting not to believe my own blood thought himself the master manipulator, a boy thinking himself above those his greater. I knew not what to do, so I allowed you free rein in the hopes you would return to your senses. But so caught up in your own mythos you are of being above and beyond any who would deign to approach you that you have blinded yourself entirely to the realities of the world, the realities of our *House!*" He screamed the last word, his voice echoing over the hollow and hallowed hall. "We are at a crossroads: either I invoke tradition and permit your sullying of the Mata name to be recorded in the annals of history, or I buck tradition and close the wound you have ripped open these last years in an attempt to restore glory to our name. I choose the latter."

Aritz lurched forward, spittle flying from the corners of his mouth as he snarled with what ferocity he could muster, unafraid though this man was. "But...but, Father—"

Nofre raised a hand. "Enough, Aritz. In due course, an announcement shall be made naming Lorente as my heir when he comes of age. Brighter days loom ahead for the Mata name, the weeks to come will bring ahead a golden opportunity, and this proclamation shall seal our commitment to this party's wishes." He flashed his teeth, shimmering white as the last vestiges of sunlight vanished from the windows before the storm clouds emerge in full. "The Mata name sees no future with you leading it." His smile was venomous, almost vindictive.

Stunned to silence, Aritz froze in place, his mouth agape. Frustration welled within him. He could almost feel tears forming in his eyes, obscuring his vision.

"Now begone from my sight," Nofre commanded, pointing a stern, yet rapturous, finger toward the door.

Numb to all else around him, Aritz obeyed. He descended the pedestal, the cold floor pain upon his heels. His skull rattled with each step he took along the ornate carpeting, the world around him and before him little more than a hazy blur. Distantly, he could hear the echoes of the footman proclaiming his departure, as though any in the room were blind to the proceedings. The ghosts of amused smiles upon the faces of the guards he passed as he exited the hall seemed to indicate they reveled in Aritz's sudden misery.

The doors slammed behind him, and Aritz could not help but stop mid-stride, carefully and intently listening at the threshold for any raucous laughter or regretful conversations that would act as a signal of everything that was said was nothing more than a spiteful jest.

But there was no such laughter, no proclamations to the Savior begging for salvation for this grave betrayal. There was only the deafening sound of silence.

A furious quiver gripped Aritz as he began the long walk back to his bedchambers. His head pounded with an uncertainty he had never felt before. Everything he was raised to believe, everything he had readied himself to inherit...it was all stripped from him in an instant. *It is not I who is tarnishing our family's legacy, Father. It is I who will save it, whether it is with your blessing or not.* He seethed with each step, flames burning within him, ready to erupt.

The long corridors of the Mata estate were remarkably empty, or perhaps those lowly servants who would "sooner trample him underfoot" were already wallowing in their own hatred and fear and had retreated to parts unknown. *No matter. Those who feel they are above me may be discarded. Loyalty is easily bought. How easy it is for Father to say his guards hold him in the highest fidelity when it is he who allows them a wage.*

Haunting silence surrounded him as he finally reached the corridor of family bedchambers. A faint odor still wafted from the creases between Alsonso's door and the frame. Lorente still did not appear to be in his room, unless he was busy playing soldier, as Nofre had suggested.

And Aritz's chambers were just as he left them, in dire need of a servant's attention, if one did not feel themselves above the work. He slammed the door shut and locked it behind him, his attention drawn to a loose floorboard in the corner. Kneeling down, he craned his wrist underneath the small opening and found the canvas drawstring back he still hoped was there. Pulling it open, he was relieved to find a small collection of gold pieces and one royal mark. Perusing the treasury had long since been an option since that kerfuffle of four years past, and once his personal stash was discovered, it immediately went back under lock and key.

But despite what his father implied, Aritz *did* possess a keen intuition for such matters. And though he did not assume he would have a need of such a large monetary collection, he knew it to be wise to keep a cache separate should a necessity present itself. And what better opportunity to make use of this considerable sum than now?

Loyalty is easily bought, he thought. *But so are a great many other things.*

CHAPTER EIGHT

CORONATION

If she never had to return to those frozen mountainous wastes again, it would have been far too soon. But for now, Kamataa was grateful for the thaw provided by the more temperate climes south of the Heart's base.

Camp tents had been pitched in an instant—as it always seemed they were—once the Acrarian forces merged into the clearing past the abandoned dwellings of the Stone Tribe. It was a day of hard travel made no easier by the cargo trailing behind them on the downward slopes of the mountain paths, a caravan once intended to be for supplies and instead transporting husks of sizes great and small.

As Kamataa surveyed the camp, wind at her back, the sun's warmth melting away any lingering frost from her withered and weathered bones, she could not help but be impressed they successfully managed to haul the Bear's corpse out of the True Heart of the Land. Even more impressive was that the carts could withstand its great weight. *It seems these people are adept at matters other than killing, after all.* The god's body lay atop a caravan of creaking and bending wood brought to an inch of its livelihood and struggling to stay assembled, and beside it was parked a convoy of separate carts holding the groaning chorus of the mindless. The area was placed under heavy guard, a task Kamataa viewed to be wholly unnecessary and rather pointless, but she was far beyond the point of caring for the redundancies of these people, so long as they remained useful to her.

Songs filled the air as the aroma of beer wafted in the breeze. Spirits had been lifted in the time it took them to traipse out of the cold, though for what reason, Kamataa could not be certain. The journey out of the mountains had proven just as treacherous as the battles that had taken place within them, if only for the environmental and occupational hazards rather than the land's inhabitants. Kamataa could not say if these melodies were sung in a toast for those who lost their lives, or for the sheer denial of what they were able to survive, but at the very least, it was a much more enjoyable atmosphere than that of the sad sods prior to their departure.

Then again, the promise of warmth thought long lost was always something to celebrate.

She felt an urge to smile, though she knew it would not fully reach her eyes. Turning on her heel, she looked back into her tent. "How's the shoulder?" she asked.

Sha'a sat in the corner, flexing and rotating her arm, notably wincing as a red stain began to pool the fabric of her shirt once again. "No worse for wear, I guess. Still hurts like a bastard, but I suppose it's better than the state of most." Her arm stopped as it appeared she hit a pain point, hissing in a sharp gasp of breath. She pressed her palm to her shoulder and Kamataa could already hear the sopping wet texture of Sha'a's shirt.

Kamataa kneeled beside her, directing her protegee's hand away from the re-opened wound with a flick of her head. "Fortune smiles upon you still, and the Moon continues to protect you. Perhaps Luck guards you and guides you more than you know." She lifted Sha'a's top to get a better look at the wounded flesh, her bandaging well past its use.

Sha'a shook her head. "Given that state of those granted Luck by Her, I'm not exactly keen to group myself in with—ow, shit!"

"Apologies," Kamataa said bluntly, pulling her hand away from the medical wrapping.

"Damn it, where's Vanta? Should she not be back by now?"

"Patience, Sha'a, patience. You face no dire wounds, by the grace of the Moon. Vanta will return in due course. I cannot imagine procurement shall go smoothly, given everything that happened on the descent."

"I hardly thought finding clean bandaging and disinfectants to be a perilous task."

Kamataa shrugged. "Nor I, but I also would have left the injured and infirmed where they fell, but such matters are not up to me." She rose back to her feet and walked to the threshold of the tent, the sound of merriment still dancing in the air. She scanned the perimeter of the camp from one end to the next, but Vanta was nowhere to be seen. Not that Kamataa knew precisely where the camp medic or the medical supplies were situated.

"Has Aritz summoned you yet?" Sha'a asked, fashioning a makeshift bandage out of her ruined shirt. Another sharp gasp escaped her lips as she put pressure on the wound.

"Oh, I needn't await his beck and call," Kamataa responded with a chuckle. "I am certain he is beside himself with uncertainty at this point. All that needs doing is a gentle nudge in the right direction. A man of ambition shan't lay dormant for long."

"And so the man of ambition will be crowned a king of fools."

"And long shall he reign." This time, the smile upon Kamataa's face felt more genuine. "Would you like me to find Vanta for you?"

A slight moment's hesitation marked Sha'a's face, but she shook her head, regardless. "No, I'll live. I know you're right. She'll be back soon." Another sharp hiss of pain. "But damn it, Kama, did you have to stick me so hard? Blessed Moon."

"Apologies. Perhaps I was a bit overzealous." Kamataa shrugged her shoulders. "But it worked out just the same." She inclined her gaze to the south, where a plume of smoke billowed from behind the largest tent in the camp. "You shall be okay by yourself until Vanta's return, then, yes?"

Sha'a nodded, wordless though with an expression that spoke well enough. The message of *I guess* was loud and clear.

"Good. Then if you'll pardon me, I must see to planning a coronation. Much still to do, and a king of fools must seek all the guidance he can get."

By trail's end, Cin practically had to drag himself to the welcoming embrace of soft soil and verdant grass. His legs flared in agony, his wounds from the Bear's assault still not quelled, his arms all that kept him afloat atop his wearied feet.

When he saw the Acrarian armies descending the Heart's pathways, he knew nothing else but to follow. The words and admonishments from both the Moon and Zarrow still weighed heavily upon him. Thoughts and doubts assaulted him for days. And exhaustion set in from now just the physical ordeal of his injuries, but the mental toll placed upon him. He needed answers, and no more would come to him the longer he wallowed in his rudimentary shelter. The Moon would not speak to him. Zarrow's presence could not be felt.

And so all that was left to him was to traipse in the same footsteps as his comrades-in-arms, and his fellow kin who he hoped still dwelt amongst the living. He knew in his heart, at the least, that Kamataa still lived. Nothing would fell that woman. And more and more, that knowledge served only to unsettle him.

He could not keep pace with the Acrarian march. His body would not allow it, and their forward momentum was nothing if not relentless. Nothing stopped them, not even the collapse of precious cargo, and the lives lost with it. For them to bring that beast's corpse all that way, only to abandon it among a pile of death and ruination, only further flummoxed Cin. He thought there was a rhyme and reason to the Acrarians, but little was making sense to him anymore. Pained screams were short-lived, shock strewn upon the faces of those with whom he had passing familiarity, and he could only pay them the same degree of attention offered by their own comrades.

The dead could not offer him answers this time.

You would face death itself for these Children of the Black Moon, you say. Would they do the same for you?

Zarrow's question continued to nag at him the further he descended the mountain. The further he descended into the doubt cast upon him by those who cared not to search for him after the battle, while he was far too weakened to search for them. His head swirled. Pangs upon pangs of regret rattled him as he continued to question why he warned the Tribes of the impending Acrarian return. He knew it would not have mattered either way. He saw them running for their lives just the same.

Questions upon questions, doubts upon doubts. And none of them would ever be quelled by Kamataa. He knew firsthand that hesitance held no place among the Children of the Black Moon. He could hardly blame Sennalhat for abandoning them for her own misgivings. But for how long Cin had spent in pursuit of everything, in pursuit of *Kamataa and Ziialhan's* aims...to have any doubt at all simply felt wrong. Those questions would find no resolution in Kamataa's hands.

The Acrarian campsite loomed in the plains south of the Stone Tribe village. From the final descent, he had felt a flutter in his chest, a sensation in conflict with the sheer exhaustion bringing his body to ruin. Even when he permitted himself a brief respite in the muck at the crest of the Stone village, it was not enough to stop him. He couldn't be Lieutenant Gaona any longer. That mask could not be known to have returned. Kamataa need not have known him to be back in her presence.

A face took shape in his mind as he felt the warmth of Illusion within him. One of the lads crushed at the bottom of a valley, mangled by wooden shards and splinters and misshapen by jagged cliffsides. An unassuming face with plain features, dark eyes, long brown hair pulled back tightly. A face entirely insignificant to Kamataa. And when Cin took that form, he forced himself back up to his feet and limped along to the Acrarian camp.

An armed crowd patrolled the northwestern corner of the campground, flanking a convoy of wagons, one of which somehow holding the Bear's imposing form. A stark anger filled Cin at the sight of the dead god, an anger overtaken by the confusion at the sight of how heavily guarded the wagons were. *Why the hell would a corpse need this many people?*

As Cin drew closer to the camp, murmurs and whispers gradually became clearer and clearer to him. Attentive fingers pointed at him, soldiers stopping dead in their tracks at the sight of him. Cin knew nothing of the man whose form he assumed, but he apparently had enough friends amongst the living who cared enough for his survival.

A stocky soldier ran up to him, throwing an arm around him with haste to assist him into the camp. "Alvar?" the man said, his voice shaking. "I saw you fall! I thought you were dead!"

Cin had no clue what this "Alvar's" voice sounded like, and so grated his voice against his throat to produce as much gravel to his words as possible. "Got lucky," he growled with a wince that was not altogether forced. "W…water?"

The soldier's pace quickened, enough to draw a sharp pain from Cin even as he exaggerated some of his real injuries. "Come, I'll take you to the med tent. Just this way."

There was life and vigor to the camp that Cin was not expecting, the melodies of drinking songs wafting in the breeze. For the briefest of moments he saw the convoy pass by, he had witnessed a people completely broken. He still wondered about that mist himself, and he could only imagine the effect it had on those uninitiated to the Tribes' supposed "wickedness." But to see so many in such high spirits already was rather strange and unsettling, to say the least.

Dizziness gripped him as Alvar's comrade nearly hurled him into the medical tent and onto a soft bedroll. Compared to many of the other Acrarian soldiers in the tent, Cin may as well have been in immaculate shape. At least he was not suffering from severely broken or severed limbs, head trauma, or other agony that justified permanently crying out in pain. *One would think they've not suffered a wound in their entire lives.*

The medic kneeled beside him, and Cin recognized her as Elena, a woman with whom he had interacted in passing a few times over the past months. Blood coated her shirt, sleeves rolled up to her elbows, her field jacket long since discarded, chestnut hair tied back in messy strands. "Alvar?" she prompted, her voice calming despite the chaos surrounding her. "Can you hear me? Can you tell me where the pain is?"

Lucidity returned to Cin's vision as he reached and pointed downward with exaggerated weakness. "L…leg," he grunted, still doing his best to disguise his voice as best as he could. "And…water?"

Elena nodded and vanished from sight, returning almost as quickly with a waterskin. Cin grasped the skin with pronounced eagerness and emptied its contents down his throat, streams dribbling out from the corners of his mouth and onto the bedroll beneath him. The water was lukewarm, but he cared little. It was instant refreshment on his dry throat, much more relief than he was able to get from allowing snow to melt in his mouth as he had been doing in the mountains.

"More," he croaked as he relaxed his head against the bedroll, a comfort he had not known in quite some time.

A pained wail pierced the air from somewhere deeper in the tent. "It will be a moment," Elena said to him, putting a light hand on his shoulder. "Stay put, I'll be back shortly."

Though Cin did not quite notice Elena's presence vanish, he could feel his own exhaustion beginning to dissipate. Re-hydrating, even a little bit, had already done wonders. The aches were still present, but his head had stopped swirling enough for him to gauge his surroundings. The faces of those who he could see were strewn with pain and anger, loss and despair, but they were not giving up. There was something watching over them, no one to abandon them to the wilds.

The immediate concern shown to him whilst posing as this man called "Alvar" felt...unfamiliar. Comforting. Reassuring. *I have known these people for a span of minutes, and yet it is greater camaraderie than...I have ever known.* The years spent wandering the Land as a child after learning the truth of his Tribe, fortunate only for escaping the wrath of the Acrarians in time. The years living under Kamataa's yoke, content with pursuing the goal of the Children of the Black Moon, but knowing no purpose of his own.

And now? Even within this tent reeking with the stench of blood and fouled sheets, he felt altogether...less lonely.

Cin inclined his head, turning his eyes toward the rear of the tent where Elena was still hard at work on quelling the pain of a wailing man. He nodded to himself, never knowing that degree of attentiveness before. He grunted, his throat still raw, and sat up, facing the main thoroughfare of the war camp.

As his attention returned to the front of the tent, he noticed a woman crouched beside the shelving units near a row of unconscious soldiers. Her hands rummaged through a bin filled with bandaging and brown bottles filled with what Cin assumed to be some sort of antiseptic, her eyes fluttering between her task at hand and whatever Elena was up to at the rear of the tent. As she stuffed a number of bandage rolls and bottles into the pockets of her field jacket, she began to sneak away, the glasses clinking together but not loud enough to draw Elena's attention.

It struck Cin as profoundly odd. *Why would one need to steal medical supplies in a war camp? Just ask for them.* But even stranger was the profile of the woman. Just before she vanished from view, her face was fully visible to him. A face that he was entirely familiar with, despite the Illusion disguising it.

Vanta? What the hell? Cin furrowed his brow. *So, she's alive at the least. Who else?* He averted his eyes back toward Elena, the medic still hard at work on the screaming soldier. He was no medical expert, but he had to assume she would be busy for some time. She wouldn't notice him slipping out.

Cin rose back to his feet, his legs still weak but in no way hindering him, and walked out of the tent, Vanta remaining well within his sight.

No one called after him as he left.

Unsurprisingly, Aritz was keeping to himself when Kamataa arrived. An aroma of scented candles and subpar food lingered within the confines of the General's tent as his attention was drawn to a letter he was penning.

Kamataa walked in without pomp or summons and hovered over him, curious at the words he was drafting. Even without looking at her, it seemed Aritz was more than aware of his presence and hunched his shoulder to hide his correspondence from her.

"Secret letters then, is it?" Kamataa prodded, a grin on her lips. In surveying his desk, she noted weaponry laid out within an arm's reach: the flintlock pistol he had kept on his person throughout the march through the Heart, and the imbued blade she had crafted for him. The rune looked plain, without any notable glimmers.

Aritz heaved a disapproving sigh. "My affairs are of little consequence to you."

"Come now, Aritz. All your lieutenants are gone now. Surely, you have need of another to confide in."

"I did not confide in anyone when my lieutenants were still alive. I hardly think it necessary to begin now." Aritz continued penning his letter, shaking his head as though disinterested and dissatisfied with Kamataa's presence.

Kamataa scoffed, throwing her head back with great exaggeration. "A pity. I had hoped there was much and more still for us to discuss."

Aritz set his pen down, his hand resting firm against the desk. He drew in a sharp, long breath and slowly turned toward her. "What *more* what you suggest we do? The savages have been put to rout. We are going *home*. We have *won*. There is no more in the way of strategy that requires our conference. If you must know, I am writing to inform my people of just *that*."

Extending out her hands, Kamataa grinned. "There. Was that so difficult to share?"

"Savior's breath, woman. If you want to be useful, you can at least explain *this*." He grabbed the blade by the hilt, holding it out to her. The blood had removed it of its shine, the carved rune dyed a pronounced red.

"What of it?" She did not reach out to grasp the steel, opting instead to fold her hands behind her back.

"Take it. Do you feel nothing from it?"

Kamataa flexed her shoulder and did as requested, hefting the steel in her hand. "It feels as a blade should."

"Precisely." Aritz's face was stern. "Whatever wicked magic you put into it is now gone."

"Huh. So it is."

Aritz's eyes widened. "'So it is?' Is that all you have to say? You promised me this rite would—"

Her attention placed firmly on the steel, Kamataa brushed him off with a flick of the wrist. "Yes, yes, I know what I said. I promised nothing. I do remember you objecting to my use of the word 'should,' after all."

"Do *not* interrupt—"

"I wonder..." she said, deliberately increasing the volume of her voice. She paid Aritz's sharp, irritated breath no mind as she paced the tent, hand stroking her chin thoughtfully, the flickering flame of the nearby candle just barely glinting off the blade's dulled sheen. "It could be we used too little of the necessary blood. Or perhaps the effect of the blood is only growing weaker with the death of the Bear. Interesting."

Aritz rushed beside her, a vein near to bursting in his forehead. "'Interesting?!' You mean to tell me that we dragged that beast down through the mountains for nothing, and you merely call it 'interesting?' We lost who knows how many soldiers when the wagon carting that wolf collapsed and sent its corpse and everyone with it careening into the valley, but you can only find your failed experiments 'interesting?' Tell me—"

"Oh, calm yourself, Aritz. We both know you care little for the livelihoods of your soldiers."

The General bit back a sneer and paced back to his desk, planting his hands atop it. He grasped the letter he had been penning and held it up to her, though the hand was in a florid script Kamataa could not quite decipher. "The numbers I have had to log as deceased are an embarrassment, and worsened only by whatever game you are opting to play here. And if you mean to inform me that all of this, this promise of advancement, has been part of some grave farce, then I shall have you—"

"Whatever you shall have of me, I assure you it shall not stick." Kamataa continued to pace about the tent, deep in thought. "Many have tried worse, and yet here I still stand."

Aritz muttered something under his breath, but not loud enough for her to hear.

She turned the steel this way and that, humming and tutting her lips as she held it in closer examination. "No, it shan't be for nothing. If there was a momentary surge of power running through the blade, then I would surmise it is more to do with the quantity. The quantity of the blood of the Tribes needs to be greater. Perhaps materials could even be forged in it. Yes, yes, that should do." Kamataa turned and flashed a smile toward Aritz.

He did not reciprocate the smile, instead offering a distrusting raise of the eyebrow. "How can you say that with any certainty?"

"Because I can say with authority that which I have confirmed with my own eyes."

"You have confirmed nothing."

"I didn't say you were there."

Aritz scoffed. "And I am to…take you at your word, then."

"As I've said before, you stand to lose nothing for it." Kamataa twirled the blade in her hand and tossed it back to Aritz, hilt-side first.

The blade landed gently in Aritz's open hand. He glanced at the steel and tossed it aside, missing the desk and sending it through the fabric of this tent. "And *why* are you so certain this shall work? How do you know of these methods in the first place?"

Kamataa planted her hands on her hips, the smile still wide on her lips. "Oh, Aritz. If I were to tell you, you would hardly believe me." *Though perhaps by now, you are beyond the stupidity of cries for witchcraft.* "With age comes wisdom. And though you may be disbelieving of it, but I am far older than I appear. The secrets of this Land are no longer hidden to me. And I would hazard to say that knowledge has been to your great benefit, has it not?"

Nothing was said in response. Aritz cast his gaze aside, folding his arms about his chest.

"Do not concern yourself with the 'why' and the 'how,' Aritz. You care only for the ends, don't you?"

"What of it?" The flame of indifference still burned brightly in the General's eyes.

"I have said this already: you will be viewed as a paragon of the Kingdom of Acraria regardless of the outcome. What have you to lose? We shall proceed forward in the pursuit of a higher cause, for the advancement of your precious Kingdom." She approached Aritz, closing the gap between them, an involuntary chuckle escaping her lips. A sense of revelry ran through her as she placed a hand on his shoulder, prompting a disgusted twinge in the man's face. "You shall be as a god yourself, Aritz."

The promise appeared to catch his attention, but he still wormed his way out of Kamataa's grasp, regardless. "Tell me," he said. "Of what benefit is all this to you? You are content to burn all you know to cinders. Your gods are defeated, their followers along with them. And yet, here you still stand."

"And here I still stand." She glanced outside, to the north where the ghosts of conquest were certain to roam the True Heart. "One god still remains, but that is beyond the point. There is no need to concern yourself with my intentions, Aritz. I know who it is I worship, and I need not fear for Her. I hold no apprehension for what is yet to come. I am merely content with what has already come to pass."

Aritz narrowed his eyes with clear intention to press her point further, but he had no sooner opened his mouth that Kamataa continued to speak.

"There *is* something I wish to investigate, though, if you will indulge me for a moment further."

"I would assume you give me no say in the matter," Aritz said, rolling his eyes.

"You would assume correctly. Consider this, if you will: when you slayed the Bear and the Wolf, you severed the connection between them and their surrogates, causing the complete mental collapse with which you are now familiar. However, the Owl has still eluded our grasp. Though this means there are still a number of able-minded Tribespeople wandering about this island—hardly a cause for concern, at any rate—it also means there is a stronger link still available to us."

Aritz narrowed his eyes, nodding along to Kamataa's words. He opened his mouth with a pronounced pause, a query clear on the tip of his tongue. "You are saying the power of this...blood—" He rolled his eyes once more. "—shall be stronger within these 'surrogates' if their god still lives."

Kamataa pointed an acknowledging finger at him. "That is *precisely* what I am saying. And it is to our great fortune that we have *just* the volunteer for such a demonstration." She walked toward the exit of the tent, the air still rich with drinking songs in the campground. She turned over her shoulder, finding Aritz watching her, still affixed to the same spot she left him in. With great embellishment, Kamataa bowed and motioned her arm toward the northern edge of the camp. "If you'll follow me, *General*, I can show you."

Again, Aritz grumbled under his breath, but fell in step beside her, the reluctance upon his face especially pronounced.

Conversations ceased in the camp as all rose and stood to attention at Aritz's arrival. The songs quieted, the drinking stopped, the arguments forgiven. Despite it all, Aritz seemed to pay them no heed, instead focused on wherever Kamataa was bringing him. From the corner of her eye, Kamataa could not help but notice the sheer displeasure it appeared the man had simply for having to be in the presence of his soldiers. *Truly a man above such sordid interactions. I cannot begin to imagine his demeanor once I have finished his war for him.* She chuckled silently at the thought, though evidently not loud enough for the General to hear her.

Soft commotion ruminated within Kamataa's tent as she and Aritz neared it. Shadows cast their way into the clearing, two forms bearing the shape of a stern conversation. When Kamataa peaked her head around the corner, she found Vanta hard at work rebandaging Sha'a's wound, unspooling a full roll along the length of her comrade's shoulder and chest. A brown bottle of antiseptic was thrown to the ground, a wince peppering Sha'a's face as though the liquid were still working hard. Kamataa cleared her throat, drawing their attention. Vanta turned and placed the bandaging atop Sha'a's thigh, while Sha'a hunched over and wrapped her arms around her chest for the sake of modesty.

"All is well, then?" Kamataa asked, gesturing with her head toward the treated wound.

Vanta nodded. "Her wound is cleaned out well enough—despite her protests."

Sha'a rolled her eyes but offered no retort.

"Good, I'll need one or both of you." Kamataa looked behind her and clicked her teeth at Aritz, who trailed behind her, his eyes cast elsewhere, face disinterested and annoyed, an impatient foot tapping away a discordant rhythm. She motioned her fingers at him, beckoning him forward.

It was clear upon his face that Aritz would not take well to the repeated commands, but he took long deliberate steps forward, regardless, and turned to face Vanta and Sha'a without so much as a monosyllabic greeting.

The silence dragged on until Sha'a, still covering herself, gestured to her bare skin with a free hand. "I don't care who you are, General, but it's common decency to avert your gaze."

Aritz shook his head and strolled past the tent, his gaze affixed to the wagons on the north side of the camp.

A smirk creased Kamataa's lips. *Have I discomforted the great Aritz a Mata? How droll.* "We have need of one of the bodies. Sha'a, you assisted with loading them up. Do you remember which of them holds the Owlsign woman?"

Sha'a pushed herself to a knee and reached for her shirt, the right sleeve completely stained in red. "We didn't exactly number them, Kama. I'll know by the faces."

"Do you feel well enough to walk?"

"My shoulder is wounded, not my legs."

Kamataa nodded. "Quite so. Vanta, if you would come along, too. Far be it for her to lift even a finger right now."

Vanta gestured to her own shoulder, her brow raised as though indicated what should be obvious.

"Pardon, I didn't see a god fall atop *you*, Vanta. Now come along, both of you."

Once Sha'a redressed herself, the trio of Eclipseborn sauntered off toward the heavily guarded wagons, a silent Aritz in tow. As was typical, the nearest soldiers stopped what they were doing to stand at attention to Aritz's presence, even as he paid them little heed. One soldier with tied-back dark hair seemed to have held particular focus on their group, but for what reason, Kamataa could hardly surmise why. He did not follow, at any rate.

When they reached the wagons, Kamataa gestured for the guards to part.

A disgruntled rifleman eyed her with disdain. "What do *you* want with them, Red? You couldn't have given less of a rat's arse about them before."

"It's not what *I* want," Kamataa responded, pointing a thumb behind her. "Rather, what *he* wants." She stepped aside to allow Aritz to make his presence known.

The soldier's chin shot out with the same violence as his own weapon. "Sir! How may I assist you?"

"Leave," Aritz commanded with a sigh. "All of you. That is how."

The periphery guards looked at one another, pointing to their own chests and those of their comrades in search of a confirmatory glance.

"Yes, *all* of you," Aritz repeated. "Begone."

Without further dalliance, the guards dispersed, off to parts unknown, but parts that would surely end in a tankard of ale.

Aritz turned on his heel and faced Kamataa and her group, pointing a finger at the collection of wagons. "Move, witch."

Sha'a scoffed at the label, but bowed with great embellishment. "The witch is at your command." As she approached the wagons, Aritz took three long steps backward, the memory of her felling his lieutenant with no more than a touch clearly not forgotten.

Nor should you forget. Do not think to forget the witchcraft that has won your war for you, Aritz.

A few minutes of deliberation passed until Sha'a cleared her throat with pomp. "I believe this is the one you're looking for."

Kamataa walked over to where Sha'a indicated and smiled, finding her mark among the groaning crowd. "There you are." She whistled over to Vanta, waving her along as a means for additional confirmation. Mindful of the need against a quick death at the hands of her companions, Kamataa climbed into the wagon, burrowing into the mindless menagerie, kicking aside involuntarily reaching hands and drooling faces, and grabbed a woman by the arms, her eyes glossed and lifeless just as the others, but for far different circumstances. Kamataa hoisted the woman up to a seated position, heaving her up to her shoulders, and then hurled her over the side of the wagon. The woman met the ground with barely a protesting grunt.

Already making his way to the woman, Aritz asked, "And what makes her such a valid...'volunteer,' then?"

It was easy for Kamataa to surmise the woman was of the Stone Tribe, given the braid and the fading traces of yellow paint upon her face. Though she looked weathered, it seemed prematurely so, a lingering youth just barely glinting past the encroaching wrinkled and salt-and-pepper hair. Kamataa reached under the Stone woman's shirt and withdrew her pendant, the rune of Foresight carved into its medallion. *You looked ahead too far, didn't you? What a foolish woman you are. To know what is to come, right here, in your final moments.*

"Kama," Aritz prompted. "Who is she? To my eye, she seems no different from the rest of this lot."

"*Who* she is, that is of little consequence, I assure you. *What* she is, though, that is far more important. *Her* god still lives, its power still flowing through her veins. Come, look at this rune here." She kneeled beside the Stone Tribeswoman and grasped her pendant by the chain, running a thumb along the rune. "This marking, it is indicative of Foresight. I believe among yours, such a person is called a 'soothsayer,' is that right?"

With a dismissive scoff, Aritz said, "They are the invention of playwrights, fit only for the stage."

"Then it is but a shame you did not find her before the next great Acrarian play was penned. Trust that I know more than you on this matter, would you?"

"Hmph, fine. Continue."

Kamataa whistled and held out her hand, wiggling her fingers. Within moments, Vanta placed a clean blade in her palm, pristine in much the same manner as Aritz's once was before its temporary imbuement of Strength. She reached into her pocket and found the engraving needle, carefully cutting a swath into the steel in mimicry of the Foresight rune. "Hold her down, Vanta, if you would."

As Vanta did per command, placing her knees firmly upon the Stone woman's shoulders, Kamataa placed the tip of the blade along the woman's arms, slowly tracing a path, a red trail following in its wake. A steady stream dripped down, but the Futureseer voiced hardly a yelp of pain. Kamataa placed the blade's rune against the flowing stream of blood as she frowned at the Stone woman, shaking her head. *My Children have watched you for some time, if you are who I think you to be. I suppose it is thanks to you we were able to overrun the Stone Tribe at all. What a lasting legacy of leadership you will leave for the ashes of your people, "Chief."*

When satisfied at the crimson coverage of the rune, Kamataa offered the steel to Aritz. "Take it. Do you feel anything?"

Raising his brow, Aritz complied and held the blade, closing his eyes as though trying to *will* the Foresight from the rune into his hand. After a moment's silence, he shook his head. "No."

Kamataa held out her hand and cleared her throat, and the blade was back in her grasp. "Let's try something else, then." She twirled the steel into a reverse grip and *plunged* it into the meet of the woman's arm, the impact impeded by bone. The hilt wavered as the blade wobbled back and forth, more and more blood streaming from the wound. A disgusted grunt echoed behind Kamataa but she paid it no mind. She was more enthralled by the sudden pained breaths of the Stone woman, the glassy haze of her eyes beginning to dissipate.

Do not think ill of this. Do not think it a mercy, either. I have met more than enough would-be despots in my life to know you deserve this and more.

She heaved the blade from the meat of the false Chief's arm, blood more vigorously spurting from the wound as a writhing pain seized the woman. Kamataa ignored her wordless pleas and turned back to Aritz, whose expression had turned far more pallid than before. "Try it now," she said, holding the blade out to him, its sheen nearly vanished from the top half of it.

"Savior's breath, woman," Aritz hissed, taking a step back with aversion. "This is—"

"The price of progress," Kamataa finished. "Do not forget what I said before. You stand to benefit either way. Now, take the blade and tell me what you feel."

A notable tremor gripped Aritz's hand, but he did as requested, gripping the steel firmly but quickly shaking his head. "This will not work, Kama."

"It *will*," Kamataa asserted, eager to continue. "We just don't have enough. Sha'a." She turned to her comrade, who looked upon the proceedings with muted interest. "Did we take any spears along in the wagons?"

Sha'a nodded.

"Good. Fetch one." Kamataa stared at the Stone Tribeswoman, feeling a grave smile crawl across her lips. Sha'a nudged her arm with a spear of Lake Tribe make, the feel all too familiar to her. Slowly, she approached the Futureseer, drawing in a deep breath, and she thrust the spear into her arm with all her weight behind the strike, the steel sharp enough to slice all the way through bone. Enough force was put into the strike to send it through the other end of the woman's arm and into the ground below. With a chuckle rumbling in her throat, Kamataa rocked the spear back and forth, watching the woman writhe and scream with each motion, bone splintering and blood spurting, the grind of steel screeching in her ear, until at last there was a *pop* and the arm came loose, a shriek piercing the air, shrill and agonic. Even with Vanta holding the woman by her shoulders, Kamataa still had to place a boot on her chest to stabilize her.

She cupped her hands beneath the stump where the Stone woman's arm once was, the blood seeping and pulsing out of the wound and pooling into Kamataa's grasp. With it sloshing about, dripping through the slits in her fingers, she turned once more to Aritz and said, "Kneel."

"I will *not* kneel before one such as—"

"*Do you want this to work or not?*" Kamataa nearly screamed the words, a fervor in her voice. She had never known an exhilaration such as this before. *Ziia, if only you were still here for this. You would adore this.* "Kneel!"

Aritz flared his nostrils and ground his teeth, staring with anger in his eyes as the blood continued to drip from Kamataa's fingers. "To hell with it," he growled, and then kneeled.

"Lift your head up." Kamataa's breath grew more excited as Aritz complied. She licked her lips and approached the General, the shrieks of the Stone woman still piercing her ears. She held her hands above Aritz's face and parted them, the red pool raining upon him, meeting him with a deep splash. As he sputtered and spat out the droplets that landed in his mouth, Kamataa pressed her bloodied palms to his forehead, holding him in place, exuding rasped breaths as her heart pounded in her chest. "Do you feel it now?"

"God, *no!*" Aritz shouted, trying to force his way back to his feet but held firmly in place by her.

Kamataa laughed. "Then there's but one way left to us." She walked back to the Stone woman. "The Tribes take for granted what runs through them. The longer they feel it, the longer it is part of them. It needs to run through you just as it does for them." She took hold of the knife again, mounting herself against the woman's hips, her cries still unceasing, her voice nothing more than an inane babble. Cognition appeared to return to her eyes, widened with fear and panic, a fire dimming as she reached feebly up to Kamataa, but to no avail.

"Don't take this personally," Kamataa warned. She raised the blade high above her head and drove it down, planting it in the woman's chest. The cries and screams were suddenly choked back as the air was driven out of her. Kamataa's first instinct was to pull down on the blade, to carve open the abdomen. But something compelled her to withdraw the steel and bring it down again. And again. Memories flashed in her mind of tyrants and fools. Chief Azantt, the first to betray her. His screaming whelp who lived with the same garishness and disregard for the poor. The fool Chiefs Ruwexi and Tenrir agreeing to a false peace.

Sennalhat.

Each blow was cathartic. Reliving the fates of those who deserved worse, and preparing herself for the retribution appropriate of a kinslayer like Sennalhat. Blood coated the Stone woman's mouth by the time Kamataa emerged from her haze, her eyes glazed over once again as the life left her. Gritting her teeth, Kamataa drove the steel into her chest once more and slit it open as she had initially intended, reached inside, and found the woman's heart. She could still feel a weak pulse as she ripped it free of the chest cavity, cutting it loose from the large veins holding it in.

When she turned to Aritz, she could only imagine what sort of monster she appeared to be. Kamataa's chest was pounding, her head thumping just the same. She held the woman's heart in her hand, and there was a clear realization in Aritz's eyes of what was next to come.

"No," he said, shaking his head profusely.

"Open your mouth," Kamataa commanded.

"No!"

"Damn it, Aritz, do it!"

"I will not—"

Kamataa rushed him, sending a knee into his stomach as she gripped him by his auburn locks. His mouth burst open as he tried to catch his breath, and Kamataa held the warm heart above his lips and *squeezed*, feeling its contents burst in Aritz's mouth. The Acrarian General coughed and moaned in protest but Kamataa clamped his mouth shut, clasping his chin, forcing him to swallow the blood. Aritz gagged as the blood and viscera flowed down his throat, tears welling in his eyes, but Kamataa would not let him go. Not until it was all gone.

Once satisfied, she released him from her grip, his mouth coated in slick red, and he fell to the ground on all fours, heaving above the verdant green grass now stained in dark tones. The air was still, not even the distant drinking songs reaching them, and the only sound to Kamataa's ears was that of Aritz's hesitant, choked breaths.

The exhilaration began to fade as Kamataa's heartbeat quelled. She stood above Aritz, her hands heavy with the Stone woman's blood, an exhausted quiver now gripping her. "Well?" she prompted, Vanta and Sha'a filing in beside her. "Anything?"

Aritz continued to stare at the ground, seeming to expect a response of vomit, but found nothing. He slowly cast his glance toward the three Eclipseborn, horror visible in his eyes...but also uncertainty. For once, he was speechless for a reason beyond his own arrogance.

Taking a tentative step toward the General, Kamataa was fully aware of the state of her face and clothing, but wholly uncaring for it. *It was worth it.*

Aritz met her gaze and narrowed his eyes, silently turning to the south, to the Forest, and home beyond, and walked away.

Kamataa smiled.

He had seen horrors in his life before, but never anything like that.

Cin kneeled in the shadows cast by the first row of tents, his heart catching in his chest. The sheer storm of blood was one thing to witness. The brutality with which it rained was something else entirely.

The look upon Aritz's face was unlike any he had seen of the General's. For the first time, the disgust strewn upon his face was not borne of arrogance, but of fear. Of a man who had lost control.

And she who wrested the control from his grasp appeared all too satisfied with it. Kamataa's face and clothing matched the color of her disguised hair. With Sha'a and Vanta beside her, she stood in grave silence, the wind at their backs, watching Aritz as he traipsed further and further away from them. The Stone woman's shrieks had long since ceased as her soul departed to the join the lost, but still Cin could hear the shrill echoes deep in his mind. It sent a shiver to his very core.

How... he wondered, his hand covering his mouth in shock, his front teeth gnawing at his index finger. *How do you stand so? How do you manage to smile in the face of such brutality?* Cin was too stunned to move. He had hoped to find answers, but instead found only questions he did not expect to have.

Zarrow, he thought, hoping his forebear's presence would return. *Are we...are we no better? Was this what you wished to warn me of?*

He received no answer, instead looking to the skies, the sun shining brightly over the sordid scene, a cheerfulness ill-matching the atrocities cast by a wicked hand. There was some shred of hope that the Moon would admonish him once more, chastise him for following in the footsteps of one who had "blinded herself with the thought of revenge," as She said.

Minutes passed, and at last, Kamataa led her pack back to the main thoroughfare of the campground, the deceased woman's body left bloodied and mangled to rot. On unsteady feet, Cin rose and snuck over to the body, hovering over it, taking in her face frozen in the grip of shock and agony. He kneeled and closed her eyelids, hoping the gesture would provide at least a modicum of rest. He did not know this woman. He did not care to know. But no part of him felt she deserved such a torturous fate.

Cin's hands shook, and—for the first time in ages—he did not feel compelled to follow in Kamataa's wake. He knew not in whose footsteps to follow.

"...Zarrow?" he croaked, his voice weak. "Are you there?"

A moment's silence passed, and then the familiar sensation of the lost hovered above him. *"Yes, Cin?"* Zarrow's voice said, its cadence calm, and perhaps hopeful.

"How long did you have to live with failing to prevent the Pale Night?"

He heard a grumble, regret heavy in its tone. *"Far too long."*

"Do the...do their ghosts still haunt you now?"

"They haunt all of us, Cin, in forms we do not expect them to take." A pressure built upon Cin's shoulder, as though Zarrow was placing a hand on it. *"The souls of the lost are not all we carry with us."*

Cin stared for a long moment at the tortured woman, dread filling him. "Has the river carried me too far down this path? I fear I don't know where to row next."

"Are your hands no longer beset by desires for retribution? Or are they too preoccupied to row against the current?"

The wind howled at the question, strands of Cin's hair fluttering behind him. He did not quite know how to answer. All he could do was look at his hands, watch them shake at the implication. "Perhaps they still are. But...there may now be a different current for me to row against."

CHAPTER NINE

ATONEMENT

THE YEAR 1556 ANNO SALVATORIS
15 YEARS AFTER THE INVASION

The emergence of the City along the southern horizon was not one Sen had looked forward to with any great anticipation. From the moment she had first gazed upon it with Narva at her side, it had filled her with feelings in conflict with one another: dread and wonder, shock and mystification. Her first instinct had been to see it burn to the ground.

To return with such expedience as to act as the torch in hand, though, she could hardly have expected that. But such was the hand dealt upon the table. Such was the wild card played upon the board.

The Owl remained in its disguise, the hallowed form of Aritz a Mata maintaining a firm command at the front of its flock. The Illusionists in the group fashioned themselves in makeshift Invader guises, Sen among them covering herself in her disguise from her time carousing with the enemy. Even in knowing the truth of the matter, many of the Tribespeople stayed a cautious distance from the Owl and its impersonated soldiers, the memory too fresh upon their minds. It was not lost on Sen that Tez was trailing behind at a deliberate pace, though she could not say for certain if it was due to her diminished stamina or another matter entirely.

It had been an unceasing march through the Forest, the dense darkness having held no mysteries or anxieties in the wake of the massacre of the Wood Tribe. Whether any survivors remained atop the trees, it was not for

Sen to know or learn. The sight of Aritz a Mata—fake as it was—was in no uncertain terms enough of a deterrent against recourse.

Hours were all that separated them from setting foot in the City, to go where no Tribesperson had voluntarily and willingly gone en masse in a decade and a half. To lie upon the Red Fields, and the ghosts that threatened in their depths. To set foot upon land belonging to a people near to extinction, its final gasps breathed only in pits that had long since stripped them of their dignity and humanity.

Sen could not help but feel a flutter in her chest at the mere thought of it. Hesitation had checkered her march through the Forest. Far too many ghosts haunted its depths, and there were only more awaiting their arrival in the south. But in breathing air tinged not with the overwhelming aroma of pine, but the lingering and acrid stench of smoke, a fury and fervor to put to flame the auspices of the Invaders filled her, motivated her. Though she was concealed beneath the guise of a false Acrarian, Sen felt not the cause to hide. She felt only the desire to burn.

The choice is only ours to determine whether we wish to be the ash or the flame. It was Ziia who had imparted upon her those words in a vain justification of erasing in prevention of being erased in turn. Sen clenched her fist as tufts of black smoke billowed from the City's cylindrical silos breaking the skyline. *It was all too obvious who should have been the ash and who else the flame, and I'm no longer the fool who held the torch to the wrong pyre.*

The Owl held up its hand in command to stop. Sen was grateful for it. The fields to the immediate south of the Forest were a steep descent to sea level, and her knees were roaring in protest with each subsequent step. She could only imagine how others were feeling.

We REST FOR NOW, the Owl said, still mimicking Aritz's voice, though with its natural godly intonations still coming through. There was no exhaustion upon its face, though Sen would have been surprised if a divine entity had the capability of growing tired. THE DAY STAYS YOUNG STILL. WE NEED NOT OVEREXERT OURSELVES.

Sen dropped to a knee as the ground leveled off, her chest thumping. A gentle breeze danced along her neck, a welcomed caress as the emergence from the Forest brought with it the stiffer and warmer climes of the south.

It still perplexed her how there could be such a steep change in temperature when her homeland was only but a day's march away without stopping. She was ill-suited to the feeling of her clothes sticking to her skin.

When she looked up, the Owl remained a healthy distance away, hands folded behind its back, gaze affixed to the south where the smoke continued to waft high and obscure the view of what would have been a beautiful coastline. Grumblings and heavy breaths sounded behind her, though idle conversations remained sparse. The time for words had long since passed, and there was certainly nothing that could be said that may have brought levity to what was soon to come.

The Owl turned, the trails of its field jacket billowing about in a sudden gust of wind. The ghost of a smile creased its lips, enough to send a tremble through Sen's limbs. She felt Tawa's presence beside her, the man standing tall, matching gazes with the god. Trickles of sweat trailed down his face and arms, droplets landing near to Sen's hand. She was far too exhausted to flinch away.

"Almighty Owl," Tawa called, his voice sounding all too distant to Sen. "The City draws near. Should we not review our plan of attack?"

Sen nodded to herself. Tawa's phrasing gave her pause, the subtle reminder that, for the first time, the Tribes had the opportunity to go on the offensive when facing the Invaders, rather than falling back on the defensive.

With a contemplative glint in its eyes, the Owl narrowed the gap between it and Tawa, bearing every bit the false grandeur of Aritz a Mata in each step, even if the traces of warmth in its presence seemed entirely out of place, given the guise. NATURALLY, I SHALL LEAD THE FRONT. TO WEAR THE FACE OF A MAN SUCH AS ARITZ A MATA MEANS TO ASSERT SUCH PROFESSED IMPORTANCE. The proclamation was heeded with muted response. FOR MY ILLUSIONISTS, I ASK YOU TO REMAIN IN YOUR DISGUISES FOR A SMALL WHILE FURTHER. THE OWL PAUSED AND FLASHED A GAZE AT SEN, WORDLESS, THOUGH THE IMPLICATION WAS STATED WELL ENOUGH.

I am not an Illusionist in earnest, but at this point, it matters little, doesn't it?

FOR THOSE OF YOU NOT GRANTED MY BOON OF ILLUSION, the Owl continued, its tone suddenly somber, IT GIVES ME NO GREAT PLEASURE TO REQUEST YOU POSE AS PRISONERS, IF ONLY FOR THE SHORTEST OF

WHILES. I ASK, AS WE CONTINUE OUR MARCH, THAT YOU OFFER YOUR WEAPONRY TO THE RELEVANT PARTIES. AN ARMED PRISONER WOULD BE CAUSE ENOUGH FOR ALARM AND MISTRUST.

The plan made sense to Sen, though to play the role of slaver, false as it was, did little to instill warmth within her. She turned over her shoulder, watching as the non-Illusionists in the group obeyed the request without protest, the false Invaders clasping spears in one hand and slinging bows and quivers over their backs with the other.

The only reluctant face in the crowd seemed to be Tez's. Sen bit her lip as she watched her sister remain in stern silence, holding her spear in a tight grip, her eyes focused directly forward, though on what, Sen could not discern. Beside her, Ket was whispering something, perhaps words offered as a manner of convincing, but they spoke in too hushed a tone for Sen to hear. After some time, though, Tez did offer her spear to the Illusionist nearest to her, but she did not look happy about it.

THANK YOU, ALL, the Owl said, its more natural tones coming through more than the false Invader accent. UPON OUR ARRIVAL IN THE CITY, TIME SHALL BE OF THE ESSENCE. SENNALHAT. The god flashed its eyes on Sen.

With an unsteady gait, she rose to her feet. "Yes?"

YOU KNOW THE CONFINES OF THE CITY BETTER THAN ANY OF US. UPON MY SIGNAL, YOU SHALL FREE OUR CAPTURED BRETHREN FROM THEIR BONDAGE AND LEAD THE ASSAULT ON THE INVADERS' ARMORY. THE REST OF US SHALL DISPATCH THEIR SPARSE NUMBERS FROM THE STREETS UNTIL WE ARE READIED TO CAPTURE ARITZ'S SEAT OF POWER.

Sen drew a deep breath and nodded. Her hands shook at the implication of *herself* being in charge. *Will they heed my words? Will they willingly follow me?* The objections, she kept to herself, though. This was hardly the time for them. She felt a firm pat on her shoulder as she caught Tawa offering a comforting grin. Sen returned it in kind and looked behind her, seeing numerous others sharing with her that same expression. She closed her eyes, a thunder still echoing in her mind, but the cries were altogether distant, the pleas fading on the wind's breath, and inside, she could feel not the dread of what was yet to come, but instead the confidence—for the first time in a long time—to proceed with the backing of those behind her.

The Owl turned on its heel and returned its gaze to the south. TAKE A FEW MOMENTS MORE TO REST. WE SHALL AWAY AGAIN IN DUE TIME. I WILL LOOK FORWARD TO SEEING YOU ALL ON THE OTHER SIDE OF THIS.

Though its godly visage was masked, Sen could almost sense the Owl spreading its wings triumphantly.

Two guards stood at the ready as the City's entryway loomed ahead. As their gazes caught sight of who approached, they stood to attention, weaponry held taut at their sides, chins and chests puffed out, straight as an arrow, unmoving as though holding in all their breath.

The Owl felt amusement at the sight, but also pity. There was a difference between worship and fear. It was to the Owl's understanding that Aritz expected his people to worship him, but it was only through fear that he did so. A god need not be feared, but a false idol? Fear was their only means of control. And this City operated under the firm grasp of fear.

"Sir!" the two guards said as the Owl approached. One was a spindly young man, sweat-soaked hair clinging to his cheeks and forehead, the buttons of his uniform halfway unbuttoned in defense against the heat. The other guard was a woman probably no older than her counterpart, long dark hair tied back in a bun, her puffy cheeks colored red, her untucked shirt suggesting a more casual attentiveness to maintaining the safety of the City's borders.

The false Aritz looked upon the pair, ensuring there was displeasure strewn about its face. It folded its hands behind its back, glaring at the young man for a handful of uncomfortable moments, and then shifted attention to his partner. A gravely grumble sounded in its throat as beads of sweat formed and streamed with greater frequency. Fear was the weapon. Fear was the tool.

"S-S-Sir!" repeated the male guard, his lip quivering. "We...we did not expect you back for some time still!"

The language of these Invaders was always fascinating to the Owl. It was spoken with quite a different intonation than the shared tongue of the Tribes, a more melodious tone to the sequence of words, flowing from one to the other as though part of a poem or song. Such a beautiful tongue for such a violent people.

AND THEREFORE, MUST YOUR DUTIES BE IGNORED MERELY BECAUSE YOU DO NOT YET EXPECT MY RETURN? The language felt quite odd to speak, but the Owl had no difficulty in doing so.

The female guard shook her head profusely, stammering as the words failed to come to her at the speed she clearly wished. "No-no-no, sir! W-W-We take our d-duties seriously every day, I promise you!"

AND WHY ARE YOU NOT IN PROPER UNIFORM, THEN?

The male guard shot his eyes downward and dropped his rifle to the ground as he buttoned his shirt all the way, pools of sweat already darkening the heavy material of the fabric. Beside him, the woman held her rifle awkwardly in one hand as she rushed to tuck her shirt back in, though there was a notable spot she missed, a tuft still trailing out near her hip. The man fell to a knee as he picked his rifle back up, his hands shaking.

"Forgive us, General, sir!" he shouted, a pronounced waver in his voice. "Y-y-y-you...in your letter, you estimated there to be a few days still until your return, s-so we...we—"

The Owl loosed its best attempt at an angry growl, modeled after its observance of the Wolf and the Bear. Both guards fell to the ground in shock, eyes wide. A dark stream colored the legs of the woman's trousers. The god stared at them both, flaring its nostrils and shaking its head.

A letter was unexpected, but hardly a problem. The Owl knew they could be used to its advantage. DO YOU PLAN YOUR DEDICATION AND LOYALTY TO YOUR COUNTRYMEN AROUND MY COMINGS AND GOINGS?

"Of course not, sir!" the woman replied. "We...it's just..."

"It is only that your letter arrived last night, and here you are now!"

IS MY EARLY ARRIVAL AN INCONVENIENCE FOR YOU?

"Of course not!" they answered simultaneously.

"Please, forgive us!" added the man. Tears were welling in his eyes. "We have meant you no offense, sir!"

The Owl grumbled, its hands still folded behind its back. A sea breeze wafted before it, carrying with it an acrid smell of salt air mixed with foul smoke. It said nothing, allowing the uncomfortable moment to stretch longer and longer.

The female guard's lip quivered as she rose back to her feet. "General Aritz, sir, is there...is there anything we might do to return to your good graces?"

"RETURN TO MY GOOD GRACES?" It allowed its eyes to flare with anger. IS THAT *ALL* YOU WISH FOR?

"Sir, I apologize! Please! I meant only...I meant only to correct our errors!" She craned her head around the false Aritz's shoulder. "The...the soldiers. There are so few, and with many of the savage captives with them. Surely, we can...help?"

OUR NUMBERS ARE NOT SO INSIGNIFICANT. CIRCUMSTANCES NE-CESSITATED MY EXPEDIENT RETURN. The Owl turned and gestured toward the Tribespeople waiting for its command, in and out of disguise. I HAD NO NEED FOR ANY GREATER THAN THIS NUMBER TO HANDLE *THESE* PEOPLE.

The male guard rose back to attention, a cautious smile creasing his lips as he pushed his sweat-slicked hair out of his eyes. "Then surely, *we* can help! An extra pair of hands to bring the savages to heel!"

The Owl grumbled once again, though not for the sake of the face it donned. The term "savages" was warrant enough for it.

"And not to mention," the guardsman continued, gesturing toward the Owl's leg. "You are yourself without a proper weapon."

An instinct ran through the Owl to reach to its thigh, where Aritz would have typically holstered one of his pistols. YES, it said. I USED IT, AND THEN NO LONGER HAD A USE FOR IT.

"But, sir, surely, protection is use enough!" the female guard said, approaching with caution. She unholstered the pistol at her thigh and held it out toward the Owl. "Please, sir, take mine. If any of these savages were to attack, you should not be without proper armament."

The Owl sneered once more at the mention of the word, "savages," and took the weapon without any hesitation. The time was near at hand.

The male guard nodded to his counterpart and approached the Owl with the same, holding his own pistol out. "And mine, as well, sir." As the false

Aritz accepted receipt of the weapon, the guard looked over to the retinue of disguised Tribespeople, all waiting in stark silence. "Do we need to rearm everyone, sir? It is odd to me that many of them are holding the weapons of savages. To travel all this way without a proper weapon to deter them was quite dangerous." He gasped, his eyes flaring open, and walked back three paces. "Ah! Forgive my presumptuousness, sir! I do not mean to come across as questioning your—"

With a raise of the hand, the guard shut his mouth. YOU NEED NOT CONCERN. WE HAD ALL WE NEEDED TO MAKE IT THIS FAR, BUT WE SHALL INDEED HELP OURSELVES TO YOUR STORES.

Chuckling, the guardswoman flashed a tentative grin. "'Our' stores? Pardon, sir, but they are much more *yours* than they are—"

Two loud bangs rang out, a scream in the distance at the noise. Smoke puffed out in two bursts, and the audible thud of bodies hitting the ground was all the confirmation needed for the Owl to know it had hit its targets. As the smoke cleared, it saw blood spattered against the adjacent walls, dust wisping along in the sea breeze, and the first among many to feel the wrath of the "savages" come to reclaim their home.

Another scream rang out. Fear was the weapon. Fear was the tool.

The Owl did not need to turn its head to signal for its disciples to follow. They were already running past, two claiming the discarded rifles on the ground for themselves, and the City became a blur of dust and screams.

Fear had arrived.

With spear at the ready, Sen scurried past the Owl at full speed, already feeling a flare of Luck surging through her arms as she dispelled her Illusion. A bullet hissed by her ear, splintering the wooden wall behind her. She turned to her right, a plume of smoke signaling the source of the attack, and she ran low to the ground, spear leveled. The Invader guard pounced, panic and confusion strewn about his face, and swung the butt end of his weapon down, missing Sen as she slid around the strike, thrusting her spear into his chest and withdrawing it as she hurdled back to her feet in one swift motion.

Along the streets and pathways of the City, as far as she could see, ordinary citizens were retreating into their homes and other nearby buildings, fearful cries sounding in the air. From behind, numerous Tribespeople rushed around her with spears and bows at the ready, fanning out in all directions in search of their next foes. Some kept their Illusions up, others dispelled them. The response on the part of the Invaders was going to be the same, regardless.

Turning in place, Sen caught sight of the Owl, still guised as Aritz, not having moved far from the spot where he killed the two guards at the front gates. The Owl held out a hand, gesturing to Aritz's large manor—and the slave camp beside it—and nodded. Go now, it said in a commanding voice.

Sen needed no further convincing. Taking a deep breath, she pushed off her front foot and dashed ahead, kicking up dirt and dust with each step. Familiar surges alerted her to incoming attackers, the sound in the air deafening as gunfire threatened her from left and right. Threads from her shirt burst off her shoulder as a bullet skimmed across the thick material, knocking her off-balance as she rolled to the side. Planting her spear into the ground, she spun on her heel and lunged back the way she came, an Invader loading another shot but hardly in enough time. The steel of her spear opened him up by the stomach and sent him to his death.

Two more shots zipped by her, passing her on either side of her head, and Sen threw her spear forward, catching one guard by the throat and pinning her to the adjacent wall. Sen drew her hunter's knife from the sheath at her hip and sprinted at the second guard, who met the challenge and lurched forward with a rifle held in front of him. He pushed his hands forward, aiming a jab at Sen's face, but Sen ducked underneath the strike, slashing at his leg with the blade in a reverse grip, but coming just short. The full brunt of the guard's next strike came bearing down on her shoulders and Sen collapsed under its weight, grunting in pain as her knees buckled from beneath her.

A kick to the ribs sent her rolling, but it gave Sen enough leeway to return to her feet, adrenaline ridding her entirely of the pain, and rush ahead again. As another sensation surged through her arm, the guard's rifle failed him, the weapon backfiring, he dropped it to the ground, leaving him entirely defenseless. With all her weight behind her as she sprinted forward, Sen knocked the guard off his feet, the blade finding its way into his chest. Sen pried it loose from his body and sheathed it before doing the same to her spear, the unfortunate guard's throat bursting open as the weapon came loose.

Sen hissed in a jolt of pain, the stray kick reminding her of the cracked rib she suffered in the last battle, but she pressed on, Aritz's manor looming ahead. Various voices overlapped as she ran from street to street, the City roused into a cacophony of madness and violence. Her head already pounded from the noise, and the closer she brought herself to the grounds where the Tribespeople waited in captivity like animals, the greater the reminder of her failure when last she breached these gates.

She shuddered with each step. A soldier came into her field of view, unaware of her presence, and just as quickly met his end as his throat opened against a kiss of steel. Sen gripped her chest, clenching her eyes shut, muzzle flashes and plumes of smoke peppering her vision from behind her eyelids. The feeling of steel chains against her wrists and ankles, unable to do anything but watch and wait for the inevitable that never arrived for her. The hot splash of blood on her face as Kamataa and Hollow removed two guards of their brains, robbing her of a fulfilled promise.

We won't be long, now, Brin's voice echoed in her mind. *And we won't be apart, either. We'll see Father in the Otherworld soon. Together.*

And yet here I still am, Brin, she thought. *I'm sorry I couldn't yet join you. Just let me make this right before I do.*

Sen shouted as she set herself ahead in another sprint, spear leveled. Another unassuming and unprepared guard was run through before he even had a chance to blink. His partner, appearing bewildered at the unforeseen strike, could not ready himself in time and received a length of steel in the side of his neck. From around the next corner, a soldier swung their rifle like a club, knocking loose Sen's spear and sending her to the ground in a dusty heap. As Sen lay on the ground, she stared down the barrel of the rifle and heard the uncooperative click as the weapon jammed, Luck screaming through her body. She kicked at the soldier's ankle, knocking them off their feet, and grabbed at the rifle, pummeling the butt end into her assailant's face until nothing remained but a bloodied pulp.

Her back ached and her ankle had twisted in the fall, but Sen tossed the jammed rifle aside and picked her spear off the ground, the alleyways leading to the slave camp but a handful of paces away. Rasped breaths heaved her chest up and down as blood and sweat glistened against her skin in equal measure. The height of the manor loomed in her periphery and her vision tunneled to the path ahead, the chaotic chorus of the battleground that was once the City that was once the territory of the Haunted fading into the background like a distant memory.

Sen gripped the shaft of her spear tighter and tighter, her palms dampening with sweat and blood, and held it at the ready. She could hear a set of footsteps ahead, tentative by the sound of quick shuffling. She lowered herself to a crouch, shifting her grip to one hand as she reached behind her for the hilt of her hunter's blade. As her spear tip broke the plane, the click of a hammer cocking alerted her and she jumped forward, thrusting blindly and receiving the fortune of meeting her target, a young lad, probably not much older than Brin, slumped against the gate to the camp with his chest opened up.

She looked down at him, her nostrils flaring and her lips quivering. A sense of pity welled within at the sight, the guard's hapless eyes looking up at Sen with fearful innocence. He spoke something in the Invader tongue that she could not understand, but the intent was clear.

Help me. End my suffering.

For the briefest of moments, Sen considered it. Pain was evident on his face, his breath little more than a weak wheeze. She trailed her hand to the hilt of the hunter's knife, but as she looked back and forth between the dying guard and the horrors waiting beyond the gate, she stopped just short of drawing the steel. Instead, she kicked his rifle far out of reach and unholstered his pistol, throwing it just as far away. Though she spoke no words of her own, Sen felt her own intent was clear.

Go to hell.

A weak hand swatted at her boot as she pushed the gate open, doing little more than inconveniencing her with a stumble. Sen swatted the guard across the face with the back of her hand and rummaged through his pockets, thankful to find a key in its depths. Closing her eyes, she steeled herself and stepped forward, passing the threshold to the camp. An all-too-familiar stench assaulted her nostrils, the very same she suffered in the medical huts in the True Heart, of the mindless many left in the care of those who needed any distraction to busy their hands, like Tawa.

When Sen opened her eyes, it was an even worse sight than the previous time she was here. For all the groaning individuals without their wits during her first venture to the camp, there were just as many now strewn about the ground, freshly severed from their connection to the Bear or the Wolf, surrounded by those still within their own mental faculties but without the knowledge and wherewithal to handle it all. Owlsigns and young Tribespeople yet to have come of age were hunched together, fright seeming to have long since departed their gazes until all that remained was the stern grip of shock.

Sen's pulse quickened as she took those first hesitant steps forward, her chest heavy as she looked upon the sordid sight. She rose her arms high, wincing against the sharp pain in her ribs, but knew not what next to say. Despite the ongoing chaos in the City streets, there were no reactions on the part of the captured. *They've been through enough, seen enough. I wouldn't be surprised if they're hoping for the violence to be a release for them all.* She drew a shaking breath, bit at her lower lip, flinching in bursts at the roar of gunfire, trying her hardest to be as those before her: desensitized to it all. To not fear it. To be as a stone.

"People of the Tribes!" she shouted, hoping some measure of authority was coming through in her tone. "Please, listen to me! The noise you hear out there—" She extended her arm backward, pointing beyond the gate. "—is the cry for your freedom! We are taking back this City, this Land, and expelling the Invaders from their seat of power! The time is now! Join us!" Sweat trickled down Sen's forehead as she looked upon the despondent faces with heaving breaths.

Her words were met only with confused glances and mutterings.

She winced, took a half step forward. "Please, listen to me! Time is precious! We—"

"Why are we to believe you?" asked a young boy, too young to have been of age by the time of the Invaders' arrival. From his skin tone and manner of speech, Sen assumed him to be of the Arrow Tribe.

"Has there ever been an opportunity presented to you like this?" Sen responded, flaring her eyes open, flinching once again at a sudden burst of rifle fire. "We are led by the Owl itself! The gods are on our side!"

"The gods have abandoned us!" shouted another voice, female, but Sen could not find its source. "Look around! Look at the state of these people!"

Sen sucked in a sharp breath and did as requested, taking in once again the horrid sight of motionless—but still alive—bodies, companions and compatriots surrounding them as though in mourning, as far as the chains about their ankles would allow.

"I heard some saying they couldn't *feel* the gods anymore, and then they all collapsed and may as well be dead! How can you say the gods are on our side if they've abandoned us so?!"

"The gods haven't abandoned you! They've just—" Sen grunted and bit back a pang of pain, grasping her tender side, a throbbing heat radiating inside her.

A lull in the battleground outside only punctuated the words left unsaid. "They've just what?" questioned the female voice.

Sen clenched her eyes shut, the thundering wave of adept warriors collapsing in her mind all over again. She growled at another pulse of pain and said with gritted teeth, "They're dead. The Bear and the Wolf, they...they were felled by the Invaders."

Another protracted silence, though this was not in anticipation of a feared fate, but rather, a sullen disbelief that such a fate could have come to pass. Scattered voices whispered amongst each other, conversations overlapping, but the content was much the same to Sen's ears. Defeat. Resignation.

"Why should we bother?" lamented a voice loud enough for Sen to hear, a person from one of the northern Tribes. "If the gods can be killed, then what hope do we have?"

Sen stepped forward, a tear falling down her cheek. "There's something to fight for. Always." She patted her hand against her chest. "I've lost plenty, nearly gave up plenty of times more. But I'm still fighting. For those I've lost, for those I hope to see again one day. You all know well enough the horrible things these Invaders have done. But you also did not see how much worse it has gotten. They hold the north now. They breached the Forest. But if we take this City, we change the game with one move. For the first time, *we* put *them* on the defensive. But we need your help to do it." She reached into her pocket and pulled out the key she grabbed from the gate guard. "This Land is ours. Let's take it back. Just follow me, and I'll—"

"Why in the *hell* should we follow a damned Curseborn?"

Sucking in a breath, Sen turned up her nose and followed the source of the voice. She had heard the voice before, that same pitying, angry, disgruntled voice within these confines. She didn't need the assistance of a Boon to remember where. She remembered all too well where Brin had been chained in this camp. And the memory of who she left behind stung all the more when faced with the realization it was one of her own Tribe.

She sauntered toward a man with fading yellow paint adorning his face, streaking down his cheeks against the oppressive southern humidity. In the spot that had briefly housed Brin, Sen kneeled, looking the man square in the eyes. "That term may have been more of a dagger weeks and months ago, Dounhar, but I've learned that there exist Eclipseborn more than deserving of the label. But I am not one of them. I'm afraid your dagger's edge has been dulled."

Dounhar scoffed. "Well, pardon me, but I seem to have been left without a whetstone. Would you be so kind as to offer one, or would even *that* be too tall a task for you?" His eyes flared with anger.

Fiddling with the key in her hand, Sen sighed. "I am sorry, Dounhar. I had thought of my brother that I closed myself off to everyone else who was in need. And—"

"And it ended so well for him, too, I presume. I saw the two of you paraded about this camp by the soldiers. I heard the Deatharms. I hardly needed to wonder what had happened." Dounhar paused, flashing a sneer in Sen's direction. "But imagine my surprise at seeing *you* still alive. How *did* you survive?" Suspicion colored his gaze.

Sen balled her fist and closed her eyes, flashes of blood shading her vision. The ghosts of warfare danced in her mind, the echo of Kamataa's exuberant laughter as she delighted in the slaughter to which she was party in the Forest. Sen felt her lip quiver, her body shuddering at the memory. "I made a mistake," she muttered, her voice heavy with solemnity.

"Hmph," Dounhar grunted. "Only *one* mistake? I am curious to know what you call the numerous other unfortunate occurrences that have followed you in your wake. Is it all the will of the gods, then?"

"Shut up..." Sen muttered under her breath.

"What was that? Do you have something to say?"

Sen didn't remember slapping Dounhar across the face until she felt the heat radiating in her palm, the Stone Tribesman's cheek already a deep red. "Shut the fuck up. What is this?" she prompted. "Would you truly prefer to live in captivity by these Invaders instead of having your freedom granted by someone born under an Eclipse?" She rose to her feet, turned in place, taking in the faces of many who were apparently sold well enough by Dounhar's words, now averted their gazes in pronounced shame. "I have made mistakes. *Many* of them. Certainly more than most. But does that mean all of *you* are innocent of such shame? If you're all the image of perfection, do let me know how to be just like you—I would love to atone for my own mistakes. I was merely under the impression that putting the Invaders to rout was a good start, but apparently, I was mistaken."

Another grunt sounded at Sen's feet. She looked down to see Dounhar crossing his arms and averting his gaze. He pouted like a disciplined child.

"I would have thought," Sen chided, "you'd jump at the chance to see your brother again."

Dounhar looked up, frown still on his face. "Grafhar is here?" There was a shade of hope in his voice.

Sen threw her hand out at her side, shaking her head. "*Somewhere* out there, yeah. He's doing more good than *you* are, sitting on your ass and bemoaning who's come to free you. I can apologize properly later, but I've already wasted enough time arguing with you as it is." She opened her hand, glanced at the light glinting off the key. She threw it to the ground, just within reach of her disgruntled kinsman. "If you want to continue sitting in your own shit, be my guest. I'm going to go back to what I set out to do: liberating our people. The key is there if any of you care to join me."

She made for the gate, the slumped form of the deceased guard catching her attention. As she reached the threshold, she heard the metallic clink of a chain coming undone. She turned to see Dounhar rising to his feet, passing the key to the person nearest to him.

The Stone man scratched at his arm, wavering on unsteady feet, his legs likely weak from the inactivity. "If you'll forgive my arrogance, I would—"

"Look, I don't give a shit," Sen interrupted. She gripped tightly to her spear and headed through the gate. "We head for the armory to turn the Invaders' tools against them. Follow me there. And if you think you see Aritz a Mata...*don't* shoot him."

The cacophony returned as Sen skirted out of the alleyway and into the City proper. She could see Invader guards and soldiers in the distance pelted by arrows just as quickly as they launched a volley of their own design. Red puddles pooled in the walkways, trails of blood leading to limp bodies in their final death throes. The air was rife with the foul stench of gunpowder, and the breeze carried with it the smell of burning despite its benign intentions.

Sen turned her attention to the west, to where the soldiers' barracks lay, and the armory beyond. She heard uncertain footsteps behind her as freed Tribespeople slunk together, unimpeded by their chains again at long last. Sen did not tarry in her approach, but she did not seek to leave them behind, either; she knew well enough they were both defenseless and useless without armaments of their own.

Windows slammed shut as she scurried along the path, the remnants of the City's guard evidently drawn elsewhere by the Tribal assault. Sen could hear in faint tones fearful whispers and shrill whimpers rumbling in the nearby houses, even as gunfire continued to echo in the distance. An involuntary sneer stretched across her lips as she glanced through her periphery at the homes she passed, relishing in the Invaders experiencing the fear and uncertainty that had long befuddled the Tribes, but feeling that pervasive internal conflict, regardless. She put it out of her mind, waving her freed flock along, the armory drawing near.

A rush of guards filtered out of the barracks as the group drew near. Sen held tightly to her spear, crouching into a readied position, but they were all of them focused on the road ahead, rushing to the main thoroughfare of the

City, seemingly unaware of the enemies at close range. Sen breathed a sigh of relief; there were far too many for her to take on by herself, even with Luck on her side.

She turned toward the crowd behind her and put a finger to her lips. More and more former slaves had joined the entourage in varying states of distress, exhaustion, and disbelief. Even as gunfire continued to roar in the air, though, their composure remained measure, standing in stark contrast to the inadvertent jolts of panic Sen felt at the sound, even as they remained a persistent backdrop.

With one slow step in front of the other, Sen craned her head around the corner of the barrack walls, nodding to herself as she found the room empty. The next few barracks were much the same, their respective inhabitants either fighting for their lives or already bleeding their lives out. She could hear subtle noise emanating from the final door on the drag, but when she pressed her ear to the closed door, she heard not the panicked murmurings of the homes she passed by, but pleasurable moans and laughter. She rolled her eyes and moved on, hardly of the mind to interrupt the throes of passion if the mood was struck during these worst of times.

The armory loomed ahead, two guards manning the gate, one with eyes clenched shut. Sen turned her head over her shoulder and sharply hissed, "Get to cover!" Before it was clear whether the escapees heeded her warning, she pounced, her attention drawn first to the one with fearful eyes. He fumbled with his rifle and could not so much as aim his weapon before Sen drove her spear into his chest. Luck burst within her and a bullet zipped behind her head, the Invader guard—more attentive than his compatriot—shouting something in his native tongue and thrusting the butt end of the rifle toward Sen's stomach. Sen jumped back and seized the Deatharm with two hands, jabbing it forward with all her might. Something cracked loud enough in the man's chest for Sen to hear, and he fell to the ground, hacking up a lung. Before he had a chance to regain his bearings or his breath, Sen plunged her knife into his throat.

A shiver coursed through her as she sheathed her blade. Adrenaline had returned to her, but she was growing weary. She pressed her hand to the armory door, hesitating as she collected her breath, and heard the rhythmic thumping of approaching footsteps. A gentle hand fell upon her shoulder, startling her, but she had no supposition that an Invader was behind her. She hardly cared to know which of the escapees was of the mind to comfort her at this point.

Drawing a deep breath, Sen pushed the door open, and relief settled into her chest as she found the armory to be well-stocked. More than just "well-stocked," at that. There was still enough to equip a small army. And a small army was exactly what she had at her disposal.

She turned, extending an arm out at her side, wincing from the throbbing in her ribs. The escaped slaves filtered into the room, their eyes wide and aghast and intimidated all the same. Several approached the weaponry with pronounced caution, others far too fearful to even draw near. *I cannot fault them for that. I'm still hesitant to draw the very weapon that killed my father.* But those who did not fear the weapons, those who perhaps had grown desensitized to their destruction, took them without pause. In the eyes of some seemed to dwell a hope for vindication and retribution. Conversations overlapped as questions regarding the usage of the Deatharms sounded in Sen's ears, a handful of people confident enough in having watched several Invaders use them that they understood the concept well enough.

Sen stood in place, pistols and rifles locking and loading around her. She closed her eyes, separating herself from the stray discussions and distant violence, trying desperately to recall the days of peace that now felt so long ago, to when it seemed the worst thing to have happened to her was inebriating herself during her brother's Trial. To be able to return to that time—miserable though it was—she would have given anything. But those memories were nothing more than ghosts long since passed from this world. And now, here she stood, helping lead an armed revolt, when in those distant days of peace, her only experience with weaponry was when it was knocked out of her hands by Tez.

So much had changed.

When she opened her eyes again, the Tribespeople stood at attention in front of her, weapons at the ready, seeming to await her order.

Wincing at the sight, Sen took a step back and shook her head. "What the fuck are you looking at *me* for? Go!" She gestured to the door and the chaos beyond it, to the symphony of war raging in the streets, and the songbirds attuned to its chorus. "This City is yours. Take it!"

A cheer bellowed through the ranks, led by Dounhar, and, at once, pride and vigor seemed to return to their souls, hope restored for the first time in ages, and freedom so nearly within their grasp again. They ran out of the armory and dispersed in all directions, their war cries disappearing into the distance, joining the discordant melody of battle, eager to add their own notes to the orchestra.

Sen was slow to follow. She had done her part. Her chest still pounded, her hands still shaking. She massaged her palms, fresh and old blood staining her skin a dark red. Nausea and dizziness gripped her at once as she propped herself up against the length of her spear. With aches returning, she took deliberate steps forward, watching as plumes of smoke erupted from the new surprise assault, indiscriminate screams joining the cacophony. She traipsed through the streets, now littered with fresh death, regular citizenry mixed among them. Sen closed herself off to them, still unsure of the degree to which they were at fault, but remembering their homes were built off the backs and bones of those she had just freed.

The height of Aritz's manor caught her eye. It was time. The final breach. She was ready.

She pushed herself forward, biting back the pain in her ribs, allowing the newly armed to take care of any who stood in her way. An unceasing flare surged in her arms as bullets passed her by like insects, their sources dropping like flies just as quickly. Her head was in a fog from all the smoke, but the manor drew ever closer. She was almost there. Almost there. Almost—

A body flew past her, a shout not far behind, knocked back by some strong force. A burly guard stepped into view, perhaps the only guard of any real strength or prowess that Sen had seen since returning to the City. She thrust her spear forward, but the Invader halted his movement, gripping her weapon by the shaft, the wood splintering in his grasp.

"Ah, shit," Sen muttered.

She lurched forward as the spear was ripped from her hands, knocking her to the ground. So far as Sen could tell, this guard was weaponless, but he held no qualms at attempting to knock her lights out. A heavy fist fell toward her and Sen only barely dodged it, dipping under the blow on her knees, hissing in pain as the sudden stretch aggravated her ribs once again. She rolled away from a successive series of punches, coming back to her feet with her blade in hand. A blow caught her in the shoulder, cracking something in there, but slowing her assailant just enough to drive the steel into his wrist and slit it open. The guard said something, probably a curse, as a stream of red burst from his veins, and Sen seized the opportunity to drive the blade into his throat.

"*Nnngh*, godsdammit, Sen," said a familiar voice.

Sen pried the blade free from the guard's flesh as he fell to the ground and looked to her left, feeling great relief amidst the chaos. "It was only inevitable that one of these days, *I'd* save *your* ass, dear sister," she said with a chuckle. She walked over and extended a hand to Tez, pulling her older sister to her feet.

Tez's face was covered with sweat, her chest heaving out rasped and exhausted breaths. She didn't seem able to spare Sen the dignity of a smile. "You did it, then," she intoned plainly.

Sen listened to the roars of Deatharms, a subtle flinch to each shot. She nodded. "Where's the Owl? I think it's about time to finish this."

A dissatisfied grumble was Tez's initial response, but after a moment's hesitation, she pointed to the central square, to the shape of Aritz a Mata putting to rout several reluctant and surrendering Invader guards.

From this distance, Sen could even see a collective of the ordinary citizenry lining the ground in blood. "That's one way to turn his people against him," she muttered. Grasping for her sister's hand, Sen attempted to lead on toward the avian god. "Come on, we should tell it we're ready."

Tez pulled away from Sen's grip, a frustrated sigh escaping her lips.

Sen arched an eyebrow. "What is it?"

Gritting her teeth, Tez shook her head. "Sorry, it can be saved for later. Let's move."

Though inclined to press her forward, Sen knew her sister was right, and walked toward the square.

The Owl was already on its way to the manor, a host of armed Tribespeople filtering in behind. Sen grunted and followed in step, Tez beside her, both far too weathered and weary to proceed at full strength. She needn't have moved with the same veracity to know what happened the moment the god burst the doors to the manor open.

Screams echoed in concert with the roar of gunfire. Steel clattered and clanged, wood snapped and shattered. Footsteps echoed and intermingled with the desperate pleas of foreign tongues hoping for a possibility of peaceful surrender.

When Sen made it to the threshold, she saw blood spattered about the floor, numerous dead among them. Those who survived were prostrate on their knees, bowing as though in prayer, pleading for mercy as though from a vengeful god. *How little they know.*

The Owl ascended the stairway and held its arms to its side, beckoning the entourage of successful Tribespeople forward. And as they filtered into what Sen assumed to be Aritz's chambers, a flutter of disbelief filled her chest, even as the battle continued to rage on in the streets. They had done it.

She looked to Tez, raising an eyebrow, and knowing not what to do other than chuckle. "Well, shit. We won."

Tez remained expressionless as she held a morose glint in her eyes. Something in her looked displeased and unconvinced. But she nodded just the same, a forced half-smile creasing her lips. "Yes. We won."

CHAPTER TEN

REUNION

Even after a day had passed, Tez hated everything about this room, this manor, this City.

Her arms and legs still pulsating with pain and exhaustion from the previous day's battles, she sat in the corner of what she assumed to be Aritz's chambers, leaning forward with elbows propped up against her knees, her chin resting atop her linked fingers. A musty stench lingered in the room, the air stale from the nearby smoke, overtaking what would have been the pleasant aroma of the southern seas had these Invaders not destroyed it.

She glanced about the room, the pervasive sound of overlapping conversations long since having faded from her recognition. Those who passed for Tribal leadership were huddled around the table at the center of the room, which carried a map of their Land, the south penned in tremendous detail while everything to the north of the Forest was little more than scribbles and vague shapes. The initial sight of it had sent a wave of angry nausea surging through Tez. There were plenty to whom she owed her fury beyond merely the Invaders, though she knew not where to start and where to end.

When could this all have been stopped? Could it have been stopped? Can it still *be stopped?* She glared at the Owl, still guised under the mask of Aritz a Mata, standing calmly in front of a large, ornate desk, its attention placed upon the face of a Sun Tribeswoman with whom Tez was unfamiliar. Teeth gritting, the question of whether this was indeed a turning point for the Tribes was one she was certain the Owl had the answer to, but was perplexed as to why no one was voicing the query to begin with.

Instead, all anyone recognized was the inevitability of the Invaders' counterstrike. *The danger of scholars being forced to do the work of warriors and strategists.* Tawa stood across from the speaking Sun Tribeswoman, and beside him the Keeper Ko Zaran, but beyond them, Tez had not personally met any of the others present, and therefore was only trusting of Tawa and Zaran being worthy of speaking with any degree of authority.

For herself, she believed it necessary for her presence here, being the only remaining Bearsign, even if it was in name only. She could not argue against having a true warrior present, even if the peak of her fighting days were well past her already. The days of saving her sister's skin, rather than the other way around as was the case the day before, were over. She knew not how best to acclimate to that just yet.

Sen's absence was—for once—perplexing to her. Tez could hardly blame her for not wanting the responsibility of being part of this strategy meeting. Over these last days, such was only thrust upon her because of her ill-advised carousing with the Invaders a short time ago, and she seemed to have felt greater kinship to the Tribespeople she released from the slave camps, which was enough of a prompt to help them adjust to a life without chains—though she stressed to Tez that it was a way of atonement and repentance, even if she did not elaborate why. But the assault on the City hinged so prominently upon Sen's success in loosing those same people and staking claim to the Invaders' Deatharms; it only seemed right for her to continue to be part of this. *She's more than earned it, despite what she may think of her capabilities.*

"...and these Invader citizens fear us—and you—for now, but how much longer will that last?" the Sun Tribeswoman continued, Tez's focus returning to the conversation at hand. "They may be hiding in wait now, but someone will be brave sooner or later, no?"

The Owl leaned against the desk, arms folded beneath its breast. It let loose a deep sigh, something upon its face not quite approaching disinterest, but still not suggesting full engagement with the woman's concerns. WE NEEDN'T WORRY OF THE INVADERS' COMMON RABBLE. THEY WILL STAY THEIR HANDS. THERE WAS NO DOUBT IN ITS VOICE.

Tez grunted beneath her breath. *Little wonder why.*

Furthermore, it continued, if we had cause to fear them, they would have taken up arms against us while their guards remained afoot. Should any remain, their numbers are too fleeting to make any difference. Of greater import is the invaders' return in truth. How fare we in the preparations?

A marked silence fell over the room as another foul breeze danced in through the window, scattering loose papers about Aritz's desk and displacing light knickknacks resting along his bookshelves. A healthy coating of dust marked a boundary against which to place the books, and judging from the density, those books had not been withdrawn from the shelves in quite some time.

Tez watched Tawa purse his lips and shrug his shoulders, Ko Zaran run his fingers through his long tufts of hair. She shook her head, frustration barely veiled behind a deep sigh.

Ko Zaran cleared his throat, the elder Keeper folding his hands in front of his stomach. "We...we have seized their weaponry, Almighty Owl, but from there, we..."

"It should be of no surprise to you," Tawa interjected, leaning forward against Aritz's map, "that we are neither strategists nor tacticians. Though our strengths lie in wisdom, we have had little need to make use of it with the battlefield in mind. We—"

The Owl raised its hand, and Tawa immediately closed his mouth. The god walked about the gathering with deliberate motion, its gaze bearing less the man it was pretending to be and more the omniscient deity behind the mask—a disparity apparent to Tez as it bore down upon her. You need not worry of your tactical deficiencies, Tawandhar. Forgive me, my question did appear posed to the group, but my query was, in fact, directed at you, Tezalhat, it said, gesturing a hand to her.

Tez bit her lower lip, her arms crossed. "I was always more the fighter than the tactician," she muttered, displeasure coating her words. "You should know that better than most." She kept her eyes on the Owl, letting the implication speak volumes on its own.

Undeterred, the Owl shook its head. YOU GIVE YOURSELF FAR TOO LITTLE CREDIT, TEZALHAT, it posited, ignoring the tone of Tez's words. WHAT I *KNOW* IS YOU UNITED THE FRACTURED LAKE TRIBE UNDER ONE BANNER IN DEFENSE OF THE NORTH—AND SINGLE-HANDEDLY, I SHOULD ADD. IT WAS *YOUR* PLANNING THAT ALLOWED THE ROGUE FACTIONS OF THE STONE TRIBE TO BE QUELLED, FOR THE LAKE AND ARROW TRIBES TO UNITE IN THE FACE OF THE INVADER ADVANCE. *YOU* DID THAT, TEZALHAT.

"I did little more than flash a spear and tell a few idiots to stop trying to kill each other, which lasted just long enough for them to die beside one another." Tez shook her head, grimacing at the memory. "And even *that*, I can barely do now."

THEN, IN THE DAYS TO COME, WHAT PURPOSE DO YOU SEE YOUR-SELF—

"What purpose do *you* see me serving?" Tez interrupted. From the corner of her eye, she could see Tawa sucking in a hissed breath, Ko Zaran's eyes widening at the impudence of a mortal deeming their words more important than a god's. Tez hardly cared, and she rose to her feet, locking eyes with the Owl. "What I have to offer died the moment Aritz a Mata drove a blade through the Bear's skull. The part of me that would be useful to you is buried somewhere in the mountains."

The Owl shook its head. YOU PLAY A GREATER ROLE IN ALL THIS THAN YOU KNOW. THERE IS A LIFE BEYOND WAR AND BLOODSHED, ONE I AM CERTAIN YOU WILL SEE.

Tez scoffed, rolling her eyes. "Those days are long to come."

AND YET, THEY STILL SHALL. The Owl held its gaze on Tez, letting the words sink in.

With a frown, Tez considered the implication, averting her eyes from the god, catching sight of the stunned Owlsigns watching the argument with dismay. *What aren't you telling me?* she wondered. *And is it worth it to ask now?* She glanced at the door, and the contained chaos beyond it, and felt an inclination to leave.

Before the thought could even come to fruition, she felt the Owl's hand press against her shoulder as though it anticipated the opportunity. A chill ran through her at the touch, whether simple nerves or some sort of divine energy. She didn't even want to look at the deity.

LEAVE US, the Owl commanded, bearing more the persona of Aritz a Mata in the words than it did itself.

A stark moment of hesitation gripped the present Owlsigns before they obeyed, all bowing their heads with reverence and departing without either gripe or protest. Tawa eyed Tez as he walked past, offering her a nod and a knowing glance. Tez recognized it as the same expression he would share with her during their escapades amongst the Lake Tribe, but there was a shade of worry coloring his face just the same.

I've never known Tawa's worry to be unfounded, but...there is more here than he should feel burdened to realize.

The door closed with a heavy echo resounding through the now-hollow chamber. The wooden floorboards creaked underfoot as Tez shifted in place, her eyes wandering around the personal collection Aritz was amassing, on display against the shelving at the opposite end of the room. *For someone who has professed to hate our very being, he seems quite intent on displaying constant reminders of us.* Arrows, spear heads, Tribal adornments and masks—it was an unsettling amount he was keeping for himself.

TEZALHAT, the Owl's voice rumbled, its tone returning more to the god than the false Aritz.

Tez turned her head, her brow furrowing.

I HAVE DISPLEASED YOU, HAVE I NOT?

The bluntness of the remark was enough to give Tez a chuckle. "I was never one to think of the gods as being concerned over whether *they* have displeased *us.* I always assumed it to be the other way around."

WE THREE WERE NEVER DEVOID OF EMOTION. MY BRETHREN WERE SIMPLY MORE...RAW IN THE SHOWING.

"And I am sure they would delight in hearing that." Tez rolled her eyes.

SPEAK YOUR MIND, TEZALHAT, the Owl said, seemingly finished with Tez's biting jabs. IT IS NOT LOST UPON ME YOUR MISGIVINGS ABOUT THE PRESENT CIRCUMSTANCES.

Tez narrowed her eyes, flashing a sneer. She walked toward the map, scanning the intricacies and accuracies of the southern scribblings, down to the topography and coloring. Small circular pieces were placed to the side, creases in the map indicating the pieces' placements in recent days. Tez looked up, peering out the window to the cloud-covered sky and the ocean beyond, remembering stories from her youth of the sparkling waves of the south. Her disappointment at the current state of the sight was palpable. Her right hand found its way to the map figures, fiddling with one between her fingers.

"We have been little more than pieces on the board for you all this time, haven't we?" She did not turn her head.

The Owl said nothing in return.

She smiled to herself. "I thought so. When you know what is next to come, it ruins the suspense of it all. There needs to be some element of drama."

DO YOU TRULY TAKE ME FOR ONE TO PLAY WITH YOUR LIVES AS THOUGH YOU WERE TOYS?

"You have not quite denied it."

THEN I DENY IT.

Tez scoffed. "Of course you do. Let me ask you this." She placed two pieces on the map: one upon the City, and one to the immediate south of the Forest. "Do you bind yourself to what your Foresight tells you is but an inevitability?"

IT IS A COMMON MISCONCEPTION THAT THERE IS BUT ONE BRANCH DOWN WHICH THE STREAM FLOWS. I MERELY ACT IN WHAT WILL ULTI-MATELY PROVE TO BE THE BEST INTERESTS OF OUR PEOPLE.

"And I'm sure two-thirds of our people will thank you for it." Tez glanced at the northern edge of the map, woefully underfilled, the Heart little more than sporadic triangles in some vague indication of mountains. "I fear to ask my next question."

The floorboards creaked behind her once again as the Owl turned. ASK.

"How many more must perish before we've 'won?'"

The Owl said nothing.

Tez winced. "How many will lose their lives upon the Invaders' return?"

Again, nothing.

"How long will this game be played?" She turned her head. "How long will you be having *me* play your game?"

Silence.

Tez cast a long, sallow glance at the Owl before finally chuckling with bemusement. "You're one heartless bastard."

The Owl shook its head. I MERELY THINK AHEAD AS MANY MOVES AS ARE NECESSARY. TO SEE THE DOWNFALL OF THESE INVADERS, THE DOWNFALL OF ONE ARITZ A MATA—AND TO ENSURE YOU HAVE A ROLE BEFITTING YOU AS YOU NOW ARE. CALL THEM PIECES ON A BOARD IF YOU SO CHOOSE, BUT EACH MOVE REQUIRES AMPLE TIME AND PLANNING. AND TIME IS SOMETHING I POSSESS IN GREAT SUPPLY.

"Yes. *You* do." Tez frowned. "The same cannot be said for our people."

OUR PEOPLE WILL LIVE ON, the Owl said, its voice rife with confidence. I WILL SEE TO THAT. WHATEVER IT MAY TAKE.

"But what about those who are fighting today? Is this fair to them, to be pieces to move? Do you not owe it to them to be forthright in what you know is soon to come?"

DO YOU THINK THEM IGNORANT OF THE FACT, TEZALHAT?

Tez narrowed her eyes. "What?"

A smile parsed the Owl's lips as it shook its head morosely. THINK FOR A MOMENT, TEZALHAT. WOULD ANY OF MY DISCIPLES BE BLIND TO MY KNOWING OF WHAT IS TO COME? THEY KNOW I WOULD ACT ONLY IN THE BEST INTERESTS OF THE TRIBES. BUT CIRCUMSTANCES HAVE FORCED ME TO…"MOVE PIECES ON THE BOARD," AS YOU WOULD SAY. I AM CERTAIN MANY OF THEM ARE WELL AWARE OF THE ROLE THEY MUST NOW PLAY. I WISH ONLY THE SAME FOR YOU.

"I was content without having to play a role."

AND HAD YOU NOT FOUND YOURSELF TO BE PART OF THIS, WOULD YOU BE CONTENT AS YOU ARE IN YOUR CURRENT STATE?

The words were a dagger. Tez grimaced, averting her eyes, staring off to the side at the swirling speckles of dust dancing in the chamber.

The Owl walked past her, its hands folded behind its back, shoulders flexing as though it were stretching its hidden wings. It stopped at the window, fingers rapping along the bottom of the frame, gusts fluttering its auburn curls. EVEN IF THE BEAR WAS STILL WITH US, THERE WOULD HAVE COME A DAY WHEN CIRCUMSTANCES REQUIRED YOU TO WITHDRAW YOUR

SPEAR. YOU ARE MUCH MORE THAN JUST A WARRIOR, TEZALHAT. YOU ARE A LEADER, AND ONE THE TRIBES WILL NEED IN THE DAYS AND YEARS TO COME.

"Years..." Tez muttered, shaking her head. *What is to become of us all?*

Sunlight poured on the Owl's face as it cast a half-glance at Tez over its shoulder. A TIME OF BLOODSHED IS SOON TO COME. IT SHALL NOT BE LONG BEFORE THESE LANDS WILL RELIVE THEIR MONIKER OF THE RED FIELDS. YOU OUGHT TO SPEND THESE BLOODLESS MOMENTS WITH YOUR FAMILY WHILE YOU STILL CAN.

"Sen...she is otherwise preoccupied right now. I..."

The Owl shook its head. I DO NOT SPEAK ONLY OF YOUR SISTER, TEZALHAT.

Tez perked an eyebrow. "What do you mean?" she asked with hesitation.

A pause prolonged as the god turned on its heel, a halo of light from behind giving it an ethereal glow. WOULD YOU LIKE A MOMENT WITH YOUR BROTHER?

She hardly knew what to say. Her legs trembled as she propped herself against the table and the map upon it. Dimly aware of her agape mouth, Tez tried with desperation to come up with the necessary words, but nothing fell from her tongue. A dammed river threatened to break its levee, her eyes heavy with tears. With shaking hands, she reached for the pendant fastened around her neck, the very ornament responsible for salvaging her mind and wits. Brin's Memory pendant.

The show of emotion did not appear lost on the Owl. It cast its glance back to the window, its focus placed to the southwest. PAST THE BORDERS OF THIS CITY, THERE IS A...RATHER REPREHENSIBLE SITE. TO CALL IT A "MASS GRAVE" WOULD BE TO PLACE DISHONOR ON THOSE INTERRED THERE. HOWEVER... Its eyes bore into Tez, inquisitive and wise, the false face breaking once more. IF YOU WISH TO GIVE BRINNOLHAT THE HONOR HE DESERVES, NOW WOULD BE YOUR OPPORTUNITY.

Stammered words fumbled in Tez's mouth. "H-h-how?" she asked, still trembling with a strange combination of relief and regret and anger. "How do you know this?"

The Owl cleared its throat. I CAN FLY, TEZALHAT.

It was all Tez could do but laugh. She knew not why. "Would it count as blaspheming if I punched you in the nose?"

NONE HAVE TRIED. The god drew in closer, tufts of feathers following in its wake. FIND SENNALHAT. BRING HER WITH YOU. YOU DESERVE THIS CLOSURE WITH YOUR BROTHER, BUT SHE NEEDS IT MOST OF ALL. SHE WAS ROBBED OF THAT MOMENT.

Despite the temptation to rescue Brin from that mass grave, Tez wanted nothing more than to stay right here. *Just another piece for you to move, am I? Do I need to be elsewhere for the next stage of the plan to progress?*

But at the same time...she knew the Owl was right. She wanted a final moment with Brin, a *true* final moment, not the memory of him being stolen away by Aritz as her father was killed in front of her.

And for Sen? Tez could not begin to fathom the guilt her sister felt for Brin's death. To give him a proper rest...it was necessary. *And perhaps part of Sen will be able to rest, too.*

Eyeing the Owl once more, Tez contemplated what more she could say, but the lingering resentment was all that threatened to make its way to the fore. Rather than begin another circular argument, she simply turned on her heel and burst through the chamber door, leaving the Owl to its own devices, where it was best suited. As she descended the stairs, her boots clattering against the heavy stone steps, she felt a weight upon her that had little to do with the pervasive exhaustion. She wanted to crumble beneath it all, collapse on the floor, and let the surge of emotion grip her, after all she had been able to feel lately was anger and defeat.

But before she could find her way to the ornate manor doors and to the streets of the City, a cleared throat off to the left bid her to forget the need for tears, if only for a moment.

"Where are you off to now?" Ket asked, leaning against a carved stone pillar with their arms crossed. They had long since discarded their overcoat and were contentedly sporting a sleeveless tunic, sweat-stained even with the light materials to aid against it. Despite their attempts at aloofness, Ket looked miserable in this heat; a Lake Tribesperson was not at all suited to the warmer climes of the south.

With an earnest smile, Tez walked over, damning the weakness in her legs—again, for reasons other than the exhaustion—and gripped Ket in a warm embrace. There was respite in the act, a feeling of warmth and calm in standing against the horrors soon to come. She pressed her lips to Ket's.

Ket returned the gesture but was quick to push Tez off them, gesturing to their sweat-coated arms. "Not that I do not appreciate it, but, as you can see...the heat is not agreeing with me."

"Of course," Tez said with a chuckle, clasping the tips of Ket's fingers as she pulled away.

With eyes glancing at Aritz's chambers, Ket raised an eyebrow. "Ill tidings? You seemed in a rush to leave."

Tez sighed. "The thing about not being a proper Owlsign is I don't need to show any reverence to that god. I couldn't wait to get out of there."

Ket scoffed. "That's not it. Don't think I've forgotten the look in your eyes after each conference you departed with Tenazt and Yhaan. This is something beyond grievance and annoyance."

That was something Tez appreciated about Ket, even in the brief time she knew them. Always so observant, always cutting to the heart of the matter. She stared down at her feet, frowning at the ground, kicking at a pile of loose pebbles. "Do you know where Sen is?" she asked, the words near to breaking off in her throat.

Brushing away a droplet of sweat from their eyes, Ket grunted an inquisitive hum. "Last I knew, she was in that training yard off to the west with some of the freed folk." They raised an eyebrow. "Why do you ask?"

Tez's head dipped again, a single tear breaking free. She detailed the Owl's account of the mass grave to the southwest of the City, and Brin's body likely to be among the interred. Her voice shook in the telling in concert with her limbs until she found herself steadied by Ket's affirming and comforting touch.

"...so I think it best if she and I...you know, attend to that. While we have the chance." Tez drew a deep breath, trying to find her center.

Ket held Tez's hands up to their lips, kissing her fingertips with a gentle caress. "What else do you know, Tez? 'While we have the chance?'"

"I mean exactly what I said, Ket. Exactly what I feared."

The Lake healer was quiet a long moment, but asked, "When?"

Tez shook her head. "I didn't want to know. I don't want to be counting down the minutes. Especially if the Owl has some 'grand plan' for me to be part of."

Ket shook their head, but said nothing further. There didn't seem to be anything *to* say.

Tez rested her forehead against Ket's, inclining her eyes toward theirs. "There's no escaping what's soon to come. All the more reason to protect who and what we can before then." She pulled away from Ket, eyes focused on the door. "I'll return as soon as I can."

Though she took a quick step away, Tez was immediately tugged back toward Ket, her mouth finding theirs in a show of passion, Ket's fingers tangling in the knots of Tez's frayed braid, Tez's hands pressed against her partner's lower back.

As the heady breaths subsided and they drifted away from one another with fear and longing rife in each other's eyes, Ket flashed a slight smile coated with hesitance and uncertainty. "Come back to me in one piece, Tez of the Stone Tribe."

Tez returned the smile, heavy though it felt. "See you soon."

Despite the unsettling hush of silence, the City felt at peace. Sen felt soaked with dread, but for this span of moments, she was content with the quiet. The moments of quiet had felt too few and far between lately.

The late afternoon sun faintly glimmered behind a thick layer of smoke as she sat by her lonesome in the training yard. Several of the freed people had gathered here at her behest to acclimate themselves to the Invader weaponry, now that they had the opportunity to do so. Spearcraft was something of a second nature to the Tribes, regardless of divine affinities, but the immediate death promised by these weapons provided with it a mental hurdle many would have a challenge clearing.

It had been a long day, to be sure. Stale sweat coated her skin, the acrid stench of burned gunpowder lingering in her nostrils. A ringing in her ears buzzed from the echoing memories of thunderclaps as Deatharms sang to the skies. Her throat was raw, her voice hoarse, from a day of screaming instructions, offering motivation, and handing out the one piece of advice from Kamataa she deemed to be of value: "Imagine the target as someone you truly wish to be dead." It was crude, but effective. *From the reception I received in the slave camp, I wouldn't be surprised if some did not need to imagine at all.*

Sen hardly thought herself capable of this type of leadership. It had exhausted her to the bone. She was happy to sit far from the rest, and her being Eclipseborn seemed motivation enough for them to keep their distance, even if they *were* freed by her to begin with. *Superstitions and ignorance are hard things to break.*

Conversations barely carried over the space between, but Sen was content enough to watch and observe. Even in these tired, silent moments, Sen could not help but feel a ghost of a smile on her lips. Many of these people had been stripped of everything they had ever known. Others had never known anything *but* this life. But in the worst of hells, they had found—against all odds—some semblance of family. People with whom those moments of happiness—brief and rare though they assuredly were—could be shared. Genuine mirth was visible upon the faces of many for what Sen could only assume was the first time in ages. Laughter and comfort had been in short supply for a long time, but it did her heart well to see it return, however temporary the moment may have been. Those with the opportunity to reunite with their true families were rare, but those who could not, found solace just the same.

But those who *could* reunite did so with great enthusiasm. There were a handful of pairings Sen had witnessed over the last day, but none struck her quite so hard as seeing Grafhar and Dounhar back together. Even now, after hours upon hours, Sen could not keep her eyes off the two of them. She felt a degree of responsibility for Dounhar's capture—and his prolonged imprisonment. Though she had hardly known him prior to these circumstances, the only face she had known was one of anger. But to see him smile and laugh, and boisterously at that, did her heart good. And Grafhar, as well, a wide and exuberant grin stretched his sallow face, something Sen felt she had never seen before. They communicated exclusively through hand gestures that Sen was unfamiliar with, but the meanings were clearly not lost on them. It was a beautiful thing.

Brushing away a bead of sweat, Sen leaned back on her elbows, staring up at the obscured sky, cautious not to draw too deep of a breath for fear of the lingering smoke in the air. As she closed her eyes, she could still feel the pulsing aches in her cracked ribs, the traces of pains from the battles in the Heart. A thick layer of bandaging quelled them somewhat, but she knew not how much longer she could continue this. The weight of war was never something she wished to carry, and it was only a short while ago that the greatest thing she bore on her shoulders was her own drunken burdens. Those burdens only felt heavier now, sobered though they were.

Slow footsteps approached as she winced at another pang of pain. She opened an eye and looked to her left, feeling a hesitant grin stretch her lips as Tez came into view. With deliberate motion, Sen rose to her feet, grasping at her ribs as she stood. Her sister appeared flustered, worried. More than she had been of late. The grin on Sen's lips quickly faded to a frown. "Tez? Is something the matter?"

In prior times, the question likely would have resulted in some sort of snide remark. But Tez's eyes remained sunken and defeated, a pronounced and discernible sadness readily apparent on her face. Her spear dragged behind, her posture screaming all manner of exhaustion—even beyond the physical variety.

She sighed. "We don't have much time left, Sen," she muttered in a hushed tone, putting a hand to her sister's shoulder.

Sen blinked at Tez, the words uncertain on her tongue. The implication was more than clear. She flashed a glance to the freed folk. Laughter and jubilant conversations had only continued.

"Don't tell them."

"What?" Sen questioned, raising an eyebrow. "Should we not be as prepared as possible?"

Tez closed her eyes, drawing a deep sigh. "It doesn't matter. The Owl has...requested something else of us."

"Something...else?"

"I know where Brin's body is, Sen."

A chill immediately gripped Sen, flooding through her veins. She brought a hand to her mouth and suppressed a shocked squeak. When she shut her eyes, all she could see was the row of rifles facing her. All she could feel was the brief sensation of her fingertips caressing Brin's pendant, the haunting warmth of blood spattering against her. Her lips quivered as she whispered, "Where?"

"To the southwest. He…" Tez paused, grimacing. "He deserves greater dignity than what the Invaders gave him."

Sen flared her nostrils with anger. "What *Kamataa* gave him. What the Children of the Black Moon gave him."

Tez hummed a curious tone as she inclined an eyebrow. Her mouth remained shut, words entirely unnecessary. There was a hollowness at the forefront of Tez's gaze, but behind it lay a visible anger. One that flared into existence from the moment of Sen's correction.

The background laughter served only to irritate Sen now. She kneeled and lifted her spear from the ground, feeling its weight quiver in her trembling hands. If the Invaders were in truth shortly to arrive, she wanted to drag Kamataa's withered bones out of that crowd and give her the same treatment bequeathed upon her brother. No matter how many bullets it took.

But first things first.

"There's something I want you to see before we leave," she said, not yet turning to Tez.

"What is it?"

Sen shook her head. "Just follow me."

Conversations quelled as she began to walk away, the collective curiosity of the freed folk apparently piqued, but not enough to inquire after her. Sen heard only her sister's footsteps crunching in the ground behind her, and that was all she needed.

A gentle wind danced before her, carrying with it the foul stench of death and smoke. Now that she was keen to it, Sen realized the putrid smell of this City was not limited solely to the training grounds. The air was oppressive, a far cry from the pristine breaths she could take in the northern plains or while traversing the mountains.

Windows and doors slammed shut as she and Tez passed by, often preceded by a yelp or a curse in the Acrarian tongue. Sen growled as she traipsed down the street, spear wavering in her hand, pistol heavy on her thigh. No part of her wished to continue to wield this Invader tool of death, but she still had a bullet remaining, and a target to use it on. She just had to choose which one.

As she drew nearer to her destination, the ghosts of memories flooded back to her, roaring in her mind. She winced and grimaced as gurgled coughs echoed, thunder clapping over and over, the grip of death reaching out toward her but never quite far enough, a weathered voice positing that no one could be more fortunate than she to hold the power of Luck in her hands. Sen stopped in place and pressed her palm to her head, groaning as a pulse of pain coursed within. She gasped as she felt a hand on her shoulder, the auditory assault ceasing, relief setting in as she turned to see Tez watching over her with worried eyes.

Rolling her shoulder out of Tez's grip, Sen pressed on. "We're almost there."

The stench worsened as she drew nearer, the corner approaching, a stone wall peppered with holes the size of bullets, stains of red painting the wall in a horrid tapestry of death. She gulped and forced down an encroaching wave of nausea. The pathway twisted around the corner and Sen's legs buckled, some type of invisible force intent on beating her to the ground. The entirety of her body shook as the shadows crept in, the alleyway beyond the reach of the setting sun's light.

"Sen?" Tez questioned, hesitation rife in her voice. "What...what is this place?"

Everything remained as it was, despite the heavy rain of that night. The red-spattered chains remained affixed to the wall, the splashes of blood telling their story on one side just as the array of bullet holes told another tale of the adjacent spot. "This is where they killed Brin. And tried to kill me. Where Kamataa took Brin from me and called it an act of mercy, while in the same breath trying to convince me everything she had done was to my own benefit. This...this is where I lived while Brin died."

It was clear Tez had no idea what to say. Sen couldn't blame her. All she seemed able to do was grasp her sister's hand, squeezing it for all she could.

The alleyway held Sen in some sort of trance. She could not break away from it, even as the shadows lined up in a row of four, phantom smoke billowing from their extensions in sharp bursts. She winced at each instance, even when no sound screamed at her.

The memory of rain felt cold on her exposed skin. Her hands shook, her heart pounding. In an instant, she felt small, and the shadows all too powerful, giants awaiting to crush the anthill she stood upon. To be crushed underfoot would have felt a release. Many would have endured a great deal to see it happen to her. But no matter what, no matter how many times the opportunity presented itself, no matter who was caught in the crossfire, Sen remained standing—if only on an unsteady plane basked in darkness, with but one shred of fortune keeping her tethered to this realm.

"What has even been the purpose of my Luck, Tez?" Sen asked, her eyes still affixed to the dancing shadows, her voice little more than a hoarse whisper. "What has my Luck brought us? Look at everything that's happened. Father and Brin were killed. Narva was killed. Mother may very well be dead by now. Our gods have been slain. Our people have been brought to the brink of extinction. And I've had to watch everything. Where is the 'Luck' in that? Is it good fortune that I have been forced to live—by whatever intervention the Moon has placed upon me—while others die right beside me? I feel it, every time." She looked down at her arms. "This...sensation of Luck flowing through me. But what purpose does it serve if it only serves me?

"I...I have always rejected and resented being called 'Curseborn,' even if I have felt as such sometimes. But...I can't deny that Luck feels like a curse all its own. It's a false fortune to force me to live while everyone I know and love dies beside me. And if I am the last still to stand, am I truly Lucky, or am I just...cursed to live? It just feels like a power that amounts to...nothing. That *I* amount to nothing."

Tez squeezed Sen's hand tighter. "Your Luck is not a curse, Sen. It's a gift. A gift to allow you to keep going. Despite everything else that's happened. Everyone we've lost. It'll never be for nothing. We..." She trailed off, a frown visible in Sen's periphery. "We all have our roles to play, and whether we like them or not, we have to keep playing them until our story ends. And ours is not yet over, dear sister." She turned toward Sen, interlinking her fingers with her sister's. "Not by a long shot."

My role...? Sen hardly knew what that was. For too long, she felt her role was simply to be frozen by the hold these shadows had over her. Whenever respite was near, they would return. A darkness to fill a void that had been widening from the night her father was taken from this world, only to grow with each successive tragedy. Even in their silence, they deafened her, held her, stripped her bare, exposed the frailty so poorly concealed and laid to witness the darkness of her mere being.

But she needed her role to be something more. To no longer be strung as a puppet by these shadows. To be afraid, but to no longer fear. All it took was a single step.

Sen pried herself free from her sister's grip and stepped forward, into the path of the shadows' onslaught, before the crumpling visage of another shade on the wall. She faced the attacking shadows, her fists bunching, and glared at the tufts of smoke puffing upward, angry tears streaming down her cheeks. She puffed out her chin, her lip quivering, and wiped away the rivers from her eyes. Her heart pounded, matching the rhythm of the shadows' attacks, but she did not look away. She focused, frowned, growled, and shouted, the memory of the Deatharms' roars competing with her voice, growing louder as she did, battling for control, battling for supremacy, until one at last faded. One vanished. And one by one, the shadows dissipated, wisping away into the darkness cast by this haunted alleyway.

As she turned toward the wall of chains, the slumped shade began to vanish in turn, its form wafting away in the breeze. Sen reached out, but was quick to withdraw her hand. *No. Let it go. Stop letting the past haunt you.*

Tez filed in beside her, and though words were probably necessary, they were unfounded.

Sen reached for her sister's hand and felt comfort in its grasp again. She needed that comfort, and she had to assume Tez did as well. She pulled her along, one foot in front of the other, the chill of the alley and the ghosts in its depths giving way to the sweltering heat of the southern air. "Come on," Sen said. "Let's go find Brin."

The sun had begun to crest beyond the horizon when Sen and Tez arrived at the site of which the Owl spoke. An odor most foul was signal enough they had made it.

Cast beneath an overhanging rock formation, the ground dropped to a small shore where an inlet hoped to reach. The waves caressed and crashed against the adjacent rock walls, long since eroded from a lifetime of interaction with the gentle sea. It could have been a hidden paradise, a hideaway for those longing for a reprieve from their Tribe for one reason or another.

But a gentle sea could not hope to hide the inhumane horrors housed in the throat of the inlet. Perhaps it, too, was stunned at the sight, deigning not to approach, afraid to swallow the truth and hide it in much the same manner the Invaders did. The sea wished for the reminder, no matter how horrifying.

And yet, Sen could not understand the sea's hesitance to rid the world of this sight. One glance was enough for her to know she would always remember it. Splinters burrowed into her palm by the time she realized how tightly she had been gripping the shaft of her spear. Pain shot up her arm, fury in her breast, and though she had to look back and forth between it and Tez, just to confirm what she was witnessing was no trick of the eye, she knew in her heart that there was no way this could be any sort of illusion. This was real. This was a nightmare in the making.

Her knees dropped to the ground just as her spear did. Vomit threatened to travel up the length of her throat, but she could not avert her eyes. Absently plucking the splinters from her bleeding palm, Sen shuddered, aghast at what lay before her. Words would not come to her, no matter how hard she tried.

What was there to say, when witnessing the tomb the Invaders thought appropriate for her people? This pile of decaying flesh and discarded bones, left to rot and be consumed by the carrion feeders, removed from the Land in body just as they were in spirit, only barely hanging on to their last remnants of home. Bodies old and new were stacked high, consuming the length of the shore some thirty or forty feet below, in varying states of decomposition.

Birds plucked at bloated and decaying skin, flies and maggots emerging from all crevices in this haunted mountain of flesh.

"Gods," Sen gasped, as though invoking those also departed would be of any help.

Tez kneeled beside her, nostrils flaring in pronounced anger, her fingers clawing swaths into the dirt below. "I thought I might know what to expect from the Owl's words, but this..." She shook her head, a deep growl rumbling in her throat. "This is something beyond. This..."

"I would see them all thrown down here themselves," Sen snarled, her eyes clenching shut. "Aritz, Kamataa, the whole pack of them, strung out here to rot until the sea swallows them whole, never to spit them back out again. I'll make sure they—"

"Not now." Tez put a calming hand on Sen's shoulder. Her face was more somber than rageful. "I'd like nothing more than for that to come to pass, but we have someone dear to put to rest. And I think I've found him already."

Tez pointed, and Sen followed the trail cast by her finger. At the far end of the shore, placed atop the pile, faint remnants of yellow paint were discernible upon a face. Dark hair was frayed and strewn about, but the ghost of a braid was visible enough to catch Sen's eye. Her legs worked before her mind, and before she knew it, she approached the ridge leading down to the discarded deceased, the horrid smell assaulting her senses, but she didn't care. Natural handholds marked her path down the ridge, her eyes not breaking from the far side of the pile, until impatience struck, and she jumped the rest of the way down, the sand below softening the impact on her tired legs.

Sen's breath heaved as she scanned the back wall, finding no path that did not involve traipsing over a mountain of dead, and instead she sprinted to the left, wading along through ankle-deep water, splashes of salt peppering her skin, the coloring murky with shades of dark red still dancing in its waves. The opposite end of the coastline was hindered much the same by the volume of bodies, and she saw no other option but to climb once again.

She glanced at the ground, the bottom layer littered with bones, their hosts long since withered away. Drawing a deep breath, Sen closed her eyes and whispered, "Forgive me," and jumped atop the pile, her feet sinking into the divots separating one body from the other. Those she did touch were soft, sickening, and though she averted her eyes as much as possible, there was no avoiding taking in the sight of maggots nesting into all that remained.

When the mountain of flesh and bone was scaled, Sen's head shot from one direction to the next, a fervor in her heart. She passed from one body to the next, trying to readjust her bearings as she felt herself sinking into the decay. Flies swarmed near her, the sound deafening, panic holding her in place, until finally, her breath stopped, the world frozen, and all she could hear was the soft crash of waves accompanying the gentle whistle of the wind.

Brin's body was but paces away. His skin was bloated and red, blistering from the heat of the sun as flies attacked his festering skin. Holes bordered with a deep crimson littered his torn shirt, his head lolled but gripped in what looked to be a permanent state of pain.

"So, this is how Hollow 'took care of you,' isn't it, little brother?" Sen growled, angry tears streaming down her face. She slunk her arms beneath his legs and back and heaved him up, and on unsteady footing, she traipsed ahead, gaze affixed only to Tez, who had remained atop the ridge, watching her all the while. At least this way, she could ignore what snapped or squished beneath her feet with every step and pretend the rancid stench was of the Invaders' creation, rather than their destruction.

With all the adrenaline she could muster, Sen threw Brin's body atop her shoulder and reached for the handholds on the wall with her empty hand. Her legs protested with great vigor from Brin's added weight. Her chest pounded, forehead already glistening with sweat. Each new height brought with it a grunt, a growl, a scream, until finally Tez's hand was within reach, and when all her strength had left her, Sen felt herself be hoisted up, falling face-first into a bed of rich green, Brin's body rolling off of her and stopping a short reach away.

When Sen had time to catch her breath, she finally allowed herself to vomit.

Propped on all fours, Sen felt the cooling ocean breeze on her face as she stared into the pile of her own bile, spittle still streaming down her lower lip. The silent moment stretched on and on, the nausea in Sen's stomach continuing to make idle threats, and as she permitted herself to finally look up, at the remains of what was once her brother, Sen could not hold in the emotion any longer.

Uncontrollably, she began to weep, her body convulsing with every sob. Her words became an indecipherable series of babbles as Brin's contorted body lay before her, and just as quickly, she found herself smothered in her sister's embrace, Tez convulsing in much the same manner, rain falling from above from Tez's face onto Sen's. Finding the strength to push herself to her knees, Sen linked her arms around her sister and held tight, burrowing her face into Tez's shoulder. Her head pounded, her chest aflame, and every part of her shook. It was hardly the reunion she had hoped for when she set off to the south with Narva. She would have hoped these would have been tears of joy at rescuing her brother. But these tears—these angry, morose tears—could at least serve as the farewell Sen was stripped of having in the first place. And it was a farewell she could share, even if it should have been shared with many others.

She pried herself loose from Tez and wiped away the tears from her eyes, though the sweat from her arms did sting. Nodding to herself, she managed to whisper, "We should find as many stones as we can. Give him a proper burial."

The two sisters looked at one another and nodded, fanning out along the ridge, jostling loose the stone handholds from as far down as they could reach. It was hardly enough for a proper cairn. Sen journeyed about the surrounding area, the stones she found more small rocks than anything else, but in these flatlands, so far away from the wealthy supply of the Heart, she had to make do with what she had.

By the time she and Tez returned with their haul, night had fallen. The amount they procured would have been enough for a child of the Stone Tribe, but from someone of Brin's size, it would have offered little more than a single layer rather than a full cairn, but this was what they had to work with.

Sen picked up her spear and traced a rectangular outline for a plot to dig. "It'll have to be shallow, but we do what we must, yeah?"

Tez nodded and ripped loose the thick grass, prying it loose with her spear. It took what felt like ages for them to dig to the proper depth—a consequence of using their spears and not having shovels at their disposal—but after being satisfied with the work, they walked back to Brin's body, lifted him with equal effort, and placed him gently in the plot of dirt. Already, he looked much more comfortable.

The stones came next. One by one, they placed the larger rocks against his legs and worked their way up, the earth coming together like puzzle pieces, until the single layer was completed and Brin was submerged entirely beneath a bed of stone. The spare rocks were piled in a triangular manner, something that should have been much higher. If Sen had her way, she would have built a cairn for her brother the very height of the mountain ranges of the Heart itself.

But as the Moon shone overhead, Sen and Tez's faces dampened with sweat and tears alike, they linked their arms around each other's shoulders and glanced at what remained of their little brother.

"It's not right," Sen muttered. "No Stone Tribesperson should be buried by the sea. He should be next to Father. How else are they to reunite in the Otherworld?"

Tez shook her head. "They've already found each other. I'm sure of it. And, now…" She sighed, another well of tears streaming down her face. "Now, I'm sure he's much more at rest. This is a much better burial than what he was given before. After how long he's waited, I'm sure he will have the best sleep of his life in the Otherworld."

Sen gulped down another sob and nodded. "Yeah. I hope you're right. I…I just want to do good by him, Tez. I…I promised him. I promised him, and he died. He won't get to…he won't get to see how much I've tried to be better for him."

"He knows, Sen. He, and Father, and Mother, and Narva. They all know. And one day, when we're all reunited in the Otherworld…we'll all know." She gripped Sen more tightly at the shoulder. "*I* know it now. I'm proud of you, dear sister. All of us would be."

Clenching her eyes shut, Sen flashed a smile, pained though it was. "I hope she's right, Brin," she repeated herself in a whisper. "Everything I would do for you…I just hope you know. I'll see you one day soon, little brother. I love you." She loosened herself from Tez's hold and kneeled beside the makeshift cairn. She had one last rock to place; she placed her lips to it with a gentle kiss and placed it atop the pile.

As she rose back to her feet, Sen's mind flashed back to the scene of the slave camp, when she sought only to free Brin and no one else. The furious look on Dounhar's face upon her return instilled in her a desire to never make the same mistake again.

She glanced skyward, where the Moon shone brightly in full. *Please,* she thought in prayer. *Carry them away. They deserve better than to rot and fester in the sun.*

Sen expected nothing from the plea, but then the crashing of the waves grew in intensity. The flow of water through the inlet grew quicker, the tide roaring, seawater colliding with the rock walls, drawing enough force to reach Sen and Tez some hundred yards away.

The water flowed back and forth between the sea and the shore, and as Sen approached the ridge, she chanced a glance over and saw flesh and bones being dragged along to the mouth of the inlet, wherever in the great ocean beyond they may have been sent along to. She did not know how long she should stand in wait, but with each successive crash of water, more departed. It was hardly a burial fit for them, she was sure. But it was a *proper* burial.

She looked up to the Moon once more. "Thank you," she whispered.

The Moon did not respond.

Smiling to herself, Sen walked back over to Tez, who was placing her final stone upon Brin's cairn. She kneeled and wrapped her arm around her sister again, content to watch over their brother for as long as they needed to. It was a peaceful silence, the gentle crashing of waves providing a wonderful backdrop to the scene. All she wanted was to enjoy this moment forever. This final moment as a family.

But the peace was interrupted by the all-too-familiar thunderclap. Sen clenched her eyes shut. "No," she whispered. "Not yet. Not now."

Tez had kept her eyes pressed shut just the same. She slunk her head forward, placing a hand gently upon Brin's cairn. "I'm glad we could give you this moment, Brin. Pray forgive us for leaving already."

Sen jolted back to her feet, glancing one last time at Brin's grave with tears in her eyes. Fire already illuminated the eastern horizon. Screams echoed once more over the Red Fields. And all that remained of her people was again to come to heel under the weight of powder and steel.

The sisters picked up their spears and ran.

CHAPTER ELEVEN

An Aria for Songbirds

The Year 1556 Anno Salvatoris
15 Years After the Invasion

Chaos roared as loudly as the screams of the Deatharms.

Ket ran down the steps, spear clenched tightly in hand, the stench of fire and burning already cutting a swath in the air. A drove of people from all Tribes shoved past them, traveling the opposite direction. Panicked conversations and stern orders overlapped one another, difficult for Ket to keep track of everything that had been said.

Tawandhar stood at the base of the stairs, shouting above the din and directing people where to position themselves.

He appears a Chief in all but title, Ket could not help but observe.

"You three! Upstairs, covering fire!" Tawandhar screamed, pointing at a trio of Sun Tribespeople running past. "You and you, outside! Halt their advance! Zaran!" He spun around, facing the elder Keeper. "Gather every one of your kin you trust with your life and meet me in the large chamber! We will *not* allow them to take the Owl!" He was growing red in the face. "If any of you came into possession of a Deatharm, now is the time to find a window and use it! The rest of you, to the streets! Stop the Invaders at all costs!"

The crowd dispersed in all directions, Ket nearly knocked off their feet before reaching the bottom of the stairs. Tawandhar pushed past them, his chest heaving, anger and fear flaring in his eyes in equal measure, weaponry at the ready for whenever he needed it. The door to Aritz's chamber, where the Owl still remained, swung open, slamming against the interior walls, sending a tremor through the manor. In faint tones, Ket could hear a loud discussion between Tawandhar and the Owl, but nothing discernible over the cacophony.

Their heart pounded as their halted steps became a sprint in step with those around them. Dread held them in its grip, Tez's words from earlier heavy upon their mind. As the door drew closer, Ket feared what waited on the other side, heralded by the chorus of screams and hellfire and thunderclaps. Deep down, they knew. But they would not flee.

It was not in their blood as a member of the Lake Tribe to flee from a fight.

The doors burst open, and just as quickly, the front line of Tribespeople fell in a heap, blood erupting from the group's chests. Some managed to stand back up, ignoring the pain, ignoring the encroaching death, blood cascading down their bodies. Two made it past the threshold, half-sprinting and half-limping, fashioning their best war cries, weakened though they were.

As the roar of Deatharms echoed from inside—those in possession of the Invader weaponry having already taken their positions upstairs—Ket awaited in a bottlenecked formation, droves trying to force their way out the doors and into the field of battle. To their left, some opted to break windows and jump through, forgoing the wait and joining the fray. For their part, Ket was sandwiched between too many to go any direction but forward, too many heads in the way for them to see what they already knew awaited.

They closed their eyes, one foot put in front of the next, falling into a rhythm in step with everyone around them. Droplets of a warm rain spattered against their face from some rows in front of them. Their heart kept pounding, pounding, pounding, eager to fight, eager to defend, eager to live. An image of Tez flashed in their mind, her last words to them repeating over and over.

See you soon.

Ket chuckled to themself. *It may very well be in the Otherworld, Tez of the Stone Tribe. But I* will *see you soon. Thank you for everything.*

A round of screams and war cries sounded in Ket's ears, and they knew their time had come. The row before them dispersed, fanning out to encircle the Invader formation. Following to the left, Ket eyed the same positioning with which the Invaders had fought in the Stone Tribe village and the Heart. It was predictable, exploitable. But there was a ferocity in their approach that Ket had not seen in those previous encounters. There was an anger in their motions, erratic and reactive. The front lines of the Invader host did not remain in place, instead seeking out their foe rather than felling them from afar.

This was good. This would make them sloppy.

Ket hurdled over a pile of fallen comrades and kept low, spear held out at their side in mimicry of a Lake Tribe stance they had seen time and again growing up while those fools raced one another to their deaths atop the Lake of Bones. But as bullets passed them overhead, Ket felt the stance to be useful, even as their balance was weighted to one side. They gritted their teeth, growled as an Invader came into their purview, and lunged forward, opening the stomach of one who was hardly paying attention to their approach. Warm blood erupted onto their legs as they pulled their spear back.

Lake and Stone Tribespeople surrounded them, forming a wall between Ket and the Invaders. Though there had only been one encounter, they were grateful for it. Already was their breath scarce.

The wall pushed forward, only to be pushed back, smoke billowing over their heads, blood bursting from their backs. Ket felt a graze of pain on their shoulder, sucking in a sharp breath, their spear hand already growing numb. Switching hands, they jabbed forward, filling the gap in the wall that had just fallen, catching a man in the groin, opening him up for a comrade's blade to the face.

More fighters filed in behind Ket, pushing them forward into the fray, providing no other option but forward. Spears lunged past them with haphazard technique, thrusts engaged with little regard for skill, hoping only to catch an enemy on the other side. Though, they were hardly one to talk, resorting only to mimicry of techniques they had seen but had never employed.

But blood fell just the same—from both Tribespeople and the Invaders. Ket felt their arm slicken already, and they could not tell how much of it was Invader blood and how much of it was from the wound in their shoulder. But each throb of pain was a good thing. It proved to them they were still alive. It proved to them they could still fight.

Difficult was it to determine if they were making any progress alongside her comrades. Ket felt as though they had remained in the same spot for quite some time, unsure if their feet had even moved, save to reposition for their next forward strike. They couldn't tell if the uneven footing below indicated a new body to hurdle or if their exhaustion was already setting in. But they had had not taken any steps backward—of that, they were certain. If anything, it was easy to take that as a good sign.

Grunts of pain sounded next to Ket as comrades collapsed, bullets finding home in the chest or neck. The crowd was encroaching over them, blood was spattering from every which direction, the roar of Deatharms covering the air as the moon shone brightly overhead in the night sky. Ket shook in place, the thrust of their spear becoming more a visceral reaction to everything around them than an instinct to survive. Gravel settled into their throat as they growled and grunted with each strike, the pain in their shoulder starting to throb with growing intensity. There was a feeling of forward momentum, the jolt in their arm at finding a true strike a source of hopefulness, and Ket watched as their comrades pressed the advantage, Invaders falling in droves with fear glinting in their eyes in the moonlight.

Blood splashed against Ket's arm, a Stone Tribesman crashing into them, nearly knocking them off their feet. Planting their spear in the ground for support, Ket froze, seeing an entry wound in the side of the man's head. The *side*. Their breath caught in their chest, gaze flaring to the front, where the Invader offensive had grown weaker. Ket shook their head, disbelief settling in, but Tez's warning playing over and over in their memory. *Exactly what I feared.*

Slowly, Ket looked to their left, and out from the dark of night emerged a host of charging Invaders, Deatharms drawn, smoke billowing from spent shots, comrades caught unawares as their skulls and necks were opened wide for all to see. "Shit!" they screamed, pointing their spear at the new arrivals. "Move, move!"

Those around them were slow to respond, seemingly confused over the source of Ket's pleas. Ket desperately attempted to shove their nearest neighbors along, but they fell before Ket could so much as grasp a shoulder. Shouldering past the fallen, they held tight to someone's shirtsleeve—who, precisely, it was irrelevant for them to know—and charged, body low and spear held wide. Despite the uproar of new Deatharms, they could hear enough footsteps clattering from behind to know their warnings had some effect.

The gap narrowed as the Invaders lined up their shots against the encroaching Tribespeople. Ket ground their teeth, the wind rippling by their ear as a bullet dropped someone immediately behind them. There was no time to stop and mourn. They couldn't stop. To stop was to die. To stop was to flee. This was a small group. Ket could stand up to them. They could fight.

Twenty paces separated them from the Invaders. Fifteen paces. Ten. Their right arm trembled, blood coating their bare arm down to the elbow. Screamed gasps sounded from behind. Ket reached behind for the hilt of their hunter's knife. Five paces. They stared an Invader square in the eyes, a visceral glare reciprocated with malice. A sickening smile creased the Invader's face, visible even in the dim light. Ket growled, pressed off their front leg, hurdled into the air, their blade half-drawn as the Invader pulled up their Deatharm and ran to the side.

A mighty force knocked the wind out of Ket, sending them flying off to the right, the blade loosed from their grip and ending up somewhere they could only guess. The ground greeted them with an unforgiving jolt. They coughed and hacked as dust kicked up around them, spear still mercifully in their grip. The world spun as Ket rose back to unsteady feet, slapping their head to restore some sense of clarity, even as their shoulder wound flared with greater anger than before. An alleyway greeted them, a charming stench of piss and shit fluttering through the air, as a beast of a man slowly approached with a sinister smile upon his face. His field uniform was stained a deep red such to the point it appeared to have been dyed the color to begin with, if only his neck and face were not spattered with much the same. A long Deatharm was propped against his shoulder, and beyond sight of him, Ket could see another new host of Invaders filtering out from the alley across the way.

With pain surging in their side as they stood up straight, Ket breathed with fury and fright, hand trembling, legs quivering. There was no way out but through, and this Invader seemed in no hurry to press the issue, laughing all the while. Tears streamed down Ket's face, accepting their fate. "See you soon, Tez of the Stone Tribe," they whispered, and pushed off their back foot, charging at the mad brute before them. As much as they could muster, a scream grated against Ket's throat, raw and untamed, and they lunged forward, the spear coming up short, and the Invader grabbed hold of it, pulling Ket toward him and ripping the weapon free of their grasp.

Ket had only a moment to recognize what approached before the brunt of the Invader's Deatharm struck them on the side of the head, sending them careening face first into the nearby wall. Wood and stone crushed their nose, and already the foul taste of blood coated Ket's tongue. They spat out a tooth, the world a blur, and as they prepared to flash a glare of pure anger and defiance at the Invader, the weight of everything crashed into their face once more.

Everything went black.

The opportunity presented itself, and Ko Seln was hardly one to back down. He lunged forward, every ounce of anger he could summon in the strike, and pierced the burly Invader through the back and out of the chest. Part of him wondered if even that would be enough to fell the bastard, but he was relieved to see the man fall as he withdrew his spear. Seln spat at him as he lay dying. "I wouldn't normally stoop to that, but you're worth neither the honor nor dignity."

Though sparing even a moment was hardly a recommendation, he offered just that—a moment—in recognition of the Lake warrior in the alley. He couldn't tell if they still lived; all he could say for certain was their face had been savaged. It was hard to tell past the blood and bone. He shook his head. *Filthy bastards.* He spat again.

Seln recognized it as a trap the moment the Tribes split in half. He had been torn on whether to stay with the defense of the manor or to scurry after those charging to their deaths, but he ultimately chose the latter, for reasons beyond his own understanding. There was no backing away from it now.

A gargled shout alerted him to a present danger, and he ducked beneath the arc of a Deatharm swung with enough force to take his head off. He rolled on the ground, taking the Invader out by the knees, sending him hurtling to the earth. The Invader's weapon fell loose on impact, and Seln grabbed it before his assailant could react. He stabbed his spear downward, planting it in the soldier's back.

The Deatharm was far weightier than he expected, but the power he felt in it as he fired a shot into the throng of approaching Invaders was nothing short of exhilarating. He moved to fire again, but nothing happened. He shook his head. "Pointless."

A strong lad filed in beside Seln, gashes coating his exposed forearm, strands of dark hair adhering to a sweat-soaked face. Before Seln could offer so much as a nod of greeting, the lad launched his spear at the adjacent alleyway, taking an Invader before they even had the opportunity to breach.

"Well struck, Ko Bhrandohn," he spoke plainly, wanting not to draw attention to his suddenly disarmed state. He had only just recently passed his Trial and been afforded the Keeper title of Ko, and may have been a little headstrong about it. But he couldn't deny the lad's spirit as he charged ahead, side blade at the ready, evading the volley of Deatharms with ease before retreating into the alleyway with spear retrieved. *Never much for words, that one.*

A moment's hesitation gripped both sides as Ko Seln itched to lurch forward. The Invaders' front line readied their weapons in a slow draw, the next wave of Tribespeople pressing their own offensive. Seln grumbled beneath his breath but followed nonetheless, headlong into the mouth of the beast. When the clap of thunder announced the next volley, he flinched, but he felt relief at still finding the strength to move. The gap closed, the spear hungered.

And arrows rained from the sky. A smile creased Ko Seln's lips as rows of Invaders collapsed, throats and heads and shoulders punctured with vicious quills. Immediate disarray seemed the result as the Invaders fell out of formation. *Thank the gods.* A jolt of energy surged through Seln at the sight, as appeared the case with many of his comrades-in-arms, and he sprinted atop the dying Invaders, slashing and jabbing and lunging with every ounce of strength in his body. Weaponry not readied, the Invaders took to swinging their Deatharms like clubs, just as they had during the battles in the True Heart. A heavy blow knocked him off-balance, sending his next strike to the side, puncturing only a soldier's arm rather than his chest. The momentum sent Seln rolling, but he was quick to find his feet again. *I had to drag Arsah's drunk ass out of my tavern every night for years. You think* that *will slow me down?!*

With a snarl, Seln shot forward again, meeting a challenger all too eager for the auspices of a melee. The soldier knocked the spear aside with a swing of his long Deatharm and rushed Seln, all the weight of it carrying the Keeper off his feet and through the door of the adjacent building. Wood cracked and splintered from the impact and the two men went rolling, the spear dislodged from Seln's grip.

His momentum sent him into some sort of counter or shelf, ceasing only when the side of his head bashed up against it. He grunted in pain but could not tarry; the bellow of the attacking Invader immediately drew his attention. Seln scurried to his left in a half-dive, half-roll as the Invader brought down the butt end of his weapon like a hammer, missing Seln's head by inches. A successive swing soared above Seln as he rose back to his feet, reaching behind for his hunter's knife. The steel scraped free, and he jumped forward, blade in a reverse grip, and plunged his fist downward, stopped only by the strength of his opponent's arms.

The soldier's musculature was winning out, even as Seln pressed the blade down with all his strength. His hands shook with the effort, every inch of him straining in the attempt. The Invader sent a knee into Seln's gut, spittle flying from the Keeper's mouth, and the steel was wrenched free of his grip. Dropping the Deatharm, the soldier spun on his heel and readjusted his grip. Seln ducked low and rushed forward, tackling the enemy by the hip and knocking him into the wall, the blade instantly coming free from the impact.

Before the soldier could react, Seln punched him in the face once, twice, thrice, wincing from each strike, his knuckles bleeding just as they drew blood from the Invader's nose. Despite his clear daze, the Invader brought his palm up and shoved it into Seln's face, fingers feeling for the Keeper's eyes. Dirty nails scratched at his eyelids and Seln hissed with pain while continuing to rain down punches on the soldier's face.

Fury drove Seln's punches as the man's fingers began to dig. The Keeper pulled his head away, spots filling his vision, his blows growing erratic. Face bloodied, the soldier swatted at Seln, both men wearied from the intense struggle. Seln aimed a right hook but sailed it high, his legs suddenly lifted off the ground as the Invader wrapped his arms around his hip.

The feeling of weightlessness was fleeting when gravity returned and introduced Seln's back to the hard counter, glass shattering underneath him. He felt something bite into him, sucking in a pained gasp.

The Invader rasped a ragged, bloodied breath as he stepped away, the scraping of wood all the indication Seln needed that he had picked up his Deatharm. Seln had hardly the energy to move. Warmth flooded his backside as he lay amidst this field of broken glass. The smells, the views, they reminded him so much of home, of his tavern.

And when he focused his eyes, not on the death encroaching upon him, but the environs where he would welcome it, he found it was not just the remembrance of home; it *was* home. A tavern. *The gods truly* do *have a twisted sense of humor. I'm to die in a tavern, am I?* He chuckled, catching the Invader's confused expression as he reached below the counter, flashing his teeth as the neck of a bottle found its way into his grasp. The Invader raised the Deatharm high, ready to smash the Keeper's face in with it.

Seln swung his arm, the bottle whipping at the soldier's face, shattering into pieces, some sort of foul piss liquid spilling everywhere. The Deatharm dropped again, and the Invader shrieked in pain. Seln sucked in a breath as he sat himself upright, his spotted vision allowing him to see the glass shards embedded in his assailant's face, his left eye completely sliced.

"Heh, heh, eye for an eye, is it?" Seln groaned, voice grating against his raw throat. He picked up the Deatharm, pain gripping him as he bent down, hefting its weight in his hands, the Invader far too preoccupied with his searing pain to pay any attention to him. Ignoring every pang of pain ripping his back open, Ko Seln swung the weapon into the Invader's face, plunging the glass shards ever deeper, the streams of blood erupting from his face. All it took was one strike. The soldier collapsed in a heap.

Warm blood flowed down Seln's legs as he trudged toward the door. He could already feel the strength leaving them. When he brought a hand to his lower back, he knew it wasn't good. He couldn't even touch the shard without the agony of it paralyzing him. The door was so closed, and the chaos beyond it.

But he couldn't reach it. His legs gave out. His brain was in a fog. But even in this forsaken City built upon the backs of the Haunted, Ko Seln chuckled, meek though it was. This was the environment he belonged in. It was how he made his living.

And to think, all those years of wanting to smash a bottle into Arsah's face. Some cruel irony, that.

It was enough to make Ko Seln smile as he closed his eyes for the last time.

Anger propelled Grafhar forward. A lifetime's worth of it, at that. Of being shunned and ridiculed, of being mocked by the gods in being granted the one Boon of no use to someone like him, of standing idly by while the Invaders stole from his people everything.

He no longer wanted to be known simply as the mute Linguist, his one purpose to transcribe his interpretations only a handful of times. He did not want to be known as that. He just wanted to be *known*. As the dedicated brother who was finally reunited with his kin after that horrid night in the Stone village. As the intelligent man who did not allow his disability to impact what he could learn.

And as the man about to drive a spear through every fucking Invader I see!

Anger propelled him, cast him through the air, falling to the earth at terminal velocity as blood burst into his face. Grafhar gritted his teeth at the fallen Invader, mustering as much rage into his eyes as he could to ensure the bastard would be sent to hell pissing his pants. A tear even fell down the soldier's face.

He withdrew the spear with a grunt, quickly casting his gaze over his shoulder at the fallen comrade at the door of the tavern. He had heard some deal of struggle inside, but was otherwise preoccupied.

A dozen Invaders lay dead or dying behind him, his spear and blade painted red. None remained behind him, those in front engaged with fierce warriors from the Sun and Lake Tribes. Countless were dead. That gods-damned trap of the Invaders worked too well. In the distance, the Tribal defensive was falling back toward the manor, their lines weakened, the Invaders' strengthened.

Quick, short breaths escaped Grafhar's lips, his brow furrowing, chest pounding, grip tightening on his weaponry. Dounhar was somewhere in the manor, turning the Invader's Deatharms against them. Grafhar would be damned to see anything else happen to his brother.

He charged forward, swinging his spear in a wide berth, catching the nearest Invader in the back of the neck, allowing the Lake warrior to drive her blade through the soldier's chest. His movement fluid, he flung his blade to his right, the steel driven through an eye, the roar of a Deatharm passing him by. Dust and dirt kicked up as he spun on his heel, lunging forward, the next Invader greeted by the force of rage through the chest and pushed back into his neighbor, who met the same fate. The spear was stuck, the skewer cut too deep, and Grafhar abandoned the weapon, pouncing on the soldier who had kept his blade safely stored in their skull. He ripped it free, a bullet taking him in the meat of his arm. A searing heat coursed through him as the bullet remained, but he would not be stopped.

Brother! I'm coming! The sorry bastard who shot him had no chance. Where before only the anger propelled him, now the pain did, too. Grafhar shouldered the Invader to the ground, driving his blade into his chest over and over until spurts of blood erupted from the man's mouth.

A heavy thud clubbed him in the shoulder blades, knocking him to all fours. On instinct, he rolled to the side, the descending Deatharm meant for his skull instead crushing the face of the soldier Grafhar had just savaged. *May as well piss on him, too, at this rate.* Jabbing his arm forward, Grafhar sliced into his assailant's hamstring, collapsing him to a height convenient enough for him to open the man's throat.

Screams and war cries drew his attention back toward the manor, the Tribal lines faltering. This trap had done its job. He would not stay here any longer. Grabbing a nearby spear, Grafhar shot to his feet and sprinted back to the main fray, ignoring the protests of those he left behind. He didn't care. The one person he wanted to protect was in danger. Pained tears welled in his eyes with each step, the spear immensely heavy as his arm felt weaker and weaker. But he couldn't let it stop him. Anger was his weapon. Pain was his ally. Both kept him strong.

And as he reached the encroaching Invader lines in front of the manor, both sent a mighty lunge into the neck of the nearest soldier, blood fountaining out of the wound. Brief glances of gratitude were shot his way, but Grafhar couldn't be bothered. All he focused on was putting steel into his next opponent. Cast in the shadows and shielded by the heavy crowd, the darkness held hidden a bite the Invaders could not anticipate. One jab after another opened throats and chests, red rivers flowing, and it only took five to fall before the Invaders redirected their attention from the manor to the sudden ghost felling their comrades. If only a little, it allowed his own kin to press the advantage again. Soldiers fell, the defensive became the offensive, and the blood of the wicked was spilling with greater ferocity than that of the Tribes.

Grafhar barely felt the impact of the next bullet in his shoulder when he was knocked to a knee. Blood sluiced out from the open wound, heat searing his flesh from the inside. With fury pounding in his chest, he glanced from one direction to the next, his immediate flanks covered by Tribespeople rushing to his protection. Unable to see past them, he took the opportunity to catch his breath, center himself against the pain, even as spittle sprayed from his gritted teeth. He winced against the throbbing pain and glanced back at the manor, shards of stone and wood breaking against the impact of heavy fire, plumes of smoke billowing from the second story windows in retaliatory answers. Grafhar looked about him, the surrounding protective wall crumbling. His place wasn't here. His place was inside.

A jolt of agony surged through his arm as he lifted his spear and pushed past his rear guard. He had hardly the strength left to allow his arm to do anything more than hang slack, his weapon practically dragging against the dirt, cutting a path in his wake. Ragged air rasped in his throat as he ran toward the doors of the manor, his vision tunneling as the exhaustion and blood loss began to hold him in their respective grips. Steel gates loomed ahead, a final pathway leading to the manor's interior. Screams sounded behind him, wood splintered above. Twenty paces numbered the gap between him and the door.

Fire surged through his abdomen, and the unforgiving earth reintroduced itself to him. Breath growing short, Grafhar propped himself up on his good elbow and looked down to see a fresh wound in his stomach, a crimson river flowing unimpeded onto the ground below. He hacked up a spurt of blood, his chin feeling warm and damp, but as pain and sweat held him, he kept his attention to the doors. Even if it was his last act, he would make it inside. He would see his brother once more.

Abandoning his spear, Grafhar pushed himself to his feet, hunched over for the pain, his gait unsteady. The world spun about him as he pushed forward like a drunkard, the songs of chaos fading behind him, the sanctity of family promised ahead. Everything was numb, or perhaps all he felt was pain. It was difficult to separate one from the other. Weakness held him, and as he crossed the threshold into the manor, his legs gave out, and he tumbled onto the cold, carved floor, his blood trailing after him. Rolling onto his back, he could still see movement upstairs. Someone was still fighting up there. He knew not who, but it was someone.

It was all the hope he needed. It was all the hope he had.

By the time he pushed himself back to his feet, Grafhar had already painted much of the white canvas beneath him in a wide swath of red. Tears and sweat and blood all streamed from him as he approached the stairs, each step above agony, each step above a trial. He choked up more blood as he neared the top, wandering eyes watching him. The door atop the stairs was wide open, familiar faces glancing upon him. Numerous Keepers held the room, the Owl's disguised form behind them, and Tawandhar looking away from Grafhar, his pained expression all that needed to be said. If Grafhar could even say anything himself, he would know not what words would be necessary. They were understood just the same.

A row of Tribespeople still manned the windows along the second story, wielding Deatharms and bows alike. Several had fallen already, blood spattered everywhere, bullet holes peppering the surrounding walls. Grafhar circled around the balustrade and stumbled and dragged himself toward the windows, hoping to find Dounhar. Hoping to find any sign he still lived.

A grunt of pain in front of the second window to the left spun a man on his heels, knocking him to the ground. Even as a pained expression flashed before Grafhar's eyes for but a moment, he would know his brother's face anywhere. Dounhar slowly rolled himself onto his back and propped himself up against the wall, blood sluicing from a fresh wound in his chest. Various other cuts lined his face and arms, and it appeared as though an errant shot took off the two forefingers on his left hand.

By the time Grafhar reached his brother, all his energy had dissipated. He collapsed before him, hands wrapped about his sweat-drenched head. Somehow, he found himself back in a seated position, his forehead pressing against his brother's.

"Gra...Grafhar?" Dounhar slurred, his breath short and fleeting. "What...what are you...doing here?"

Grafhar's hand shook as he raised it to sign, but his body would only allow him to raise it halfway. Apparently, another bullet had taken him in the meat of the right arm. Slowly, his fingers worked out the shapes of his words, his brother's eyes focused intently upon them. *I will not let you suffer this alone. Not again. Not anymore.*

A tear streamed down Dounhar's face as he nodded, blood spurting from his mouth in a violent cough. He fell against the wall, his back thudding against the reinforced wood, and he gripped tightly to his brother's hand. A pronounced strain colored his face as a weak wheeze escaped his lips, the intention of words apparent but undelivered.

Resting his wearied head against the wall, Grafhar squeezed Dounhar's hand with all the strength he had remaining, just to ensure the last thing he felt before passing on to the Otherworld was not pain, but comfort.

He closed his eyes, content in the thought that, at last, he had made his voice heard.

The doors shut downstairs with a resounding echo as Ko Zaran shouldered past the hand holding him in place.

"Elder, you cannot!" shouted the Keeper steward, Ko Camalice, fear and anger alighted in her gaze, her long dark locks enshrouding her face.

Zaran spun on his heel and held her by the back of the neck, his old hand shaking from the nerves. "Ko Camalice, I will do what I must to protect what remains of our people, to ensure the memory of our Land survives for the future generations." He exchanged a silent look with the Owl, who only nodded in response.

Camalice winced, acceptance apparent upon her face, but denial gritted its way through her teeth. Her fingers flexed about the spear in her hand, her nostrils flaring.

"I have watched you grow from nestling to proud Owlsign, to one of the most brilliant Learneds of our era. Even if you are not understanding of what drives me to do so, you must know what I must. The True Heart of our Land may be lost, but its *soul*, it lives on in you—" He pressed a finger to her chest, and then pointed at several other Keepers in the chamber. "—and you, and you, and you, and all of us here. It is the duty of we Keepers to protect the very heart of the Land, but should that fall...I take it upon myself to uphold its soul."

With lip trembling, Ko Camalice nodded, still seeming to be unwilling to accept what must be done.

Even as he drew a deep breath, Ko Zaran was wholly unsure he could accept this fate himself. But he was the last remnant of the Keeper elders. It fell upon him to protect everything the Land stood for. He turned back toward the entryway, where blood cut a trail along the formerly pristine floors, where scholars-turned-warriors fought with all the might they had, wielding weaponry unfamiliar to them, all in the name of defending what was rightfully theirs.

He had seen much in his years. Over these last weeks, he had seen enough to cover a lifetime. Deep down, he held a notion that the history books would not properly pen these waning days. He feared they would one day become forgotten. It was an unfair fate, one he hoped desperately would never come to pass.

But as the great Keeper elder Ko Zaran stood at the threshold, a god at his back, brethren in tow, trusted allies besides, and ferocity ahead in the face of adversity, he felt a swell of pride, that these Owlsigns would risk everything for a final chance at life, to deny what had been long stricken upon them these last fifteen years. That on this night, these songbirds would croon a final mournful aria in an elegy for the lost, not just to join solemn rank amongst the departed, but to also pen the memory in proper detail for those who still remained.

Turning his head over his shoulder, Ko Zaran nodded. "I look forward to the day we all meet again. Tawandhar," he directed, his eyes focusing on the Stone Learned. The man perked up at the mention of his name. "Though you bear not the rank of our Tribe, you have more than earned a place amongst us. Defend my people and our god well, Su Tawandhar, honorary Keeper."

Tawandhar paused a moment, seemingly stunned at the honorary title Su being bestowed upon him now. To be granted the honorific was a tremendous privilege to outlanders and was doled out very rarely. In Zaran's lifetime, it had been bestowed only upon the Stone Wolfsign Sharrabha, long may she rest. But after that silent regard, Tawandhar flashed the ghost of a smile and bowed. "The honor is mine, Ko Zaran. I shall protect the soul of our Land with as much strength and vigor as you."

Despite everything, Ko Zaran could not help but smile. He took one step beyond the threshold and said, just barely above the approaching din of chaos and death, "Lock the door behind me."

With slow deliberation, the elder Keeper descended the stairs, the door slamming shut behind him, spear wavering in his grip. Rows of warriors lined the ground floor, dropped to their respective battle stances, while the diminishing numbers above signaled the Invaders' impending breach. The front doors were shut, locked, and barred, a row of stern Owlsigns standing in wait to press their weight against them, for what good it would do.

As Zaran reached the bottom step, he stood with chest puffed out, head held high, spear propped up beside him. Many turned to regard him with solemn silence before returning their attention to the door. The roar of Deatharms became not echoes but warnings, the screams and war cries of brave Tribespeople growing closer and closer. The front row of spearmen lined themselves against the door, pressing themselves against the entryway, tears in their eyes and chests heaving panicked breaths. The wood of the door splintered as a bullet passed through it, just over everyone's heads, the inevitable near enough.

"In me, the soul of our Land dwells, and whence to the Land I return, my soul shall anew." Ko Zaran whispered the words, a variation of a mantra uttered during the funerary rites of those departed Keepers in sending them to the Otherworld. It felt only appropriate. He took a step forward, and another, the words dancing in his mind and setting his soul at ease. To remind himself of the inevitability of death, but the renewal of life, he would welcome what awaited him and those around him on the other side of that door.

He said the words again, this time louder. "In me, the soul of our land dwells, and whence to the Land I return, my soul shall anew."

Nods of approval caught his eye in his periphery as those remaining in this vanguard—a menagerie of Stone, Lake, Sun, and Wood folk alongside the Keepers—joined the utterance, truncating it.

"Whence to the Land I return, my soul shall anew."

The promise of death roared closer outside, the shards of wood that exploded inward now accompanied by spurts of blood. But Ko Zaran would not be deterred. He drew closer to the doors, his nostrils flaring, chants of the Keeper mantra carrying through the crowd, row by row, no longer a tender whisper, but a rhythmic declaration, one that the elder Keeper was more than happy to join.

"Whence to the Land I return, my soul shall anew."

More shots fired, more splinters, the doors crumbling, wavering on their hinges. Those brave warriors holding the door faltered in much the same manner, falling to their knees, blood soaking their clothing, but not surrendering just the same. Their mouths moved in mimicry of the chant coursing through the crowd.

"Whence to the Land I return, my soul shall anew!"

The chant became a chorus, unceasing, unbowed, unbroken. Bullets hummed past Ko Zaran's ears as he raised his voice above the approaching chaos and the death it promised. He would not be deterred. He would not cower. And in this storm of steel and splinters and screams, it was his and their voices that roared loudest against the inevitable.

"My soul shall anew!"

There was a crash at the door, a succession of heavy thuds caving in the wood. Those propping the door up were inevitably battered by the force, the chant slurring from their bloodied lips.

"My soul shall anew!"

The bar broke, the weight on the other side too much to hold.

"MY SOUL SHALL ANEW!"

Ko Zaran charged forward, spear leveled, all the screaming Tribespeople at his back, and thrust his spear forward the moment the initial wave of Invaders burst through, goring the first hapless soldier who breached the entryway.

A wall of spears descended upon the Invaders, the doors only half-opening for the weight of the deceased Tribespeople pressed against them. As the soldiers bottlenecked their way into the manor, they were greeted only by the sharp quills of death, spears cutting through their first ranks with ease. Bullets and arrows rained down from the second story as the remaining few loosed every piece of ammunition they had left. So focused were the Invaders on breaching the entrance that their initial ranks were nothing more than fodder.

But the doors pressed wider. The sounds grew louder. And as Zaran thrust his spear into the heart of another unprepared soldier, the next volley of Deatharms cut through Owlsigns at the front. Blood and splinters peppered the elder Keeper's vision as those beside and in front of him were pressed against him. With the instinct only to press his own offensive, Ko Zaran thrust his spear once again, opening the throat of a female soldier, but to do more than that was to stretch beyond his own capabilities.

The next volley struck him. There was no avoiding it. Ko Zaran fell on his back, pain seizing him as pools of dark red flooded out from his stomach. Heavy footsteps passed him by, the Keeper mantra fading from a battle cry to a sullen chant uttered by a select few, returning its status to a prayer for the fallen. As Zaran reached for his spear, the familiar face of Aritz a Mata—the *true* Aritz a Mata—sauntered inside, displeasure and fury plastered across his face. Not a drop of blood stained his face or arms, though the threads of his field jacket were coated in a particularly wide swath of dark red, faded though it was.

And here he stands, so unwilling to sully his hands. I will not be defeated by him!

The shaft of the spear found its way to Ko Zaran's hands. The Invader General approached, either inattentive or disinterested in the dead and dying about him. The opportunity could not be passed up. With his dying breath, Ko Zaran lurched his arm forward, summoning all the strength he had remaining, and leveled his spear toward Aritz's heart.

The Invader side-stepped the blow, tucking the spear between his arm and his side, and pulled it out of Ko Zaran's hand, deftly spinning the weapon about, and in the same motion, plunged it into the Keeper's heart. He hardly offered Zaran a second glance.

With his mouth lolled open, Ko Zaran turned his head toward the stairs as best as he could muster, watching with dread as the Invaders ascended the stairs, the sounds of chaos fading to nothing, until all that echoed in Ko Zaran's ears were the final words to a song carrying upon the winds of memory the final pledge of a brave people.

My soul shall anew.

Our *souls shall anew.*

At the sight of the bloodshed, Sen could do little more than stop in her tracks.

So different the City had looked hours ago, when a stark quiet had punctuated a tense and tenuous peace. Where it could have very well been that ghosts walked the streets previously, now it seemed only inevitable for the long and bloodied history of this part of the Land. Once again, the Red Fields soaked themselves in the foul stench of death.

Her pistol weighed heavily upon her thigh, the urge to draw it and spend her final shot all too enticing. From afar, she could see the parade of Invaders returning to reclaim their symbol of vain dominance, built upon the backs and bones of those to whom the territory belonged. Screams echoed in the air in accordance with the roar of the Acrarian weaponry. Burned gunpowder wafted its distinctive smell along the wind's breath, carrying with it the horrid smell of the fallen. Anger coursed through her limbs as she held her spear to the point of splintering, the shards burrowing into her palm.

When she felt her sister's presence beside her, Sen asked, "Did the Owl indicate that *this* was to be the result?" She gestured her arm widely to the carnage before them.

Tez sighed and shook her head, sweat dripping down her cheek and onto the ground, her natural endurance still long in the making. "I thought it best not to know. The knowing would have...I don't know. Somehow, I feel it would have been worse to know."

Sen had snuck into this City under cover of night to break into a slave camp and free her brother. She had helped lead a counteroffensive to liberate those she failed before. And yet, this time was cause for greater fear than she had experienced previously. As smoldering flames illuminated the night sky, she felt frozen in place, all instincts telling her to charge ahead but all sense forcing her to stay where she was. "And did the Owl tell you what we needed to do after returning here?"

"Only that my role was still to come." Annoyance colored Tez's voice.

"And mine?" Sen pressed.

Tez scoffed. "Perhaps count yourself Lucky the Owl is not dictating *your* story, as well."

Sen grimaced. She didn't know what to make of that. "There has to be *something* we can do. Something we *must* do." She placed one foot in front of the other, slowly sauntering forward, crouching along in spite of her wearied legs. At the street's first home, she slid up against the side, peering her head around it, narrowing her gaze toward the east. Tez squatted beside her, but the longer her monitoring of the street produced nothing of note, the more intense her feeling that she should be doing more than merely sitting on her hands.

"What are you thinking?" Tez asked in a whisper, her spear resting before her feet.

With a sharp shake of the head, Sen sighed. "I don't know. I really, *really* don't know." The more she watched the Invaders filtering in through the main gate of Aritz's manor, the more she wanted to charge ahead, screaming at the top of her lungs, damning any and all who would stand in her way.

"Fuck what the Owl told you, Tez. We can't just abandon all of them to die. It can't be worth it."

Tez grasped Sen's shoulder firmly and spun her around, her eyes averted, her face sunken with what appeared to be grief. "Say it isn't worth it. What would we do now? Hmm?" She raised an eyebrow. "It's two of us against how many of them? As much as I hate to admit it, there is a time and place for everything. There's a time to fight, and a time to die, and this isn't the time for either of them." With a grimace, she spat on the ground, the grief shifting to visible frustration. "Damn the Owl."

Sen opened her mouth to respond, but her breath caught in her chest as a pair of voices echoed against the distant chaos. She clung herself back to the wall, spear held tight, closing her eyes to focus on those who approached. It was the Acrarian tongue being spoken; that much was clear. A casual conversation, at that, judging from the light laughter. With great caution, she peered around the corner, finding no one, and sidled past Tez to the other side, the voices growing louder.

Gritting her teeth, Sen shared a nod with Tez and glanced at the road, the wind kicking up dust and dirt from the bloodstained earth. The voices numbered true; only two approached. Footsteps and conversations drew ever closer, and with a sharp breath to quell the exhaustive dread lingering in her chest, Sen dashed around the corner, spear leveled, the soldier nearest to her falling before he even recognized what happened. There was no time to wrench the spear free from the Invader's chest as a heavy impact to the arm knocked her off her feet. She wheezed against the sharp pain in her side and reached behind for her knife, but a thrown spear cleared through the soldier's skull before she could even get back to her feet.

She was far too tired to crack a joke. All Sen could do was waver back to her feet and free her spear from the dead body's grip. Tez did the same, the surrounding ground coated in blood and viscera.

"You okay?" Tez asked, prying her weapon free, disregarding the spilled brain matter. A ghost of concern coated the words, but Sen could only assume that her sister was also too deep in the throes of exhaustion to speak more than a handful of words at a time.

Sen inclined her head skyward, the Moon shining brightly upon this wretched scene. "We need to...find a place. Somewhere we can observe what they're doing." She turned to Tez, grimacing against another pang of pain. "You're right. No point fighting right now. I..." An involuntary grunt gripped her as she placed a hand on her tender ribs. "I've had enough beatings and running these last few weeks. At least one of them, we can control tonight."

Tez nodded, words to the contrary unnecessary. She nudged her head toward the row of homes on the far side, windows covered for what little defense they could possibly provide on this night. Despite the roars echoing from within the manor, the streets remained quiet as though none dared to dwell upon its war-torn passes. After the events of the last few days, there was little reason why.

Aching muscles answered Sen as she crouched below the windows, damming up her emotions behind heavy eyes, ears perked for any more soldiers claiming the opportunity for an evening stroll, but hearing nothing beyond Tez's footsteps behind. The ground sucked at the underside of her tattered boots, and whether it was mud or blood caked beneath her, she cared not to know. All she remained focused upon was the looming landmark that was Aritz's manor, a dun beacon of depravity and excess, a monument to a monster, and a hive for its thralls to return to. There had to be some sort of home or building with an adequate view of the horrid sight. It was just a matter of getting there without hesitation or discovery.

The pair of squelching footsteps receded to a singular set, and Sen turned to find Tez standing in the middle of the walkway, mouth agape, some sort of twitch holding her as she stared down the length of an alleyway. Sen furrowed her brow and scurried back toward her sister, grabbing at her arm with a heavy tug. "Tez!" she hissed through gritted teeth. "What are you doing? We can't stay here. We have to go now!"

Tez did not move. Rather, she pointed her spear down the alleyway, something calling her attention.

On instinct, Sen held her spear at the ready, anticipating another host of patrolling Invaders. What she did not expect, though, was a solitary Tribesperson walking the streets on unsteady feet, bearing all the appearance of one halfway into the grave. She lowered her spear, narrowing her eyes at the approaching figure, their face swollen and battered and caked in blood. Between them and Tez, there seemed to be mutual recognition, but it was not until Tez began to pace toward them that it hit Sen.

"Ket," Tez whispered, her voice raw as it escaped her throat. Concern flared in her eyes as she began to make her way to the Lake healer. A tenseness seemed to relieve itself from Tez's shoulder at the sight of her lover, regardless of the sorry state they were in.

Sen couldn't help but feel the same, but she still put a hand to Tez's shoulder. It brought back memories of how quick she was to flee after a phantom of Brin when she thought he had escaped the slave pits, all the while Narva chastised her for blindly chasing after him. She wanted to believe this visage of Ket to be true, but she could not quell her own hesitation.

Not that it mattered to Tez. She just as quickly brushed past her sister's grip, attention unbreaking from Ket. From the Lake Tribesperson's approach, there was no questioning the regard was mutual.

The feeling wouldn't leave Sen. She had fallen for enough traps of late to know when one approached.

When the shadow descended upon Ket, Sen was already grabbing at Tez to pull her back. The sisters watched in horror as a woman clad in Invader field regalia plunged a blade of Tribal make into Ket's chest, twisting it with a sickening lurch.

Tez screamed with bloody fury, bearing more the demeanor of a rabid beast as she tried desperately to pry herself free from Sen's grasp. Ket's wearied body dropped to the ground, and Tez wailed in Sen's clutches. *"I'll kill you, Invader bastard!"* she shouted, heedless of the attention she was drawing to herself. *"I'll fucking kill you!"*

Sen winced as she pulled Tez back to the main drag, her sister flailing in her arms, promising vengeance upon the offending Invader. The dam broke and Sen could not stop her eyes from streaming, her sister's piercing wails all too familiar to her own memory of Narva dying in her arms, of when she was ready to give up on everything, when she had lost it all, lacking any and all of the ferocity Tez was exhibiting.

But for all her instinct to run, something compelled her to stay.

The Invader remained hovering over Ket's body, staring not at her felled opponent, but at Sen and Tez. Or rather, only Sen. The wind howled in Sen's ear, and as she narrowed her eyes, the image of the Invader changed to one of darker complexion and long, flowing locks of hair.

"Vanta," Sen growled. It was a trap not just for Tez, but for Sen, as well. Sen wanted nothing more than to charge the Eclipseborn and fell her, just as she had done to Ziia and Zara. She knew Tez would hardly object to pointing to steel Ket's killer.

But the roar of Deatharms continued. The stench of blood was still foul in the air. And just as her sister said, Sen had to remind herself that there was a time to fight and a time to die. And this was not the time for either.

Against Tez's protesting screams and swinging fists, Sen dragged her sister back down the street, returning to their reconnaissance task, running and stumbling until she reached the final house at the end of the lane. She flung the door open and threw Tez inside, following after her and slamming the door behind her, the time for pleasantries long since passed.

Tez shot to her feet and ran toward the door, blocked by Sen. She grabbed her sister by the collar and tried to push her aside, but Sen stood her ground. "Let me through, Sen! I need to—"

"I want to kill her as much as you do, Tez!" Sen shouted, grasping Tez's shirtsleeves in kind. "I have cause just as you do." She hushed her voice on the chance Vanta had followed after them. "And I know this is little more than another fucking game Kamataa's ilk is playing upon us. But now is *not the time.*"

Her face a dark, angry red, Tez clenched her eyes shut and loosed a furious growl, the remnants of the Bear still bellowing within her. She threw her hands down, fingers curling like talons, and she jabbed a furious finger into Sen's chest. "I'll see her dead for this. I'm not going to rest until I see her neck snapped. That's a godsdamned promise, dear sis—"

A clatter from upstairs cut her off. Sen crouched, picking her spear up off the floor, and peered to the staircase. Placing a finger to her lips for silence, she slowly made her way to the second story, cringing as the wood creaked underfoot with each step. She turned the first corner, greeted with nothing but silence, and finished her ascent, coming to the second-floor landing and finding nothing at all.

Sen frowned as she scanned the room, some sort of small dining hall with a short table and two chairs, a stew pot still simmering in the corner with a weak flame underneath. They weren't alone; Sen knew that much. The flare in her arms was all the confirmation she needed of that.

With ease, Sen sidestepped the downward thrust of a paring knife, spun on her heel, and thwacked a man in the face with the butt end of her spear. A burst of blood erupted from his nose as he fell on his back, scurrying backward to join a young woman who had emerged from the shadows. They yelled at Sen and Tez both in overlapping foreign voices, the words little more than grating noise to Sen's ears.

"Shut up!" she shouted, drawing the flintlock pistol from the holster on her thigh. It immediately quieted the pair. They didn't need to know there was only one bullet left inside.

Tez eyed Sen, her focus shifting from her sister to the trembling Invader couple. "Well?" she questioned. "What are we waiting for?" She spun her spear into position, drawing a yelp from the two.

"What indeed..." Sen murmured beneath her breath. She stared at the Invaders, two cowardly sods who were probably not much older than she was, garbed in some sort of eveningwear of light make. Judging from how stale the air was in here, she could only hazard to guess that they had neither cleaned nor washed themselves since the war was returned to these lands. *They're not even worth the spilled blood.*

Glancing behind her, she made note of the windows, offering a perfect vantage point of Aritz's manor. The street below connected to the gateway to that monument of greed. If there was any place better to observe, Sen wasn't sure they'd find it.

She pulled up a chair and sat by the window. "Watch them, Tez. No sudden movements, yeah?"

Tez scoffed. "Ah, 'watch them?' Do you really think they'd show us the same mercy?"

"I don't think them capable of showing us anything. We'll switch off as need be."

"Sen..." Tez sighed.

"Another time, another place, dear sister. Remember?" Sen raised an eyebrow and nodded, watching as Tez rolled her eyes and stood in front of the mewling and whimpering couple.

We *are creatures fit for mercy,* she thought, peering her head past the shutters and out toward the manor, from where gunfire still raged. *But I fear the next hand to be shown by those* unfit.

The pounding at the door sent a shiver down Tawa's spine. He closed his eyes, muttering a prayer beneath his breath to no one in particular, begging for deliverance from a figure standing ten paces behind him, knowing such intervention would not come.

Voices resounded on the other side, the melodic yet harsh tones of the Invader language sending angry chills through his veins. To either side of him, his Keeper companions quivered, sweated, murmured with apprehension and fear. It was to them this final line of defense fell. And yet, when Tawa turned his head over his shoulder, all he saw was the Owl standing in stark, calm silence, hands folded behind its back, something resembling contentment or acceptance strewn across its false face.

Tawa hardly knew what to make of it. Perhaps there was nothing *to* make of it. It mattered little. His whole world was now this small room, and the heavy oaken door gradually giving way to strike after strike, the sounds echoing through the chamber, the thuds growing more and more hollow as the wood began to splinter off into nothing.

Fanna, he thought, his spear readied for the moment it needed to be. *I am sorry. I wish only I had the strength you possessed to survive this day. But to see this day...I can only say you would be proud of your daughters and all they have done for our people. I will see you soon, my friend.*

A tear strolled down his cheek, his heart pounding in step with the rhythmic assault from outside. It wouldn't be much longer. Each Invader shout was punctuated by a resounding thud. More splinters clattered on the ground. The hinges creaked and cracked. The Keepers whimpered and shuddered.

Tawa's limbs felt heavy, everything coming down to this moment. He knew there were too many beyond the door. Too many for this inexperienced lot to defend against. His only wish was to see the Owl to safety.

TAWANDHAR, the god's voice called.

Tawa turned on his heel and stared, raising his eyebrow, questioning what there was to say at this time.

The Owl, however, shook its head, placing a single finger to its lips, and then tapping its temple with that same finger. DO NOT FEAR, its voice continued in Tawa's head, unheeded by the surrounding Keepers.

Slowly, Tawa returned his attention to the faltering door, feeling nothing but dread despite the Owl's insistence to the contrary.

STILL HAVE YOU YOUR OWN ROLE TO PLAY, TAWANDHAR. DO NOT WASTE IT.

Narrowing his eyes, Tawa scoffed to himself. *What does that even mean?*

The butt of a Deatharm burst through the door, and Tawa's heart sank. Two Keepers rushed ahead, lurching their spears forward into the newly created opening, a single pained grunt the only response. Blood came away from the blow, a brief flow dripping down the door's length. A clicking could be heard on the other side, and Tawa's first instinct was to drop low and turn his body sidelong, facing away from the impending blow.

The shot sang through the chamber, screaming through its cavernous depths, a Keeper quick to fall as a bullet took her between the eyes. A pair of hands reached through the holes and found the lock, turning it, and before any sort of counterstrike could be met, the doors flew open, striking those nearest to their wide berth. A sea of Deatharms filtered into the chamber, a deadly wave crashing against their shores as they had for these last fifteen years.

Tawa backed away until his rear foot rested against the desk, all that separated him from the Owl. He gritted his teeth as the soldiers barred their only exit, lining up in a half-circle with Deatharms held at the ready, freezing the defending Tribespeople in place. If there was any solace in this moment, it was to see the growing confusion upon many of the Invaders' faces as they locked gazes with the god wearing their General's face. Perplexed murmurings rumbled through the crowd, though their weapons did not waver.

Nor shall my own, Tawa thought. *Should this be my role, I will not waste it.*

A hush fell over the proceedings, all the chaos in the hall receding to nothing as footsteps clacked against the ascending stairs. The wall of soldiers opened, and in through the gap approached that all-too-familiar face. A face with whom Tawa had grown strangely familiar over these last days.

But it was only now that he had felt the anger and fear requisite of encountering one Aritz a Mata in the flesh.

The Invader General sneered, his eyes narrowed. Slowly, he glanced at the assembled Keepers, his gaze casting a wide arc and stopping only when he noticed the Owl's disguised form. Aritz took in the sight for an uncomfortable, prolonged moment, saying nothing, his hand hovering over the small Deatharm holstered against his outer thigh. And then he laughed. Soft at first, but growing more and more boisterous in the passing, the soldiers eventually joining in, even as the laughter did not reach their eyes in earnest.

Tawa shuffled to the center of the desk, blocking the clear line of sight Aritz had had of the Owl. "Why do you stay?" he asked through gritted teeth, his head turned slightly over his shoulder. "Fly, you fool!"

The Owl said nothing, remaining stoically in place with hands folded behind its back.

The laughter ceased, the room falling to a hush once more. Aritz paced back and forth, his eyes not breaking from the avian god—and Tawa between them. He said something in his deep voice, the first time Tawa had heard it since the night Fanna was murdered. Tawa could not understand the meaning of the words, but the intonation was all too clear. Arrogant, spiteful, hateful. Some sort of rousing speech to rile up the soldiers, judging from the smirks upon some of their faces.

The words faded into nothing more than noise to Tawa, a hypnotic melody. But when Aritz drew his weapon, Tawa would not hesitate for a moment.

At half a step, Aritz's hand rested against the handle of his Deatharm.

At a full step, Tawa angled a diagonal swing with his spear.

At a leap, the spear tip knocked the Deatharm loose from Aritz's hand.

Upon landing, Tawa shouted, "Fly!"

And the Owl jumped backwards out of the adjacent window, diving to the ground below. A tuft of feathers fluttered into the chamber, the air rippling outside against the might of heavy wings. A shadow was cast upon the room, and in that renewed darkness, a tense silence finally broke into a moment of chaos.

Spears were thrown as shots rang out, blood spilling in all directions. Soldiers were pierced in the chests and legs, some wounds mortal, some superficial, and likewise for the Keepers in the face of the Deatharms' on-slaught. Some bodies dropped while others wavered on their feet, and all the while, Tawa lurched ahead at Aritz a Mata, freezing the Acrarian General with a spear aimed at his throat. It would only take a moment for it to end. To avenge everything and everyone that was lost due to this man's hubris. For Narva. For Fanna. For the Bear and the Wolf. He desperately wanted to.

But something knocked him back, a searing heat exploding in his arm, only narrowly missing the meat of his shoulder. Tawa grunted but main-tained his footing, the moment lost as Aritz spun on his heel and found his Deatharm on the floor, clicking the hammer back, ready for his deadly counter. Tawa closed his eyes, awaiting the thunderclap.

But a dismissive female voice deterred it from ever coming. "Ah, ah, ah," he heard and understood, but the words beyond that may as well have been nothing.

A young soldier with vibrant red hair entered the chamber, flashing a glance at Aritz, who only averted his gaze with what appeared to be disgust—or perhaps even distrust. The woman laughed with amusement coloring her voice, swaying from side to side, her Deatharm still smoking from the shot she had just taken at Tawa. Blood new and old stained her skin and uniform, but she seemed wholly unperturbed by the fact. By the way she was licking her lips, she even seemed to enjoy it.

And when she spoke again, Tawa's breath caught in his chest. "A shame, truly, that you could not put up more of a fight. Though, I must say I am disappointed the Owl fled. We were so close, indeed."

Tawa's nostrils flared. "You are Kamataa."

The Eclipseborn woman raised an eyebrow and chuckled. "Ah, so you have heard of me. Stone Tribe, are you? Perhaps you are familiar with

Sennalhat, then? I do wish I had met her on this battlefield, and yet I did not see her. There is much she and I still must settle, but alas, it appears this is another battle from which she chose to run. How pitiable."

"Pitiable is only those who would betray their people as you have. You blind yourself to the Invaders' atrocities, and for what?"

"For what? Oh, if only you knew the depths of your arrogance and ignorance. For, as you can see…" Kamataa reached beneath her uniform top and pulled at a chain. A glowing ornament hung slack against it. The rune of Illusion dispelled its faint glow as she ripped it from her neck. A light enshrouded her form until from it emerged the image of a woman aged beyond anything, cavernous wrinkles covering her face to bear her the appearance of a weathered oak, while wispy milk-white hair rolling past her hunched shoulders. "I have seen and known far too much to know what you see as atrocities by the Invaders is only the beginning of the Tribes' crimes against the Eclipseborn. The Moon shines bright upon us this night. For the first time in centuries, She smiles."

The remaining soldiers whispered amongst one another, shock coloring their respective tones. Even Aritz stared at Kamataa with wide eyes. It was easy to surmise this as being the first time any of them had seen the Eclipseborn's true form.

Tawa spat at the ground before her. "If you think the Moon would bless this carnage, then you are even more mad than I thought."

"Madness is but a matter of perspective." Kamataa tapped the barrel of her Deatharm against her shoulder, tutting her lips. "Madder still would be to continue to arm yourself when you have no means of escape, no means of victory. You have lost." She paused, smacking her lips, and then turned to Aritz, speaking something in the Invader tongue with slow, methodical intonation.

Aritz remained silent for a moment, but did not protest, even as his face remained averse with shock.

Kamataa smirked. "Stand and die, or surrender and serve a purpose. What say you?" She clicked back the hammer on her Deatharm and held it out at Tawa, the barrel aimed squarely at his forehead.

Tawa had known defeat, but never like this. He looked at the surviving Keepers, all their attention placed upon him. Whatever he elected to do, it was clear they would follow. His chest pounded with the decision. And the Owl's words pestered him once again.

Is this *my role to play? Or is my part yet to come?*

He closed his eyes and let loose a heavy sigh. And with a grunt, he threw his spear on the ground, sending it clattering and echoing against the hard floor. One by one, the Keepers followed suit, their weapons discarded, each resounding thud a further punctuation to a sentence already written.

Flashing her teeth, Kamataa chuckled to herself and holstered her Deatharm, approaching Tawa with far spryer movements than he expected from a woman of her advanced age. There was a dark flame burning in her eyes as she held Tawa's gaze, until finally she said, "You chose wisely. And there is work still to be done."

Tawa sunk within himself, a pit opening beneath him as the Invaders encirclied the surrendering Tribespeople. All he could do was avert his eyes, chance one last look at the spear he discarded, a final connection between him and his closest friend.

It was over. They had lost.

INTERLUDE

SIGNIFYING NOTHING

The woman shifted in place, a deep and bestial growl rumbling at the back of her throat, her basest animal instincts threatening to return to the fore at the next provocation.

Aritz licked his lips in anticipation. Her façade was breaking. He had her.

And yet, even with that clear and present anger, there managed to be a hint of amusement coloring her cheeks, the ghosts of her composure slowly returning. She smacked her lips, her fingers rapping against the handle of the pistol. "A 'categorical' falsehood, you say. You must pardon me if I am not at all convinced of your claim."

Throwing his hands out at his sides, Aritz scoffed and shook his head. "Is it of any consequence to me, your denial of the truth? Am I to care that you remain unconvinced? There are few to none in this nation—*my* nation—for whom your denial is of any matter. If you yourself saw what you saw with your own eyes, then you are well aware that what you are so adamantly in pursuit of did not, in fact, happen."

"The extent to which it did or did not happen is irrelevant, Aritz," the woman barked, turning her nose up at him. "The Harvests were an unequivocal truth—not an inconvenience to label as a myth for but a technicality."

"The strength of your arms truly impresses me, I must confess, for the length to which you are stretching the concept of the truth."

"Facts are not a concept."

"And yet, your 'facts' venture into the realm of absurdity. Pray tell, who would you expect to believe them?"

"It is *because* of that so-called 'absurdity' that people may believe it." The woman's gaze was sharp as steel, the waning sunlight glinting in her eyes in a fireball of fury. "The very notion of the Harvests, the brutality and gruesomeness by which they were carried out—there is none so morbid that they would fabricate such a farfetched tale. The only fabrication comes from those who sought to write it out of their history entirely."

Aritz flashed his teeth, half in anger, half in command. "You will find that what is put to writ is not for *you* to decide."

"Nor should it be for you."

"And yet, decide I have. I do not regret omitting your savage lot from memory."

"Denouncements of 'savagery' are ever rich coming from *your* lips, Aritz." The façade was breaking once more, the control she had once displayed slipping further and further away. There was a twitch in her hands, a bead of sweat trickling the side of her forehead.

All the while, Aritz regained control for himself. The pit she had tried repeatedly to stamp him into was far shallower than previously indicated. He felt himself breaching back to the surface. He licked his lips, tasting the supposed richness of which she spoke, savoring the anger instilled by his utterances of "savagery." Leaning back and crossing his arms, Aritz chuckled and permitted a sly smile to return. "And they shall pass my lips again and again, passed from lip to page to pen until it shall be recorded in not just the tomes but the minds and spirits of the nation that it was I who purged wickedness and savagery from the good nation of Ferranda, for it is *I* who rose above my mortal limitations and became a symbol and paragon for these dear citizens of mine."

Raising her brow, the woman dropped her arms to her sides, stared at Aritz intently, the wrinkles on her forehead creasing, until she let loose a bemused laugh. "If you truly think you have 'purged' wickedness from these shores," she said, "then I must insist you do a more thorough job."

Aritz reached his hand out. "Then, if you would offer me the gun, I will certainly—"

Her nostrils flared in anger as she aimed once more at the Founder's head, yet another threat promising to be little more than hollow. "*No.* I believe *I* will be the one to clean up your mess. A wound festered upon my people's lands from the moment you set foot on it. Those common folk wandering the streets, those patrolling this manor in fear and service of you, those children who are raised to learn nothing more than a heroic fiction—they are all a symptom, but it is *you* who are the disease, a blight covering this island and threatening to spread until you are plucked out, root and stem."

"Then why *haven't* you done so yet?"

"You have not yet told me what I need to hear."

Rolling his eyes, Aritz shook his head and turned toward the window, the crashing waves calling to him from the southern shores. "And you will do *what* with those words, precisely? Do you require me to repeat your false recollections of this so-called 'Harvest' in the mirror thrice and your gods will at once reappear? Will your people rise from the earth and drag me to hell? Will my coerced admission provide you the succor and retribution you so desperately seek? Is that it?"

"There is little retribution remaining in this world," the woman said, a hollow visage gripping her eyes, the anger fading but doing its utmost to remain in control. "But what remains is reserved for someone who is as monstrous as yourself. There will be no hands to take you to the hell where you belong; mine shall be more than sufficient." She clicked the hammer back on the pistol. "We need not dawdle any longer, if you wish to end this. Just tell me what I wish to hear."

Another bluff. You've kept your cards close to your chest for far too long, woman. With slow, deliberate steps, Aritz drew closer to her, narrowing the gulf, the pistol remaining steady in her hand. "And if I remain silent?" he asked. "Shall this monster continue to roam the earth, undeterred and unabated?"

The assailant remained silent, even as Aritz drew ever closer.

"Do you fancy yourself a hero, woman? A monster slayer? A god killer? There is indeed such a person in this room, and we are both well aware that it is not you."

"Not yet," she affirmed, her face remaining frozen and plain.

"Amusing," Aritz responded with a scoff. "But what know you of gods, of monsters? Surely a god can neither bleed nor die, and yet I proved both to be false. Does that make your gods false, or does it mean I am of a divine purpose beyond your own? Or it could be I am indeed a monster—but only to those for whom a monster is necessary. You and your people could never stop me; therefore, it must be that I am not a man, but a monster, is that not right?"

"You are a monster for your ill deeds, you fool, and a low man besides. The corpses you bled speak loud enough for that."

"The corpses I bled served a purpose unfulfilled and were thusly laid to rest accordingly. Beyond that, what more am I to confess? Our war had ended. It was time to move forward."

"There are ways to move forward beyond defiling the dead," the woman growled.

"But if I defiled the *living*, you would be more accepting, yes?"

"You *did* defile the living."

Aritz laughed, halting his advance, a gust of wind at his back and a faint creaking of wood groaning in his ear from behind. "It is impossible to defile that which is not sacred. I merely gave your profane ilk a purpose. If I am to be labeled a monster for it by your kind, then so what? You know nothing of the necessity of monsters. Kingdoms and empires are started not by the kind of heart, but by the strong overcoming the weak, the sacred surpassing the profane, a light blanketing the shadows. It is the "monsters" who lurk in the night of the battlefield and stake claim to victory, not those who proffer hapless pleas for others to pen false confessions to ease their own feelings of defeat and despair. It is not those who grovel in decades henceforth, but those who rise to a station equal to the divine."

He licked his lips, gnawing at his bottom lip, the salt air peppering his skin through the window. "Answer me this, woman. For what purpose would *any* of this serve? The Acrarian Kingdom has become a global empire, spanning from the homeland to the east to the New World to the west. What difference do my actions on a small island nation like Ferranda even make in your grand machinations? Your words would be but a sentence easily stricken from the annals of history, erased just as easily as your people were. What cause have I to fear you?"

The woman flashed a ghastly grin, her face cast in shadow. "There is great cause, and greater reason still. You forget that word has surely spread to your King and Queen of your actions at your Acrarian estate."

"Your actions, not mine," Aritz interjected, anger puffing out of his nostrils.

"It is not to my recollection that they were mine, either. Categorically, was it?" She sneered, all manner of devilry in her expression. "But it would not be the first time there have been parties witness to the *divine* Aritz a Mata willfully slaughtering his own people. Memories linger and echo and do not fade, and those echoes of twenty-five years past are only ringing all the louder in the wake of your own recent familicide."

Aritz's lips quivered, his teeth rattling. "Neither of which I had anything to do with!" he bellowed, spittle flying from his mouth in a viscous spray. His pistol was so nearly in reach, but his hand was far too gripped in the throes of anger.

"The story of Aritz a Mata is already penned with lies. What are a few more?" The woman chuckled, the passing shadows still blanketing her face, a trickle of light only barely finding its way to her eyes. "But I will grant you this: today, it may ultimately matter for little. As it will tomorrow, and next week, and next month. But the winds will blow, and they will carry on whispers and secrets that will inevitably become news and proclamations. Already do they travel from your homeland. I wonder how long it will take them to reach your 'New World?'" She smacked her lips, a shine dispelling the darkness from her expression. "I made a promise twenty-five years ago. I accepted a role. And today is the day I see it through."

Clenching his eyes shut, Aritz rotated his shoulders, rolling his head in a wide arc, feeling the invigorating crack of bones within. The sickening crunch of steel opening Lucrecia's head sounded over and over in his ears. The otherworldly shriek of his children just before their heads rolled along the white marble of his bedchambers. He shook in place, screams and blood haunting him, assaulting him, sending a tremor of grief and rage coursing through him. He ground his teeth, his hands balling into fists, nails burrowing deep into his palms.

When he opened his eyes, the woman remained just where she was, stood in place, still as a statue, an envoy of little more than empty threats. "Who even remains," he growled, "for you to keep your promise to? If there are any still wandering *my* lands, I'll be sure to keep you alive just long enough for you to watch me expunge every last bit of malice and wickedness from this nation. Then—and only then—will you know the depths of a monster."

She sneered once more and opened her mouth to say something, but Aritz was on her in a flash. The roar of the pistol sounded in his ear as it discharged into the ceiling, splinters of wood raining down to the floor, the room filled with nothing more than a ringing of white noise. Aritz's shoulders ached as his hands wrestled against the woman's for control of the weapon, arms thrown in all directions. Despite her diminutive size, this woman was strong, a strength hidden in her grip. Aritz snarled at her, pushing and pulling against her in this tug-of-war, the barrel of the pistol slowly finding its way toward his face.

He kicked his right foot out in a flail, meeting his assailant's ankle in a stroke of good fortune. Her leg collapsed from beneath her, her momentum falling with it, and as she hit the floor with a hard thud, her grip loosened from the pistol, giving Aritz all the necessary leave to grasp it for himself.

Hovering over her, his chest heaved, his lungs straining with the effort. No longer was he accustomed to these bouts. He looked forward to this being the last one.

Aritz clicked the hammer back and aimed at the woman's face as she continued to eye him with those wild, furious eyes. "Tis a pity that these twenty-five years will have come to naught. You should have pulled the trigger at one of your many opportunities."

For a brief moment, the woman's attention was paid not on Aritz, but to the side, and as she returned to him, there was no disappointment in her gaze. No fear, no anguish, no despair.

Just that same, mischievous smile she had given him so many times already.

"The night is still young, Aritz," she said. "And my luck has not yet run out."

Glass shattered, and a gun fired.

CHAPTER TWELVE

Dust

The heady aromas of heavy stouts filled the air as Kamataa leaned back in her chair, feet propped up against the table, content for a number of reasons.

Content that this long, drawn-out conquest had at last reached its conclusion.

Content that, after all the lives lost among her brethren and sistren—Ziia, Hollow, Zara, and even those from centuries ago like Ruhr—she had finally claimed vengeance and retribution against the Tribes in the name of the Blessed Moon.

And, content that she no longer needed to maintain appearances. Here, in this tavern, in the sight of gawking soldiers and murmuring gossipers, she was free to exist with her Illusion dispelled, her true form displayed for all to see, and none of these fools had the courage to speak a word about it. She had never felt it necessary to *hide*, per se—she did not make it a secret from Aritz of her natural-born origins—but to merely exist in this space, her stark-white hair flowing past her dark shoulders and framing her heavily wrinkled face, was liberating, in a sense.

She could feel the daggers being drawn by their gazes, but she cared not. She knew they dared not raise a hand to a hero among their lot, the woman who helped lead Aritz a Mata to an impossible victory, who laid bare the secrets of the Tribes. Both the truths and the lies.

The salt-infused breeze fluttered in through the open windows, the ordinary stenches of this City returning to blanket the acridity of spilled blood and fouled trousers. The lesser soldiers spent much of the night and morning disposing of the deceased soldiers and collecting the departed Tribespeople, much of the duties in and around Aritz's manor. Stray skirmishes had made their mark elsewhere in the streets, even right in this tavern, where signs of battle made their mark on the splintered bar and cracked walls, while blood and broken glass still stained the floorboards.

Contributing to the cleanup was beneath Kamataa. She knew it, and so did everyone else. Everything she had worked for all these centuries had at long last been accomplished. If any deserved a long respite, none could argue against her.

She couldn't remember the last time she felt truly relaxed. Not needing to have thoughts of revenge ruminating in the back of her head. Not needing to look over her shoulder for someone who may have outed her for what she truly was. Here, Kamataa could sigh with relief, a weight on her shoulders lifted, and drink deep a heavy brew. She knew not what it said of the Acrarians that their first order of business after reclaiming their City was to reopen the tavern, but there was always a call for libations when the days called for celebration or mourning.

The drink spilled from the corner of Kamataa's mouth as she placed her mug down and surveyed the tavern's clientele. *All these sunken faces and defeated voices. We* won, *you fools. This Land is now yours. Show some enthusiasm.* She chuckled softly, taking another swig of stout, craning her head toward the ceiling, staring blankly at the rot stains on the ceiling, wondering how much longer it had left before it all came crashing down on everyone inside. She had only to hope she would be long gone before that ever happened.

Creaking footsteps sounded against the aching floorboards as the halted conversations quickly became suspicious whispers. Raising a curious brow, Kamataa looked toward the door and grinned, pleased to not only see Sha'a and Vanta joining her, but doing so out of their Illusions as well. Both tied their hair back at the napes of their necks; for how thick their hair was, there was no sense in allowing it to flow freely in this oppressive heat. Vanta had discarded her field jacket, the top two buttons on her shirt left undone to permit a breeze to cool her, even if it did expose a fresh wound on her chest. Sha'a moved more gingerly, her shoulder evidently still tender, but her Sun Tribe origins seeming to allow her greater tolerance toward the heat even in full uniform.

The chairs on either side of Kamataa scraped against the floor as her companions took their seats. "I had a feeling we may find you here, Kama," Sha'a said with a smile, grunting with effort as she leaned into her chair.

"You're missing quite the festivities outside," Vanta added, rolling her eyes. "They're preparing a march."

"Celebratory or funerary?" Kamataa asked.

Vanta shrugged. "I haven't a clue. The wagons are out, at the very least. The big one, too. Think I saw a few of the living with bound arms, as well. Not much longer until they're off."

Kamataa raised her mug, dwindling to its last drops. "Sound the keening bell," she said derisively. She turned toward the bar and loose a sharp whistle, grabbing the barmaid's attention and stilling the air otherwise. Kamataa raised three fingers and gestured toward the table. The barmaid eyed her with a hesitant sneer but eventually nodded, setting about her work at the taps.

If any of the tavern's patrons had been unaware of Kamataa's undisguised presence, they were no longer. All eyes were upon her, Sha'a, and Vanta as the barmaid brought them their stouts, the contents splashing out from the mugs as they met with the table.

Flashing a smile, Kamataa dug through her pocket and flicked a silver piece toward the barmaid as a show of thanks. The barmaid didn't bother to catch it and allowed it to instead slip through the floorboards. Kamataa smirked and shook her head, and then grabbed her mug by the handle, holding it up to her companions in a toast. "To our fallen."

"To our fallen," Sha'a and Vanta repeated in unison.

They clacked the mugs together, the liquid from each sloshing together and spilling onto the table, and they drank deep. The contents were mostly head. *How rude*, Kamataa thought. *Show your heroes greater respect.*

Conversations slowly resumed in the tavern as whatever misery lingered became altogether more enchanting again than watching the three Eclipseborn with suspicion, and Kamataa breathed a contented sigh. The toast felt good, but with it came the memories. She stared into the foam still coating the top of her mug, wondering what recollections lay in the liquid ripples underneath.

Sha'a cleared her throat. "So, then," she said. "What now?"

Kamataa raised an eyebrow and grunted with curiosity.

"Nothing, it just feels…almost surreal. Everything we've worked toward, it's…it's done now." Sha'a closed her eyes and nodded to herself. "When I close my eyes, I remember it all. My parents abandoning me, leaving me to the Acrarians' wrath. Back then, I never would have thought I'd be sitting here with you, with the Acrarians, toasting to the demise of a people who wished me dead. And now…" She chuckled. "Now, I hardly know where to go from here."

"You gave us a home, Kama," Vanta added. "I thought I had nothing. But, nine years ago, you found me when I had nowhere to go and showed me a direction and kindness that I wouldn't trade for anything. And now, wherever we go from here, I know I can do so without having to worry about some close-minded elder wishing death upon me for something that was beyond my control. You've done more good for us than we could ever express."

Kamataa smiled, feeling a tear well in her eye. "Trust me, children, when I say you have done just the same for me. I wish only that…" She trailed off, biting her lip and sighing into her mug, the reflections still not clear before her. "There are more who should still be at this table with us. Hollow, and Zara, and…" She looked off to the side, a frown setting into her face. "It still does not feel right for Ziia not to be here. We all knew the risks, of course, but…if there was anyone who should have been able to see this through to the end with me, it should have been Ziia. She always was the more…level-headed one. Stoic as the stone that banished her. If only it wasn't another stone that took her away." She gripped the handle to her mug with enough force that she felt it begin to crack in her grasp.

"And Cin as well," Sha'a muttered, rapping her fingers along the side of her mug. "We shouldn't forget him. We don't know that he died. He could still be out there somewhere."

Kamataa opened her mouth, but just as quickly closed it and nodded. *Forgive me, Cin, but I* did *forget.* For the others, it was difficult to erase the images from her mind. Ziia discovered Sennalhat's treachery and was rewarded for it by having her brain spilled. Hollow met his end with a bullet to the face, though from whom, Kamataa had never learned. Zara's head and neck were crushed in a fall, a sight far too gruesome to adequately recollect.

But Cin? Swatted away like a fly? That wasn't how he would meet his end. Fortune would not allow that of him.

"He's alive. I'm sure of it," Kamataa said, forcing a small smile. "The Moon saw fit to grant him Luck for a reason. He would not be felled so easily." *But if you're still out there, Cin, then where? And why have you not returned?*

"Would that we all were afforded the same Luck," Vanta lamented with a sigh. She took a deep gulp of her drink, at last venturing beyond the foam. "Is this what you and Ziia expected in the end? The defeat of the Tribes?"

Kamataa pondered the question for a moment, but slowly shook her head. "I don't think anything is ever fated to go according to plan, and this ended up far sloppier than I expected. I hardly believed the Owlsigns of all people had it in them to overtake the Acrarian City, to reclaim this territory—tenuous and ill-defended though it was both before, during, and after. Perhaps I was too dismissive toward the Owl's escape from the True Heart. The weakest of the gods was ever the more dangerous. In Aritz's eyes, this was nothing short of an absolute victory. But for me? Retire and rest though I wish, I cannot help but be obliged to tie up the final loose ends. The Owl is one of them, but that may as well be a lost cause."

"And the other?" Vanta asked, taking another swig of her stout, seeming to already know the answer.

"Who else?" Kamataa scoffed. "Sennalhat."

Sha'a chuckled. "Come now, Kama. There's no way she could have survived."

"She's alive," Vanta affirmed. "I saw her myself. Her and her sister, after the battle had already been won."

"Why didn't you go after her, then? You could have—"

Vanta shook her head. "Not my place. Not my kill." She stared at Kamataa. "She's somewhere in this City, and we'll find her. But the honor shall be yours, Kama."

Sha'a looked unconvinced but said nothing further.

With a smile of gratitude, Kamataa bowed her head toward Vanta. "Thank you. Much like Cin, she's far too stubborn and Lucky to die, but eventually, her Luck will run out, and it shall do so by my hand. On Ziia's life, I swear it." She gritted her teeth, her eyes flaring merely at the thought of putting Sennalhat in her place. *If it is amongst the filth of her people she wishes to die, then I am more than happy to grant her that.*

"It's ironic, though," Sha'a muttered, pursing her lips.

Kamataa raised an eyebrow.

"It was Luck that allowed Sennalhat to keep her head, but also Luck that her little scheme with the Owl fell apart so quickly."

"True," Vanta said in agreement. She took another swig of her drink. "All the citizens running north for their lives—I'm sure none of them expected to bump into us."

"And all the greater motivation for Aritz to return home with the greatest of speed," Kamataa said, tutting her lips. "To think he was content to mope in the Forest for a time yet and lick his wounds."

Vanta pointed an amused finger at Kamataa, stifling back a laugh. "Licking his wounds, or maybe trying to catch a glimpse of the future?" She shook her head with joy creasing about her eyes.

"I *still* cannot believe you managed to convince Aritz that there was 'magic' in Tribal blood," Sha'a said. Propping her elbow on the table and resting her head atop her hand, she flashed the widest smile to the Eclipseborn elder. "I was beginning to believe it myself."

"It's ever fascinating what a mind wishes to believe," Kamataa admitted, placing her mug back on the table, resting her hands behind her head. "I have known men like Aritz a Mata for centuries. Men who would stop at nothing to be remembered. To leave behind a legacy that spans generations. Little do those fools know, they are all just that: fools." She licked her lips, slowly taking in the despondent faces around the tavern and the dreary words escaping their mouths. "The only way to endure through the ages is to ensure you are there to witness the ages. The faces change just as much as your own must. Aritz expects a portrait of his deeds will immortalize him, but let me ask you this: do you know of the great Lake Tribe Chiefs Ruwexi and Tenrir?"

Her companions were quick to shake their heads.

"Really?" Kamataa asked with exaggerated shock. "The two Chiefs who signed the accord that ended the Lake Tribe's Long War?"

"Can't say I've heard of them," Vanta admitted. "Though the Arrow Tribe wasn't exactly comprised of storytellers."

"No, no," Sha'a interjected. "The Sun Tribe *boasts* of the exploits of supposed great men regardless of the Tribe, and I'd never heard any—"

"Precisely," Kamataa interrupted, jabbing a finger toward the two of them. "In the end, what did their promises amount to? What did their *legacies* amount to? The Lake Tribe never stopped fighting amongst itself, the dumb bastards. Skirmishes resumed before the ink was even dried upon the parchment on that day.

"The point being," she continued, dampening her throat with more stout, "Aritz heard an opportunity to draft the legacy he intends to pen to history. To be the mastermind behind an industrial revolution beyond what his homeland had already achieved? Why, he would be nothing short of a god to his zealous followers. Or, rather, unwilling followers, from the looks of them."

Not a shred of happiness lingered on the faces of the nearby Acrarian soldiers. Such a stark difference from before the northward march, when these same faces would be colored with eagerness and exuberance.

Kamataa shrugged her shoulders and held out her hands. "I hadn't steered him wrong yet, after all. He would have been gored by the Bear at the first opportunity without me, and we would be having a vastly different conversation now if that had been the case. But instead, if he wanted to, he could call himself 'godslayer' and have *that* be his legacy."

"Oh, *please*, no," Vanta groaned. "It's bad enough having to listen to him style himself as 'the Sword of the Savior.' Is that even a title granted in his faith?"

"I think it's a load of horseshit he invented merely in the interest of self-importance," Sha'a said with rolling eyes. "Much like his precious 'Savior,' but that's a different story."

"But you see what I mean, don't you?" Kamataa asked. "The ego of a man such as Aritz a Mata knows no boundaries, no limits. I laid the trail for him to slay two gods, and in an instant, I have his ear. In that moment, I could have told him that to drink the blood of the dying Bear would permit him to ascend to an existence beyond mortal ken. I could have told him he would have had the power of a god in the palm of his hand. I could have told him any number of things, and he would have been more a fool to distrust me than he would to believe me, especially after I won his war for him.

"Ultimately, I elected the half-truth, that which offers just enough of a morsel for him to believe, and just enough promise for him to pursue it. Imagine what his legacy will amount to when *that* is brought to light." She could feel the sinister hold of her smile, but she cared not. Her companions did not appear perturbed by it. "The only enduring legacies are those which we ourselves direct. Blind ambition and bold beliefs are but an enemy to those who wish to be remembered. They're merely too self-enamored to see that."

"And when the truth is revealed?" Vanta prompted, finishing off the last drops of her stout a bit too eagerly; she inevitably hacked up a few droplets before resuming as though nothing happened. "What would you have us do?"

Kamataa brushed the concern aside with a swat of the hand. "Oh, it would be ill form not to see the look on Aritz's face. I've grown fascinated with the full breadth of his emotions. I do wonder what his next act will be after being forced upon his knees to have a human heart burst in his mouth."

"That is a mental image I will *never* rid myself of," Sha'a groaned, seeming to lament the diminished supply of alcohol in her mug. "I am almost afraid to know what was going through your mind when you decided to do that."

"I believe my thought was, 'This will be fucking hilarious.'"

"Blessed Moon, Kama." Sha'a shook her head, feigning disgust but chuckling behind the mask.

Flashing her teeth, Kamataa leaned forward and rapped her knuckles on the table in an arrhythmic beat. "Right, then. I suppose we've dawdled enough here. The fools outside surely need *some* direction in preparing for Aritz. We don't need another wagon collapsing as did the Wolf's. Shall we continue the act?"

"Gladly," Vanta said, popping back up to her feet.

Sha'a nodded, scraping the chair behind her, and heading for the door, offering a sneer toward the quieted crowd eyeing her.

With careful deliberation, Kamataa rose and offered a nod to the suspicious crowd. They could watch her all they liked, but it would not change a thing. Nothing would shake this contented feeling.

Especially when she had the opportunity to oversee a *very* big delivery.

The hazy sunlight beaming in through the window did not at all help the stench of piss and shit permeating through the air.

Tez was exhausted. The hours passed and not a single one of them was spent resting. Not that she *could* rest, even if she wanted. The image of Ket being run through by Vanta did not leave her mind. The desire to hunt down that Eclipseborn was even more pervasive.

But instead, she remained in this chair, the pale moonlight having turned to dawn's rays having turned to a high afternoon sun behind her, her spear still held level atop her lap, her eyes not breaking from the two Invaders sitting before her, cowering, shaking, grumbling, relieving all over themselves. Her eyes were heavy, her head swirling, but it was an anger—focused squarely upon the two in front of her, even if they were not directly responsible for it—that kept her alert.

She and Sen had taken shifts between watching by the window and watching their two captives. Much of the morning's window observances were comprised of a monotony of Invaders hauling the dead out from Aritz's manor and into respective piles—one for their own people, and the other for the Tribes. What had perplexed Tez particularly was *why* the Tribal corpses were loaded so unceremoniously into the same covered wagons that the

Invaders had brought with them on their northward march and into the mountains. Surely, whatever they pilfered and stole from the Stone village and the Keepers' realm were of greater value to them than a collection of the dead. Not to mention, the bodies of the *Invaders* who were felled were simply carried off elsewhere with none of the care and attention paid to the Tribal bodies with respect to transporting them. It would not have surprised Tez in the least if the soldiers' bodies were being carried off to the hidden mass grave where she and Sen had found Brin. *Hell, it would surprise me if Aritz even gave them* that *much.*

For now, though, the noise outdoors consisted only of harsh commands and sarcastic barbs, the meaning lost to Tez's ears but the intent more than recognizable. The density of voices came in waves, and it now appeared a larger number of Invaders were gathering in the street below. Their voices were loud enough to feel as though they were inside the house. Grunts, creaking wheels, and splintering wood echoed in the background, often punctuated by what Tez assumed to be Invader curses.

Tez brushed away a bead of sweat as it trailed down the length of her forehead, her shirt clinging to spots where the chair's backrest marked her shoulder blades. Behind her, Sen smacked her lips, her ringers rapping along the armrest of her seat. Her foot was tapping rhythmically along the floorboards, probably an anxious twitch, or a shake only a stay in the tavern could quell for her. Tez could hardly blame her sister for that. She had every inkling to do so right alongside her.

The captives whispered to one another, tears glistening in their eyes. The man held tight to his partner's hand, his arm shimmering with sweat. A long string of words escaped his lips, hushed as though to guard a secret from Tez, even if the dumb bastard should have been well aware that Tez had no knowledge of his people's language. Regardless, his eyes danced with caution, fluttering between his partner and Tez, the words never stopping.

All it took was a soft growl from Tez to shut him up. *You think me and my people are beasts? Then I'll gladly play the part,* she thought as the man curled back into a ball, the crotch of his trousers still stained and pungent, while the woman slunk backward as far as the confines of the room would take them. There seemed to be an understanding that any traversal beyond this room would go poorly for them. Tez had not released the hold on her spear in quite some time.

Deep down, she wanted to *dare* them to try something. To give her a reason, *any* reason. She had no qualms to have been over and done with them in the middle of the night; fewer Invaders made the world all the better. She wasn't used to Sen being the more level-headed one.

Sen grunted behind her, and from the creaking in her chair, it seemed she was leaning forward.

"What is it?" Tez asked, not breaking from her watch over their captives.

"Hmph," Sen murmured. "I don't know, but...looks like they're all gathering. There's a lot of them outside the manor."

"A lot of who? The soldiers? Is it not normal for them to line up outside Aritz's manor to kiss his ass?"

"Well, if it was, I was never invited." Sen's tone was deadpan, the words seeming more a reflex than an intentional quip. "But no, it's...I don't know, this is strange."

"What is?"

"They're...lining up? Like a march or something."

"A bit early for their victory parade, don't you think?" Tez rolled her eyes. "Their dead aren't even cold yet."

"I'm not sure I'd call it a parade—those usually require people watching. The street is empty otherwise." Sen huffed a long sigh. "So much for watching patrol routes. Unless this is what they plan to do every—wait, what the fuck?"

Tez arched an eyebrow, ensuring she masked her confusion to keep up appearances in front of their captives. "What?"

The floorboards creaked from behind. Peering over her shoulder, Tez could see Sen having risen to her feet, her head nearly peering out the window.

"Sen, what the fuck are you doing?" Tez hissed. "Get back inside. Unless you want to alert all the Invaders that we're in here."

Sen complied, but still did not return to her seat. She seemed too stunned to move or speak.

Tez cleared her throat. "Sen?"

"Tawa."

"What about Tawa?" Tez half-turned in her seat, the chair scraping beneath her. She held the tip of the spear out toward the captives, the weapon wavering in her hand, exhaustion in her arm be damned.

"He's...he's down there. Alive."

Tez breathed a sigh of relief. "Oh, thank the gods." *At least someone else made it out of this.*

"He's chained up, Tez."

"Oh, fuck the gods."

Sen waved her over, motioning to join her at the window.

Tez flashed a sneer at the two captives and pointed her spear at them. A sharp gasp burst from the man's mouth, and he slid himself backwards, knocking his head into the wall with enough force to loose a splinter. "You stay right there," Tez warned, despite the couple's attention being focused squarely on the man's head in search of an open wound. Keeping an eye on the pair, Tez filed in beside her sister, reluctant to take her eyes off the two Invaders in their midst.

A click sounded, and Sen stepped out of Tez's way. "Take a look; I'll watch them." She did not narrow the gap, but the familiar readying of the Deatharm was all the indication the captives needed to cease their mewling.

Following Sen's instruction, Tez leaned against the window frame, her forehead resting atop her arm until she was near enough to sleep that she needed to voluntarily jolt herself to stay awake. She narrowed her eyes, parsing through the sea of bloodied and dusty field jackets and a mist of dense dirt, and unmoving within the waves of Invaders stood Tawa. Mercifully, he appeared unharmed, though for what reason, Tez could not guess why, but he was surrounded by several Keepers who were in much the same state. Battle-worn though not to the gravest extent of others, with defeat and anger and loss all evident upon their faces, even from this distance.

Despite the relative health of the surviving fighters, though, the bindings about their wrists could not be ignored, nor the intent of their placements. *New flesh for the slave camps,* Tez lamented to herself. *They start anew.*

She shook her head and drew a sigh, pushing herself away from the window and toward her sister on wearied legs. "At the least, we know the Owl still lives."

"Though for how long, who can say?" Sen muttered. "I don't know whether to feel relief that Tawa still lives or remorse."

"The line between the two has grown far too blurred." And relief was growing shorter and shorter in supply.

The sound of creaking wheels and heaving wagons drew Tez's attention back to the window. A heavy sensation of dread weighed upon her chest, but she could not bring herself to draw further from the window. She peered through the opening with much the same dejection, watching the bound Keepers and Tawa march forward, flanked by several soldiers, the supply wagons trailing behind them. "I wouldn't think they'd need this many for transporting to the camp." She turned toward Sen. "Was this normal?"

Sen was quick to shake her head.

Tez was well-aware of the bluntness of the question, but stepping around the ocean of dark memories was near impossible when dry land was nowhere in sight. She furrowed her brow, gnawing at her lower lip, observing intently the proceedings below, fingers rapping along the shaft of her spear. At any moment, the procession would turn to its left, depositing the Keepers and Tawa into their new profane dwellings. Biting back a surge of furious tears, Tez watched Tawa's head remaining high, his teeth gritted, bearing every resemblance to the brother he never had, the Chief under whom he could have felt cast into the shadows, but embraced everything about it, and the man upon whom that light shone. The spirit of the Stone Chief Fannalhen lived on in Tawa, just as it did within his surviving children.

But even as the march drew closer and closer to the entryway to the slave camp, it did not turn. It kept heading straight on, and all the wagons followed in its wake.

"What the hell is going on..." Tez muttered.

The floorboards groaned underneath two steps as Sen backed up toward the window, still keeping her Deatharm lined up on the captives, but not saying anything besides.

Tez watched with morbid interest at where the march could possibly be going. She could not see too far down the street, but all that lined either side were rows of homes, and a tavern or two. Those, and…

"Sen," Tez said. "What goes on in that place where all the smoke is billowing out of?"

Sen hummed in confused acknowledgment. "The factory?"

Tez shrugged. "I guess?"

"I haven't a clue, but why?" She lowered her arm and shuffled over toward the window. "Is *that* where they're going?"

"It'd seem so. There's nowhere else to go down that way so far as I can tell. But why…"

"I think *some* sort of labor goes on in there. Maybe Tawa and the others are just going to be kept in there?"

"But then what is the reason for the wagons of dead?" Tez gripped the windowsill, grimacing. "None of this makes sense." She shot a look back toward the captives, who were whispering to one another. At Tez's glare, they quieted in an instant.

Groans both human and wooden roared beyond their field of view. As far as seemed wise, Tez craned her head out of the window and glanced to the east, the shadows approaching in a staggered manner, starting and stopping in intermittent bursts. Another wagon approached, and whatever lay within was *big*. Big enough to require an entire group of soldiers hauling it along. There was even a scream cut off by a crunch, though it apparently did little to deter its forward momentum.

Tez rested her spear against the wall beside the window and wrung her hands with great apprehension. An initial row of soldiers appeared out from the corner, some five spread out, pulling the wagon along by the strength of two sturdy shafts. There seemed to be enough space for a sixth, but judging from one man's distress, that may have been the cause of the scream and crunch.

A large mass protruded above the wagon as it came into view. It appeared to be bloodied, matted fur, dark in color and darker where wounds had made their mark, and looked almost too large for the confines of the wagon. Tufts poured through the wagon's slats where the mass appeared ready to burst the frame apart. It was only when Tez saw the heavy foot hanging low and cutting a trail in the dirt below that she realized.

"*Gods*," she muttered. "The bastards brought the *Bear* all the way here."

"*What?*" Sen pushed Tez aside, her mouth agape. "What in the hell…"

The wagon struggled, its wheels holding on for all their worths. One wheel carried a red stain along its rim and a damaged axle for its trouble. Numerous Invader soldiers shouted at the poor sods tasked with hauling a god's corpse through this blasted heat, the slow pace evidently an inconvenience for those performing none of the work. Particularly the one spitting on the ground and scratching at his groin while he screamed his throat hoarse.

The procession continued, the soldiers and captives and wagons all pressing on in the same direction. Tez squinted, trying but failing to see through the obscuring veil of dust kicking up into the air. She couldn't be certain, but it seemed as though figures moved along into the factory down the way. And wherever this lot was going, she had no doubts that it would be where the Bear's corpse was headed, too.

"I don't understand," Sen whispered. "What are they…"

"Keeping the Bear like it's a trophy," Tez barked, sneering. "Fucking bastards."

As Sen opened her mouth to respond, another voice sounded from below, clearly discernible, even if the words were uninterpretable. Tez was unfamiliar with it, but Sen seemed to know it all too well. She gripped the windowsill, fingernails digging into the wood.

Curious, Tez raised a brow and followed Sen's sightline, spotting what appeared to be an elderly woman accompanied by two others. The old crone was shouting something to the people hauling the wagon holding the Bear. The wagon stopped and one of the frontmen appeared to be voicing something to the woman, disgust plain on his face.

She responded by punching him in the stomach, doubling him over.

Tez gasped, but Sen stood and fumed.

"Kamataa," she growled.

Her eyes widening, Tez felt a flare of anger rising within her. She had never seen the woman out of her Illusion, but Sen clearly had. Which only meant the two with her were Sha'a and Vanta, their faces no longer disguised by the Boons of Illusion long since stolen from their rightful owners.

"So, this is what happens when they learn who you truly are, isn't it, Kamataa?" Sen whispered. "You think you have all the cards now, don't you?"

Tez glanced at her sister, but redirected her focus to the one behind Kamataa: Vanta. When she closed her eyes, she could still see her plunge the blade into Ket's chest. Her chest pounded, the world around her little more than an angry haze. The longer she glared at Vanta, the further away everything felt. The groaning wagons below and the creaking floorboards behind her seemed so distant, a memory of sound. Slowly, she reached for her spear, her hand taking hold of it. Every instinct compelled her to jump from the window and offer Vanta the same treatment she gave to Ket.

Sen seemed to sense this and barred the window with her arm. And then she gave Tez a shove to the left.

The downward thrust of a knife occupied the space Tez had just left.

She slid to a knee, hand fumbling for her spear, when she looked up to see the captive woman glaring at her with a perplexing mixture of rage and fear filling her eyes. The woman looked stunned, unsure of what to do next. The knife shook in her hand.

Beyond her, Sen wrestled with the man, holding his wrists back while he tried to assault her just the same.

Tez shook her head. "You just *had* to give us a reason, didn't you?" She lurched forward, the woman trying to punch the knife through her but failing. Tez sidestepped the blow, her attacker's momentum propelling her past and to the spot where Tez had just pushed off from. Telegraphing a downward plunge, the woman rushed forward, growling, and Tez caught her at the wrist, twisting her arm one way and another, the knife prying loose and clattering on the floor.

The adrenaline pumped through Tez just as it seemed to for the woman. Sharp talons clawed at the flesh of Tez's neck. She hissed at the pain and tossed her attacker aside, slipping on the hilt of the blade in the process. Both tumbled to the ground, Tez ramming her elbow onto the hard floor. Pained spittle burst from her mouth as she gripped the woman by the shirt collar and pulled her to her feet. Frightened tears streamed down her face, but Tez was hardly in the comforting mood. A heavy headbutt opened the bridge of the woman's nose, the bones shattering and blood sluicing down her cheeks and into her mouth. The Invader groaned in both pain and fear and pushed against Tez, the Stone warrior's boots sliding against the wooden floor. Tez blinked away spots in her vision, her rear heel touching the table leg next to where she had sat previously. As she gritted her teeth, a moment of fearful recognition seemed to flutter in the Invader's eyes. The woman feebly swatted against Tez's arms, and Tez spun her around and threw her down.

She barely heard the sickening crunch of bone. All she saw was the blood painting the table in the aftermath. The woman's face was frozen in shock. Tez blinked and saw Vanta's face. Then Ket's, and then his unnamed woman again. She shuddered, her hands shaking.

Only the piercing of flesh by steel broke her from her trance. She turned to see Sen skewering the man along the length of her spear.

Sen kicked her attacker off the weapon, retrieved the Deatharm she had dropped at some point, and rushed over to Tez. "Are you okay?"

Tez's heart still pounded, but she nodded, words ill-formed on her tongue.

"Good. Get your spear; we need to get outta here. If we didn't cause a commotion just now, then the Invaders really are fucking idiots. And I want to know just what the hell they're doing in the factory."

Drawing a deep breath, Tez retrieved her weapon and followed Sen, out of the window adjacent to the alleyway and into the streets below. And into the dust beyond.

Voices sounded from well behind, but she could not discern whether they were the commands to shout to the sods pulling the wagon, or those drawn to the commotion they were part of. It was all drowned out by the sound of the woman's skull smashing against the table.

She wanted to hear the same sound again when next she encountered Vanta.

Memory

Vivat Rex

The days passed, and there was little sign at all that Lord Nofre would change his mind.

It had been a foul birthday for Aritz. What should have been a celebration and veritable feast had instead devolved into a meal of obligation, a feast fit for none but the servants who would oft pilfer for scraps. Felicitations for the commencement of his eighteenth year should have been marked with a cake crafted to strike fear into the waistlines of men throughout the kingdom. Instead, he received only a cut of some week-old slop from the pantries, while his parents discussed the impending arrival three days hence of Their Majesties, King Ferrand and Queen Catelina, paying Aritz little heed whatsoever.

Truly, it had been the worst of his birthdays, in all of his years. Even more so than the year Alsonso vomited all over the cake in a fit of spiteful food poisoning. At least there had *been* a cake on that occasion.

But in the space of the past three days, Aritz felt as though he may have been one of the servants, cast off beyond the peripheries of his father's grasp, a shadow hidden from an all-seeing light. He confined himself to his bed-chamber, emerging only when called for the midday and evening meals, but was otherwise regarded with open disdain rather than concealed. No words were exchanged with him, nary a glance, and barely an acknowledgment of his presence. Even his servant had chosen not to attend to his bedchambers. Whatever the servant's name was.

Gazing out the window to where the mountains kissed the skies, their crests enveloped by an alpine mist promising a torrent of rain, mired in clothing with three days of grime settled upon it, an odor rising from his pores—this was not how Aritz envisioned his first days of adulthood, the first days of being officially named heir to the Mata name and fortune. Instead, he bore every resemblance to the wistful and dramatic adolescents characterized by the visiting theater troupes whose visits he oft slept through.

"This shall not be how my story ends," Aritz had repeated to himself over the last three days. And when a raucous commotion resounded through the corridor, the echoes dancing off the walls of the hallways long since vacant of serving staff, a smile creased his lips, the first in four days. One arrival kept him going. Two, in truth. And as he licked his lips, he nodded with satisfaction that his next chapter may yet still be penned.

"Father may think he can disinherit me," he muttered, narrowing his gaze to the approaching storm clouds. "But Their Majesties will surely not take kindly to a House's firstborn being spurned of what is rightfully his." He rose and tossed aside the robe he had been adorning since his pallid birthday feast. Dark stains colored its underarms, and even throwing it several paces away ridded him of some of the lingering stench that had plagued him since the servants began to think of themselves as being above their wash duties.

He grabbed a long, blue, silk robe, elegant in its make and fringed in beautiful gold, and fastened it about himself. The cut exposed some of his chest and the hairs still gradually filling a blank space. It may not have been the regality meant to receive the royals, but if his next chapter was still yet to be written, then it needed to begin with a statement. Having no time to wash and feeling a slick layer of grease running through his auburn locks, he tied his hair back, letting the back tuft out in a curled puff at the nape of his neck. Appearances mattered, and he could not cast dismay upon the opportunity to play up the role of the betrayed firstborn.

When Aritz ventured into the corridor, it may as well have been inhabited by ghosts, the distant echoes very well serving to be not the proclamations of the King and Queen's arrivals, but the spirits of those long since passed, haunting these walls for they had yet to be embraced in the arms of the Savior. Not that Aritz believed in any of that; it was just another matter he had to remain glib and silent on with his standing among the great Houses of the Kingdom. But as he absconded through the halls, it was hard not to feel an overwhelming presence bearing down upon him, as though something was watching him. It was unnatural for there to be so much silence within this part of the estate. Even Lorente and Alsonso's chambers were vacated. Aritz sneered at the sight of that.

"How nice it must be for them to be informed of a royal visit. I am certain Their Majesties have a wealth of eagerness to greet a family of usurpers and thieves." He wrung his hands and stood in the middle between the doors to his brothers' bedrooms. Wondering, planning. But nothing came to mind. Whatever was fit for them could wait until after matters had been set straight. There was little time for much else.

With head held high, Aritz hummed a tuneless melody to himself, sauntering down the empty corridors, following the inviting echoes to their source, which he could only assume was the receiving chamber of the great hall. Applause and cheers roared in the distance as his boots clacked and squeaked against the pristine white marble underfoot, grimacing slightly as his heel caught for the briefest of moments and left a black scuff against the white canvas. He shook his head but pressed on. "Better a boot print than a bloodstain," he muttered. "We would never hear the end of it were that to spill."

The great hall drew closer, and so, too, did the raucous commotion. If Aritz had to guess, almost the entire household had gathered within. Not just his parents and brothers, but the guards and servants, as well. And yet, here he was, discarded like a forgotten memento. *A poor play, Father. A very poor play, indeed.*

By the time he reached the great hall, it sounded near to the reception for an acclaimed troubadour's performance. The doors were wide open, flower petals scattered about to mark the path the royals were meant to take—a tradition that forever seemed obtuse to Aritz—and an elegant carpet laid in gold and gems was spread out as a replacement for the typical one that adorned the hall's floors.

Aritz halted himself as the crowd quieted, and he pressed his back against the wall adjacent to the open doors, crossing his arms. Nary a whisper sounded from the hall, the silence broken only by a scarce cough and a cleared throat. Footsteps clacked upon what seemed to be the raised dais where the carpeting did not reach, where the seating for the Lord and Lady of Mata would surely be occupied by Their Highnesses.

"My family, my friends, my household," shouted a commanding voice.

Father. Aritz sneered.

"It is my greatest honor and privilege to welcome to our home our most esteemed guests, a privilege that is but once in a lifetime. May I present to you all: our High Mother, our Queen Catelina of the House of Nabarres; and our High Father, our King Ferrand of the House of Jaen, the Third to Bear His Name, Blessed of the Savior, and Protector of the Kingdom." Nofre's voice resounded throughout the great hall, a measure of authority as sharp as a well-honed blade.

The crowd erupted in thunderous applause, and then, in an instant, fell to complete silence again as the lordly chair creaked.

To rouse a people to cold quiet by merely the act of rising to one's feet. Such a display of power. Aritz nodded, staring straight ahead at the wall across from him.

A set of heavier footsteps thumped against the dais, followed by a heavy clearing of a throat. "Lord Nofre, Lady Aldorisa," proclaimed a rich, bass voice. The King's voice. "I speak on behalf of both myself and the Queen in tremendous gratitude for this marvelous reception you have provided us. You speak of both honor and privilege, but please rest assured that such honor and privilege are altogether my own."

"Please, Your Highness," Lord Nofre responded, seeming to artificially deepen his voice to match that of King Ferrand. "Think nothing of it. The hospitality of the Mata estate is ever yours. The capital is such an arduous journey—for you and Her Highness to venture all this way is nothing short of a boon to us all."

Aritz rolled his eyes. *All this talk of honor and privileges—is this truly* all *there is to lordship?*

"Why, Lord Nofre, you belittle yourself and your House!" The King offered a deep laugh. "The contents of our previous discussions, it would bode ill of me—and to us all—were they to be kept to private correspondence. This is a day for celebration—not only for you, not only for your family, but for your *legacy*."

"'Legacy,'" Aritz whispered with a scoff. "Of what consequence to Father is our family's legacy, truly?"

Fingers snapped, and another set of footsteps scurried into action. A heavy thud resounded against the marble of the raised dais, followed by the unfurling of parchment paper.

"I do not speak falsely when I profess you to be one of the greatest merchant lords of our Kingdom, Nofre. You are shrewd, determined, ambitious—and it is your ambition that will see you rise even further above your already lofty station." The King paused and walked along the dais.

Aritz peered his head round the corner, discrete so as not to draw his father's attention, and found the King—every bit as plump and boisterous as he imagined—standing beside a table, the unfurled parchment resting underneath his finger. Aritz slunk back to the wall, resting his head against it.

"When the Duchy of Attaviano and their great adventurer, Omerago da Vespindi, discovered that vast expanse far beyond the western oceans, they had to know they were on borrowed time. It was to their great detriment that word spread to our shores. An ill-kept secret, to be sure. The Duchy has hardly the men to claim all of it for themselves—a want for which we thankfully lack. I know not what lay within the frontier of this New World. But I needn't send Omerago da Vespindi to find out. I need only send the Kingdom's greatest merchant lord."

A collective gasp seemed to grip the household. Several "ooh's" and "ah's" were uttered, though Aritz had to wonder if they knew what any of this meant. They would never see a single mark from any of this, nor the fabled expanses of this so-called "New World."

But for Aritz himself? It seemed quite the adventure to embark upon.

"Your Highness," Lord Nofre proclaimed, still exaggerating his voice beyond a natural tone. "Are you certain? I am beyond honored, but—"

"But nothing, Lord Nofre," King Ferrand interrupted. "I gaze upon this estate and find not only a man of means, but a man of cunning and wisdom. You built a commercial empire from nothing. Now, you shall help turn our fair Kingdom into an Empire of its own. It is my *own* honor to bestow unto you this task, to secure these expanses in the name of Acraria, to establish these trading routes, and create a prosperous and rewarding future for our land and our people." He paused and laughed boisterously once more. "Come now, Nofre, back to your feet. You have long been clamoring for the rights to this expedition. There is no need to be coy."

"Of course, Your Highness, of course. I fear I am just...overwhelmed. I have awaited this day for ages."

"And I am certain your family has, as well. The House name 'Mata' will no longer be just a standard bearer for the Acrarian Kingdom—it shall ever be a symbol of prosperity for the *world*."

And may that symbol be fashioned in mine own image, Aritz thought. He pushed himself off the wall and turned toward the door.

"Your children, and your children's children, will be eternally blessed in the light of the Savior as staunch champions of our Kingdom."

"Then we should ensure that *all* the children are present, should we not, Father?"

A deathly silence fell over the great hall and Aritz strode in, the ends of his robe fluttering behind him as he sauntered along the carpet and toward the raised dais where his family and Their Highnesses stood in varying degrees of shock or confusion.

For the first time, Aritz was able to take in the King's appearance. In his brief surveying, he had assumed Ferrand to be portly and overweight, inevitably the goal of any monarch from a lifetime of indulgences and feasts. But he was surprised to have found himself mistaken. While King Ferrand had some girth to him, yes, much of it was due to a thick musculature which had left him with a minimal chin and thick arms. There was no hiding the protruding stomach, but he did not look unhealthy by any stretch of the imagination.

Conversely, the Queen was a paragon of beauty. Catelina's face was framed by wavy blonde locks cascading down her shoulders, her piercing eyes, prominent cheekbones, and pursed lips, all bearing every resemblance to a sculpture cast in perfect marble. She sat in Aritz's mother's chair, hands folded in her lap, glaring at the spurned heir not with anger or malice, but curiosity, a reaction matched by the King himself.

The same could not be said for Aritz's family. The color had darkened on his father's face to a deep red, such that it was a wonder he had not already burst from rage. Behind Nofre stood Aldorisa, Lorente, and Alsonso. It had been some time since Aritz had seen his mother without a drink in her hand, but it meant her general disinterest had been replaced with a capacity for attentiveness, her mouth agape, too stunned to produce words.

It did not take long for Aritz's brothers to cower behind their mother's skirt. All it took was Aritz flashing a sneer for them to turn tail and hide. *And Lorente was to be a soldier-at-arms? I shall say a prayer for the state of the Kingdom's armies.*

"Pray forgive my intrusion, Your Highnesses," Aritz said as he reached the dais, kneeling with respect to his King and Queen. "I confess I overslept, else I would already be standing beside my brothers."

The King regarded Aritz with silence, narrowing his gaze at the young Mata. After a moment's hesitation, he nodded in acknowledgment. "Then I was *not* mistaken, was I, Lord Nofre? It was my recollection that you had *three* sons, not the two you presented before me and wrote of in your missives."

Ah, so I had been long discarded, was I, Father?

Before his father could address the "oversight," Aritz rose back to his feet and put a hand to his chest, offering a slight bow. "I offer my humblest apologies on behalf of my Lord Father, Your Highness. I am Aritz a Mata, *firstborn* son of Lord Nofre and Lady Aldorisa."

"*First*born, you say?" King Ferrand raised a brow and turned to Nofre. "Lord Nofre, I was under the impression that Lorente was your firstborn—is that not so?"

Again, Aritz interjected before the words could escape his father's lips. "Do not think ill of my father, Your Highness. We have had a recent...disagreement, shall we say. One that I do wish we can put behind us soon."

Nofre did not meet his son's eyes. "I disinherited him four days past, Your Highness." The bluntness of his words ill-matched the edge of the King's glare, but it did little to deter him otherwise. "The disagreement begins and ends there. Lorente shall be named my heir when he comes of age."

King Ferrand regarded the Mata patriarch for a long while, the illusion of grandeur and warmth dissipating into an air of complete authority. He stood in silence, his chin puffed out, daggers in his eyes.

But it was the Queen who spoke first on the matter. "The law is clear on the matter, Lord Nofre." Her voice was smooth as honey, but still commanding. "One may not spurn the rights of inheritance—title and all—without written petition to the Crown."

A sputtering of nonsense erupted from Lord Nofre's mouth.

"Aritz is not guilty of treason to either his House or the Crown, is he, Lord Nofre?" Queen Catelina raised an eyebrow.

"N-not as such, Your Highness, but..."

"Conspiracy or sedition, my Lord?"

Nofre blinked with frustration, but shook his head. "No, Your Highness."

The Queen unfolded her hands from her lap and gestured with palms facing out. "Then I fail to see the reasoning to disinherit him so. As long as he remains a faithful servant to the Kingdom, then he—"

"He is neither a—" Nofre bit back the interjection and held his hand over his mouth.

Ferrand took a heavy step forward, his face plain, but with enough authority to drop the Lord of Mata to his knees with barely a glance. "Do you deign to think your words are of greater import than those of Her Highness?"

Fear flared in Nofre's eyes, the first time Aritz had ever seen his father gripped in the throes of terror. For a moment, he pitied him. But though it was well worth it to at last see him grovel on his knees, Aritz knew this expedition was beyond just his father's glory.

It could be for his own.

He gestured his palms toward both Nofre and King Ferrand in a placating show. "Father, please." Aritz inclined his head toward his Lord Father, showing deference to him, and then turned to the King. "Your Highness, I fear I have unearthed some ugliness best kept within our halls. This...*momentous* occasion should not be sullied by familial difficulties. If you would but pardon this matter, we will resolve it in private after Your Highnesses have made your return to the capital. My Lord Father and our family needn't be punished nor kept from receiving this great boon from you." He offered a deep bow to the King and then another to the Queen, masking a smile threatening to emerge.

Nodding along to Aritz's words, Ferrand relaxed his posture, his stomach once again protruding as he slouched, and he gave a slight smile. "Very well, Aritz. I pray these...disagreements shall be overcome in due course. I know not the root of this strife, but resolve it with the utmost of haste. The hands of a young man such as yourself are hands in which I would gladly place the future of your family."

Good. What passed for a sincere smile creased Aritz's lips. "You are too kind, Your Highness." As he glanced back at his father, he almost could not stifle the chuckle building within him.

A tremor had gripped Lord Nofre. The realization that his decision to disinherit Aritz had been summarily ripped from his hands and buried beneath the marble flooring seemed to have broken him. A feeling of defeat was apparent on his face, but he did not appear willing to give his son the satisfaction of victory.

Folding his hands at his waist, King Ferrand returned his attention to his favored merchant lord and said, "Then, if that shall be all for this matter? Lord Nofre, I would endeavor to discern the details of your voyage. I believe it is your plan to depart within the fortnight, yes?"

Nofre stammered, but rose to his feet and gave a hesitant nod. "Y-yes, Your Highness."

"And you shall have a marvelous new galleon for this expedition, recently completed and in need of a captain. I can think of no man more deserving than you, Lord Nofre."

"Ah...ah, thank you, Your Highness."

"She has been christened the *Chariot.* A powerful vessel, perhaps the most powerful in all the continent. I will see to it that a capable crew is at your disposal before your departure."

Nofre bowed deeply. "That is very kind of you, Your Highness. Thank you again."

Aritz took a step forward. "And I shall volunteer to be your first mate."

Disdain colored Nofre's face. "I beg your pardon, Aritz?"

With a smile, playing up the innocence in the face of Their Highnesses, Aritz ascended the dais and put a hand on his father's shoulder. He could feel Nofre flinch at his touch. "If only that I may prove my loyalty to our House and to our Kingdom—if ever it was called into question. I would see this New World with you, Father, to see the glory that awaits the House of Mata, and the glory we shall bring to the Acrarian Kingdom. Permit me this, dear Father, that I may prove myself as heir to the Mata name and legacy."

A brief glance at Their Highnesses showed approval in his proclamation, pride upon Ferrand's face that water was flowing beneath the bridge and hope on that of Catelina for a new beginning for both the Mata family and the Kingdom. Such was the interpretation Aritz wished to believe, at any rate. He knew his Lord Father would be a fool to deny him.

But when Lord Nofre pulled Aritz in close, he brought with it none of the warmth of a reconciliatory embrace. Rather, he firmly gripped Aritz's shoulder and pursed his lips beside his son's ear, the King and Queen's view of his face obscured by Aritz's head, and whispered, "Begone from my sight."

The shadow of a grin slipped across Aritz's lips. An involuntary reaction, one heeded not by amusement, but disbelief. That, even when faced with royal decrees to the contrary, he would still play this pointless game, even if he was too gripped by his own cowardice to proclaim it at large. All Aritz could do was stand and wait as though this was an intimate and private conversation reserved only for father and son.

"Believe as you may that you can manipulate any and all to get what you want—even Their Highnesses," he continued in a harsh and low volume. "But I will be neither swayed nor deterred, even if I must make myself to be a liar in the eyes of the King and Queen. Know this, Aritz: there shall *never* be a place in our legacy for a petulant and conniving *child* like yourself, and so long as I breathe, you shall never be my heir. This I swear." And he pulled away.

Aritz maintained what composure he could, managing not to tremor with the anger building within him. Instead, he nodded with feigned grace, and then glared toward his brothers. He could already spy a dark stain trailing down Alsonso's leg. "If I may beg your forgiveness once again, Your

Highnesses," Aritz proclaimed, holding his arm out at his side with a wide flourish. "I am afraid I must depart. There is…much for which I must prepare, and I am but one who jumps into tasks while they are still fresh in my mind."

King Ferrand nodded and smiled widely. "But of course, our young Lord. Ambition awaits no man. I wish you the fairest seas."

Aritz approached the King and lightly grasped his hand, bowing before it and pressing his lips to the ring adorning Ferrand's pinky finger. "And the safest of trails to you on your return to the capital." He turned to the Queen and offered her the same respect, kissing the jewel resting on her finger. "And you, my Queen: the safest of trails to you."

"The fairest of seas, and the brightest of futures," Catelina responded with a warm smile. "The Savior's light shines bright upon the Mata family."

And may it glow ever brighter. Aritz bowed once more and turned on his heel, descending the dais and sauntering once more down the carpeted pathway and out of the great hall, paying no extra heed to the observant crowd of servants and guards, or to his family.

That shadow would be bathed in bright light soon enough.

The dusk of the next fortnight brought with it a commotion of a different kind. There was a liveliness in the manor's halls that Aritz had not seen in some years, an excitement borne of the promise of prosperity and the hope for a lucrative future.

It had been a day since the porters and crewmen arrived in full at the Mata manor, and several hours since they departed to the shipyard to ready the *Chariot* for her maiden voyage on the morrow, the docks an hour's ride to the west. Visitors came in droves to his parents' bedchamber to proclaim well wishes and safe travels to Lord Nofre, their conversations stretching the limits of what was acceptable within the confines of an enclosed space. After a while, the echoing voices stopped giving Aritz a headache. The processions had finally receded to but the scant remnants who had missed the opportunity to be part of the earlier crowds, and whose lonely and sad footsteps sang in a soft aria for the opportunities lost.

Aritz reclined in the reception chair of his bedchamber, feet resting atop the nearby stool, his elbow propped up on the armrest. He eyed a bottle of wine on the side table, the waning orange sunlight glinting off the glance and illuminating the contents within. As the days continued to pass between the morning of the King and Queen's departure and the bottle's eventual arrival, Aritz had grown concerned. It was his intention to bequeath this unto his father before his voyage, and no small fortune had been spared in its procurement. That it arrived but two days past was nothing short of a relief for Aritz.

He rose to his feet, drawing a deep breath as he grasped the bottle by the neck. With a nod to himself in the looking glass, he opened the door and found the corridor once again empty, the celebration long since departed. His footsteps clapped against the naked floor, the door to his parents' chamber wide open. He stopped short of the threshold and lightly rapped his knuckles against the thick wood before peering inside.

An exasperated yet curious mutter sounded from elsewhere in the chamber, and Lady Aldorisa emerged from the adjacent changing room, a measure of surprise on her face. "Oh. Aritz," she said, deadpan. "Apologies, I thought there was yet another visitor for your father."

Aritz forced a smile. "No, Mother. It would appear I am the sole unwanted visitor remaining."

The slightest of cracks formed in the mask of his mother's face. Though Aritz did not believe her to be party to his father's decision, she also had not raised any objections to the matter. How much of it was keeping up appearances and how much of it was coming to an accord, it was not for him to know. It still came across as a betrayal, regardless.

Still, a mournful grimace could not escape her lips. "Aritz, you—"

"No, no, Mother, tis quite alright," Aritz interjected, raising his free hand. "We needn't act to the contrary. It does not mean *I* wish not to see *him*." He showed the bottle of wine to Aldorisa. "Is Father here? I would like to give him this."

Aldorisa approached and took a closer examination of the bottle. "Where did you get this, Aritz? This is not from our stores."

"I...put in a special request." He paused, his lips curling upward for the briefest of moments. "I had hoped to be able to share it with him upon his official proclaiming me as his heir, but, well..."

The words hung in the dense air between them. Aldorisa sighed and wrung her hands, the words she clearly wanted to say falling short of her tongue.

"It's okay, Mother," Aritz assured. "It does not mean I cannot still gift it to him. I would rather the air was cleared between us before his voyage should the worst befall him on the journey, Savior forbid." He took a step past the threshold. "Is he here?"

Aldorisa shook her head. "After the thirtieth visit, he departed elsewhere. Perhaps the great hall, if you do wish to 'clear the air,' as you say."

"Thank you, Mother," he said with a bow. "I'll look for him there." He turned on his heel and trod down the corridor.

"Aritz," his mother called.

He stopped, his heels squeaking against the marble flooring, and he turned his head over his shoulder.

Something unreadable was apparent upon Lady Aldorisa's face. A modicum of frustration, yes, but something else, as well. Sadness, perhaps? Fear? Apprehension? It was difficult to discern. It was an expression with which Aritz had no familiarity as it pertained to his mother. Anything beyond disinterest was a shock.

She sighed, her breath rife with resignation. "Whatever may happen, I ask only that...you respect your father's decision. For the sake of the family."

Though he wanted to grimace, though he wanted to shout, Aritz allowed his lips to crease into a smile, even if it was far from genuine. He did it for her. *For the family,* he thought mockingly. And without another word, he turned back to the corridor and set off for the great hall.

Much of the idle conversation seemed to filter in through the windows, the servants and guards enjoying a beautiful summer's evening, the air crisp and vibrant as it wafted in from the mountains.

All the fewer people to be forced to ignore.

A single guard stood in front of the doorway to the great hall as Aritz approached. The man eyed him with suspicion, but no malice beside the fact.

"Is my father here?" Aritz asked, finding no sense in belaboring his visit.

The guard furrowed his brow and nodded. "He is, but requested none disturb him."

Aritz stared blankly at the guard. He kept his face plain but forced a hint of anger into his expression.

It worked. The guard let loose a heavy breath and rolled his eyes, glancing at the bottle in Aritz's hands. "But, if you must, Young Master." He moved to open the door, but Aritz shouldered past him.

"I can make do, but thank you." The door groaned as he forced it open, the hollow and hallowed great hall waiting in silence for him. None stood within, save for the footman who stood readied at attention, for whatever reason necessitated his being there, and Lord Nofre, whose attention was paid to the world beyond the northwestern window, where the mountaintops were surely glimmering in the waning sunlight.

The footman drew a deep breath and began to proclaim, "Presenting, the—"

Aritz shoved his empty palm into the man's face to silence him. "Save your breath. My father knows who I am." His footsteps did all the talking as he approached Lord Nofre, echoing off the hard marble flooring now stripped of the ornate carpet from a fortnight past.

A tuft of wind blew in through the opened window, Nofre's untied hair billowing behind him, his hands folded behind his back. He seemed to have no inclination to turn toward his son.

As Aritz filed in beside him, he presented the bottle of wine and cleared his throat. "Father."

A sliver of attention was paid to him. Nofre glanced at Aritz in his periphery but offered no more than that. "What is it, Aritz?"

Permitting his hands to tremble and his lips to frown, Aritz closed the gap between himself and his father by another two steps. "I...wanted to offer this to you, Father. Think of it as an olive branch."

Nofre grunted and turned to his son, his brow raised. "An olive branch?"

Aritz nodded. "I understand your reasoning, Father. I understand the need for a lasting legacy for our family. I understand you may wish not to have any more to do with me. But it does not mean that I wish ill of you. Before your departure, I would rather we..." He paused, grimacing in a gesture not wholly ingenuine, though not for the reasoning his father may have suspected. "I do not wish matters to be left on such poor terms."

Smacking his lips, Nofre unfolded his hands and stroked his chin pensively. "You speak as though you do not expect me to return."

"I fully expect you to return, Father. It is more that...should the worst come to bear, I fear the regret would be too much."

"No gesture will change my decision." His father's glare was sharp and stern.

Aritz nodded. "Nor do I expect it to. Just share a drink with me. I am still your son as you are still my father. Indulge me this once more."

Though the acquiescence on his father's face appeared more obligatory than voluntary, Nofre still gave his son a tentative smile and nodded. "Very well, Aritz," he said with a sigh. He snapped a finger and craned his head toward the man at the door. "Footman! Two glasses and a corkscrew, if you would, please!"

The doors groaned loudly behind Aritz as he took in his father's smile. Silence still hung between them—the events and revelations of the last fortnight could not be remedied so easily—but he still felt relief at being able to stand here, his father not banishing Aritz from his sight.

A moment later, the footman returned with the glassware and corkscrew as requested. He handed a glass each to the two Mata men, set to work on releasing the cork from the bottle, and then presented a healthy pour to Nofre and Aritz both. He nodded to either man, seemingly unsure what next to do with the bottle. There were no tables set up in the great hall.

"You may leave it anywhere," Nofre assured. "If my son is so eager, then it must be a delicious vintage."

Aritz nodded. "I've been told wondrous things about it, Father."

The footman smiled and placed it by the lordly chair before scurrying back to the door for whatever important duties awaited him there.

Raising his glass, Aritz declared, "To a prosperous journey, and a safe return home."

"Hear, hear," Nofre responded, bringing the glass to his lips and drinking deep. He nodded along with the notes as they danced upon his tongue.

With a grin, Aritz reciprocated the gesture and made to drink just the same…only for the wine to slosh about before reaching his lips and instead spilling all over his chin. "Ah, damn it," he muttered. He turned back to the footman, the man already appearing eager for his next task. "Ah, excuse me! Could I ask you to bring a towel? Apparently, the aroma was intoxicating enough."

Haste took hold of the footman as he departed, the door slamming shut behind him.

Nofre smacked his lips and hummed with soft approval. He looked at the bottle but seemed to notice the lack of a label. "This is delicious, Aritz. How did you procure this? It does not appear to be one of ours."

Aritz shook his head, wiping away the dripping liquid from his chin. "You're correct, it's not. I thought an occasion such as this required a more…unique note. I feel we oft ignore the talents of those in the Northern Marches."

"Mmm," Nofre grunted in affirmation, coughing twice as he finished the glass a bit too eagerly. "I would have to inquire to Pandrea upon my return. I was unaware the Northern Marches were rich with vineyards." He coughed again.

Chuckling, Aritz strolled over to the window with glass still in hand, his eyes affixed to the north, and the Marches that lay beyond the mountains. He tossed the contents of his glass out the window. "They are not."

Nofre opened his mouth as though to question further, but he coughed again. And again. His face was colored in a deep red, and he dropped to his knees.

The footman would return at any moment. Aritz dropped the glass, allowing it to shatter upon the marble, and slid over to his father, holding him in his arms, letting him fall slack in his grip. "'Curiosity pays its weight in gold,' does it not, Father?" he whispered. "You were always keen to inform us of that. And shall I say, I have always known where my curiosities should be directed."

His father's breath grew short, a ragged rasp between fits of coughing. He gripped at this chest, his face now purple, his hand trembling to a stop.

Aritz hushed him. "Now, now, Father. It is in *my* hands His Majesty was keen to place the future of our family, after all. I am merely...correcting the course you set us upon."

His face contorted into wordless, pained anger, a fire raged in Nofre's eyes, threatening to burn his son to cinders if it only maintained the strength to be more than smoldering embers. But instead, a long, weak breath wheezed out from his throat, fading to a faint whistle, until it was nothing more than the part of the wind at Aritz's back.

Looking down at his father's slack body, Aritz licked his lips and drew in a deep breath. And with an emptiness in his chest, he shouted, "Help! My father, it's...it's his heart! Somebody, please!"

CHAPTER THIRTEEN

BLOOD MACHINE

Though he had never much been a fan of the loud roar of machinery inside the factory, it was rather cathartic to finally be walking amongst this realm again.

Aritz had been to the very depths of hell and back. Felled two gods. Crushed a savage people beneath his heel. And even after being subjected to devilry against his will on this return home, an impostor took his face and his name and slaughtered fair citizens without discrimination, without remorse. The streets of this monument to the Acrarian will had been bathed in innocent blood.

At least now, the blood plaguing the earth is from naught but a society of wickedness and filth.

Against all those odds, to walk within this factory, within this testament to achievement and symbol of progress, it was quite soothing, regardless of the oppressive noise. He could barely hear himself think, but such was preferable when faced with the memories of the return journey south.

The conveyor belts running into and out from the larger machines had revolutionized production in the Acrarian homeland, and it had done much the same in this new land. That this city had become the monument it was now had much to do with the success of the machinery. It had never once crossed Aritz's mind that it would wear down, that it would falter and perish. Never had he the inclination that such had happened in Acraria, but it was also a realm beyond his understanding. It was not he from whom the prospect of steam power was realized. But he was more than happy to use it to the best of his ability for the benefit of this new land that he had won, that he could now lord over, shed the guise of the warrior, and become the ruler he had always envisioned himself being. The next chapter in a book long being penned.

But if Kama was speaking truly, then the golden age of this new nation was soon to be realized. There was no better time than now to take this country newly won, still in its infancy, and raise it to a standard not only meeting that of the Acrarian homeland, but *exceeding* it. Aritz closed his eyes, feeling the warmth of the whirring and spinning machinery around him. A nation crafted in his own image, a new industrial revolution with himself as its chief architect, the visionary who had both the gall and the means to attempt such a profane experiment. One that may have appeared morbid to outsiders, but none would argue for its efficacy, should it have proven to do so.

All this—*all* of it—for this land to become the jewel of the Acrarian Kingdom that Aritz knew it could be. A nation and economy fit for an empire with himself as its central figure. A nation defined not by its size but by what it shall provide to the Kingdom, a centerpiece of Their Highness's expansion and influence across the world. Everything was within his grasp now, everything his father once saw fit to deny him. A true lordship rather than being a lord of the spice trade. A regional governorship to permit him to shape this nation as he saw fit. Future lands and holdings for himself and his descendants, prosperous and absolute rule, so long as he received the means for exploration and conquest. A history in the making. His would be the greatest name in the Acrarian annals. He longed for it, yearned for it.

He opened his eyes, a contented sigh escaping his lips. *I am but too far ahead of myself.* Soldiers passed him by, apparently electing not to interrupt his daydream, judging from the wide berths they took around him. *The daydream proves to be greater than this reality. There is much still to do.*

And though he tried, the illusion was long gone by the time he next closed his eyes, his mind now altogether preoccupied by the duties awaiting him in the adjacent room, and the memory of blood sluicing down his throat. The foul taste still sent chills through him. An involuntary burp traveled up his throat at the thought of it, but he suppressed it and walked toward the adjacent room, the whirring machinery leaving a ringing in his ears.

Hesitation marked Aritz's step as he approached the threshold. He had willingly been party to this, but at the same time, the very sight of it was a bit too much. He was reminded of a trip he once took to a slaughterhouse as a child, a venture his father insisted he embark upon with him. It had been a harrowing experience, but a worthwhile one. The production and delivery of meat had been a prevalent mystery for him up to that point.

And as he took a step into the room, seeing the savages strung up and bled dry, their lifeblood pooling and collecting in troughs underneath, Aritz could not escape that same sensation. The feeling of familiarity when faced with a gruesome reality. *But it is a necessary reality,* he assured himself. *Just as the cow is brought to slaughter so that we may provide for ourselves and our kin, so, too, must these animals in order to carve a brighter future.*

At any rate, it was a mercy. These very people were groaning and pissing themselves over the entire length of the journey back south. Despite how lowly these creatures were, Aritz still recognized the cruel state he had left them in. He would have done much the same to a wounded dog begging and whimpering for what little life it had remaining. It was better to slit the throat and let it end than to watch the mind wither to nothing while the body decayed for reasons that could not be stopped. He was ending the lives of these blighted minds while also ridding this land of their poison. So long as he thought in those terms, he had no reservations for this task.

It hardly meant feeling a hint of disgust was beyond him, though. He could feel his stomach turning already. With a grimace, he approached the nearest bleeding man, his eyes lifeless and devoid of any and all light, but a sharp, rasping breath still grating against his throat. Aritz lifted the man's chin by the strength of a finger, a tongue lolling out from the mouth, breath worse than a feral dog's. The trickling of blood into the trough gave the initial impression that the man was relieving himself in front of his betters. *Sickening,* Aritz thought.

Shaking his head, he dropped the savage's head, the man's face blanketing in a sheet of stark white, and looked down the row of people, men and women, some who could barely be considered adults, sizes large and small.

None with even a shred of cognition toward what was happening to them, the only signs of life coming from the pervasive drone of grating groans and heady breaths.

In here, though, it was merely another noise in concert with the crash of machinery.

A procession of voices coming from the direction of the main assembly lines drew Aritz's attention. Whoever it was, they were loud enough to stand out against the competing sounds of the factory. Aritz held few doubts to whom the voice belonged.

He adjusted his coat and traipsed around the blood-filled trough and walked back toward the entryway, eager to rid himself of the foul stench of impending death.

But he still was yet to acclimate himself to the face of death awaiting him in the factory's main corridor.

"*General Aritz*," Kama said with great flourish, bowing to him in a quite embellished manner.

When first she revealed her true appearance, Aritz had every inclination to gut her where she stood. Even knowing the truth of her origins beforehand, being fully aware that she was borne to these…creatures, to see her with the mask removed, the façade dispelled, it was more than a shock. It was every representation of the unnatural affront to nature her people represented. As the woman straightened herself out and glared at Aritz, that wave of revulsion returned. That she was aged beyond anything Aritz had ever seen, her face not beset by wrinkles but rather her wrinkles were beset by a face, called to wonder just how old she truly was. *How many years has she seen?* he could not help but contemplate. *How many* centuries *has she seen?*

Beside Kama and her tufts of thinning white hair stood her two accomplices, more of the savages who had been long hidden among his ranks. *For how many more must I keep a close watch over my shoulder?* Their field uniforms looked nothing less than tarnished when garbed upon them. When all this dust had settled, Aritz had every inclination to change the attire for his soldiers, so these now-fouled uniforms could forever be relegated to the stains of time, these memories washing and flooding over them.

Aritz opened his mouth to address them—beyond the words he truly wished to say—but the factory doors crashed open, followed by a strained grunt and a roar of anguish. Strings of curses, some of a derogatory nature that even gave Aritz pause, were thrown out from the mouth of a guard at the front of the large delivery wagon, his face not just slick with sweat but entirely drenched, beside him two others. *Should there not be more among those who were to pull and steer?* Aritz raised an eyebrow and craned his head, noticing wobbling wheels on either side of the wagon. One wheel had a notable smear of red along its rim, not yet removed from the dust and dirt outside. When at last the wagon cleared the threshold of the door, the front line collapsed, nearly taking the arms of the pulley down with them.

Kama held her arm to their new arrival with a flourish. "Aritz," she said with malice coloring her tongue. "I am sure you are—"

Holding out a hand to quiet the old woman, Aritz did not so much as spare Kama a glance. Of greater import was the mass of matted and bloodied fur threatening to collapse the wagon to splinters. He rushed over to the men, hovering over their exhausted forms. "Back to your feet, soldiers," he commanded. "While we still have wheels with which to haul this monster."

The lead man, the one with the colorful tongue, looked up at Aritz with despondent eyes, almost near to tears, his chest heaving with heavy breaths. "But—sir—we—"

"Now!" Aritz reiterated. His voice would have echoed if not for the machinery drowning him out.

A collective groan chorused among the soldiers—and in louder resonance from behind the wagon—but with pain in their eyes, the front men rose back to their feet and screamed every ounce of effort they could summon into their arms and legs, the wooden frame voicing the same agony, creaking and cracking to what may have soon been its last breath. There was precious little room to work with, the rows of assembly lines impeding much of the forward momentum, but a path was clear enough for them to pull ahead. Aritz took several steps back to permit them a wide berth with which to pass through.

The gargantuan paw of that demonic beast trailed out from the back, its claws filing against the factor's stone flooring, cutting a swath through it as though it were chalk on a board. It seemed impossible that even in death, the bear's claws remained just as sharp as they were when the beast was disemboweling his soldiers deep in the mountains, its roar threatening to summon all the north's snow and blanket them all.

Aritz gritted his teeth as the beast was carried along. He still felt the tremble up his arm from driving steel through its skull, the hot rush of steaming blood sluicing out and bathing his hand in a torrent of red. When he closed his eyes, he could still see its jaws so near to closing over his throat, before he could open up the beast's instead.

As the wagon passed him by, though, he found himself meeting eyes with a different beast.

Kama awaited on the other side, upon her face a wide smile—eager, sinister, venomous. The crevices in her cheeks stretched to their limit against the strength of her mouth. She folded her hands at her waist, bearing the appearance of a kindly grandmother, even as her eyes gave all indications to the contrary.

Aritz sighed and approached, wishing only to get their interaction over and done with. He had not spoken to her since the...rituals she performed on him in the north. He had yet to find a drink stiff enough to purge him of the memory and everything associated with it. For now, all he could do was repress the hell out of the experience and avoid any and all reminders of it.

Reminder number one, however, appeared ill-inclined to permit him to forget.

"Kama," Aritz spoke plainly, paying little heed to the trailing soldiers practically being dragged along with the wagon. "What is it?"

"Why, so hasty, Aritz," she responded, putting a hand to her chest in feigned offense. "I am doing quite well after this final skirmish, thank you for asking."

"I didn't ask. What do you want?"

Kama laughed. "I wish only to see how you fare. I ensured this morning enough would be readied for you to begin in earnest, after all."

Aritz gestured to the machinery. "I would hardly know where to begin, Kama. I am not privy to the details of your sorcery, let alone the mere meaning of the symbols you carve."

"I assure you, Aritz, it is quite simple. I will ensure a diagram of the runes and their meanings is drafted for you." She turned toward one of her accomplices. "Sha'a, would you be so kind?"

"There is no need," Aritz said, stopping Sha'a before she could take a single step. "It shan't be myself or any of my men performing this task. I will not have them sullying their hands with your witchcraft."

"But you'll permit this 'witchcraft' to strengthen everything in this factory?" Kama scoffed. The offense upon her face appeared more genuine.

"I told you. *Our* hands will not be sullied. *Yours* are already tainted. The task is best left to you. Or one of those two." He pointed to Sha'a and the other one, whatever her name was.

A hint of disapproval marked Kama's face.

"What is it?" Aritz asked, raising his brow. "Surely it is not beneath you to make use of your natural-born talents."

Kama narrowed her eyes. "Of course not. My knowledge is at your disposal. Just as it was for…" She extended her arm, pointing toward the beast rising above the confines of the wagon. The soldiers collapsed once again, and the wagon seemed to thank them for it.

Aritz understood the implication. *So, you* do *think yourself above this work.* He scoffed. "So long as you have knowledge still to offer." He left his own unspoken words hanging in the gap between them.

Slowly, Kama nodded, and the smile returned to her face. "But of course, Aritz." Her old eyes drifted in the direction of the adjacent room, where the mindless savages continued to be drained of their life. "Have you ensured the blood stays separated by Sign and Boon?"

"Why in the hell would I have done that?" Aritz asked, flummoxed the question was even raised. "It was *you* who organized them as such!"

"But it should have been well clear that—"

"Then *you* should have prepared for that." To feel anger and annoyance toward Kama again, rather than revulsion and nausea, was something of a relief. Her goading seemed almost intentional in that regard. "*You* should well know that I haven't the faintest clue what any of that means, nor do I have any intention of doing so. Why should I waste any of my time learning it?"

Kama shrugged. "It could mean the difference between a machine with sustained durability and a machine that can speak any language."

Aritz sneered, feeling his nostril twitching. "It's *your* oversight. Will this be a problem?"

Throwing her hands in the air, Kama gave a nonchalant smile and walked over to the room, her mobility defying her true ancient appearance. "The effect may be diluted, but it's still worth the attempt. We have plenty of others to make use of—and plenty more who have still kept their wits about them. Trust me, Aritz. All shall be well."

"Trust," Aritz muttered. "Right." He closed his eyes, a chill running up the back of his neck. He felt the savage woman's heart bursting down his throat again, the horrid warmth choking him, a fire rising, a promise, a pledge, and then...

"Come along, Aritz," Kama called. "Allow me to show you."

He hesitated, the memory's sensation fleeting until he at last felt hollow once again, the emptiness he had hoped would have long been filled. He shook his head, renewing his focus, and followed Kama, past the beyond-exhausted soldiers still groaning and whimpering beside the wagon. Judging from the splinters left behind in its wake, the transport seemed moments away from collapsing atop at least one of them, and not a moment too soon.

Kama was gripping one end of the trough by the time Aritz entered the room, Sha'a taking hold of the other. The blood sloshed about, splashing on the floor, coating the ground in a slick and viscous red while streams continued to sluice in absence of a destination where the trough had once been. The pair, appearing to be unimpeded by the liquid weight of the vessel, placed the trough beside the machine nearest to the room. Kama placed her palm against its metal surface, clearly not fearing the heat residing within it.

Aritz's initial reaction was to speak out and warn her against doing so, but she was old enough to figure it out for herself. Age and wisdom and all that. *Though I've met plenty of fools among the elderly—they may just be the greatest fools of all.*

If Kama felt pain at the touch, she did not show it. Instead, she drew what appeared to be a calming breath and glared at the machine's frame as though discerning some great secret. Whatever words of wisdom it offered, it was beyond Aritz's expertise, but Kama seemed well adept at interpreting what it had to say. She removed her hand from the searing metal, her palm clearly scorched from the heat, and reached into the trough of blood.

Whispering something indecipherable to Aritz's ears over the surrounding noise, Kama allowed the blood to pool in her cupped palm and trickle out through the slits of her fingers. She bunched her hand into a fist, flexing her digits and running them along the length of her palm. A slight smile creased her lips, and a chuckle along with it.

In the span of a blink, she turned on her heel and slapped her hand against the machine's frame, the impact resounding through the factory. It even drew the attention of the exhausted soldiers, even if it did not rouse them back to their feet. The startled breaths were more than enough indication.

The blood stuck to the hot frame, steam rising as it already began to boil. When Kama returned to where she left a smear, she produced a swath that then became a stroke. With the intricacy of an adept artist, she painted her hand along the machine's body until it was well coated in the drained life of the savages from the adjacent room. The faintest of winces broke her expression as she made a fist, her fingers slow to close, her arm shaking with the effort.

Insanity was all Aritz could label it as. Insanity and stupidity. *She shan't be shirking her duties by burning off her skin. I will make certain of it.*

As she sucked in a pained breath, Kama held out a hand, and the accomplice not named Sha'a produced a carving knife, not unlike the one Aritz had seen her use back in the mountains in her first demonstration of this claim to power.

When this had all been but a curiosity. But now, if it were not to work...

An ear-shattering screech halted further doubts from Aritz. Kama jammed the tip of the blade into the machine and dragged it by the strength of two hands, the steel screaming against the heavy frame. Aritz clenched his eyes shut and threw his hands to his ears, the very noise causing an eruption of anguish. It pained him to his core, enough to draw water to his eyes.

The horrendous noise ceased and Aritz felt calm once more. Until Kama set right back to it, inflicting the same pain again. The collapsed soldiers, some paces back, cried out in both anger and pain, screaming curses at Kama for her transgressions. The witch ignored their words, though it could very well have been that she did not hear them to begin with.

When the screeching ceased again, Aritz did not bother to open his eyes or unblock his ears. His instincts prepared him well as the woman made another pass, a final, merciful pass through the metal. When it was all over, and the initial silent seconds stretched into truthful, genuine quietude, Aritz breathed a sigh of relief, his hands shaking, that stretch of minutes a greater torture than he had ever experienced in all his days.

His chest thumped as he took two heavy steps forward. "What. The hell. Was that?" he prompted between breaths.

Kama handed the blade back to her subordinate and wrung her hands as though to remove the lingering blood, but doing naught else but smearing it further into her scored flesh. She did not seem at all bothered by what should have been agonizing pain. She said nothing, only motioned Aritz forward with a wave of the hand, waiting beside whatever was imperative enough to rupture the eardrums of all present.

Aritz filed in beside her and narrowed his eyes at her carvings, symbols that were clearly of this land, but the meanings of which far beyond him.

Seeming to sense the confusion, Kama pointed to the first of her runes. "Strength." She pointed to the one below it. "Endurance." And the one below that. "Restoration." A long breath escaped her lips as though the experience was tiring for her as well. "The Strength to withstand whatever you may throw on this assembly line. The Endurance not to break down in the most hectic of times. The Restoration to fix itself should any parts become rent."

His initial instinct was to reach out and run his fingers over the carvings, the indentations pooling with savage blood, the edges still flaked with metal that had been shaved away. The presence of close heat was enough to rip Aritz away from that idiocy, warmth close enough to dance upon his palm, but he still regarded the runes with great deliberation. "Impressive," he muttered, his voice only barely rising above the surrounding noise. "Let us test it, then."

"Hold, Aritz," Kama said, raising her unburned hand. "This is not the same as carving a rune into a blade. This thing is massive." She looked upward, taking in the height of the machine, a smokestack atop it carrying the mechanism's breath to the skies. "It will take some time yet. I ask for your patience."

"Patience," Aritz repeated, smacking his lips. He flashed a sneer at her. "Forgive me if my patience has worn thin. I believe it is within my rights to doubt after your previous...gifts to me have proven faulty."

Kama did not immediately respond. A ghost of a smirk creased her lips as she continued to wring her hands, her thumb massaging the burned flesh of her palm. "Fear not, Aritz," she said at last. "Rest assured that I shall do all I can to ensure your gruesome blood harvest goes as smoothly as possible." Ghosts walked again as her smile returned in full.

The accusatory glare and words left Aritz's mouth agape. *My "gruesome blood harvest," you say? My memory must be betraying me—I never thought myself of the mind to paint my factory in savage blood!* A thousand and one words to say came to Aritz's mind, but before he had a chance to unleash them upon the old crone, the factory doors crashed open once again.

"General! General, sir!"

With an exasperated sigh, Aritz turned on his heel to see two soldiers running toward him. "What? What is it?"

"There've been two murders, sir!" shouted the lead soldier, apparently attempting to carry his voice above the factory's mechanical rhythm.

"We are but a day removed from retaking our home," Aritz responded, rolling his eyes.

"No, sir! Screams and struggle were heard not long ago. Those nearby investigated and found one with a skull caved in and the other with their chest run through. A spear wound, from the look of it."

"And the hunt continues," Aritz muttered, pulling his flintlock out from the holster on his thigh. "Come, show me."

"Of course, sir. Right this way!" The soldier turned back toward the door and jogged to the exit.

"Aritz, allow me to accompany."

Stopping dead in his tracks, Aritz spun toward Kama with anger in his eyes, her comment not yet forgotten. He felt some measure of surprise at seeing what appeared to be hatred in her eyes, though for what reason the flames were there, he did not care. "No!" he declared, pointing his pistol at her, directing the nose between her and the unpainted machinery. "You still have plenty to work on here. I want this all working by the time I return. Is that understood?"

Kama's upper lip quivered. She outstretched her fingers, flexing them, balling them into fists with the same speed. Even the burned one, with no difficulty. "Very well," she said, lacking the vigor and haughtiness that had oft colored her words.

A sharp, snorted breath puffed out from Aritz's nostrils, and he turned toward the factory doors. Before he walked too far away, he called out over his shoulder as he walked past the wagon, "And while you're doing nothing, you may as well get started on *this* beast. Unless blood from a fucking god will dilute things further!"

The wagon finally collapsed as though in response.

His ears rang as he emerged onto the streets, the soldiers awaiting him there. He followed them without further word, off to the scene evident of apparent stragglers still pursuing their wicked goals, whatever they were.

And yet, that did not bother him so. Not so much as the sensation of heat still gripping his hand. Or the heat that should still have held Kama's...but clearly no longer did.

CHAPTER FOURTEEN

WHAT WE FIGHT FOR

The Year 1556 Anno Salvatoris
15 Years After the Invasion

Exhaustive fire continued to burn in Sen's chest. Even when a suitable hiding place was found, she could not stop running. The shadows provided ample cover, the tight quarters even more so, but everything within called for her to run.

She hadn't stopped since that day four years ago when she learned of her birth as an Eclipseborn. Escape had been her goal each following day. Into the comfort of a drunken haze. A fleeing of a different kind.

When the worst had come for Brin and her father, she ran from the realities of what she deemed her own responsibilities in the matter. To feel she had nothing at all remaining, a life no longer worth pursuing.

When blood stained the mountains and her survival rested upon divine intervention, the two lives she led—one by birth and one by consequence—both lay smoldering amongst the ashes. Nothing remained to run to, only to run from.

She wondered if there was greater comfort amidst the ashes. No longer did she feel she could be the flame. It was dwindling, flickering, the torchlight blown about by the heavy winds of change, threatening to extinguish with a final push. All Sen knew had been piled into the ash. All she remembered, all she lived.

And now, huddled against her sister, her heart pounding, bones aching, blood spattered against her flesh and tattered clothing, all she wished to do was run once more. To run from this land of pain and sorrow, this City stained by dark memories and wicked deeds.

But the only place remaining to run to was where the ashes lay smoldering, where the dust called and cursed her name.

For the time being, at least, the voices calling for her knew not a name to curse. Only a people, an eviscerated people known only as savages and animals.

It was difficult to discern whether the dwindling commotion had been from the uproar over their killing of their two hostages, or if they were far enough away from it for it to have even mattered, anyway. It had been a blind fervor that led Sen and Tez to this spot. Everything between when they alighted from the second-story window and when they sat themselves among the muck and grime of these tight quarters was a blur to her. A horrid, nightmarish blur. It could very well have been but a few buildings down where Sen had opted to hide, or it could have been halfway across the City. She knew not where she came from. Her presence of mind led her only to position herself in relation to the proximity of the factory.

The billows of smoke were still well within her line of sight. They weren't too far from it, and whatever mysteries lay within.

She and Tez had not exchanged a word since their flight. Sen had never seen her sister so gripped in shock as she was when she opened her assailant's skull on the table. At this point, she couldn't be certain if all the bloodshed and death of these last weeks had finally caught up to her. Caught up to them both.

It wasn't long ago that Sen had killed her first—the Chieftain of the Wood Tribe, purely out of mercy. It had haunted her for days. But now, after the battles she fought and the lives she took, just to survive for another minute more? She couldn't feel anything. She was numb to it all. And that frightened her. She had no intention of slaying those two captives. But she also felt no remorse for their deaths.

She closed her eyes, letting loose a shaking breath. *I don't want to become like Kamataa, delighting in the slaughter of my enemies. I don't even want to have enemies.* Her head tapped against the wall, wincing from the impact of the heavy stone against her skull. Her spear, once an obligation for her to hold so she could act as a training dummy for Tez, now felt an inextricable part of her as she gripped it firm in her hands, resting the tip against her forehead, the steel somehow cold and refreshing against this oppressive southern heat.

A distant crash called her attention, a burst of dark smoke peppering the southern horizon. She inclined her head, a heaviness settling upon her chest. Sen knew the time she and Tez could stay here was dwindling. It only forced her to grind the shaft of her spear even tighter.

"Tez," Sen whispered, her throat dry and her tongue like sand. She turned to face her sister, feeling the weariness settle into her eyes.

Tez looked far worse for wear. Still, she had that blank, cold expression on her face. Her upper lip was stiff, a sense of pain holding her in place. Before her feet rested her spear.

"Tez," Sen repeated. "If there was a time…it would be now."

Closing her eyes, Tez sighed. "Do you remember when we first heard that the Invaders had taken these lands?"

Sen raised an eyebrow, unsure of the purpose of the question. "Not…particularly."

"I didn't think you would. You were too young to understand it back then." Tez gritted her teeth. "I remember Father receiving panicked missives from Chief Han'e, from Fen-Osenta, that something terrible had happened. At the time, I don't think Father put much thought into it. I don't think he *understood*. But when Han'e arrived in our village a broken man, I saw something I still can't believe to this day." Slowly, she turned toward Sen, her eyes opening to reveal weary anger. "He got on his knees and *begged*. Like a dog. He lost his home and people to the Invaders and the Wood Tribe both and it had reduced this hero of the battlefield to a beggar stripped of everything he once held dear."

She paused, letting the words simmer between them. "It is the only time I ever saw fear in Father's eyes. *Our* Father, Bravesoul himself, saw what the Invaders had reduced the proud Han'e to, what they had taken from him, and it was then that he understood. Father may have come across as stubborn in maintaining Stone neutrality whenever Han'e returned to the village and plead for help in retaking the Sun Tribe's lands. But he understood what we are now learning." Tez looked past Sen, her focus placed upon the billowing smoke beyond. "The Invaders take, they burn, they destroy. And those who get in their way just become smoke clouding the wind's breath."

Sen loosened the grip on her spear, her hands shaking from the effort. She hardly knew what to say. The words hung in the air: the stern warning and the acceptance of defeat. "You've never been one to give up, dear sister. That's always been *my* job."

Tez scoffed and shook her head. "Sen, the Invaders have taken *everything*. We have lost *everything*. It's no longer a reality reserved for the southern Tribes—it has happened to us *all*. I give up because we have nothing left to uphold! Who besides us remains? Who is there left to fight for? *What* is there left to fight for?"

"There's *always* something left to fight for," Sen murmured. "Even when it seems there's nothing." She released herself from her spear and held Tez by the back of the head. "Even if it's just you and me. There is *always* something, Tez. Some of us just have to wait longer than others to find out what."

Gesturing in the direction of the smoke, Tez flashed a sneer. "And will our answers await us in there? Is that factory our calling?"

"It might be." Sen shrugged, maintaining what confidence she had been able to muster, even as the reality of it all threatened to pull her back to the pit. "It might not be. But we insult ourselves and everyone who has fallen to the Invaders if we merely sit here and wallow. And regardless of whether it is by our lonesome or with a legion of the lost at our backs, we need to go in there and stop whatever it is they're doing to our people. If there is but one small victory we can grasp from these jaws of defeat, then let it be that. *This* is what we can still fight for."

"A 'legion of the lost?' What, are we the Haunted now?" Tez rolled her eyes but rose to her feet, regardless. With pronounced effort, she picked up her spear, not quite bearing the image of the fearless warrior she once was, but she at least appeared a bit removed from the one who had been ready to give up a moment ago.

Half a smile creased Sen's lips as she rose to her own feet in kind, the shaking in her hands quelling as she held firmly to her spear once again. "We very well could be," she said. "But I don't plan on standing around and waiting to join their ranks."

"And what are we going to do once we find our way into the factory? *If* we find our way in?"

A stark silence hung between them. Sen looked down to the ground and kicked at a pebble digging into the ball of her foot. She opened her mouth with a smack of the lips. And then closed it again.

"You haven't a godsdamned clue, do you?"

With a sheepish shrug, Sen said, "In fairness, it's not quite easy to form a plan when we don't know what we're facing in there."

Tez shook her head. "The more things change..." she muttered, pushing past her sister.

Sen raised a finger. "It's as I've always said—"

"Luck hasn't been on our fucking side in quite some time," Tez interrupted, sneering at Sen from over her shoulder. "Let's get this done with."

There was a life to Tez's words and motion that Sen was relieved to see again. So despondent had she been in the wake of everything that had transpired during the battles in the True Heart. Sen knew not how to mend the fracture left when Tez was stripped of the Bear's Endurance, for she left only further pain in saving her. She did not know how to fill the hole left by Ket's death, for she was still climbing from a pit of her own left by Narva's death. She could not understand what it was like to have lost so much, for she always felt herself as having little to lose.

But what Sen knew full well, what she was more than confident about, was her ability to annoy her sister into action. And that was more than enough for now.

Do I have a plan? No, she admitted to herself. *But I've made it this far without one. And try as I might, the Moon seems far from done with me right now.*

She caught up with Tez, who waited at the mouth of their hideaway alley, holding up a closed fist to signal Sen to wait. Slowly, Tez craned her head around the corner, the pathway evidently clear from the way she rushed forward to the next alleyway across the street. Sen followed her, her first step a slip against the soft mud underfoot, but she caught herself by the end of her spear and ran after her sister.

The factory was not far. The acrid and foul stench of the smoke was proof enough of it. By Sen's estimation, they were only a few streets away.

The City seemed quiet enough around them. Beyond the procession of wagons, and the soldiers parading them, Sen had barely heard a peep from anyone or anything today. The people seemed to still be hiding in their homes, fearing reprisal, that the next chapter of this book of warfare was yet to be written, that its next act was about to take center stage before them. *What little they know,* Sen lamented. *If only such were in my power.*

She pulled ahead of Tez, placing a finger to her lips. Her heart thumped in her chest as she rested against the wall of the next alleyway, a closed and shuttered window beside her. She peered around the corner, finding soldiers far in the distance, nowhere near enough to call attention should they spot her. Nudging forward with her head, Sen scampered across the next gap, sliding into a close with broken glass littering the path. She sucked in a sharp breath, feeling a shard cut into her leg, but stifled the pained gasp she wished to loose. As the glass crunched beneath her heel, Sen crouched low, feeling and hearing Tez close behind, and breached the dank walkway.

The factory loomed ahead, its smokestacks visible beyond the next row of homes.

Voices sounded down the road but seemed to be moving away from her. There was an edge to the words, the conversation not at all casual. Sen could only wonder how much of it had to do with her own actions. *The more moving away from the factory, the better.*

When the road cleared, she sprinted ahead, feeling a warm wetness trickling down her leg, her trouser leg clinging to where a glass shard had cut her. A small fire burned at the spot of the wound, but there was no time to tarry. No time to fuss. At the mouth of the alleyway stood the gate to the factory.

During her brief time among the Children of the Black Moon, Sen had not ventured over to the factory; much of her time had been spent hiding in the barracks. She had seen it from far away—her initial memory of it was seared into her memory, when she and Narva overlooked the City for the first time—but to stand before it, it truly made her feel small. The only building of an equal or greater height was Aritz's manor.

A lone wagon stood in wait outside the factory—one of the wagons the Invaders had been loaded with the Tribespeople with rent minds. As Sen approached it, she could hear the faint groan of its inhabitants—mercifully still alive, unmercifully still in this sorry state. She winced at the reminder of the horrid proceedings in the True Heart and passed the wagon by, crouching beside the nearest window, Tez kneeling beside her.

"Whatever you need to see, make it fast," Tez whispered sharply. "We're wide open here."

With a nod, Sen peered her head toward the corner of the window, narrowing her eyes in a hope to spy what was happening within. "Damn it," she whispered, and wiped at the window with her hand, coming away with nothing. The view was no better. "There's…something on the other side of the window. Probably grime. I can't see through it."

"Shit," Tez muttered. "Now what?"

Sen glanced back at the wagon, and the doors beside it. The entryway to the factory had been left open, enough of a gap for them both to squeeze through without drawing any unwanted attention. She smacked her lips and nudged toward the door. Though the glare in Tez's eyes seemed to indicate protest to the proposal, Sen offered a shrug as if to say, "What other choice do we have?" Without further argument, she scurried over to the wagon, placing a hand along its side in a request for forgiveness from the people inside, and lined up beside the door.

To call the interior "loud" would have been a tremendous understatement. Something—or several somethings—was hammering away in a discordant symphony of noise, echoing violently against the walls. There were metallic crashes and slams, the sharp points of impact sending a crushing sensation through Sen's bones. She could feel herself collapsing merely from the sheer cacophony of it all. *But at least we won't have to worry about keeping quiet.*

Once again, she peered around the corner, finding several Invaders inside, but all of them turned away from the doorway. Sen took one breath, two breaths, three, and scampered around the door, finding the nearest thing to hide behind, not even taking the time to recognize just what it was. Tez rushed beside her with the same urgency.

The interior of the factory both stunned and frightened her. Peering around the stacked wooden pallets they had hidden behind, Sen gazed with wide eyes at everything within. Screeching metal behemoths roared in rhythm with one another, moving platforms carrying objects between one another with great speed. From the top of each monster protruded a thick tube that ascended through the ceiling, which Sen could only assume was the source of the smoke that littered the sky.

Scattered about the factory floor were the other wagons, though whether the dead and mindless still dwelled within was beyond Sen's recognition. Even if they were groaning inside, she would not be able to hear them against this noise. For what purpose they were brought here, though, it was still not immediately clear. Sen scanned the perimeter of the factory, the far ends of either side of the floor flanked by rooms with what seemed to be space for closeable doors, with whatever good that would do. Beyond one of the wagons, she could see a flurry of movement cast by a series of shadows. She furrowed her brow and peered her head around the other direction, still not getting an adequate angle to see around the wagons.

Another stack of pallets was within reach some paces away. From Sen's line of sight, it appeared to offer a better view of the proceedings. She tapped Tez on the shoulder and inclined her head in that direction and rushed ahead, sliding behind the coverage and hissing in another pained breath against her cut leg. The blood was seeping through the fabric of her trousers. A problem for another time.

From here, no wagons impeded her view, and though one metal behemoth blocked some part of the factory floor, Sen could perfectly see who was hard at work on the other end of the floor. A collection of nameless soldiers stood in wait with hands placed on their hips—Sen recognized a couple of them as being part of the caravan that hauled the wagons here—but past them was the unmistakable corpse of the Bear, resting atop a bed of shattered wood. Apparently, the wagon it was placed in finally collapsed under its weight.

Even from this distance, though, the pool of blood underneath the Bear was not lost upon her.

Sen felt her jaw drop. She looked at Tez, who had the same shocked reaction. "What the hell…" she muttered, barely able to hear her own voice. The soldiers standing in front of the Bear pointed toward it, looking to one another, looking beyond the god's corpse. Someone appeared to be on the other side of it.

There was no point in being surprised when she saw Kamataa emerge from behind the Bear like a rodent breaching from a hole in the earth. Her hands were coated in dark red—the Bear's blood, it was safe to assume—which she then tossed into the frame of the metal behemoth as though she were bailing water out from a flooded room. Sha'a and Vanta appeared beside her, kneeling next to the Bear's corpse and mimicking Kamataa's motions. Back and forth they went, back and forth, in a rhythm matching the sounds of the factory.

It was hypnotic yet horrifying. Sen kneeled back down, hiding away behind the stack of pallets. She covered her mouth and gnawed at her index finger, disbelieving what she was seeing. And then she thought back to the various wagons placed around the factory floor. *No...they wouldn't. Even for them, that's too...no. No, no, no. There's no way.* When she looked at her sister, she had to wonder if the same thoughts were running through her head. All she could say for certain, though, was that the fury in Tez's eyes was not reserved exclusively for the desecration of a godly body. Sen could *feel* the air change next to her when Vanta came into view.

Sen put her hand over Tez's, softly shaking her head. She understood the urge, but there were only two of them against Kamataa and who knows how many Invaders. The trembling in her grip should have been message enough for her sister.

Thankfully, it was. Tez closed her eyes and drew a long breath. When she opened them back up, she appeared focused on the adjacent room.

Sen followed her line of sight and looked back at her sister with a silent accord. Shadows moved in the room, hanging above a long, rectangular object. Ignoring the heavy flutter in her chest, Sen rose back to a crouched position and scurried along, slipping on something wet beneath her, cursing the alley of broken glass as her leg stung with pain. She hadn't realized how much she was bleeding. *This visit may have to be quick yet.* Her leg now throbbing with each heavy step, she scurried along to the door's threshold with Tez.

She felt far too frozen to keep walking when she looked inside. Nothing could have prepared her for it.

How could anyone prepare to see their own people strung up like animals to be bled out? Anger, fear, sadness, hatred, they all coursed simultaneously through Sen at the sight. A row of Tribespeople, all Tribes mixed together, were hung by the wrists, tied tight, their feet dangling just out of reach of the floor. Their stomachs were opened up, not wide enough to gore them, but still wide enough for them to continuously drip and sluice blood onto the ramps jammed into them, allowing it all to slide down into the trough below. All of it accompanied by one of the foulest odors she had ever smelled.

It was beyond inhumane.

"And they call *us* savages," Sen murmured. "This isn't even torture. This is...pure evil." Her spear quaked in her grip as she took a cautious step forward, faintly hearing clinking chains in the next room over, a door linking that room to this one. In her periphery, she could see a bound foot pacing back and forth, a face eyeing her with no intention of looking away, but she could not break her gaze from this more horrifying sight.

What made it worse was the seeming acceptance of these victims. Sen did not recognize the faces, at least by name, but she knew these were all people with families, with homes, with dreams and aspirations, and all they amounted to now was being bled dry for purposes she neither knew nor wanted to know. None exhibited any pain or protest. All any of them could do in response was rasp out their weakening breaths and await the end, an end far too prolonged. If any of them had been given food or water, it was clear that it was only enough to keep them alive.

Being kept in their mind-broken state was horrid enough. They deserved mercy, and this was anything but.

Sen grabbed Tez by the arm and pulled her into the room, the wall helping to mute the hammering sounds of the metal behemoths, but only a little. What echoed more in here was the trickling of blood into the trough rather than the rhythm crashes outside.

The flow was enough to drive her mad.

She positioned herself at the center of the trough, her eyes meeting the sparkless gaze of those strung up. Deep down, she wished she could have done so much more for them. What she offered was hardly a mercy, but it was at least a hope. One that wished whatever nefarious purpose this blood was for…it would not be done.

With a shove, Sen tried to topple the trough over, but far too much blood had pooled in it already. It was too heavy for her to do on her own. "Tez! Help me," she pleaded.

A moment's hesitation held Tez in place, but she just as quickly acquiesced, and after two further attempts, they were successful. The trough fell over with a heavy clang that resounded through the room, piercing Sen's ears as blood crashed against the floor and wall, covering the hard stone in a crimson tide. It did not take long at all for it to puddle about the entirety of the room, soaking the soles of Sen's boots. She stood in it silently, wondering if this river of blood was her own recompense, a place she deserved to be.

Her chest pounded again. She didn't know what to do now. *How many more of these do they have? How many more lives are at stake?* The blood kept trickling down from these victims' stomachs, collecting in the puddle. Sen knew she could free them, but then what? Where would she go with this mindless flock with not a thought of where they were or how to function? But at the same time, she couldn't leave them like this. It would be to subject them to the same cruelty. They couldn't be long for this world, though.

Sen groaned against a throbbing pain in her head. She rested a hand against it, unable to look away from them. "Cut them down," she said plainly.

Tez turned to her, placing a hand on her shoulder, her feet splashing in the red puddles underfoot. "Sen. What would we—"

Quick to shake her head, Sen stared back at her sister. "I've made the mistake of leaving people to a worse fate. I promised myself I would not do so again."

"And what are we gonna do once we free them? At this rate, it's not going to be much longer until they—"

"I don't know! But anywhere is better than here. Come on, just—" Sen gritted her teeth and grasped the ramp hanging from the bare stomach of the first man in the line, biting down the rising nausea as his stomach let go of it, the sound and the smell all too sickening. "*Fuck,*" she groaned. She looked at the binding, too high to reach with her hands but still well within reach of her spear. Luckily, it was just rope. She positioned the tip of her spear against it and began to saw it back and forth. Frustration settled into Sen's heart as the binding would not come undone against her spear's might. A tear trickled down her cheek, pain roaring inside her, the face of the unwitting prisoner blurring behind the veil filling Sen's eyes, the knowledge that elsewhere in this house of horrors, another face was assuredly strung up. A face Sen wished she would be able to see one last time. *Please,* she thought. *Please be okay.* Wet footsteps and clinking chains filled her ears against the backdrop of crashing on the main floor of the factory.

Tez still appeared unconvinced. "Sen. Your heart is in the right place, but you need to know you can't save every—*shit look out!*"

On instinct, Sen dove to the side, splashing and sliding through the pooled blood. Everything happened so fast. Agony roared through her as she landed on her wounded leg. Tez lurched forward, thrusting her spear into the space Sen had once stood. A Deatharm sounded, the bullet biting into the chest of the man Sen had been attempting to spurn free. Tez's spear knocked the pistol loose, sending it careening into the wall next to the door of the adjacent room.

By the time Sen looked back up, Tez was backing away, growling and heaving her breath toward the new arrival.

"Vanta," Sen snarled. She tried to push herself back to her feet, but all she could do was writhe against the shooting pain in her leg.

The Eclipseborn splashed her feet in the pooled blood, hardly bothered by being disarmed. She was plenty dangerous enough without it. "I'll have you know, Sennalhat. You'd make a horrible Sneak. I only came to collect the last wagon, when what do I find but a trail of blood leading me here." She held her arms out, gesturing to the mess. "You'd do well to leave less evidence of your presence."

Sen managed to push herself up to a seated position, damning the slick floor underneath her. "The hell are you even doing with all this? Haven't our people suffered enough?"

"I won't waste my breath," Vanta said, slowly approaching through the viscous puddles. "And you aren't long for yours. I know Kama would prefer you for herself, but...I'm sure she'll forgive me."

Tez blocked her path. "You won't live long enough to ask for it."

"Nor shall you to prevent me." Vanta's hand shot forward, and Tez swatted it away with the shaft of her spear. Her motions were cautious, despite her rage. Vanta, by contrast, needed only a touch. She could afford to be deliberate in her motions. One mistake by Tez, and it was over.

Sen slid herself back as far as the room would allow, using the end of her spear as leverage to rise to her feet, but failing as the pain was too much.

Tez slashed and jabbed at Vanta, snarling with each attack, limited by the small confines of the room, but all Vanta did was back away, duck, dodge each strike, and goad Tez into pressing the attack. The Stone warrior did not fall for it. She played defensive, her shoulders already slackening, the exhaustion of these last sleepless days draining her already. Her next thrust was weak, barely a challenge, and all Vanta had to do was pry the weapon away from Tez. The momentum of Tez's attempt to maintain her spear sent her flying backward to join her sister in a heavy splash.

Disappointment flashed on Vanta's face. She tossed the spear aside and cracked her knuckles, a metallic splash to her feet as she approached the sisters. "Pardon me if I appear vexed, Sennalhat. I simply find it hard to believe after watching *this* pitiful display that you actually are the one who killed Ziia."

Sen outstretched her wounded leg, rising to a half-crouch on the strength of her good leg and spear. "For what it's worth...I also killed Zara." She smirked. "Luck has always been on my side."

"And all things eventually end."

"Too right," a male voice said.

And manacled wrists clasped around Vanta's throat, the chains digging into her flesh. The Eclipseborn's feet stamped in the struggle, splashing blood in every direction. A deep purple colored her face as she reached back and clawed at the arms of her assailant, the death sentence sealed at that moment, but not sealed enough to diminish her attacker's strength. A last breath cracked out of her throat, and as though worrying the time had come for them too soon, the assailant threw Vanta's body to the side, her head crunching against the overturned trough.

All things end, indeed.

With effort, Sen pushed herself the rest of the way to her feet, her eyes affixed to Vanta's dead form. She couldn't look away. Because she knew her heart would be ripped asunder once she looked upon the face of their protector, their rescuer.

Once she looked at Tawa.

There were no words to be said. Tawa simply smiled at her and Tez, streaks of blood clawed into his forearms and sluicing down into his manacles. A tear strolled down his cheek, and he closed his eyes, no pain on his face, nothing but a shred of acceptance shining through as he fell backward, the Otherworld awaiting him while the pool of blood on the floor claimed him.

A clamor of commotion on the main floor was all that kept Sen from rushing to Tawa's body. It didn't mean, though, that the tears were not to come. She raised an unsteady hand toward his lifeless form, this man so near to family drifting further and further away the more she tried to reach him. Her body was numb as another life was stripped away, and she could not do a thing to stop it. Dropping an arm, Sen simply allowed the tears to flow.

Everything else was a blur. The glass crashing. Tez dragging her through the window. The running. The painful, agonizing running. Again, she had to run. She barely remembered stopping. It was only when Tez was binding her leg with fabric from her own shirt that Sen realized they were far from the City. Where they had laid Brin to rest. At this point, it was as good a place as any.

It was only when Tez held closely to her that she realized her sister was crying. Sen leaned into Tez's shoulder, the stones comprising Brin behind her, and they stared in silence at the crashing waves to the south. The weight of their brother's presence loomed heavily on Sen, and an even greater force drew her eyes back to the east, where the darkness cast by the smokestacks still loomed on the horizon.

"We have to go back," Sen murmured.

"Why?" Tez asked.

It was a valid question. The number of things they had to lose was growing fewer and fewer, as was the number of things left to fight for. But there was still *something* to fight for. There was always something.

"Because Mother may very well have been among those set up to die."

CHAPTER FIFTEEN

POWER PROMISED

The Year 1556 Anno Salvatoris
15 Years After the Invasion

Droplets of blood fell from Kamataa's hands as she awaited Vanta's return. She had always been averse to using the Acrarians' weaponry—so imprecise, so slow to use. For her to resort to using it was more than enough to hold Kamataa's attention.

But the seconds stretched on, and she could not break away from staring at the room where there were assuredly intruders. Vanta was never one to take her time. Speed had always been her ally, a trait she learned whilst growing up among the Arrow Tribe. It was enough for Kamataa to begin moving away from the machinery, the false runes only half-completed. Her ears were already offering her great thanks.

The exhausted soldiers shouted something in her direction as she moved further away from her task, their voices far too soft and unassuming for her to register them. In response, she flashed them a glare coated in ice, stopping them all in their places. *If you think you may lord over me, then the least you could do would be not to tremble at the sight of me.*

The same curiosity seemed to have held Sha'a in its grip. While the men continued to shout at them with all their false bravado, Kamataa wrung her hands, wiping them against her uniform jacket, prompting even greater protest from the other soldiers. She narrowed her eyes toward the room, the machinery clanging away in her ear, and where once she held an amused curiosity toward Vanta's exploits, there was instead a sensation of dread and concern.

One that was punctuated by the thud loud enough to carry across the factory floor. She nodded to Sha'a and began to walk over, one of the soldiers finally chasing after her with whatever words he thought were disciplinary.

She broke into a run at the sound of shattered glass. The blood coating the floor of the room immediately gave her pause. She reached for the pistol at her thigh, never having the same hesitation about such weaponry as her protégé.

"What the *fuck*?" exclaimed the soldier who had followed her. A look of pure revulsion colored his face, more so than he already had when glaring at Kamataa. He stopped dead short of the blood, the act of slaughtering Tribespeople apparently easy enough for him, but to walk through their remains was where he drew the line.

Kamataa clicked the hammer back on her pistol, shouldering the soldier out of the way and knocking his face into the corner of the doorframe. The floor squished underneath her boots, reluctant to give her command of her own feet. Foul was the scent assaulting her nostrils, a round of voided bowels signaling that at least some of the Tribespeople in here had been bled dry. But she cared little for that. Her attention was paid instead to the man lying on his back in the middle of the floor, his face spattered with red splashes. She recognized him as the man who signaled the surrender in Aritz's manor.

Far too reluctant was Kamataa to look beyond the pale of this dead Stone Tribesman, because she knew what revelation the body next to him held. She drew a deep breath and holstered her weapon, her feet caught in between the slow march toward the truth and the rush to disprove it all. But there was no preventing what had already happened. There was no manner in which she could undo it all.

All she could do was pry loose Vanta's skull from the overturned trough and carry her in her arms, eyeing the shattered window where the intruders had clearly escaped from.

Where *Sennalhat* had escaped from.

A growl resounded deep in Kamataa's throat as she rose to her feet, Vanta's corpse hanging slack in her arms, blood and brain matter still sluicing from where her head was bashed open.

"Savior's breath!" cried the accompanying soldier. "Absolutely vile!"

"Surely, you don't mean her," Kamataa responded in a plain tone, all emotion gone from it.

The soldier groaned with pronounced disgust. "Get that away from me. I don't want to look at it."

A loud bang erupted just as soon as Kamataa freed her hand. The smell of spent gunpowder was an enchanting delight when compared to the stench of death.

And it was all the more satisfying when accompanied by the soldier's pained wails as he clasped his stomach, streams of black and red bursting out through the slits of his fingers.

"There," Kamataa declared as she kicked him over and onto his back, stepping on the wound with the full force of her boot. "Now you don't have to look at her."

A shrill scream became a meek whimper as the soldier reached after Kamataa's boot, his glistening-red hand doing little more than offering a brief tug of her trouser leg as she walked away. The further she drifted from him, the more he came to sound like a mewling babe, until nothing more was uttered from his foul mouth beyond his keening groans.

The remnants within the factory—the other soldiers huddled about the Bear's corpse, as well as Sha'a—were standing in a half-circle as Kamataa approached with Vanta's body. In part, it seemed they were drawn by the gunfire. But it was also apparent they were equally roused by the return of their General.

Aritz strode in with pomp and purpose, flanked by two guards, his head held high and his brow dropped low. A scowl painted his face as he stopped before the gathering, glancing one direction and then the next, his focus paid to both the bloodied machinery and his own soldier adding his own life to the canvas. "What's happened?" he asked.

One of the useless soldiers stepped forth. "The damned savage has gone and—"

"Quiet," Aritz commanded, and the soldier shut his mouth, backing away with clear shame. The General stayed his gaze on Kamataa. "I was addressing *you*. Speak. I heard gunfire upon my approach. What's happened?"

Kamataa's lip quivered, her nostrils flaring. A long breath escaped her nostrils as she kneeled to the ground, placing Vanta's lifeless form in front of her. Her eyes were still frozen open in shock, even as her skull caved in. "O Blessed Moon," she murmured, the world around her irrelevant, "carry again into Your warm arms Your humble servant Vanta. Bless upon her—"

"Kama," Aritz called, his voice echoing above the machinery.

"—in death the light of Your radiance so bestowed upon her in life—"

"Kama," Aritz repeated.

"—and lead her again into the eternal flow of—"

"*KAMA!*"

"*WHAT?*" Kamataa bellowed. She gestured to Vanta. "Are you blind to what has happened here?"

"I asked you a question." Aritz appeared unmoved by the funerary rites she needed to perform. He raised his eyebrows, his expression plain, but a hint of impatience peppered his gaze.

Swinging her arms about herself, Kamataa directed the General's attention to the chaos at her back. "Look around you, Aritz! We had intruders! They spoiled the samples! They killed Vanta! Still, they live, wandering about to who knows where! It will only be a matter of time before—"

"Why is one of my soldiers dead?"

Kamataa froze with her arm half-raised. "I just told you. Those intruders killed Vanta and—"

"I said, 'one of my soldiers.' Your companion's life is nothing to me. Did these intruders also kill my soldier?"

Her lips puckered with anger. Grinding her teeth, Kamataa bunched her hand into a fist, her arm quivering as the rage gripped her. She peered down once more to Vanta's damaged face, the image replaced for the briefest of moments with Sennalhat's, and glared back up at Aritz with hateful eyes. "No," she snarled. "I did."

Aritz grunted, his hand hovering over his thigh holster. "Enlighten me, then, why I should not offer you the same treatment."

"Did you forget, Aritz?" A deep chuckle grated against her throat. She raised her crimson-stained hands to her face, the color matching the fury nestling into her chest. "I am the only one who can perform this for you. Do you not wish to be a symbol of Acrarian ingenuity? A godly figure for whatever you wish to do with this wretched isle?" A smile stretched across her lips. "You need me. Else all this shall go to waste."

Smacking his lips, Aritz moved his hand away from his weapon and sauntered to his left, peering his head over Kamataa's shoulder. "Hmph," he grunted again, looking toward the tainted room. He raised his hand toward it. "And does *that* not qualify as a 'waste?' You permitted that to occur in my absence. What more could you offer than wasted savages and wasted opportunities?"

"That was not my fault," she asserted, her eyes narrowing. "That was the intruder. I would imagine the very same responsible for the murders you were just investigating."

"And such an individual will be dealt with in due course."

"You won't be able to stop her. She has survived worse than the might of the Acrarians. But she cannot survive *me*."

"Whoever this individual is," Aritz said, rolling his eyes, "she clearly has naught to fear from you if she still lives."

"Luck has kept her alive, but it shall soon run out. I will make certain of it."

"And why should I allow it? You are needed *here*, are you not? You just said as much." Aritz turned his hands, extending his palms toward her. "If the purpose you serve to me is aught else but to imbue this machinery with the power you claim resides in the blood of these...things...then for what reason must you not face the consequences of felling one of my soldiers, a man who is to be your comrade-in-arms?"

Kamataa scoffed. "Still your tongue, Aritz. These men care not for me, and you care not for them. If anything, I offered you the mercy of quieting another voice oft pestering your ear."

One of her supposed comrades-in-arms stepped forward, shooting an accusatory finger at her. "Sir! She is a savage and a traitor! Please permit me to take her to Execution Alley and—"

"Your bullets would be wasted, I assure you," she said with a sardonic chuckle, not even bothering to glance at the man. "They're best saved for your own head—at least then, they would be offering us all a service and kindness."

"Why, you—"

"That's enough," Aritz commanded, his voice crackling like ice. He walked forward, crouching before Kamataa, Vanta's corpse filling the wide chasm between them. A long gaze he held over her fallen comrade, her *true* comrade-in-arms. A mark of sadness filled his lips, pity glinting in his eyes.

It gave Kamataa pause.

"I will suffer no more distractions from what I have requested of you, Kama. Has any of this worked thus far?"

Her jaw dropped. Her hands hung before her, now begging to be painted in the red of one Acrarian General. "What?"

Aritz glanced to the machines, where the false runes Kamataa scribbled into their frames glistened against the dun light filtering in through the grime-soaked windows. "I have been away for some time. I see you opened the beast as I asked. I do not notice anything amiss, nor do I notice anything different. Pray, enlighten me."

"Enlighten *me*, Aritz," Kamataa retorted. "With what regularity have you frequented the factory? I must admit, in my ten years of servicing you, I have seen you spend not a minute within these walls. Would it be fair of you to determine what is amiss or different?"

"Do not think me ignorant, nor yourself an expert on industry. I have known machinery and its workings since I was but a boy—and great machinery beyond the confines that limit us here on this land. I am no fool, Kama, and you would be wise not to forget that fact."

"Is there not a saying that 'with age comes wisdom' in your mother tongue?" Kamataa remarked with a scoff.

"The wisdom of the aged is ill-adapted for the wisdom of the young."

"Is that wisdom of your own, or is it arrogance?"

"It is *experience*." Aritz rose to his feet, towering above Kamataa's kneeling form, a giant blotting out the weak light shimmering onto the factory floor. He began to take slow paces to the left and right, hands folded behind his back. "I first learned the sting of betrayal and deceit when I was just a boy primed to become a man. I was ready to reach out and claim what was mine, what had long been promised to me, what had been my right and no one else's. It was only when it was so near that I could skim my fingers against it, so warm, so invigorating, that it was torn away, put so far from my reach that I realized power promised is not power gained. Power promised is but a hollow pledge, upheld only until it is more convenient for a man to continue to hold it for himself.

"I am no longer beholden to promises, nor do I believe in them, Kama," he continued, stopping but a few paces away from her, drawing a deep, contemplative breath. "The only power in this world is that which one claims for themselves, and that which is promised to them is little more than empty, vapid falsehoods uttered by opportunists interested in only their own gain. My father was an opportunist. My brothers were opportunists." He stopped, holding Kamataa's gaze for a long, long while, the silence broken only by the persistent rhythm of the factory's machinery. "You, Kama, are an opportunist."

The laugh was involuntary, but Kamataa could hardly help herself. "You don't live to my age without taking advantage of every opportunity at your disposal, Aritz."

"Chief among them a witchcraft that you 'promised' would work to my benefit."

She smiled. Malice coated it, and she cared little for how much of it showed. "And?"

Another disapproving grunt escaped Aritz's throat. "If there is anything the promises of opportunists have taught me, it is to know and accept when I have been fooled." He raised his arms toward the machinery, still chugging away despite their now-tainted exterior. "You have fooled me from the beginning, haven't you? Am I so wrong to doubt whether this heinous method was to work at all? Or did you merely wish for the means to take part in your wicked rituals en masse?"

"Oh, and your soul is pure and undefiled, is it, Aritz?" Kamataa tsked her lips, feigning disapproval. "A man of your...stature surely did not take your betrayal lightly. Are your own hands not stained as mine are? And no, I do not mean that of these Tribes—we both know you care not a whit for them. What of your betrayers—your father, your brothers? Are your hands clean of their blood?"

If there was conflict in his heart, Aritz did not show it. He maintained the same sharp glare in his eyes, one that threatened to pierce her at the first provocation.

Light footsteps approached Kamataa from behind, hesitant hands hovering above her. Sha'a hummed with bemusement, her caution not to touch her kin as pronounced as always. "It matters little how pure you believe yourself to be, Aritz," she said. "You are party to this little harvest whether you wish to be or not. These ghosts shall follow you wherever you may roam. Are you prepared for that?"

"If I am not? If I need not be?" Aritz's hand roamed toward his pistol holster once more. "What is to stop me from silencing all in this room?"

Kamataa smirked. "What indeed? You give only further credence to the claim roaming about already that Aritz a Mata will stop at nothing to achieve his ends. Your legend—famous or infamous—is already being penned."

"And has it been your hand holding the pen, Kama?" Licking his lips, Aritz was beginning to lose the steel to his gaze, giving way instead to a soft anger that was gradually hardening. "Was this lie you crafted one merely to sully my name, my legacy?"

"Heh, you attribute far too much credit to my own name, Aritz." The old woman rose to her feet, finding at last the strength to pull away from Vanta. She held her arms out at her sides. "All of this? It was simply because it amused me, entertained me. This war against the Tribes was mine long before it was yours. The history of my people is long and drowned in rivers of blood, and is there no better poetry than to let flow the rivers once more, to pay back in equivalence that which was taken from me and mine? Is it not—"

Aritz held up a hand to silence her. "I do not care. At all. I've not the patience for the ravings of a madwoman."

"If not for this madwoman, you would have lost this vain war of conquest of yours, and you would not be alive to speak with me. You should be on your knees and *thanking* this horrid madwoman."

"And if there was aught else to do but slay the savages' gods, why had you not done so yourself?" Aritz shook his head at her. "You are but a slave to your own weakness, leeching off the exploits of your betters. A true opportunist to your core. Even to go so far as this—" He gestured once again to the blood-stained machines. "—shows how weak you are. Hiding behind falsehoods as grounds to pursue your own gruesome self-interests."

"But what difference does it make in the end, Aritz, hmm?" Kamataa scoffed, crossing her arms across her chest. "Ultimately, we all get what we want. This Land is purged of its tyrant Tribespeople and is free to be reshaped to a realm befitting it. You can now claim this reforged land in the name of yourself or your King and Queen or whatever the fuck you wish to do with it. After centuries, my dream has at last been realized. We all win—surely, you do not intend to tarry on how this Land was won?"

The General said nothing.

Deep down, you assuredly do not care for the methods, Kamataa thought. *You care only that your name shall ever be written in the stars. You damned fool.*

Aritz turned away from her, his attention appearing fixed to the machinery, his face pensive and considering. Apparent in his expression was the pronounced disregard toward those around him—Kamataa, Sha'a, his soldiers—and remained still as a statue, hands folded once more behind his back, his shoulders tensing as a deep breath escaped his mouth.

The silence stretched on. Sha'a took a step forward, falling in step with Kamataa, flashing her a curious shrug and a suspicious glare.

Kamataa responded with much the same, beads of sweat raining down her face as the factory's heat beginning to swelter in a hellish accord with its machines' discordant harmonies.

"Kama," Aritz called over the pervasive noise. "To what Sign do *you* belong?"

"Heh," she scoffed, offering a smile to Aritz's back as though the answer was obvious. "I belong to the Owl, of course. Should it not surprise you? It is the only of the three still living, and I am clearly in control of my own wits still."

Aritz turned and did something Kamataa could hardly expect. He *grinned,* flashing his teeth in a show of malice. "No," he said. "No, you do not."

The smile vanished from Kamataa's face, though amusement still colored her voice. "Oh? On what authority have you to determine that?"

"I am not the ignorant outlander you claim me to be, Kama. I have seen well enough the aptitudes your people possess. They exhibited their capabilities on the battlefield. I saw numerous faces, numerous fighters, all in possession of various realms of prowess, all endowed by those wicked beasts they call gods with abilities beyond the limits of their own humanity. Loath as I am to admit it." Slowly, he stepped toward Kamataa, his heels clattering against the hard floor. "With all this power at their disposal, it was only inevitable that I'd find it odd they elected to fight with spears and arrows—" He stopped, turning a sharp gaze toward Kamataa and Sha'a. "—rather than their bare hands."

Kamataa raised her brow, inclining her head to one side, offering nothing in return in the way of words.

Aritz continued his pace, circling around the two Eclipseborn, his presence bearing heavily down upon them. "When first you showed your hand and revealed to me you could kill my lieutenant with little more than a touch, I admit I was horrified. It was an image that stays with me. It shall remain with me until the end of my days, I am certain. But if the people of this isle were in possession of such wicked magic...why would they not have employed it on the battlefield? Had they done so, I am not so arrogant to not have recognized they could have slaughtered us with ease. And yet they did not. Because it is not a power natural to them, is it, Kama?"

She watched him prowl about her and Sha'a, a predator waiting for the perfect opportunity to pounce upon its quarry. To break face would have been to present him the opportunity. To that end, Kamataa maintained her stern expression, intent not to give a single inch.

"Insofar as what your lot do can ever be considered 'natural,' eh? Savior's light or no, the world is better off without such wickedness tainting it. And yet, you manage to sink even further below those wretched depths. It's little wonder you claim they are not 'your' people. I believe it to be more accurate to claim that *you* are not *their* people."

"The semantics of it matter little," Kamataa said. "They are departed from this world all the same."

"And here *you* still remain, living lifetime upon lifetime. Do not think me blind that I would pay no heed to your claim to having lived centuries. I cannot say I've seen others live to such an advanced age. How curious."

"You simply have not looked hard enough."

Aritz laughed. "Oh, no. My eyes are well-attuned. They see plenty. As a matter of fact…show me your hand."

Glancing down at her palms, Kamataa shook her head and gave Aritz a questioning glare. "For what purpose? You cannot see past the stains of blood."

"Oh, but I can do much more." He lurched forward, grasping Kamataa with great force by the hand.

"Hey!" Sha'a called, taking a step forward. Rifles and pistols clicked in unison as the soldiers and guards readied themselves for the slightest provocation.

"Now, now," Aritz chided, at last drawing his pistol from its holster and aiming it at Sha'a's face. "I am merely confirming something that had gripped my curiosity."

Kamataa winced against the strength of Aritz's hand. "I know not what you are playing at, Aritz, but do recall that Sha'a could kill you with but a single touch. That 'unnatural' power of which you remain in fear."

Aritz grunted in acknowledgment. "Too right." And he shot Sha'a in the knee.

Blood burst from Sha'a's shattered kneecap as she fell to the ground. She seemed too shocked to scream initially, her eyes bulging from her eyes. Only when she met the floor at full impact did she howl to the Moon, her agonic cries harmonizing with the mechanical rhythm of the factory.

Reaching behind for a blade, Kamataa shouted, "You bastar—"

The butt end of a pistol cut off her words and she collapsed in a daze, still alert, but the world spinning about her. Everyone sounded miles away, Sha'a's pained screams an alarm to drag her back. All she could feel was the harsh tug at her arms and the thorough examination of her hands.

Blurring into focus was Aritz's face.

"Just as I thought," he said, his voice echoing in her skull.

She groaned with discomfort, the side of her head throbbing with pain. "*Nngh*, wh-what?"

A hard force knocked her onto her back, and the dizziness gradually began to quell. Off to the side, the sound of steel scraped against the floor. She reached to her hip and found her blade missing from its holster.

"You seared your flesh against the machinery earlier, did you not?" Aritz asked. "And yet, here you are now, hardly a scar to make its presence known."

With a wince, Kamataa pushed herself to a seated position, staring Aritz down with a grimace. She had been too careless. She clenched her fist.

The Acrarian held his arms out to her and Sha'a, a pistol in one hand and the blade in the other. "How curious, the powers that lay groveling at my feet. Life and death itself. What simple poetry this moment holds. And you would say all this might—this power to take life in an instant, or to restore it just the same—is held in the same breath as those you told me were little more than meek scholars?" He shook his head. "I think not." He lowered his arms, turning his attention to Vanta's corpse, a puddle long since pooling beneath her head. "I can only imagine what else differentiates you from the rest of the beasts."

Straining against the heavy weight of the world, Kamataa rose to a knee, her balance still yet to return, and watched as Aritz approached Vanta, kneeled beside her...

And drove the blade into her chest.

Barking out a protest, Kamataa lurched forward, only to slip and fall to her stomach.

Weapons clicked into place around her.

In his crouch, Aritz clucked his tongue and shook his head, allowing the hilt to protrude out from Vanta. "I long wondered why these two had driven their blades into that wolf before I felled it. But now...now it all makes too much sense. This...harvest, as you have called it, I am of a mind to cut my losses and move on. It is a harvest bearing no fruit at all. But there are secrets to your *own* blood that I believe you are keeping from me—perhaps a promise that may yet be fulfilled."

"And what?" Sha'a growled, her legs trailing behind her as she remained on the floor. "What would *you* even do with such a weapon? You have no need of it—any of these fools around me could kill with a blade without any extra assistance."

"It's not about the need," Aritz said, sauntering over to Sha'a. "It's about the *possibility* of needing it."

The nose of the pistol rested against Sha'a's throat.

Before Kamataa could say anything, blood exploded out from the back of her companion's neck.

Red droplets spattered against Aritz's face as his gun propped Sha'a up at the throat, the wound sluicing fresh blood down the length of the pistol. A deep chuckle rumbled in his throat. "A productive tool will do what it will, but there is always the chance of failure, of uncertainty. But if one were to remove that uncertainty and replace it with something beyond a shadow of a doubt, then all that remains is...inevitability."

Sharp, ragged breaths stabbed at Kamataa's chest as she turned her gaze to Vanta's defiled form, the blade jutting out from her chest, and Sha'a's limp body, still twitching its last involuntary movements. The scream that erupted from her throat was something beyond human, more akin to a wounded beast, a mother bear watching helplessly as her cubs were slaughtered before her. She snarled, spittle frothing from the corners of her mouth, and jumped to unsteady feet, reaching for the hilt of the blade inside Vanta, but the brunt of a rifle's strike sent her hurtling to the floor. Even as she hit the ground, a successive strike caught her in the small of her back, an almost vindictive blow, knocking the wind out of her. Her eyes watered—both from the attack and the lives ripped from her hands.

Sinister and sadistic was Aritz's smile as he glanced up at his guard and nodded. Grabbing a fistful of Sha'a's hair, he lifted her head off the pistol, its frame now soaked in dark red, and let her drop to the floor without ceremony. Little regard was paid to Kamataa as he walked past, pulling loose the blade from Vanta's chest, and then handed it to the nearest guard. "We're done here. Put these on the desk in my chambers."

"Yes, sir," replied a voice.

Kamataa did not turn to face its source, but it sounded too familiar.

"What of the wagons, sir?" asked another man.

Aritz shook his head. "For now, back to the camps. We've no use for them here. We'll determine what to do with them later."

"Aye, sir."

"And what of her?" a third voice added.

Glaring up with hateful eyes, Kamataa felt her nostrils flare, her body tremble with rage.

And yet, Aritz regarded her with the same demeanor he likely would have an animal. "It matters not," he said pitiably. "She has nothing left. No one to protect her." He drew two steps closer. "I am a man of means and a man of results. Both have been dependent upon my slaves being alive—not fed to a blood machine on a fool's errand."

Spittle rained down on her.

"Goodbye, Kama." And Aritz walked off, his self-assured stride all the more irritating.

The remaining soldiers spared her only a brief glare of disdain before setting about their tasks, their muttered insults fading into the rhythm of the machines painted in the errands once believed by a fool.

Crawling to Vanta, Kamataa gripped her by the collar and dragged her beside Sha'a. Her breath quickened, her nails clawing into her palms. She wanted to scream, but had no voice with which to do so. She wanted to cry, but her well of tears had long since dried. And as Kamataa glanced upon the remains of the last of her Children, she felt alone for the first time in centuries.

And just as she had done for centuries, she seethed.

Somehow, to hold these weapons felt wrong. The constant drip of fresh blood against the battle-worn flooring of Aritz's manor only punctuated the fact.

Attendants and guards glanced at him with curious regard as he traipsed up the stairs, carrying the General's new toys with the same caution he would show a newborn. But for all his care not to drop or lose these tools, he could not escape the feeling of revulsion in the same breath.

After all, despite his preference not to associate with any of the Tribes, despite the abandonment of they who he considered to be his family, the blood dripping from the blade and pistol was still that of his kin. It was gross, perverse. Just as Kamataa proffered this lie purely for the sake of her own satisfaction, Aritz played along, and at the end, he showed much the same perversion as did the Children of the Black Moon.

The door to Aritz's bedchamber opened with a wide creak. The room was still a mess from the final confrontation, where the Owl's trusted few had made their last stand, and the Stone man amongst the Keepers declared their surrender. Papers and books were scattered everywhere, furniture was overturned, blood marked the floor and carpeting. But the desk remained just as it should be. Despite all the chaos elsewhere in the manor, the desk was untouched. There was a sensation of power radiating from it, strangely enough, the very seat of Aritz's power. How curious that it survived in spite of everything that occurred here these last few days—much like Aritz, himself.

With slow deliberation, he approached the desk, holding the weapons out before him in each hand. The blood dripped and puddled onto the finely crafted oak, staining an otherwise unmarred canvas. It was almost criminal to ruin the image in such a way, but such was Aritz's request. It was beyond his right to deny him.

But it was also beyond his will to follow him any further.

The pistol clacked against the desk with a wet thud. Would that this Land had never been introduced to the Acrarians and their weaponry. As he pulled his hand away from the pistol, he felt a weight lifted from him. No longer would he be party to their destruction. If his last act with an Acrarian weapon was to halt Kamataa in her tracks, then that was more than enough for him.

The same weight bore upon his other hand, the weight of the Tribes and their people housed within this blade. But it was one from which he was reluctant to part. Because it would be removing the last remnant of who he truly was.

The Children of the Black Moon were gone. The Acrarians made clear there would be no home for someone like him.

"If not here, then where?" Cin muttered as he peered into the blade's stained steel, the light obscured by the crimson encompassing it, his Illusioned reflection only barely visible. "Zarrow. Where would I go?"

The spirit of the lost did not answer.

"Thought as much. Something I need to figure out on my own."

His hand moved to the blade's hilt, his fingers wrapping around it tightly. Out the window, the southern horizon looked peaceful, untouched by the death and anger that had gripped this Land for ages upon ages, even before the Acrarians' arrival.

"I don't know where I may go," he said, less an admission to Zarrow, should he have been listening, and more an assurance to himself. "But I know where I may start."

MEMORY

A New World

Three months. Three blasted months at sea.

When Aritz embarked upon this journey, he underestimated just how horrid it was to spend a quarter of a year on a ship, surrounded by the foulest odors this side of a Silk Isle brothel. At least there was an escape from *that* smell. Apparently, to be a man of the sea was to forego the auspices of cleanliness in favor of constant imbibement, even amongst those of royal employment. All he could ever hope to do as a means of escape was remain in his quarters, emerging only to accept the chef's offerings.

It was a sign of the Savior's mercy when he heard the calls for land.

Rising to his feet again as the ship rocked against the waves, Aritz brushed crumbs off his robe and tied it tightly against his chest, the warmth of his quarters short-lived whenever he opened the door.

The *Chariot's* crew had congregated on the port side of the deck, gripped in the throes of wonder at the promise of respite from this long sea voyage. The galleon's floorboards creaked underfoot as Aritz walked toward the helmsman, his focus at least paid to his duties. A favorable wind continued to push the ship along to the west, carrying with it a salt air that Aritz wished never to have to smell again. It was disgusting compared to the crisp mountain air he had been most accustomed to.

"Helmsman," Aritz called, his back facing away from the rest of the crew. The top deck of the ship held the helmsman's post, the large wooden wheel that he treated as though it were his child. There was space for at least a dozen men on this level, but the helmsman preferred to be on his own for one reason or another, perhaps to ensure no one would get in his way. Aritz had respect for that, at the least. "There is land ahead?"

The helmsman was near skin-and-bones, his clothes sopping and ragged, his beard and hair patchy and unkempt. He had more the image of a beggar come to ask for scraps than the man trusted with the navigation of the greatest galleon in the Kingdom, but he came personally from the recommendation of Their Highnesses. Aritz just couldn't remember his name. At the young Lord's approach, he raised his arm off the wheel and pointed to the west. "See for yourself, my Lord."

From this height, Aritz could see the formations breaking the horizon. An emerald green dot breaking the impenetrable blue of the promising horizon, sharp ridges rising from it to indicate some sort of mountain formation. Even without a spyglass, the land's approach was clear as day.

"I must say," Aritz called, ensuring his voice carried over the sea breeze. "I was not anticipating this New World to be so near so soon. Their Highnesses' charts estimated at least twice as long."

The helmsman shrugged. "They may have underestimated the *Chariot's* speed. There is none faster in the whole of the continent. The Attaviani could never craft something so magnanimous, and Omerago da Vespindi is unfit to steer even his own shite into a chamber pot."

"How comforting," Aritz responded with a grunt. "Are we certain, though? I expected Vespindi's discovery to be much...grander."

"Trust me, my Lord. Those southern twats are known only for two things: overexaggerating and overcompensating. I'd not put it past Vespindi to have gotten lost for half a year at sea only to return to say he discovered gold in a mermaid's teat."

"Forgive me if I do not feel at all encouraged. I would rather escape this feeling that Their Highnesses may be disappointed."

"I'm just pulling your tail, my Lord," the helmsman said with a laugh, clapping Aritz on the back of the shoulder with a heavy hand. "This is a happy occasion for you, for the Kingdom."

"For my family," Aritz added.

"Aye. They're part o' this too, my Lord. Apologies, I hoped a joke would lift your mood."

"No, no, tis no bother. It's been a long two years—I needed every minute of the mourning period. The situations with my mother and my brothers did not help matters when all I wished to do was pay respects to my father."

"And look at the reward awaiting you. The faith placed in you by Their Highnesses has never wavered, and for good reason, my Lord. You have earned it." The helmsman walked away from the wheel and stood beside Aritz, grasping the young Lord's shoulder. "You have every right now to smile and laugh."

Glancing at the man in response, Aritz managed to force a smile. The laugh was quite far behind. He was far more distracted by the stains upon the helmsman's teeth and the wretched yet familiar odor exuding from his mouth. A quick inhale through the nose told Aritz all he needed to know. *I had thought our wine stores had been lighter of late. That* would *explain his unusual friendliness.* The faint sound of glass rolling along with the rocking waves gave him all the confirmation he needed. *He's remarkably coherent for a man however many bottles deep. As long as he takes care not to crash the ship into one of those gold-teated mermaids.*

The sun sparkled against the crystalline waves as the distant mountains rose higher on the horizon. If it was indeed the New World that lay ahead, then the new chapter of the Mata family legacy would be soon penned. *If only you could see this, Father. If only you were not so stubborn.* Aritz turned to the helmsman. "How long until we reach land?"

A range of wrinkles creased the man's face as he squinted his eyes to assess the distance and the positioning of the sun. "Two, three hours tops, my Lord. By midday we shall kiss solid ground once again."

"I don't believe I have ever been inclined to kiss dirt, but I may make an exception just this once."

"Yes, my Lord! Yes! It is well worth it—all the works of nature that adorn this world are deserving of such admiration!"

Aritz raised an eyebrow. *Perhaps I won't, then.* A shiver ran through him as another gust rolled past, setting strands of hair free from the binding tying it back. *The warmth of my chambers is calling me to return if there are still hours yet until landfall.* He broke free from the helmsman's friendly grip and descended the stairs to the lower deck, the crew still entranced at the port side by the approaching New World. "Back to work, all of you!" he shouted, scattering them to their various stations aboard the galleon. "There shall be plenty of time to gawk once we're ashore."

He paid little heed to the acknowledgments and hasty apologies as he descended one deck further and entered his quarters. As he closed the door, he breathed a sigh of relief that the warmth had not left. The comfort of his bed was all too alluring.

As his head hit the pillow and he closed his eyes, all Aritz could picture—as he had quite often these last two years—was Nofre a Mata's final choked breath, the realization apparent in his eyes that nothing would stand in the way of his son's ambitions.

Nothing at all. This seabound jewel would be but the first step.

To finally be away from a full crew's worth of odors was nothing short of a blessing. That of but a dozen men was more than manageable.

A plume of white smoke wafted into the air along the approaching shoreline. Aritz stood at the bow of the rowboat, leg propped against the edge, water splashing against him as the oarsmen fought against the gentle waves taking them ashore. He didn't necessarily find it surprising that this isle was inhabited, but he also was not expecting the lookouts to find signs of life so quickly. It was an advantageous location, to be sure. From what his men could tell—and from what was apparent the closer the landing party drew to the island—the northern reaches were rather inaccessible by the shore, the land rising to a higher elevation, the seaside terrain itself turning from sandy coastlines to rigid cliff faces.

Whoever settled here first certainly was well aware of the fortune on which they sat.

Even at this distance, Aritz could see a flurry of movement on the land ahead, within what appeared to be a small village of some sort. He narrowed his eyes, the wind setting his bound hair free in more and more loose strands.

He pushed it back out of his field of view and scratched at his unshaven face—his beard still yet to be fully grown-in. The sea's chill still peppered him, but there was a tease of warmth fluttering in from the west as the rowboats—four of them in all—came but minutes away from the shoreline.

Once near enough, the sailors in Aritz's boat jumped overboard, the water only coming up to their waists, while the Lord himself remained standing upon the wooden frame, maintaining the stance and keeping a steady focus in order to not lose his balance. Whoever looked upon him from this new land would need to be aware of his own importance to this crew.

The boat wedged itself into the sandy shores until the stern's rudder was fully planted within, and Aritz took a long step forward, savoring the sensation of soft sand beneath his feet. Despite his previous conversation with the helmsman, he did not feel inclined to fall to his knees and bring his lips to the dirt.

As the rest of the landing party came ashore beside and behind him, Aritz ensured he was well-prepared. At his thigh lay a holster with a flintlock pistol inside, a weapon he was not quite used to, but was offered in bulk by Their Highnesses along with an armory's worth of rifles and sabers. One such saber lay sheathed at his waist, its hilt ornately carved and set with blue and gold trim, but already he found movement with it to be cumbersome. He never did enjoy his fencing lessons as a boy, especially when this Age of Industry had produced such wonderful and faster weaponry such as firearms. A saber felt antiquated.

Successive splashes signaled his sailors' departures from their respective rowboats as he broke from his self-inspection. Offering a nod to them, Aritz turned toward the seaside village, spying collections of small homes—*hovels* would have been a more apt term—composed of what appeared to be straw, stone, and mud. *How primitive,* he thought, scoffing to himself as he took the first step forward into the New World.

It was a wobbling, unsteady step. He underestimated the impact three months at sea would have on his balance. But he righted his course, refusing to fall before his men. Submitting himself to such shame would have been unacceptable.

His boots sunk into the sand as he closed his eyes against the warming sun, a heavy air bearing down upon him that he absolutely treasured. It was a fair bit more oppressive than what he had grown accustomed to, but it was far more comforting than the chill the sea had offered him. The one thing that *did* remind him of home was the air itself. There was a crispness to it, something untainted. Even though those northern mountains were still far, they still managed to make their mark even in these warm, more humid seaside environs.

When the sand gave way to a dirt-lined pathway, a host of people filtered out seemingly from nowhere to observe their approach. Aritz found it odd. To them, it seemed he was a curiosity. He could say the same for them. Their skin tone was darker than he had ever seen on another person, more of a red-brown clay appearance. Their clothing appeared rudimentary, almost as though they ran out of materials. Animal hides, from the look of them, a sleeve missing on their shirts. For those who still held on to their hair, they fashioned them in two buns tied at the back of their heads. Many had painted on their faces two vertical red lines crossing over their eyes and traveling from crown to chin.

Hushed words were mumbled among the people, some pointing fingers at Aritz and his men, not in any semblance of a threat, but rather in a conversational manner, as though they were deciphering a mystery revolving around his presence and origins. The words carried loud enough to reach his ears, but not in any tongue he could decipher.

Furrowing his brow, he strolled along the main pathway, the hilt of his saber tapping against his hip with each step, his fingers flexing in the area of his pistol. Even with the landing party trailing behind him, he felt exposed. Already he was suspicious of these people and the way they gawked at him as though he were a novelty. They all kept their distance, perhaps falling into the same hesitation, but Aritz was hardly inclined to trust them.

A loud, booming voice echoed over the village, deep and resonant to the point it silenced everyone in an instant. Aritz would never have admitted it in front of his men, but it actually startled him, even as it had little effect on the villagers surrounding him.

All attention seemed to be drawn toward the center of the village. A circle expanded down the way, a pocket of people opening wide, and sitting by his lonesome was a man of tremendous brawn, greater than Aritz had ever seen before in his days. The man had arms like tree trunks, his biceps larger than Aritz's head. Even as he sat, he was taller than the person nearest to him, a fact only punctuated by the tall tufts of tied hair sticking out from the back of his head, like the feathers of a noble bird.

Stranger still was the wide, gregarious smile plastered across his face. He held a thick hand out as Aritz entered the circle of curious onlookers, and gestured to the seat across from him. Or, what passed for a seat, at any rate. It bore more the appearance of a chopped tree trunk, the table nothing more than a slab of oak unpainted and unfinished.

Aritz accepted the seat regardless, unbuckling the saber from his hip and resting the hilt against the table. The smile did not vanish from the man's face, so he clearly did not take the act as a threat. In truth, Aritz was simply irritated by the added weight of the weapon.

A deep chuckle rumbled in the man's throat, and he began to say...something. It was clear he did not know the Acrarian tongue, and Aritz had no inclination to continue listening.

When at last the man stopped talking, Aritz simply shook his head. "I know not what you are saying," he muttered, gesturing with his two forefingers from his chin to the direction of the man's round face, hoping it would get the message across.

With a grunt, the man crossed his arms and nodded, the gestures apparently translating as well as Aritz hoped. He turned his head to the side and shouted a single word with enough vigor to sunder the earth around them.

It was to Aritz's surprise that there was not even a whimper of shock or surprise at the sudden bark; his own heart had jumped at the shout. If they were used to something like this, they were a strange people indeed.

A petite woman emerged from the crowd in garb equivalent to the man across the table. She said something in their language, likely an acknowledgment if Aritz was to judge from the inflection.

Words flowed from the man's mouth, something of an inelegant language now that Aritz gave himself the chance to listen. When the words stopped, the man turned back to Aritz and mimed something with his hands. He pointed to the woman, and then to Aritz. Next, he held up his thumb and pressed it to his own forehead, before removing it and offering an affirming nod. He raised his eyebrows, seeming to expect a response.

Aritz hadn't the faintest idea what any of that meant, but he looked at the woman and nodded, regardless.

She approached in stride, fleet enough on her feet that Aritz reached down to the pistol on instinct. The calmness with which she held out her hands seemed an attempt to relax him, and with cautious movement, she held the back of Aritz's head with one hand and pressed her thumb to his forehead with the other.

A surge burst through him. Aritz felt himself go rigid, the sensation not quite a pain but far from comfortable. It was over in an instant, but it felt an eternity. His eyes went wide, his hands shaking, his heart pounding. The woman backed away as though nothing was out of the ordinary, but Aritz could not help but glare daggers at her. If he hadn't been so gripped in place by whatever *that* was, he would have reached for the saber, finally having a use for it. Instead, all he could muster was a meek, "What the *hell* was that?"

The woman smiled, shaking her head. "Relax. You will be okay in a moment."

Aritz's jaw dropped. "Did...I hear that correctly?" The words were familiar, though a bit stilted, and the accent was far different from what he was accustomed to. "Did you just speak my language?"

She tapped her thumb against her own forehead, smiling sheepishly. "That is what *that* was for. Do not worry."

"I...I don't understand. A moment ago, you couldn't—"

The man across the table laughed, his burly chest heaving up and down with each breath, the wide smile still stretching across his face. A string of words flowed from his lips.

Before Aritz could question further, the woman spoke, "The Chief says, 'It is clear the gods do not bless you as they do us. Your reaction is an understandable one.'"

Narrowing his eyes, Aritz remained seated with muted confusion, looking back and forth between the man and the woman. "'Chief?' 'Gods?' I...what are you talking about? Who are you people? *What* are you people?"

Smiling, the woman turned back to this "Chief," and spoke in their own language. The Chief nodded and said something in response, nodding to Aritz once he was finished.

"He says, 'Welcome to our land,'" the woman continued. "'My name is Han'e, and I am the Chief of the Sun Tribe. My linguist here, Wik'na, will translate for us. Is this acceptable to you?'"

Aritz scoffed. "'Acceptable?' If you wish for this to be 'acceptable,' you can begin by explaining how any of this is possible."

The woman, Wik'na, maintained a calming smile. "I merely employed my boon granted to me by the owl. It is so infrequent that I have the opportunity to use it as all of our tribes share a common tongue for the most part, so I am happy to be useful here."

None of that made any sense to Aritz. "A boon? Given to you by an owl? Forgive me if that means nothing to we uninitiated."

Han'e chuckled as he listened to Wik'na's translation, planting his hands against his knees in his wide, seated stance. "'Not *an* owl,'" he said through the woman. "'*The* owl. One of the three great animal deities who guide us and fulfil us.'"

Aritz narrowed his eyes. "You speak of them as though they are gods."

"'Because they are.'"

That was enough to raise an eyebrow. *Just my luck to run into a pack of animal worshipers.*

"'You appear unconvinced. Or, perhaps unfamiliar? From where have you come to our shores?'"

The candidness of Han'e's response took Aritz aback. Even as a man who did not hold the teachings of the Savior in any serious esteem, he could not deny the fact that they were blatant blasphemers. It did not sit right with him. Aritz grunted, a hummed grumble grating against his throat, and said, "We have sailed from a land far to the east. It has been about three months since we left our homeland. We are—"

Han'e raised his arms, startling Aritz. "'Three months? No, we will discuss this further over a feast.'" He stood and shouted something to the gathered crowd that was not translated by Wik'na, and then turned back toward Aritz with a grin, gesturing him forward with his curled fingers.

Hesitation marked Aritz's step as he did not immediately rise to his feet. Instead, he kept his eyes peeled upon Han'e, who had redirected his attention elsewhere, conversing with his surrounding attendants—or whatever this rudimentary equivalent was. Slowly, Aritz reached for the hilt of his saber, fastening it back to his waist as he got up from his seat. He was suddenly grateful to have brought the cumbersome thing along with him. *I wouldn't put it past this lot to cannibalize us in celebration of the beasts they supposedly worship.*

Judging from the approaching footsteps of his men, he did not find himself alone in that line of thinking. One sailor filed in beside him, his rifle strapped along his shoulder, but seemingly inclined to slip off at any given notice. "My Lord..." he whispered.

Aritz nodded, resting his hand on the hilt of his sword. Though he felt he was rightfully suspicious, the emptiness in his stomach protested any potential refusal. It growled as though to illustrate the point. "Aye," he murmured, wrapping his hand over his gut. "But on the possibility of eating something that has *not* been stewing in a hot barrel for three months?"

The sailor responded with a hesitant half-smile.

Han'e waved Aritz over with both arms, shouting something that Wik'na was not around to interpret. The smile remained ever broad upon his face as he disappeared into the parting crowd.

"I suppose we could do worse for dinner guests."

As Aritz led his sailors through the throng of natives, the people of this Sun Tribe gathered around them, offering casual observations to their neighbors as they walked on by. There was never a sense of threat in their tones, but it had made the Lord of House Mata uncomfortable just the same. He kept a suspicious eye on the onlookers as he followed after Han'e's imposing frame, the mountain of a man not even bothering to glance back to ensure his guest was following.

Eventually, they arrived at some sort of longhouse, still composed of the same primitive materials as all the other huts, but this one offered some wealth of space, probably for these such occasions. Han'e entered first, but his attendants moved to the side as they apparently awaited Aritz and his party to set foot inside.

The interior was nothing special. Two long tables filled the room, sets of benches on each side to accommodate whoever opted to eat or meet here. The smell was rather off-putting as the room carried a lingering odor of raw fish. From where, Aritz could not determine, since there wasn't so much as a pot over a flame in this longhouse, only the two tables.

Han'e sat himself at the center of the front table, Wik'na seated beside him. Aritz grunted to his men, and they all fanned out to either side of him, resting their weaponry against the floor in a collective clatter. With the same methodical caution as before, Aritz unstrapped the saber from his belt and leaned it against the frame of the table, the hilt jutting out above, the ease of reach all too enticing should things have gone upside down.

And yet, the Sun Tribe Chief maintained the same cordial smile that had been on his face since Aritz's arrival. If he felt at all threatened by the presence of what Aritz could only assume was advanced weaponry to the man, he did not show it. From the look of him, it would probably take an entire firing squad just to put a dent in him.

Almost as soon as all were seated, platters of local food were brought to the table—fish and grains and fresh greens from the look of it, much more plentiful than Aritz had anticipated. A tankard of what likely passed for alcohol was placed in front of them, hardly bearing the enchanting aromas of Silk Isle wine, but still not offensive in the least. Han'e poured himself a large mug, then offered the same to Aritz. The Chief held his mug up in a toast and shouted something.

"'Let us feast!'" Wik'na repeated with much the same enthusiasm.

Aritz took a sip of the liquid in sequence with Han'e. He may as well have been drinking piss. Food was passed around shortly afterward, and though he assumed he would hold the food in the same low esteem, he was pleasantly surprised to find the fish was quite delectable and wonderfully seasoned.

For what seemed a long while, Han'e droned on and on about the people who inhabited the island, the different individual tribes to which they belonged, and the various geographical differences separating the land, from the warm and humid climes of the south to the harsh mountainous terrain to the north. A long while was spent warning Aritz of the dangers lurking within the forest separating the north from the south—not only the disorienting depths, but also the dangerous and overprotective people who lived within it. If anything, whoever these people were, it appeared they had instilled some measure of fright into Han'e. That which had the capacity to cause fear in a man such as the Sun Tribe Chief was something Aritz would have rather taken seriously. Aritz chewed thoughtfully at the decadent fish platters while taking only courtesy sips of the horrid drink while he listened.

"'...but you have landed in a quite beautiful area of our land,'" Han'e continued through Wik'na. "'The sea is wondrously close to us, and the Haunted Tribe are fortunate to hold similar lands to the south. The Arrow Tribe to the west has tamed wild horses, and what magnificent beasts they are. Crops and livestock abound here, as well. And here I am rambling—I must apologize. We have never received outlanders such as yourselves, and many do tell me I am quite the overzealous host. So eager I have been, I have neglected entirely to ask you your names.'"

It took great effort for Aritz to maintain the appearance of being engaged in the conversation, but beyond the comment about the area's natural resources and potential, he had largely ignored Han'e's words. Except the part about the forest; that seemed quite important. He offered a respectful smile, the same he would give to visitors at his family's estate when their words held nothing of interest to him. "Chief Han'e," he said. "We truly must thank you for your hospitality. Our names are hardly important, but one name of which I am curious is that of Omerago da Vespindi. We had departed from our homeland some three months ago in search of lands he claimed to have discovered to our west. You state you have never played host to our people before—so am I correct in assuming Vespindi never arrived on these shores?"

Han'e raised an eyebrow and shook his head. "'No, not at all, I am afraid. If such a man were to have come ashore here, it would have been cause for much uproar. Much as it has been for you.'"

Aritz leaned back and stroked his chin, deep in thought. *Interesting, indeed. Then it is either Vespindi's discoveries lie further to the west, or he found nothing and this is as far as the world goes.*

"'Is this man Vespindi a friend of yours?'" Han'e asked, inclining his head.

"No, no, nothing as such," Aritz responded. "Perhaps a 'contemporary' would be the correct word. A fellow explorer, if you will."

"'An explorer?'"

Aritz nodded. "The world is large, far larger than you can even imagine. We would be remiss not to see all of it. I am fortunate to have the opportunity, myself. It was a wish of my father to embark on this journey."

The smile dissipated from Han'e's face, replaced instead with a remorseful frown. "'From your tone, it sounds your father has since departed from this life.'"

"He has." Aritz forced his voice to shake ever so slightly. "A sudden heart attack on the eve before his intended departure two years ago. I have spent the intervening years mourning him, as is the custom of my people. To say those years have been challenging would be an understatement. I hope I have not offended by opting not to partake in much of the drink, but I lost my mother to alcohol since then, too." *Though I fear I would be inclined to vomit should I have been forced to drink another drop of this dog's urine.*

Han'e offered a sympathetic bow. "'You have my deepest condolences.'"

With a deep sigh, Aritz turned his eyes askance, looking past the platters of food and to the thatched walls beyond. "And I lost my two younger brothers as well—one to war, another to an accident. Now I...I am all that remains of my family. My House's legacy rests entirely upon my shoulders."

The Sun Chief looked entirely bereft of words. Any man would struggle to devise the correct response to such a tale.

It is a tale I have perfected quite damn well. If it works on Their Majesties, these primitive sods have hardly a chance. Aritz fashioned a forced smile onto his face, allowing his eyes to mist for just a moment. "It is thanks to the King and Queen of my people that I am permitted to be here at all. Because of them, my family's name shall continue to live on."

Han'e inclined his head with curiosity, the remorse still plain on his face. "'King and Queen?'" he asked.

"Think of it as...well, think of it as yourself. As a Chief." *Only with substantially more power and influence than you have ruling over dirt.*

With a nod, Han'e's smile returned, though less exuberant than before. "'Perhaps I should adopt such a title for myself! Wik'na, inform our people I wish to be known from now on as 'King and Queen Han'e!' Hah!'"

Aritz held out a hand in confused protest, opening and closing his mouth in search of a retort, but too dumbfounded to respond.

The air outside the longhouse had cooled, a gentle sea breeze rolling in. Aritz turned over his shoulder to find that the sun had long since set. He had been in here for much longer than he realized.

Han'e seemed to take notice of the encroaching nighttime for the first time, as well. "'Where does the time go? It is getting quite late. Where do you plan to go now?'" he asked, curiosity apparent in his tone.

Aritz shrugged. "Back to our ship, I suppose. We have taken advantage of your hospitality far too much already today, Chief Han'e."

Quick to shake his head, Han'e rose to his feet and planted his hands on his hips with authority. "'Oh no, it is far too dangerous to navigate these waters when night falls! It would be my honor and privilege to offer home and hearth to you. Please, I must insist.'"

Exactly what I hoped you would say. Aritz stood in turn, his saber rattling against the table. He put a hand on it before it could topple over. "Who am I to decline such humble insistence?"

Han'e reacted with animated excitement, interspersed with boisterous laughter and wide gestures. Over the course of the next half hour, the Chief passed along details to Wik'na, who led Aritz and his sailors to another larger hovel—not as big as the longhouse, though not as frail as the normal dwellings—that seemed to be constructed exclusively for nights such as these. There was only one surface adequate for sleep, which simply meant Aritz's men would have to sleep on the ground. Wik'na offered Aritz the same exuberance as the Chief, bowing several times before departing and allowing the Acrarians to relax in sustained peace and quiet.

"Quite a friendly bunch," one of the sailors said, a thicker man with a thick and bushy mustache.

"A primitive and blasphemous bunch, aye," Aritz answered, folding his arms behind his back as he examined the thatches in the wall. "But a friendly bunch as well; this is true."

The mustached man filed in beside Aritz, concern apparent on his face. "So, this is not the New World that Vespindi discovered then, is it?"

"It would appear not."

"What do we do, then?"

Aritz considered the question for a moment, then flashed a smirk. "Who's to say this 'New World' need only be relegated to but one land?"

"My Lord?"

"Think back to the Chief's words," Aritz said as he turned his head, his eyes lighting up. "After all the advantages of this land he informed us of, how can we *not* offer this to Their Highnesses? I am certain we will put it to much more efficient use. And if Vespindi's New World lies only further west from here, I see no reason not to take advantage of what we have discovered for ourselves."

The sailor's eyes widened. "Then, sir, you mean..."

"All that shines under the Savior's Light shall be held by Their Highnesses. And I feel inclined to assert their hands are far less tainted than those who currently hold this land." Aritz turned on his heel, facing his sailors. "I believe we are about to need a larger landing party."

The midnight air came alive with the sound of screams and crackling flames. Where once had stood the Sun Tribe's rudimentary homes along the shores stood instead the smoldering craters left behind by the *Chariot's* cannonfire, nothing remaining of the previous inhabitants but blood, bone, and crumbled stone.

A smile, one that was at last genuine, stretched across Aritz's face as he watched his sailors take the village, rifles singing in concert with the *Chariot's* mighty roar. The animal-worshipers sprinted in all directions, trying desperately to outrun the might of the superior Acrarian forces. All Aritz had to do was stand and watch, his fingers rapping along the hilt of his saber.

Those who evaded the gunfire all seemed to be sprinting northward, where the arboreal ridges of the forest stood in wait, peaking out over the horizon. Aritz could only laugh at the sight, remembering the warning Han'e had given him about the dangers lurking within. *I have had enough of dirtying my hands for one lifetime. I am more than content with allowing others to do so on my behalf.*

As the deadly chorus rang on, Aritz surveyed what still stood in the village. The cannons had taken clean the half of the village nearest to the sea. What he could not help but notice was the largest hovel in the village—beside the longhouse where he had supped earlier in the day—still stood. Were he a betting man, he would have assumed that to be the good Chief's dwelling. Aritz did not take Han'e to be a man to run, but was he a man to hide?

With his hand still resting atop the hilt of the blade and his other arm dangling in the vicinity of his holstered pistol, Aritz strolled toward the Chief's supposed hut. He whistled a tune to himself, nothing to mimic any mistral he had heard in his youth, but simply a melody of his own making as the percussion of gunfire continued to thump behind him.

A flickering flame cast two shadows inside the hut, and Aritz drew his flintlock, clicking the hammer back with his thumb. He took one step past the threshold, then two.

A blur of movement caught his eye. His arm was but a hair faster. A body thumped on the ground, accompanied by a wooden clatter beside it.

Before Aritz could examine the body he felled, a moving wall seemed to close in on him. With little time to reload his pistol, he drew his saber in a quick motion, slashing in a diagonal arc, knocking back the approaching wall, which reacted with a pained grunt as it fell back toward the flame, kicking up dirt in the motion. Aritz tutted his lips, flicking blood off his steel before returning it to its sheath.

Now afforded the luxury of surveying his surroundings, he noticed the body of the translator, Wik'na, bleeding out from the throat, seizing as she drew her final choked breaths. A spear—if one could call a sharpened stick as such—lay motionless and useless beside her. And ahead, Han'e lay on his back, still breathing, propping himself up against the strength of an elbow as his free hand pressed against his stomach. He was bleeding, but it was only a surface wound. Against the light cast by the flames, Aritz could see fear in the Chief's eyes as he glared at the pistol, faint wisps of smoke still dancing out from the barrel. *He needn't know I've a need to reload.*

Aritz crouched down, looking between Wik'na's fleeting corpse and Han'e's horrified expression, pointing from one to the other with his flint-lock. "Oh, was I interrupting something, then?" he said with a chuckle. "My deepest apologies for your loss. I do wish you'd have followed your people's example and ran than hide like the coward you are. What a shame."

Han'e hissed a pained breath and muttered something, his face maintaining a combination of fear and rage.

Shrugging, Aritz continued to laugh. "I am sorry, but it does not appear I can understand you. If only your translator still lived. Hmph, a pity."

The Sun Chief growled, but said nothing further.

"I must say, your hospitality is greatly appreciated, Chief Han'e. I trust you have no objections to our taking it upon ourselves to become situated in this new land. You have my gratitude for highlighting all the wonders your land has to offer. Of course, if you *do* object, I more than welcome you to speak up." He held out his empty hand as a prompt for the Chief to respond.

There was nothing for Han'e to say. He merely lay there, silent.

"Such kindness. I happily accept your offer!" Aritz offered a wide grin, matching the exuberance and enthusiasm Han'e once exhibited. "I am certain Their Highnesses will laud you for your generosity, as well. It shan't be forgotten. And I, myself, I will long remember this day. I am, after all, penning a legacy that shall last generations. Tonight is but the first chapter I shall write."

Han'e continued to glare at Aritz with hateful, fearful eyes, frozen in place by the presence of the Acrarian's weapon.

As Aritz rose back to a standing position, he waved the empty flintlock around, spinning it along his finger, listening to Han'e's anxious gasps in so doing. He strode about the hut, circling Han'e, who would not take his eyes off him. "I would assume there is no harm in telling you, of all people, the truth of the matter." He sighed, his tongue rife with the taste of bitterness at the memories. "The Mata name was on the verge of being soured beyond repair. My father shamed us before the King and Queen, my brothers tried to usurp what was rightfully mine, and my mother was a willing participant in it all. I needed to correct those grievous errors.

"And so I poisoned my father. None were any the wiser. How could *I* have caused him to have a heart attack? Their Highnesses certainly did not question it. I had to wonder if they were relieved that I would indeed carry on the family name.

"I had a brother training to be a knight, a brother who would have inherited my father's titles had I not set things right. He wanted to be a knight, and so I sent him off to war in the Northen Marches to quell some sort of rebellion or another. And a catspaw traveled with him. Oh, how I mourned such a treacherous tragedy.

"My youngest brother was a scholar in waiting, so eager to learn from whatever he could get his hands on. Tis a shame when accidents happen. You cannot control fire. The loss of life was horrid—as was the loss of knowledge that came with the library's destruction.

"And my poor mother, beset by it all, finding comfort only in the drink. Comforts begat comforts until they granted her the eternal comfort of a long and endless rest. May the Savior rest her soul."

Aritz stopped behind Han'e, hand resting on his hip, a satisfied smile on his face. "Their Highnesses have long respected a man of ambition, and I am but offering them the Mata Lord they deserve. My father thought too small, and I have long intended to correct that. I will begin with this land, with these precious resources you have graciously offered me. I assure you, we will put all of this to much better use than you ever could. The removal of the taint of your presence shall allow this isle to shine ever brighter under the Savior's light. And so, I must ask you, Chief Han'e..." He raised the flintlock toward Han'e's head, clicking the hammer back.

With a shocked gasp, Han'e shuffled toward the threshold and scampered off into the night, suddenly seeming to forget the superficial pain scoring his gut. The ground had hardly puddled with his blood.

Satisfied, Aritz holstered his weapon and chuckled. "I must ask you to give us leave of these lands, and you to away to another. You can keep your life as a show of my own generosity." Taking one last look at Wik'na's corpse, Aritz whistled his melody once more and sauntered back out into the night air, rejoining his chorus of conquest.

Three sailors approached, rifles slung over their shoulders.

"Status," Aritz demanded.

"This village is ours, my Lord," one of the sailors responded. "They didn't stand a chance. None had the gall to fight back."

"Good. Quell the embers and rest. We needn't scorch this land before we have taken five steps upon it." Aritz turned his attention to the southwest, and all the unclaimed promise it held. "The ashes may pile at a later time. But for tomorrow, we may simply carry our flame elsewhere."

And that flame itself promised a new world crafted in a new image.

CHAPTER SIXTEEN

A Bleeding Stone

The Year 1556 Anno Salvatoris
15 Years After the Invasion

As the waves crashed before her, Tez looked at her sister with a heavy heart, her very soul weary. To look at her sister, the fire still burning in her eyes despite the defeat in her voice, she could hardly bear it. "Sen," she said, her voice tired, the feeling of sand grating against the back of her throat. "Even if Mother *is* there...what can we even do right now? We've lost. We've lost everything."

Sen curled herself up, bringing her knees to her chest, resting her head on Tez's shoulder. Pebbles clattered behind them from atop Brin's makeshift grave, rustling around against the wind's breath. The tides had continued to send the piled corpses out to sea, but the horrid stench still remained, forever staining the world below.

Tez had seen her sister in these depths of anguish before—back when there was a chance to save Brin's life. So much had happened since then. On that day, it seemed so easy to let Sen go, to know it would be futile to argue to the contrary. But now? It was no more than a quick march to a quicker death. Or a fate worse than it.

"We can't leave her there, Tez," Sen asserted, even as her tone was anything but assertive. "I can't allow it. *We* can't allow it."

"You know I would want nothing more than to rush in there and save Mother," Tez agreed. "But stop and think for a moment, Sen. We still have our lives. Think of everyone who we've had to say goodbye to. Father, Brin, Tawa,

Narva, Sharrabha…" She clenched her eyes shut, drawing a deep, pained sigh. "Ket. Would it be fair of us to rush to our deaths, when we were among the lucky who escaped it?"

"It doesn't matter, Tez." A tear trickled down Sen's face, another for the collection, another to implant in the earth. "I can't accept that."

"It doesn't matter if you *can't*, Sen. It matters that you *must*!"

"But how is that *fair*? So many have been taken from us, and of those who still remain, is it fair that *I* am one of them? Is it fair that I have the opportunity for life when in that factory, not only Mother, but countless others are merely awaiting the inevitable? I can feel them cursing me from the Otherworld already."

Tez reached out and grasped Sen's hand, clutching it tightly, reluctant ever to let it go for fear of what Sen would do should she be let free. "If you are to be cursed, then so am I. But it does not make it right to do so. We're still *alive*, Sen. I don't want to give that up. I don't want *you* to give that up."

Sen shook her head. "A life in hiding is hardly a life at all. Storm clouds are sure to follow us wherever we may go. This Land isn't our home anymore. But if we've lost everything, I want to hold tightly to all that remains. *Mother* remains, Tez. I'm sure of it. And I cannot—"

"Sen, please." Tez felt her sister's hand trembling, a cold sweat dripping from her forehead. Some weeks ago, these would have been the moments where Sen would have run away into a drunken stupor, eager to leave the problems of the world behind, if only for an evening. "We will find home. So long as we have each other, we will have a home. You have to believe that. We still have something to fight for: us."

"And Mother."

"Mother is *gone*, Sen."

"You don't know that!"

"I know what awaits us should we go back! You know it, too! Why do you feel the need to throw your life away like this?"

"Because if I stand atop our people's ashes with my head held high, then I am just the monster they all claimed me to be!"

"You were never a monster, Sen!"

"I know, damn it!" Sen ripped her hand free, clenching her fingers in front of her face, a sobbed gasp escaping her throat. "But do you not think those who reviled me are angry that they are beneath the ground and I am not?"

"No, I don't think so, Sen, because they're *dead!*" Tez spun onto her knees and grabbed Sen by the shoulders, glaring at her sister's face even as Sen averted her eyes. "And I'll be damned if I'm letting you join them in the Otherworld just yet."

"As if I even end up there."

Tez slapped her—not hard, but enough to grab her attention.

Sen winced as she brought a hand up to her cheek, massaging at the red spot that marked the point of impact.

"Contrary to what you still think—even after being told otherwise by a literal *god*—you belong with us. You are part of us. And if I let you run off to your death, Father will never let me hear the end of it when I join you all." She gripped Sen's shoulders once again, this time ensuring she was making eye contact with her. "I'm your sister. I have to protect you. We have to protect each other."

Gritting her teeth, Sen looked past Tez to the ocean beyond, tears still streaming down her face. "I know, Tez," she said, another sob bursting from her mouth. "But no matter what you tell me...I can't leave everyone behind."

"You can't save everyone, Sen."

"But can you fault me for wanting to try?"

"Yes! Because it's unreasonable to try! You feel you need to prove yourself so much that you've blinded yourself to the fact you've already done more than enough. No matter what you say, no matter what anyone else says, you. Are. Tribe. Nothing will ever change that."

"Tez..." Sen muttered, bringing her hands up to her shoulders, meeting her sister's hands with a shaky grip. "To run is wiser. I know that. But I would never forgive myself if I ran. To run would be to abandon everything that is part of me. I've run more than enough in my life. I ran from the reality of being Eclipseborn. I ran from properly processing Father's death. I already ran from the Tribes once when I thought my only place would be amongst other Eclipseborn. But I can't. Run. Now." She pulled Tez's hands off her shoulders and held them before her face, still quivering with a potential myriad of emotions and reasons. "If there's even the slightest of hopes that I can save Mother, then I have to take that chance. I can't ask you to understand. I'm only asking you to accept it." Determination settled into her face, even as her eyes were rimmed with cracks of pink.

The wind howled at Tez's back, her frayed braid wafting along its flow, strands of hair obscuring her vision. The moist, soft grass underneath her was seeping in through her trouser legs and dampening her knees. "Are you trying to save Mother, or are you trying to save everyone?"

Sen winced, again gritting her teeth. "I don't know. I only know that I am going to do what I must. What I can."

"And what will you do with all our kin if you do save them? These people stripped of their wits and their minds with nowhere to go?"

Her lip quivering, Sen remained silent, the possibility of a retort dwindling by the second.

"You need to be realistic, Sen. We can do nothing to help them." Tez's lip curled downward, a reserved breath puffing out from her nostrils. "I don't know how many times I need to say it. You've done more than enough. It's not running. It's merely a matter of knowing when it is best to walk away."

"The Owl laid that path for *you*. But did it say of *me*?" Frowning, Sen broke herself away from her sister, remorse apparent on her face. Her eyes drifted back to the east, where the shadow of the City still loomed ahead, puffs of dark smoke still billowing to the heavens. "My fate could very well remain there."

"Your fate is tied to wherever I go, dear sister. Damn the Owl, but that was its plan for me. And my plan for *you* is to make sure what's left of our family remains together."

A tentative smile cracked Sen's lips, her face glimmering in the waning orange sunlight.

Tez raised an eyebrow. "What is it?"

"Have you ever known me to stick to a plan?"

"Sen, please," Tez said again, feeling the emotion welling within her. She was beyond the point of exhaustion, physically and emotionally. It took all her might to keep the tears dammed up. "Don't."

Slowly, Sen turned her attention back to Tez, the smile remaining, wan though it was. "I just want to do some good, Tez. I want to give back for what I took away. I was here, Tez. I was here before it all began. I could have ended all of this with a single shot. I could have taken Kamataa's life, Aritz's life. But I didn't, and we all suffered for it."

"You can't take the entirety of that burden for yourself, Sen."

"But I do. Gods forgive me, but I do. I want to save everyone in the City, but I am too much of a fool in the thinking. I want to save Mother, but I would just be the same selfish girl I was when I decided only to rescue Brin while others looked on in disbelief. Blood is on my hands, Tez, blood that I cannot wash away. If there was but one thing I could do to cleanse myself of it, I would do it in a heartbeat. But that time has long passed, hasn't it?"

Tez frowned, bunching her hands into the folds of her trousers. "Then what will you do?"

Sen shook her head, casting her gaze downward. "Whatever I can. If Mother still lives, I will set her free. If I can free others, then so be it. I do not want to be a bleeding stone, dear sister. I will mend what I can. And if I cannot stop what is going on already..." She stopped, sighing deeply into the earth.

"What?" Tez inclined her head. "What will you do?"

"Then I will offer retribution to those responsible. Aritz and Kamataa. Blood may coat my hands, but theirs are drenched in it. They've bathed in it. And the greatest good I could offer anyone is to ensure they never spill another drop of blood again."

Tez allowed the moment to stretch on in prolonged silence. She looked off to the side, where their spears lay in wait, their shafts damp from the ocean spray coating the grass. Past Sen, the small mound of stones remained quiet, save for the bugs crawling about in their depths. A part of her wanted to admit that Sen was right. That it was worth it to offer the bastards the judgment they deserved. The memory of Brin being carried away by the Invaders while her father bled out from Aritz's assault would never leave her. She knew it would always haunt her. Fear and pain had paralyzed her, made her feel weak. An uncertain future was laid out before her. One she knew would be filled with hardship, regardless of what came next.

If there was something she could do that would mitigate that hardship, even a little bit, she knew she'd have to take the opportunity. *Gods, Sen. I wish you weren't so fucking stubborn. It's rubbing off on me.*

"I'm not letting you do this, Sen. Not alone, anyway."

Sen clenched her eyes shut, furiously shaking her head. "Tez, you can't. The Owl—"

"Oh, fuck the Owl. I don't give a shit what 'fate' has predicted for me. This could all very well be 'part of the plan,' for all I know. But I told you already: I'm your sister. I have to protect you. I may want you to go wherever I go, but for now, I suppose I have little option but to go wherever you go."

The cautious smile returned to Sen's face. "You told me I'd be walking right to my death. You're content with walking along with me?"

Tez scoffed. "You're not dying when I'm there to save your ass."

"There are few things in this life I know I can count on, and that's always been one of them."

Rising to a kneeling position, Tez held out a hand to her sister, pulling her up to her feet. The stains of wet grass colored her trouser legs, her imprint left in the ground below. Tez walked over to their weapons, picking up the spears and tossing one to Sen. Suddenly, it didn't feel so heavy in her hands anymore. It was amazing what a spot of anger could do.

As Sen inspected her spear and hovered a hesitant hand over the holster housing her Deatharm, Tez walked over to Brin's grave, unsure if or when she would get the chance to see him again. She closed her eyes and kneeled before it, pressing her two forefingers to her lips and placing the kiss upon the pile of loose stones. *May the gods be willing, we will not have to meet soon, little brother. But if you are watching, I pray you will lend us your strength. We carry you with us, always. All of you. Our legion of the lost.*

Wet grass sloshed underneath Sen's feet as she approached Brin's grave to offer what Tez could only assume were the same wishes. Placing a comforting hand on her sister's shoulder, Tez smiled down at the memory of Brin, and the fearful image of him being taken away from her forever became the prideful visage of his face during his celebration ceremony, the happiest she had ever seen him. When next they met, Tez could only hope that would be the face that greeted her.

The sisters turned and faced the City, the day's light already falling behind them. "We shall have the cover of night on our side by the time we return there," Tez said.

Sen nodded in agreement. "All the better. This is it, isn't it?"

A heavy breath escaped Tez's lips. "This is it."

The time for the final Tribal offensive was at hand. They took their first steps, ready and eager to spit in the eyes of fate.

It had felt like an eternity since he was last afforded the chance to sit down.

As Aritz returned to his manor, feet clacking against the hard floor, servants stopping their activities to bow and pay their respects, even at the expense of the structural integrity of whatever they held, he let loose an enormous breath. He knew not when it would all sink in, but it was over. This damned conflict, all the fighting against savage beasts, all the bloodshed...it was no more. This land was his, and he had every intention of petitioning King Ferrand and Queen Catelina to allow him to use it as he saw fit.

He knew the days and weeks ahead would be a logistical nightmare. He had a new gaggle of workers with whom to contend—many of them without their wits. Training them to be useful would be a challenge, to say the least. He ran the risk of insubordination, if Kama had her way. How many of her ilk still lurked within his ranks, he knew not. Savior willing, she would be the last remaining. A sign of greater divine intervention would be her removal or disappearance entirely, but he had grown weary of such bloodshed. His life had been filled with it. The last fifteen years produced nothing but bloodshed. It was his hope that the next fifteen would produce something else entirely.

A new home. A new legacy. A new chapter in the book of Mata. His ambition knew no bounds, and he could hardly wait to see where it would lead him.

But such was a thought to worry about tomorrow. For now, he needed his rest. He yearned for it. He was afforded hardly a moment to enjoy the comfort of his bedchambers last night. The maidservants were hard at work putting everything back in its place when last he was there. Far too disruptive to have a well-earned sleep.

As Aritz ascended the steps leading to his chambers, his legs protested, roaring with the effort. It seemed it was only now that he could recognize the extent of his exhaustion. Weeks of constant fighting and traveling were enough to keep one's mind off such aches. That, and the futile attempts to purge some of the...unpleasantness of the return journey from his mind. He feared what memories would unfold in his dreams when next he slept. He prayed the nightmares would soon cease. Only pleasant dreams were to loom ahead.

He had to catch his breath by the time he reached the top of the stairs, one of the doormen opening the passage to his bedchambers for him at first sight. Though Aritz's legs bore more the temperament of a disobedient child, he forced himself to press on, the call for a long lay all too enticing.

"The maids completed their work a short time ago, sir," the doorman said, standing beside the opened door. "Please let me know if it is not to your liking."

Aritz managed a tired smile as he walked past the man, meekly rapping his shoulder with a light hand. Even *he* was surprised at his own gesture. Clearly, Aritz was more exhausted than he thought. "Do not trouble yourself, son. I am certain it is perfect for now."

"Very good, sir," the man responded, closing the door after the General upon his entry.

Placing his hands on his hips, Aritz surveyed the room, finding it...far from his liking. The paraphernalia along the shelves was askew and out of order, shards of wood and glass still littered the floor, someone's plate remained on a table with breakfast food still upon it, the sheets upon the bed were of a disagreeable color...

He was simply too tired to raise a fuss about it. Another thing to worry about for tomorrow. Along with the decisions of what new trophies would adorn the shelves after this expedition. He had not been blind to the photographs taken by that one man throughout the journey. By some miracle, he had managed to survive, as did his pictures, supposedly. Aritz strangely looked forward to revisiting those moments frozen and captured in time.

From his periphery, his bed was beckoning him. But a glint cast from the setting sunlight caught his eye first. Aritz walked past the war map, its northern territories soon to be filled in to the same detail as the south, and approached his desk, where his flintlock pistol rested, its once-polished sheen diminished by the stains of red now coating it. He picked it up, turning it about in his hand, unaware of any physical changes to it, but all too eager to test if any...unnatural properties had been picked up. The sight of it was ghastly, at the very least.

As he returned it to the desk and turned to face his bed, Aritz stopped mid-stride, holding a curious finger up. "Wait a moment," he murmured, glancing back at the desk. "Where is that dagger?"

He kneeled to the ground, examining the underside of the desk on the chance it fell and slid underneath, but there was no steel waiting for him. He bit at his lip with befuddlement, scanning the various shelves and bookcases throughout the chamber, wondering if it had inadvertently been placed elsewhere from the pistol, but again, he had no luck. It was altogether missing. Aritz frowned and huffed a breath, his brow furrowing. He tried to picture the face of the man he handed the weapons to, but came away with nothing more than a plain face with no distinctive features or markings. A ghost of a man walking among the living.

With slow, deliberate steps, Aritz strode to the door and opened it, catching the doorman from earlier by surprise.

"Ah, sir?" the man said, hastily adding an Acrarian salute. "Was there something you needed?"

Feeling the large frown on his face, Aritz nodded. "One of my guards had dropped a couple of items off in my chambers some time ago. Were you watching my doors at that time?"

"Ah, yes, sir, I was."

"Did anyone happen to enter after his departure?"

"No, sir. After he left, no one came this way again until you."

Aritz grunted, stroking his chin. "Curious. Very curious. He wouldn't have..."

The doorman raised an eyebrow as Aritz trailed off into his own thoughts. After a moment's silence, he cleared his throat and asked, "Is there something I may help with, sir?"

It took a moment for Aritz to register the question, but he grunted once more and cast a sharp glare at the man. "Do you know the name of the guard who dropped the items off? He was not part of my normal retinue." *Or he could very well have been. It is not for me to remember their names.*

In response, the doorman opened his mouth, but was quick to shut it again, perplexed into silence. He cast a long glance into the middle distance, pursing his lips, but at last shook his head. "I must admit, sir, I do not. I presumed he was a newer recruit—I had not seen him before today. I am sorry."

Aritz shook his head. "Tis no fault of yours," he muttered, before turning on his heel and closing the door behind him before any further questions could be asked. He crossed his arms, staring ahead at the chamber that now felt far larger than it had before, far lonelier than it had before.

It appeared his well-earned rest would have to wait another night.

CHAPTER SEVENTEEN

A Child of the Black Moon

The City found itself in the grips of a long rest as the clouds covered a night sky, obscuring the light of the Moon. It was to Sen's assumption that there would always be some drunkard or braggart stumbling around the streets at all hours of the night, shouting into windows or pissing themselves before passing out in a ditch somewhere. Projection though it may have been, she could not deny the dread she received from the overbearing silence.

For once, the City was asleep. It did not sit right with her.

Sweat trailed down her neck and back as the oppressive heat remained even into the late hours. The dirt crunched underneath her feet, pebbles kicking up as she dragged the butt of her spear through the dusty earth. The flintlock, still housing but one bullet, weighed heavily at her thigh. Though her eyes were wary of hidden eyes lurking in the shadows, she sensed nothing, felt no warnings from the Moon surging within her.

The only ones in the streets were herself and Tez. Hiding, a valid option, was wholly an unnecessity.

All the better, as it brought them back to the factory that much quicker. But at the same time, the reality of what had happened within since their flight from its horrors arrived just the same. Whatever lay beyond those doors…Sen was unsure if she was ready for it.

A wagon remained outside, the same one that had been waiting when she and Tez had snuck inside earlier in the day. Mindless groans and murmurs continued to drone on as Sen approached, those within still managing to hold tight to the bare requirements they needed to be considered "alive." Sen felt uneasy. It had been hours since they were here last. That the wagon had not yet been brought into the factory, away from prying eyes, did not sit well with her. Something was amiss.

Sen held up her spear and turned to Tez, putting a finger to her lips. She nudged her head toward the door, drawing a deep breath. *Are you ready?* was the intent of her wordless gaze.

Reluctance still coated her sister's face, but she had, at least in part, returned to the Tez she had long known, the Tez who would do anything to protect her family. She nodded in acquiescence, crouching into an attack position.

Pushing the fear and anxiety down, Sen closed her eyes for a brief second longer than a standard blink and shuffled to the factory door, the thumping of the metal beasts still pounding rhythmically within. Slowly, she pushed the door open, a creaking groan the answer, and slid her way back into the hell within the moment she could squeeze through. Hiding behind the nearest thing she could find, she let her heart thump away, her shoulders heaving up and down while she waited for Tez's arrival.

With her sister cleared through, Sen spun around on her knee, spear in hand, and froze in her tracks.

Bodies. Blood. Everywhere.

Sen tightened the grip on her spear as she rose back to unsteady feet, her eyes shifting from one direction to the next, and she approached the nearest body. A young woman's frame, blood pooling underneath a caved-in skull.

Vanta, Sen realized. She was not able to see just how gruesome a sight it was after Tawa threw her into the trough. Purple bruises lined her throat where Tawa's manacles had marked her flesh, her mouth frozen open in a final gasp for air. She shuddered as she remembered just how close they had been to having it all end right there and shook with anger at the thought of Tawa having to pay for it. It took every ounce of restraint for Sen to ignore her corpse, to not drive her spear through her just for the satisfaction...but it seemed something had already beaten her to it. *I don't recall Tawa having the opportunity to stab her in the chest.*

Furrowing her brow, Sen exchanged a glance with Tez, who mirrored the same confusion, and pressed on, finding another familiar face coated in blood. Sha'a, her throat left entirely opened, the hole the size of a bullet. It was easy to determine the cause, but who pulled the trigger was another question entirely.

One Sen could not help but ponder the answer to as she surveyed the rest of the factory floor, and the numerous soldier bodies scattered about it. Her breath caught in her throat as she drew nearer to them.

They were not just killed. They were *savaged*. Throats were cut, chests were scored through, entrails were ripped from the guts previously holding them. Indentations marked where there once existed faces, now instead caved as though the strength of a heavy stone crushed them. Eyes were frozen in shock, bodies gripped in pained spasms only to remain in the same position, petrified by the throes of agony. Blood had splattered across the floor, more an angry painting than a reminder of death. Whoever, or *what*ever, did this, they seemed more beast than human. No human could produce something this visceral, this horrifying—not just the capacity to do so, but also the endurance to survive long enough to fell six men trained in the Invaders' brutal art of war.

The signs of battle were evident all around Sen. The blood covering the floor did not belong exclusively to the Invader soldiers. There were droplets that had fallen much too far for them to have been sourced from these bodies. Whatever was responsible, it didn't escape unscathed. Or so Sen wanted to believe.

Her hands trembled as she examined the gruesome scene, her mouth agape, her nose hardly phased by the horrendous odor filling the room. After everything she had experienced, the stench of a mere six corpses barely registered. But it mitigated nothing at all. She couldn't look away. Fear gripped her, as did anger, curiosity. And that search for the answer led her eyes astray, to the blood beyond the bodies, to the droplets moving further and further away from the scene.

Judging from the nudge on her shoulder, Sen could only assume Tez had reached the same conclusion.

They were far from alone.

Sen drew a long, deep breath, her chest far too heavy to catch it, and slowly inched forward, crouching into a readied, attacking position. Tez lined up beside her, taking much more measured and assured steps ahead, her prowess with a spear, should it have been necessary, making her the obvious one to lead. For as much as relief could carry her at this point, Sen was relieved to see that confidence return to her sister.

A room loomed ahead, adjacent to the thumping metal beasts. A trough—one that Sen could assume was or had been filled with the same Tribal blood as had been in the opposite room—was placed beside the door. Red smears colored the nearest metal beast, what passed for crude runes cut into its frame. *Whoever carved those runes either did a shit job of it, or they've never seen a Tribal rune in their life.* Drops of blood continued ahead in the direction of the room, the spacing between drops growing larger and larger until it eventually stopped some paces before the room as though whoever was bleeding had vanished into thin air.

Vanished...or healed. Sen gritted her teeth, closing her eyes, trying to find her center even as Tez continued to press on. The rhythm of the metal beasts thumped and thumped with the same cadence, but as she focused her hearing, clinging to the long-lost hopes she would one day be a Wolfsign just like Narva, she could hear something in between the crashes of steel.

A voice. No, a *scream.* Not one of pain or fear, but of anger, rage. One lacking concert with the metal beasts, instead singing to its own shattered melody.

Flaring her nostrils, Sen opened her eyes back up to see Tez crouched and waiting just outside the room. Sen let the tremors course through her, flowing down her arms, the butt of her spear rattling against the floor. She understood what lay beyond that door. She was ready to face it. No amount of Luck would protect her this time. She had Tez for that.

Loose residue crunched under her feet as she approached the threshold, the shadows within the room jostling in place, bookended by an accompaniment of erratic and furious movement. Sen peered her eyes around the corner, the walls lined with much the same horror as the room across the factory—only with Tribespeople bearing much more horrid appearances. Blood streamed down their bodies from numerous puncture wounds, from slashes to their throats, limbs now strewn about the floor. If there had been any life remaining within any of them, it would have been nothing less than pure hell. It was an even worse state than the soldiers left on the factory floor.

Sen steeled herself and slowly worked her gaze down the line, to the blur of ancient fury at the far end of the room, a face cast in shadow, much like the heart of the woman to whom it belonged. Entering the room in full, Sen leveled her spear and took in the sight of Kamataa driving a half-spear into the stomach of a hanging woman over and over and over again, beyond the point of any signs of life. Even in this darkness, Sen was not blind to the sprays of red coating the old crone's stark white hair, such to the point that she needed not the fire-haired Illusion in which she had draped herself. So intent on goring this dead woman that Kamataa seemed to not have been cognizant of Sen's arrival.

It was only when Sen looked upon the corpse's face that she had any intention of making her presence known.

The suspended body turned and swayed against its chains, the face of a Stone Tribeswoman shining in the shadows, her strength long since slackened and departed, but it was all too clear who it was, even with red face paint faded to nothing.

A growl grated against Sen's throat until it erupted into a scream. She charged forward, spear leveled, the gap between her and the old Eclipseborn narrowing by the instant, narrowing to three paces, two paces, one, and he lurched her weapon toward Kamataa's stomach, all the power she could manage instilled in the blow.

Without a glance, Kamataa spun around the assault and swung her arm with enough force to knock Sen aside and into the murky glass window that separated the room from the factory's main floor.

The breath escaped Sen's chest as she felt gravity's push. The pain and the sound of broken glass came all at once, her arms flaring both with the sensation of Luck and the agonic burn of slashed flesh. She landed past the glass shards and rolled several yards away, skidding to a stop past Tez by the butt of her spear. Pushing herself back to her knees, Sen took a cursory glance at her arms, but they were marked by nothing more than surface-level cuts. Nothing she needed to concern herself with.

On the other side of the broken glass, Kamataa exhibited none of the wicked and exuberant joy with which Sen had been familiar. The woman who delighted in shooting a defenseless Tribeswoman in the face at point blank range instead appeared hollow. Draped in the shadows, her eyes were two sunken holes of darkness, her expression one of a shattered woman sharing much with the shards of glass cast in her wake.

The only thing seeming to restore life to that sallow face was taking in Sen's presence. The longer Kamataa stared at her, the deeper the shadows were cast over her face. She bent down and emerged just as quickly, leaping past the opened window she had just created and onto the other side, a half-spear tucked under each arm as though they were venomous quills emerging from her sides.

Tez remained three strides away from the Eclipseborn woman, holding her spear in a readied position, walking sidelong in step with Kamataa until she reunited with her sister.

Sen, for her part, groaned away a pang of pain, the throbbing in her ribs returning, and rose back to her feet, damning the sharp protests of her slashed flesh.

Stopping several paces away, Kamataa relaxed her arms, the half-spears falling slack at her waist. A smile did not even make its way to her lips. "You have kept me waiting for far too long, Sennalhat."

Tufts of rageful breaths billowed from Sen's nostrils, her knees bent in anticipation of a forward lurch. "You godsdamned madwoman," she growled. "My mother...you killed...my—"

"Your mother was long gone, and you have taken far more from me than I from you, Sennalhat."

"Oh, cut the shit." Sen dashed forward, screaming a raspy war cry, and lunged her spear toward the old woman's chest.

In a swift motion, Kamataa engaged one of her half-spears and turned the blow away, the momentum carrying Sen into her guard. Sen spun on her heel and rolled on the ground, evading a quick counter from Kamataa's off-hand, landing in a half-crouch with her spear held out to the side, tucked beneath her arm.

"Knowing the state your mother was in," Kamataa said, her tone taunting, "would you not say I did her a kindness?"

"Enough of your 'kindnesses' and 'mercies!'" Sen sprang back to her feet and sprinted, swinging the spear in a wide arc, the force spinning her around on her feet, the blow easily evaded by the old Eclipseborn, turned aside with one half-spear while the other found itself closing in on Sen's throat.

The strike was answered with another scrape of steel. The weapon vanished from Sen's sight in a blur of motion.

Resistance slackened on her spear and Sen spun on her heel to reposition herself, the weapon held leveled once again. A flurry of strikes rang in her ears against the pounding metal as Tez held her own against Kamataa's dual strikes. Even as she was pressed into a closer quarter than was comfortable against the half-spears, Tez was compensating more than well enough by her speed of movement, something that had served her perfectly before being stripped of the Bear's Boon.

Sen knew her stamina would not last. She ran forward, her feet sliding against the hard floor as she unleashed a series of successive jabs, each blocked by half-hearted swings, the tips of their weapons only barely kissing in the attempts. Her chest heaving, a fire in her side, she leaped, bringing the spear down in a downward strike, her steel meeting only the hard ground below as Kamataa backed away, simultaneously blocking a blow from Tez. The half-spear nearest to Sen was inside her guard, too close, just on the outside of the shaft of her spear. Kamataa's arm twitched, and Sen pushed the shaft forward, pressing against the lighter weight of the half-spear, the tip of Sen's weapon grinding and scraping against the floor. She reached to her lower back and drew the hunter's knife from its sheath and cut a wide swath in the air, finding a brief moment of resistance in its arc.

Kamataa hissed a breath as blood splashed from her shoulder, but hardly enough to deter her. No grimace adorned her face, nor did groans of pain escape her lips. She merely stepped away, the same fire glowering in her eyes past the dark pits which hid them. The same fire that burned with violent hatred.

With a shout, Sen pressed forward again, Tez at her side. Her feet skidded against the floor as she swept her spear at Kamataa's legs in a wide arc,

Tez thrusting toward the woman's chest. The Eclipseborn planted one spear against the ground, meeting the full brunt of Sen's swing, while allowing Tez's strike to pass her by, sidestepping it and carrying Tez into her, her other spear well within striking distance. Tez dropped her weapon, grasping Kamataa's arm before she had the opportunity, and flung her over her shoulder, the crone's old frame landing on the ground with a heavy impact that, once again, hardly seemed to slow her as she retained control of her weapons.

The bodies of the Invader soldiers were but a few paces away, the pools of blood emitting a rank odor. Kamataa slowly rose back to her feet, half-spears hanging loosely in her grip. Her eyes shifted to the side, seeming to catch sight of those she savaged, but betraying no thoughts or indications of remorse or regret.

Taking the opportunity to catch her breath, Sen sheathed her knife and pressed a hand to her cracked rib, wincing back a sharp hiss at the touch. "So, did Artiz dispose of you, or you of him?" she asked with a pained smirk. "I remember telling Ziia he'd hardly welcome us into his fold were he to know what we really were."

Her shoulders rising and lowering as she heaved angry breath after angry breath, Kamataa gritted her teeth and growled, just over the clanging of the metal beasts, "You have not the right to say her name."

"The right to determine who can and can't say one's name was a right you forfeited long ago, Kamataa."

"It is a right that I *alone* shall determine!" the old woman shouted. "Those names will be remembered as martyrs, while those to be forgotten are of they with traitorous hands, hands I shall forever rip from the pages of history."

"The only traitorous hands here are *yours*, Kamataa. Look around you. The blood of Tribe and Invader alike pollutes these walls!" Sen snarled and leveled her spear once again. "Can you earnestly say you have not betrayed everything you once were, everything you once stood for?"

Kamataa bared her teeth, at once more beast than human. "Blood repays blood as betrayal repays betrayal. The Acrarians betrayed me just as the Tribes did, and *this*—" She gestured to the bodies beside her. "—shall be the price they must pay for it. If it is the will of this Land that those loyal to me shall meet their end, then I will suffer this Land's people no further—regardless of whether they are native or Invader. I shall endure as I always have, waiting for another to burn it all down and rise again from the ashes."

Sen flared her nostrils, taking a hesitant step forward. "You yourself have burned down enough that you would be alone in those ashes with none to rise again with you."

A long sigh escaped Kamataa's mouth as she rolled her shoulders, shaking her arms about. "And what, Sennalhat, is so wrong with that?"

Before Sen had the opportunity to respond, she was pressed onto the defensive, bringing her spear up just in time to block a twin diagonal slash that knocked her back. As she regained her footing, Tez jumped forward, swinging her spear up and using her own strength against that of Kamataa's to pry loose the old woman's weapons. Sen saw an opening as Kamataa's stomach lay exposed, and charged, lurching with all her might only for Kamataa to kick at Tez's shins and knock the tiring warrior to a knee, freeing her to block Sen's blow just in time, pushing the spear tip away with one half-spear while ensnaring the weapon with the other.

Cursing beneath a growled breath, Sen gave her spear a tug but came away empty, the old Eclipseborn smirking while Tez was regaining her stamina. Sen snarled, two more attempts to pry loose her weapon coming away futile. *Still two more I can use...and something I've been saving for her.* She let go of the spear, allowing the butt to clack against the floor, and reached back and drew her knife free, holding it in a reverse grip aimed a bladed punch at Kamataa's throat while she was still otherwise entangled. The first blow missed, Kamataa ducking her head underneath. A successive strike found skin, but barely a nick.

A third found its way into the back of the old woman's hand, sending a half-spear to the floor.

Kamataa hissed and jabbed the butt end of the weapon into Sen's gut, knocking the wind out of her and sending her sliding backward. Sen gritted her teeth as she coughed out a weak breath and reached for the pistol at her thigh, drawing it, clicking the hammer back—

And watching it scatter across the floor as Kamataa knocked it loose from her hand. Armed with only her hunter's knife, Sen growled and tried to press into the woman's guard, but she was too slow on the draw. Kamataa barreled into Sen with her shoulder, pushing her backward, and before Sen could raise her blade, a wall of steel crashed into her, knocking loose what remained of the air in her lungs and sending her knife flying from her hand. The sound of clanging metal burst in her ears in its heavy rhythm as the world spun around her, the face of the hateful woman blurring in and out of focus in front of her.

Just barely, she could see the half-spear raising above her, the shadows dancing along its steel tip, but her arms would not cooperate, feeling nothing but a cold numbness as she wavered in the dark.

She closed her eyes when the next flash of steel came, but with it did not come a rush of blood nor a burst of pain. Instead, the pressure upon her released and she collapsed to her knees, slapping her palm against the side of her head in an attempt to redirect and narrow her focus. The faint sound of clashing steel was discernible over the horrible clanging next to her, and she saw Tez pressing on Kamataa like a violent torrent, thrusting and jabbing and swinging her spear and overwhelming the limited range of Kamataa's single half-spear.

A fire had Tez in its grip as she wove in and out of step with the old Eclipseborn, her pattern of movement unpredictable, her battle motions even more so. They were the same tactics that had made her such a phenomenal dualist—no maneuver repeated, no pattern revealed. A thrust followed an upward swing followed a kick followed a jab of the butt end, the fervor and speed at which she attacked unsustainable in her state, but it was enough to put Kamataa furiously on the defensive.

Tez practically danced around Kamataa, the old woman unable to keep up. Everything was a constant motion, and though she was showing clear signs of fatigue, Tez kept pressing, scoring slashes against steel and surface cuts, but nothing that could impede the Eclipseborn.

Sen wobbled back to her feet, her head still throbbing and swirling. As the sounds of battle continued, she scanned the shadows around her for her blade, for her pistol, for *anything*, but they were well hidden in the darkness. She gritted her teeth and looked back to the two combatants, Tez's rapid fury slowing a step, Kamataa's defensive growing less frantic. Tez had to have hoped that the old woman would not have been able to keep up with such speed and force.

But when Tez's footing slipped from beneath her, Sen quickly realized it was her sister who could not keep up with Kamataa. Sen lowered her shoulder and sprinted forward, aiming to offer the same treatment to the old crone as was shown to her. She took one big step, then two.

At the second step, Tez unleashed a heavy and defensive swing as Kamataa aimed a fatal strike. Tez's strength won out, sending the half-spear flying out of Kamataa's grip.

Three steps.

At the fourth step, Tez spun to give herself extra clearance and lurched forward.

Five steps. Six.

On the seventh, Kamataa sidestepped Tez's strike, tucking the tip of the spear underneath her arm.

Eight steps.

She kicked at Tez's stomach, knocking the wind out of her and prying loose the full spear.

Nine.

She leveled the spear, aiming her blow.

Ten.

She thrust.

Sen met Kamataa at eleven and barreled into her hip, setting her off-balance.

The spear went well wide of the intended target. But it still scored the inside of Tez's thigh.

Against a backdrop of pained and hissed groans, Sen wrestled with Kamataa on the ground, clear of any weaponry to aid them. Pinning the old woman's shoulders to the floor, Sen brought her fist down like a hammer on Kamataa's face, just as she had to done to Fann when they were kids all those years ago. She landed two clean hits to the crone's nose, blood spurting from what was already a clean break, but Kamataa kicked her knees up and flipped Sen onto her back, a pain shooting through her as her rib roared in protest.

As Sen writhed on the floor, Kamataa rose, slowly encircling her before leveling a heavy kick to the side. Sen cried out breathlessly, the world dimming around her, but she held on, swinging her arms in the vain hope she would find purchase on the old woman. Such was not the case.

A weight pressed against her chest and her throat tightened. Cold, clammy hands dug into her flesh, wrapping around her neck. Her vision tunneled such that she could only see Kamataa above her, blood dripping from her shattered nose that was already beginning to heal and reshape. Sen clawed at Kamataa's wrists, warmth sluicing down her fingers, but already her strength was waning. And then a breath—somehow both warm and cold—danced into her ear.

"You deserve far worse than this, Sennalhat," Kamataa whispered. "Consider this a mercy."

Sen allowed her hands to drop, barely feeling the impact of the floor. The thumping of the metal beasts became little more than a distant echo. The tunnel before her began to close until it was but a faint speck of light.

Then she heard a grunt as something splashed on her face. The pressure on her lifted, her airways opened, and a burning yearning for air overtook her. Sen rolled onto her side, hacking as she breathed freely, her eyes watering, but not so much that she couldn't see Kamataa's feet standing beside her.

The old woman appeared distracted. "W-what?" she asked. "You? You're..."

"Alive, yes," responded a new voice. A familiar male voice.

Kamataa's feet wavered, her balance unsteady. She groaned as blood rained down; it sounded as though she was pulling something out of herself. "This...but this...is..."

The newcomer grunted in acknowledgment. "It is."

There was a steel clatter on the floor beside Kamataa's feet, near enough that Sen could kick at it. It was a knife, coated in blood—both fresh and dried.

"Y...y...y-you..." Kamataa's speech was growing slurred, her legs continuing to wobble. "Trai...tor. C...c-c-ci—"

"The greatest traitor of all was you. Goodbye, Kamataa."

Sputtering and wordless denouncements mumbled from Kamataa's mouth, but eventually they ceased just as her legs gave out. Kamataa collapsed in a heap, unmoving.

Sen stared with her mouth agape, her lungs still burning as she drew in more breath. The hairs on the back of her neck stood up as footsteps approached, a hand gripping her shoulder. Her first instinct was to swing a fist, but it seemed it was well anticipated—a second hand gripped her fist, gently placing it back at her side.

"Hello, Sennalhat," the voice said.

As the hands lifted from her shoulder and fist, Sen pushed herself to a knee, blinking in a fervor to regain her sense of focus until the figure before her returned to a former clarity. She couldn't quite believe it was actually *he* of all people who saved her.

"...Cin?"

She had long considered him dead, not seeing hide nor hair of him since the battles in the True Heart. But here he was, looking no worse for wear. His Illusion was dispelled, displaying his piercing eyes and sharp nose, his dark hair fluttering past his shoulders. As ever, a morose, apathetic demeanor colored his expression, but something deeper shone in his eyes. Relief, perhaps.

Cin helped Sen up the rest of the way to her feet, steadying her as she wavered. Before Sen could question his presence, he walked toward Tez, offering her a helping hand, which Tez graciously accepted. She had been in an uncomfortable seated position when Sen looked over, but it was immediately apparent that she could not fully put weight on her wounded leg. A dark stain already dampened the length of her trousers, but she voiced no complaints.

With mouth still agape in shock, Sen asked, "Cin, what are you doing here?"

Wrapping his arm around Tez's waist and lending her his shoulder for support, Cin scoffed dismissively. "I would think it to be obvious right now."

Sen narrowed her gaze, unsure what to make of the comment, and turned to Kamataa's body, the old woman still unmoving. She wanted not to draw too near for fear of it being a trap. "Is she..." she began, half-turning her head over her shoulder. "Is she really...?"

Cin nodded. "Yes, Sennalhat. She's dead."

"How?" Tez questioned, notable strain in her voice. "You only threw that knife into her shoulder."

At the mention of the weapon, Sen looked at the knife on the floor, kneeling beside it. It looked no different from any other hunter's knife she had seen, beyond the dried blood robbing the steel of its shine.

"She played with fire, danced too close to the flames. I don't think she expected to burn." Cin grunted, walking toward Sen at a slow pace to accommodate Tez.

"I don't understand," Sen said. "Why? Why this, why *any* of this? What happened, Cin?"

Cin shook his head. "I long grew up believing I knew the face of my enemy. I believed my ancestors had provided me with a more than adequate idea of it. But when one's sins of the present become greater than the sins of the past, what is one to do? What was *I* to do? Against whom was my fight, when both sides forded a river of blood of their own making?"

Sen remained silent, unsure of what to say.

"Who I believed to be my comrades are no more than ghosts, and ghosts were all we were fighting in truth when we should have been fighting one who remained in the land of the living for far too long."

With great caution, Sen kneeled and picked up the blade that felled Kamataa, disinclined to fully grasp it for whatever dark enchantment it may have held. She held it up, motioning it in a quick gesture. "And this? Everything going on in this factory? All of this was…"

Cin nodded. "Kamataa's wicked fascinations and heinous persuasions, yes. Empty promises of power as a lure for Aritz, simply for her own amusement. All lies, of a sort. The truth of this matter may forever taint Aritz's name, even if Kamataa had hardly the foresight to recognize that. This was nothing more than a game to her."

Tez fidgeted against Cin's shoulder, raising her leg off the ground. "A game you didn't wish to play, then."

"Do not think me a hero," Cin said. "I hold no love for the Tribes, and I never shall. But I am also not a monster as she was. Or a monster of a different sort as Aritz is. Our interests…simply aligned at this moment."

Sen shifted in place, unwilling to part with the blade just yet. "And what now? Now that our interests no longer align?"

"Hmph," Cin grunted. "I did not say our interests began and ended with Kamataa's death. We…also have a mutual interest in remaining alive, do we not?"

"Right," Sen muttered, a feeling of suspicion rising within her. "And where would we go?"

Cin threw his free arm up at his side. "Away. Far from here."

"That's it? We just leave?"

"Do you see a better alternative, Sennalhat? The Tribes are defeated. The Children of the Black Moon are now gone. The Acrarians would see us dead without a second thought. Do not make this more difficult than it needs to be."

"That's what I was telling her earlier," Tez murmured. "Sometimes, she's just too stubborn to listen."

"Shut up," Sen said, looking to the ground and shaking her head, free hand on her hip. She sighed. "Fine. Away, then."

Cin nodded, his face not quite exhibiting a smile, but something close enough to one.

Against the rhythm of the metal beasts, Sen spent the next several minutes fumbling in the darkness in search of her weapons. Her knife was not far from where Kamataa slammed her into the wall of steel, and her spear was gathering blood in the puddles left by the savaged soldiers. Her last piece, the Deatharm that had been knocked out of her hand, sat in the shadows some paces away, its nose pointed toward the opened door. She picked it up, the lone bullet still remaining within it, and holstered it with a heavy sigh. The weight of it on her thigh was just as heavy.

For the first time, the air of the City felt refreshing as she stepped outside, finally free of the stagnant and dense murk of the factory. Still, the streets remained silent, the only noise the distant crashing of waves to the south and the gentle whisper of the wind. Sen turned and waited for Cin to emerge outside with Tez, her sister now managing some weight on her leg, but propping herself up instead with her spear. The bleeding seemed to have stopped.

With downcast eyes, Sen nodded to the two of them and turned her attention to the north, slowly making her way to the City's nearest exit. But with each step she took, the weight at her thigh grew heavier, itching to be discarded. She stopped, Cin and Tez walking past her, and she looked past the factory and the row of homes beside it until her eyes caught sight of the garish building towering over all. She could not rip her eyes away from it.

"Sen," Tez's voice called. There was no command to it, no anger or frustration. Just a soft, despondent acceptance of what she knew her sister was about to do.

Sen looked over her shoulder, clenching her eyes shut, unwilling to spare Tez what could very well have been the final time she would ever see her. "You said it yourself, dear sister. Sometimes, I'm too stubborn to listen."

The ground crunched underfoot as Cin approached. "Sennalhat, what do you—"

The words were cut off as Sen held the blade out to Cin, the weapon that had killed Kamataa. "Take it."

Cin hesitated, his hand twitching but staying put, his mouth left agape. "You fool. This may be your last opportunity to—"

"I am well aware, Cin. But Aritz is a monster of a different kind, is he not? It may be best for us to keep the monster's toys far away from his chest, don't you think?" Sen smirked as she pressed the hilt of the blade into Cin's chest, forcing him to take it.

Her former comrade took hold of the knife, still stunned by Sen's decision.

Sen passed him by, rapping him on the shoulder with her hand, and approached her sister, still averting her eyes.

"You're godsdamned lucky I only have one good leg right now," Tez said. "I'd be dragging your ass northward kicking and screaming if I had to."

"I have to take advantage of the one time in my life I'm able to outrun you." Her eyes met Tez's, and she saw the tears forming in her sister's eyes.

"I'd say you don't have to do this, but if you never listened to me before, why would you start now?"

"I listened all the time," Sen said. "I just rarely did what you told me to do."

Tez sighed. "You fucking idiot." She pulled Sen into a tight embrace, sobbing into her ear. "I'm not going to let you go."

"Eventually, you'll have to, because it'll be sunrise and you'll have wasted your one chance of escape."

"Shut up," Tez growled before pulling herself away, resting her hand firmly atop Sen's shoulder. "You're a stubborn, impulsive wreck, but I've always been damn proud to be your sister. We have been far too lucky to have you in our lives."

A slight smile curled Sen's lip. "Don't go soft on me. Someone's gotta keep Cin alive. Luck'll only get him so far." She turned over her shoulder, glancing back at Cin's bemused frown.

"Give him hell, Sen."

Turning back to her sister, Sen nodded and pulled her back in for one last embrace. "I love you, dear sister."

"And I love you."

The sisters pulled apart, exchanging one last smile with one another, and Sen turned on her heel, wiping away a tear from her eye with the back of her hand. She bared her teeth at Cin in what passed for a smile, but one that she could not put the full effort into. "Don't let my sister boss you around too much," she managed to say before the words were choked off by a sob.

Cin continued to frown, holding the blade gingerly in his hands before returning it to a sheath at his waist. He nodded wordlessly and turned his back to Sen, muttering something indecipherable beneath his breath as he walked away.

Tears glinted in the moonlight upon Tez's face as she wiped a sleeve at the stream running down her cheeks, and then followed after Cin.

Sen watched them vanish around the corner, resigning herself to the fate she had written, regardless of what had been penned by the Owl. Inclining her head skyward, she looked upon the glow of the Moon, basking in Her light. "Allow me this one last thread of Your power," she said as though in prayer. "One last thing to set right. One last monster to slay."

The dust danced around her in concert with the wind, and Sen took a step forward. The spear rested in her hand and a single bullet awaited her command, one that would ensure Aritz a Mata felt the full strength of a legion of the lost.

CHAPTER EIGHTEEN

The Spellbinder and the Gunslinger

Shadows fluttered and danced past the flickering torchlight in front of the manor, pulsing in much as the same manner as Sen's chest. Kneeling beyond the reach of the light, she watched the front gate, a pair of inattentive guards standing in an approximation of a watch, appearing lulled into a false sense of security. Rapping her fingers along the shaft of her spear, she closed her eyes, drawing a deep breath, the air dense around her, a thick and smoky humidity filling her lungs.

The faces passed her by in her mind's eye. The people she had known all her life, lost to this senseless and violent struggle. Her parents and brother, victims to another's bloodlust, duplicity, and madness. Narva and Tawa, victims caught in a crossfire they should never have had to walk into. Sharrabha, ever brave and loyal, stricken by forces beyond her control. Even the faces that loathed her, betrayed her and her people. Rantalha with his stark and measured stoicism. Fann with his ugly expression and uglier personality. She even had to wonder where Koelhe wound up in all of this, if she had managed to gather her wits, or if she had instead been cut to pieces and fed to a wild beast—whatever to sate the Invaders', or Kamataa's, wicked fantasies.

All those faces, all their praises and admonishments, adulations and condemnations, whether they were friend or foe—their fury was Sen's fury. Their pain was her pain. Their sadness was her sadness. And their vengeance was her vengeance.

On unsteady, trembling legs, Sen rose. Her head throbbed, the sensation of a welt forming. Her side pulsed with red-hot pain, the wrappings meant to help mend her rib only doing so much. She felt the weight of a thousand lifetimes pressing down upon her, threatening to crush her at the first wrong move. To stop and allow it to do so, though, would be to fail her people, betray their hopes, let all of this to happen without any recourse or retribution. Despite what many in her village would have said, she knew she was better than that. She was worth more than that.

The first step was the most difficult, yet also the most liberating. It was a release from the chains holding her in place, the foul memories ensnaring her in the belief that she would be nothing more to the Tribes but a blight casting darkness across the Land. Those bindings were left behind the moment she emerged from the shadows and into the reach of the light, the nearest sentry eyeing her with curiosity at her arrival.

No longer was she the one to bring the shadows. She was there to *purge* the shadows. In her people's tongue, "Sennalhat" translated to "Child of Light."

And she had every intention of living up to her namesake.

The guard inclined his head toward his partner and barked something in the Acrarian tongue, drawing his attention. He took a quick yet hesitant step past the threshold of the gate, his eyes narrowing, taking in Sen's appearance, her features surely fading in and out of the dancing torchlight.

"How slow you are to recognize," Sen muttered as she picked up her pace, quickening to a skip, then to a light jog. By the time she reached for the hunter's knife at the back of her waist, she had broken into a sprint.

And by the time the sentry opened his mouth to alert the manor, the familiar surge was flowing through Sen's arms. Nary a noise escaped the man's lips by the time the Moon's good fortune guided the blade across the gap and into his throat. Tufts of dirt kicked up in Sen's wake as she burst forward at full speed and ripped the knife free of the dying man's throat in stride, dark blood sluicing out of the open wound until met with a heavy and lifeless thud upon the earth.

With the dripping steel in one hand and the spear in the other, Sen charged toward the adjacent guard, his motions far too sloppy to ready himself in a proper fashion. He raised his rifle above his head, apparently unloaded, and brought it down with a downward thrust. With ease, Sen slid on the dirt around the point of impact, dust wafting behind her, and she cut a wide arc at his legs, cutting deep across both and sending him to the ground with a cowardly yelp. He moaned and writhed in the dirt, blood pooling underneath him.

Sen, for her part, spun back to her feet in a swift motion, the threads of her trousers tearing against the dirt, the cloud of dust catching up to her by the momentum of the draft she cast. She looked down at the whimpering guard pitiably, driving her spear through the back of the neck, silencing him in an instant.

The memory flooded back to her of her first kill, when she was forced to kill the Wood Tribe's Chieftain—not in a show of murderous anger, but in a display of a hopeful mercy. But as she looked down at the two she just killed—and however many more in between the Chieftain's death and where she stood now—Sen felt that pang of murderous anger, an indignation at being ripped further from the hands that had once been inclined to show mercy. The perils of survival forced her to drift and drift to one she did not want to be, one that barely felt a shred of remorse for those she had no choice but to fell.

As she ripped free her spear from the guard's neck, Sen turned toward the main doors, the threshold she had crossed in signal to a short-lived victory. Whether victory or defeat lay beyond those doors for her this time, she did not know. She knew not how quick one would arrive or how short-lived the other would be.

All she could say for certain was that, for as long it needed to be present, she had no qualms about putting her anger and frustration to good use.

Blind was it that carried her to the doors, and she only had the briefest of recognitions before she realized she kicked the door in, the stunned gasps and stunted breaths snapping her from the trance.

Her feet clattered along the floor as she allowed her dance of death to resume.

Aritz shot to his feet when he heard the crash downstairs. The indentation at the foot of his bed began to vanish without his weight upon it. The ocean breeze sharply whistled against his closed window as though shrieking in response to whatever was happening outside his chambers. Shouts and screams echoed just the same, the sound of steel scraping against his floors.

By the time he reached his desk, his flintlock pistol near in hand, his door flew open. Spinning on his heel, he picked up the gun and cocked the hammer back, his finger but half a second away from pulling the trigger.

"Apologies, sir!" shouted his doorman, seemingly undeterred by the weapon that nearly took his head off. Sweat glistened against his forehead as heavy breaths rasped against his throat. "I must ask you to remain in here." He turned away just as soon as he finished speaking.

"Hold there," Aritz commanded, but the lad did not listen. "Tell me what is happening right—"

"I'm sorry, sir, there's no time! I pray you forgive the insubordination just this once."

The doors slammed shut after him, and footsteps scampered away into the distance.

Aritz did not think the sound of gunfire could ever startle him again, but he was shocked by its sudden roar just the same. He winced against the persistent rhythm assaulting his ears, expecting them to cease momentarily.

But they did not stop. One after the other, they continued.

"What are these fools aiming at?" Aritz growled. "Do they intend to level my manor to the ground with their ineptitude?" An angry puff of breath escaped his nostrils as he lowered his flintlock, his arm slackening at his side. He shook his head as he patrolled his chambers, willing to allow that doorman to give him an order just the once. *If they are to act as a wall, let them. So long as I remain, their deaths shall be worth it.*

A memento on his shelves caught his eye as the chaos continued to unfold outside. He holstered his pistol and walked over, examining a marred card placed face down, one that he had placed haphazardly on the shelf in an effort to empty his pockets upon his return. But the closer he drew to it, and the louder the noise grew, he could not help but be reminded of that night.

The savage girl in the northern village. The game she had somehow managed to cheat at. The defeat at his hands that she reveled in. And the damaged card he kept as a memento of all of that. The promise of another challenge, another round.

Aritz couldn't help but chuckle. "Is that you, girl?" he wondered. "Not for long, I promise you." He picked up the card and flicked it between his fingers, smacking his lips. There was a faint hope within him that she would somehow make her way to his chambers. Just to ensure she could not best him twice.

There are things one may cheat their way through. But cheating shall carry you only so far, girl.

He rolled up his sleeves and deposited the card in his trouser pocket before sauntering back to his desk, a faint smirk finding its way to his face. Heavy footsteps thumped outside, rifles continued to roar, his useless guards shouted their meek war cries and meeker death throes, but he could not find a shred of anxiety within himself. He had a full expectation of what came for him. The Savior truly shone His light upon him, and Aritz felt greater excitement than he had felt in ages.

A final thread to pull. A last knot to unwind. And a girl who, by some wicked fortune, still lived, now about to learn how quickly her luck could run out.

With a contented sigh, Aritz leaned against the front of his desk and waited. The brush of his pistol's handle against his fingers delighted him in the anticipation.

The cacophonous wall assaulted her more than the gunfire that produced it.

Bullets zipped past Sen's head and arms as she wove her way in and out of the guards' reach, driving her spear from one unskilled combatant to the next. Four had already fallen by her hand, her arm coated in spilled blood. Servants ran at the sight of her, some managing only to get in the way of the defending guards, others running straight into the line of fire only to be felled in an instant. Screams and battle cries competed for dominance over the roar of gunfire as Sen ignored the burning in her exhausted lungs, not permitting herself even a moment's rest.

A quick glance upward revealed four guards looking down at her from the parapet, covering the surviving responders on the ground level. Luck flared in her arms to the point of numbing her, the bullets continuing to stop short of her feet or backfiring on those who fired at her. Approaching her on the ground were three men, one with a long blade of some unfamiliar description and two with pistols. Caution marked their steps as they did not hide the fear in their eyes at coming into such close contact with one they assuredly thought of as a savage.

For one night, allow me to prove them right.

Plumes of smoke erupted as Sen shot forward, a bullet deflecting off the tip of her spear. The lead guard met her challenge and lunged, allowing all his momentum to carry him toward her. Sen deftly spun around him, grabbing him by the back of the collar and using her own momentum to twirl and throw him into one of his compatriots, knocking them both to the ground. She skidded on the floor as more bullets passed her, locking eyes with the other gunman. Flashing her teeth, she evaded a haphazard shot and jabbed with her spear, taking him in the chest with ease. Even as she withdrew the spear, the man did not seem inclined to relent, and tossed the emptied pistol at her. On instinct, Sen held out her hand, catching the hot barrel and just as quickly throwing it into the attacker's face, square between the eyes. He collapsed in a heap, never to rise again. Her palm seared, but the pain only renewed her focus.

The threads of her shirt frayed against passing bullets, and she jumped at the pile of two she had created, the blade wielder having the presence of mind to roll out of the way, but the man on the bottom offering nothing but the briefest of screams before a downward thrust opened his throat. Sen turned to see the other combatant holding the blade out at his side, beckoning her to charge him. She feinted left, convincing him well enough that she took the bait, and redirected to the right, slashing her spear in a wide horizontal arc that she was surprised to have blocked, the steel of the man's blade moving quickly enough to deter her advance.

Wielding the steel in one hand, the guard unleashed a flurry of quick slices for which Sen had no remedy other than to duck and dive. He was inside her guard, the spear too cumbersome in these tight quarters, and she had not the time to draw her hunter's blade from her waist. Sen gritted her teeth as her lungs burned with the strain, her throat dry, the aches growing far more apparent. Steel flashed in her field of view while shards of wood kicked up at her feet from the force of nearby bullets, Acrarian curses sounding from above with growing regularity.

The kiss of cold steel found its way to her arm, but only barely. Sen hissed at the sudden pain and flailed her spear for what good it could do, accomplishing little more than pressing the shaft into her attacker's side. Instinct told her to move her head to the right and she was thankful for it; a sharp bite took a bit of her ear, but it gave her just enough leeway to grab at the guard's wrist, pressing it upward, the blade pointed to the sky. Sen dropped the spear as a punch was aimed at her chest, her free hand catching it in the nick of time. Warmth trickled down her neck as a part of her ear dangled helplessly. She growled through the pain, clawing at the man's sword arm, an inferno of Luck scorching within her. Wooden shards peppered her ankles and calves in a discordant rhythm, her arms crumbling under the pressure of her attacker's superior strength.

A strength that waned as the fire of her Luck reached its zenith and the guard slumped against her, his weight nearly knocking her to the floor. A second's glance showed a bullet-sized hole in the back of his head.

You really want me alive, don't you? she wondered to the Moon.

The moment for gratitude passed as the gunfire persisted from above. The stairs loomed ahead, and the only way through the hail of bullets was to brave it head on. Fresh blood dripped down Sen's arm and ear as she picked her spear up off the ground and charged with a scream, ignoring every ache, every pain, every struggle for breath as she pushed herself to her limits. Awaiting her at the top of the stairs were two guards with their rifles lined up on her, their brows furrowed as the weapons refused to fire.

A smirk creased Sen's lips, and she threw her spear forward, taking the first guard in the chest. The second guard leaped toward her, descending the first three steps in a single bound, swinging his rifle down like a club, a strike easily avoidable as Sen sidestepped the blow, cutting at his hamstring with her hunter's knife and letting him fall and tumble down the rest of the steps. A final twitch signaled his end.

The Luck raged within her to the point of agony. She could feel the bullets redirect around her, splintering the handrails for the stairs as they passed her by, screams sounding in her ears as misfires landed in the leg of a guard beyond her. Adrenaline propelled Sen forward upon reaching the top of the stairway, the bleeding man frantically reloading his rifle while dropped to a knee. The pistol inside Sen's holster thumped against her thigh as she sprinted forward, blade in hand, sliding on the slick flooring in advance of the bullets passing above her. Her steel planted itself just above the man's clavicle, and he fell to the ground against the force of Sen's slide.

Two remained, and she knew for certain it would not remain the case for long. It was only a matter of time before a new host of guards and would-be reinforcements stormed the manor, drawn to the noise, and all the good fortune passed to her by the Moon would matter for nothing if Sen had collapsed of exhaustion. She was lightheaded enough as it was. The world drew in and out of focus in front of her, but she could not stop. Though her body was failing her, her mind would not surrender, and that was more than enough.

Sluggishly, she closed the gap between her and the remaining guards, one advancing and the other staying back. Sen felt as though she was floating—she could hardly feel her feet as they thumped against the floor. All the might and anger and retribution within her may as well have been lifting her off the ground.

The guard dropped to a knee and lined up his shot as Sen charged toward him. A plume of smoke erupted, and a hot gash cut across Sen's side, opposite of where her rib was cracked. If not for the Luck flaring inside to numb her to all else, Sen would have writhed in pain. But as it was, all the bullet served to do was knock her slightly off-balance—which she immediately regained and cut a deep slash against the guard's throat, and followed the maneuver by flinging the steel into the eye of the remaining soldier.

Her feet skidded against the floor, stopping just before the final felled opponent. Sen ripped her blade free of the man's eye socket, doing her best to ignore the sickening pop in so doing. One step forward was all it took for her to drop to her knees, shuddering. The fire in her limbs quelled until she was no longer numb to the pain assaulting her all over. A sudden wave of nausea rose and spilled out in front of her. Sen bent over on all fours, staring into the puddle of her own making, watching it, waiting for a second wave that never arrived.

The foul stench of death surrounded her, rising with her as she stood back to her feet. She clenched her eyes shut, drawing a deep breath, the manor gripped in a grim silence. Her hand trembled, resting beside the handle of the flintlock pistol, the Deatharm, the weapon that killed her father, caused so much pain and death and destruction for her people. The thought of using it one more time was enough to threaten another wave of nausea.

But when Sen opened her eyes again, staring at the ornate door overlooking the stairs, knowing who lay beyond its threshold...the revulsion ceased. Her fingers brushed against the grip until wrapped firmly around it. Slowly, the weapon was drawn from its holster, shaking in her grasp until her hand steadied. Beads of sweat stung her eyes and dampened her face, mixing with the blood trailing down her cheek from her ear. One foot stepped in front of the other, the one step became two, three, and Sen's pace quickened to a jog, to a run, to a sprint. The door approached, a thick oak barrier the only hindrance between her and the end goal of everything she fought for, everything she did, everything she survived.

Without breaking stride, Sen lowered her shoulder. The wood cracked, the door breaking from its hinges and swinging open. Sen took a half step beyond the threshold and cocked the hammer back, raising the pistol, the unfocused image of a man standing some paces before her. Her finger brushed the trigger, applied pressure, pulled.

She barely heard the all-too-familiar thunderclap as the pistol fired.

Nor did she hear the second one a fraction of a second later.

The flintlock flew out of her hand, emptied of its last bullet, and the fire erupted in her shoulder, a slick warmth immediately following it.

An impact spun her around, knocking her against the cracked doorframe, enough to elicit a gasp of pain as she crashed into it. Instinctively, she pressed a hand to the source of the fire, her fingers coming away fresh with blood. She gritted her teeth, wincing in response to her slackened arm, and eyed across the room.

Aritz a Mata mimed Sen's movements, holding a hand against his own shoulder, red ribbons sluicing out from the slits between his fingers, but he did not waver on his feet. He just stared at her, a ghost of a smile on his lips, a tuft of smoke billowing from his freshly fired pistol.

"Shit," Sen growled through gritted teeth. Pushing herself back up to a fully standing position, she reached behind and grabbed her hunter's knife, preparing to charge.

A motion that seemed to give Aritz no cause for alarm or panic.

With her wounded arm dangling, Sen rushed forward, blade held out, the floating sensation returning...but she felt her balance vanish almost instantaneously. Her strength waned, her vision blurred in and out of focus. As she circled around the table where the map of the Land had been crudely sketched, a wave of dizziness assaulted her, spinning her around in place, her sense of positional awareness dissipating.

Her stomach lurched. She felt as though someone shoved her to the ground. In a last gasp of desperation, she swung her blade in the same arc tracing her path to the floor, but her arm came away with nothing. Her blade clattered against the ground in a distant echo.

The air grew tight in her chest. Panicked spittle erupted from her lips. "Wh...wh...what..." she stammered, gasping for what little air she could grasp. Her eyes watered as each breath drew only a painful choke.

Footsteps—distant or near, she could not tell the difference—thumped in approach. A shadow hovered over her, heavy and menacing, death itself coming to claim her.

And out from death's shadow dropped a card. A simple, meaningless card. But even as the world darkened around her, the light tunneling, she could still discern the mars on the card. The same one Aritz had taken the night he killed her father and kidnapped her brother.

He had kept it all this time—for some reason. A reason Sen would never be able to fathom. Time was too short for all that.

She felt a sharp tug at her hair, forcing her eyes up. It was the only thing she could feel. And all the light would show her was Aritz's satisfied grin.

"You rest now," the Acrarian said in the Tribal tongue, the intonation hesitant. "It is over."

When Sen's head dropped and thumped against the floor, she did not feel it. The warmth spread from the wound in her shoulder, her sides, her ear, all the wounds radiating a surge, cleansing and invigorating, yet eating away at everything she was just the same. The light faded to a dot, a single mote holding all she knew the world to be. As though miles away, she could see the memory of her hand trembling on the floor until fading to a final twitch. A final spasm gave way to the dark.

And the dark gave way to an ethereal light. There was no more pain.

Aritz stood over the dead woman, finally allowing himself to acknowledge the pain scorching the inside of his shoulder.

"Fortune indeed smiled upon me," he remarked, glancing at his smoking pistol. "Had this shot gone errant..." He shuddered to think of it. Shuddered to think how close he had been to losing his life to this...creature.

Straining with the effort, he lifted his arm just high enough to place the pistol on his desk. He nodded in silence, flashing a brief glance at the deceased savage before returning his gaze to the weapon. "And to think, what saved me at all was the wickedness of these people. Such cruel irony. For them, and myself." He gazed out the window, to the seas beyond and the horizon unending, still awaiting morning's first light. "I only pray, dear Savior, that You cast Your light away in aversion to what deeds I had to commit in Your name. But this Land is now Yours." *Mine, truly. But we needn't say such things aloud, do we?*

Footsteps echoed downstairs, shocked murmurs halting the impending advance. Some seemed to have accepted the worst had happened before they made it three steps inside. It was a shame all his competent soldiers had perished in the northern campaign. He did not look forward to training these half-wits in the art of such intricate matters as ensuring he was alive.

Someone finally had the presence of mind to ascend the stairs, their pace slowing near to a crawl, from the sound of it. When they at last reached the threshold of his chambers, a sharp gasp escaped their lips. "Sir! Are you well?"

Aritz sneered, turning to face the soldier, a young lad, waves of auburn locks falling short of his shoulder. He looked so much like Lorente. That alone instilled in Aritz the desire to cast him from the window.

"I still live, as you can see," Aritz deadpanned, gesturing to his indeed living form with his red-stained hand.

The soldier holstered his weapon and ran toward him. "But, sir! This wound! It needs attention."

Aritz rolled his eyes. "Then stop gawking and pay it the attention it requires."

Fear roared in the lad's eyes as he rushed to the door and shouted, "Medic! Now! The General is wounded!"

Do not make it sound as though I'm dying, you fool. I survived worse on this campaign than you did kicking rocks and hiding behind your mother's skirts, I'm sure.

A flurry of movement sounded from downstairs, but Aritz was keener to the reasoning for the lad's continued presence. "What?" he asked.

The soldier frowned and walked over to the corpse lying beside the war map. "All of that?" He raised his arm toward the main foyer, and the destruction that assuredly lay outside it. "All of it was from this one woman?"

"If you have not found any of her compatriots out there, then I would presume so."

"They truly are savages, aren't they?" The lad sneered.

"Savage or no, I cannot help but admit," Aritz said, pursing his lips, "that she has earned my respect. The faces are many that I refuse to remember, but hers is one I shall not forget."

A silent regarding smile creased the soldier's mouth.

"Or that shall be so until the day one woman wielding nothing but a goddamned *spear and a knife* will not be enough to slaughter my entire household guard."

At Aritz's sudden imposing glare, the lad seemed ready to piss his pants.

"Now make yourself useful and get her out of my sight. I've a nation to build, and no longer savages to suffer."

The rest of the evening passed in a blur. He remembered medics wrapping flimsy bandaging around his shoulder and being offered some foul-smelling liquid to numb the pain. There were faint recollections of the savage's body being carried off, and the stench of blood and departed bodies being removed.

But all Aritz had a mind to focus on was his map.

And all the possibilities of expansion that it now promised.

Sen opened her eyes to a realm of pure, white light. Threads of mist wafted around her ankles, a pleasant aroma dancing in her nostrils. A gentle warmth surrounded her, dense and palpable, moving along with her with each flick of the wrist.

She looked down at her body, the scars and memories of battles that seemed to have lasted a lifetime now disappeared, vanished from her body as though they never existed at all. The wound in her shoulder had closed, no longer eating away at everything she was. No more did she feel the throbbing pain in her side where her rib had cracked at the True Heart, nor the flares of fresh agony from where bullets had torn at her flesh. The aches, the pains, they had all vanished, nothing more than memories floating away on the wind's breath.

"What..." she muttered. "Where am I?"

Turning in place, the landscape surrounding her changed shape, rolling hills and verdant moors stretching as far as her eyes could see, but lacking the sharp green hues with which she had been long familiar. Everything was bathed in the bright light to the point of being washed out, but despite that, there was still a pleasantness to the view. There was no anger or hatred in it. Only a subtle, unspoken peace.

But how she got here—and where she was, for that matter—was a different question entirely. Instinctively, she slapped at her own face, the possibility that this was some strange dream not outside the realm of her imagination. But she didn't even feel the slap—or, at the least, she felt no pain from it. She felt the touch, the sensation of her own palm swatting her cheek, but she did not wince from it. There was nothing lingering in the aftermath.

She narrowed her gaze, flummoxed. Looking down at her hands, expecting something, anything, to indicate even a faint memory of pain to show, Sen watched as there wasn't even a familiar tremor in her limbs. No urges to blind herself to the struggles of reality. No desire to indulge in the vices that had long ate away at her. All she felt was the warm mist enveloping her, comforting her, stealing her from all that shackled her in place.

And when a faint, familiar voice sounded in her ear, the realization came at once.

"Sen."

Her breath caught in her throat. An involuntary sob broke free. Sen turned, slowly, wishing to prolong this moment for fear that it was indeed a dream and she was to be ripped from it the moment she laid eyes on him.

The moment she caught sight of her father. And her mother. And Brin. All three of them bunched around one another, waiting for her, the memory of her family's hut looming behind them.

Fannalhen maintained the same strong, burly image he had always sported, a smile reaching his eyes, but sadness quite clearly welling within them. He looked just the same as he always did before all of this happened. The wounds Sen associated with her final encounter with her father were not present.

And the same could be said for both her mother and Brin. They did not anguish, but at the same time, they did not revel. Hesitant half-smiles marked their lips, and though there was a clear happiness at this reunion, it was not inherently a joyous occasion.

Sen had every intention of rushing forward, leaping at them, embracing them all and never letting go. But the circumstances were enough to give her great pause. "I don't understand," she said, an almost breathless quality to her voice. "How are...*where* are..."

Dennalhir nodded, offering Sen a tight smile even as her brow wrinkled with forlornness. "This is...the Otherworld, Sen."

"The Otherworld?" Sen repeated, taking two shocked steps toward them, glancing at her surroundings, the ethereal landscapes casting their light around her. "But, that...that means...I...I'm..." She broke off and looked down at her hands, gasping a choked sob.

A sea of arms engulfed her, warmth surrounding her. She found her face immediately burrowed in the crest of her father's chest, just as it was on the night he was killed. But blood did not coat her face on this day, and she instead felt nothing but the comfort a daughter was to feel when supported by her father. The love she was to feel when embraced by her family, an embrace she herself had pushed away for so long. To feel her mother and brother holding her just the same was something she longed for, but never thought she could experience again. She just wished it didn't have to be here.

"This means...I failed," Sen murmured. "I couldn't stop him. I *should* have stopped him. But I—"

"You didn't fail, Sen," Brin said. "You never did. There were just...bumps along the way. But that doesn't mean you failed."

"But I have every opportunity to—"

"You've had every opportunity not to place the weight of the world on your shoulders," her father assured. "This was something no one person could stop on their own. And you should have no shame in accomplishing what you did."

"We watched you all along, Sen," Brin added. "We were with you the whole time."

"Which means you saw all the bad things I did," Sen said, tears streaming down her cheeks. "All the mistakes I made. I nearly took part in all of—"

"But at the end of the day, you didn't," Dennalhir reminded her, just as she had done the day before the battle in the True Heart. The final conversation Sen ever got to have with her mother. "When the time came, you fought for what was right. You fought for the good of our people. And that alone was more than enough."

"We'll suffer you blaming yourself no longer, Sen," Fannalhen said, kindness and warmth coloring his words. He gripped Sen tighter, pulling her into his chest. "We're proud of the woman you've become. We never stopped believing in you."

Sen pulled away, wiping away the tears from her cheeks. "All of you?" she prompted.

"All of us," added a new voice. A welcomed voice that sent Sen's heart aflutter.

She looked to her right, gently pushing Brin out of the way—something she was more than happy to be able to do again—and saw Narva standing several paces away, the same goofy smile adorning his face. To stop the tears from flowing once again was a futile effort, and she gladly allowed them to stream as she broke away from her parents' grasp and sprinted toward Narva, practically jumping into his arms. A moment's embrace gave way to their lips meeting, the fire and passion once robbed from them now able to be experienced, late though it was.

"It's good to see you, too, Sen," Narva chuckled, remorseful though it was. His hands trailed down her arms and gripped her hands.

Sen interlinked her fingers with his and looked into his eyes, unable to keep herself from asking the heartbreaking question, "Could you ever forgive me?"

With a smile, he shook his head. "There's nothing to forgive. The time for blaming yourself is long past."

"Now is but a time for rest." Tawa emerged from behind his son, placing a hand on Sen's shoulder.

Sen inclined her head against Tawa's hand, looking up at him with sadness, joy, and a whole wealth of emotions she did not know how to properly process.

There was but one hole still to fill. Sen turned to her family, her hands still interlinked with Narva's. "Tez is still out there somewhere."

Fannalhen nodded. "She is. And she'll continue to fight, for as long as her body allows it."

Dennalhir wrapped an arm around her husband's waist and offered a gentle smile. "And when it is at last time for her to join us, we will be ready for her. However long it takes."

Brin inclined his head in agreement. "However long it takes."

Sen looked to each of her family members, to Narva and Tawa, and returned the same nod. "However long it takes."

But until such time, she knew she had no other recourse but to accept the defeat. Because she knew defeat was not everlasting, and peace was inevitable to follow.

If she had her wish, her reunion with her sister would not be for a long time. But she did not lament her present reunion with so many she held dear. It was more than enough.

The warmth of the Otherworld promised a long, comforting rest.

EPILOGUE

An End, and a Beginning

The Year 1581 Anno Salvatoris
40 Years After the Settling

It all happened so quickly.

A fiery pain surged in Aritz's shoulder from the moment the glass shattered. His flesh seared from the inside, and an involuntary gasp escaped his lips as his pistol flew from his hand. A slick warmth already began to sluice out from the blazes burning within him. All the strength left his arm as he lurched forward, all his momentum pushing him against his will.

And right into the woman's grasp.

He never saw her return to her feet. In the span of a blink, she was simply...there. With a knife in her hand, the steel pressed against Aritz's throat.

The night was still young, indeed.

But Aritz would not concede in such a manner. He would not meet his end at the hands of such a clumsy assassin. The very thought was preposterous.

The woman seemed to find humor in the possibility, though. She flashed her teeth, her shoulders bouncing against the deep chuckle rumbling in her throat. A firm hand held Aritz by the back of the throat, forcing him to look her in the eyes, those wild and untamed eyes.

His wounded flesh stretched against the angle the woman held him. Aritz sucked in a heavy breath, spittle frothing out from the corners of his mouth. There was not a waylaid intention for him not to scream, but it was not a pain to which he was accustomed. He had been shot with an arrow before—and vowed never to return to those mountains ever again as a result—but he had never been the victim of a bullet lodged inside him, having only suffered a graze the last time one of these savages drew so close to him in here. The flare traveled down the length of his limb, his hand spasming.

The cold steel against his throat only made it all the more uncomfortable.

"For the sake of argument," the woman said, "let's just agree that you are telling the truth. The Harvests did not happen—as such. We could argue that whatever we wish to call such slaughter was all the work of Kamataa, and you had no part in it at all."

Aritz moved his mouth to protest that her words were accurate, but he was wary of the blade cutting into his throat should he have done so.

The woman scoffed. "But what does that matter? What does it disprove? That you drew the line at treating a people like animals to the slaughter? Do you believe yourself to be a noble sort because of it? Killing an overmatched people in their homes and turning their lands into a battlefield is a just cause, is it? Am I to laud you for your refusal to indulge Kamataa's sick inclinations?" The grip on the back of Aritz's neck grew tighter. "It changes nothing. Deny your involvement all you want, but under your watch, the Harvests still happened. We who survived them do not forget. We will ensure your people always remember."

The urge to fight her for the blade was too great. Aritz's unwounded arm twitched with anticipation, his fingers curling and uncurling, her sides left entirely exposed.

She seemed all too aware of where his mind was headed.

Before he could process what had happened, Aritz felt himself pushed off his feet, meeting the hard oak of his desk with a resounding thud, the bullet wound bearing the brunt of the impact. Something between a gasp, a breath, and a scream escaped his mouth. Vomit threatened to expel itself, but it did not rise high enough. Beads of pained sweat trickled down Aritz's forehead and onto the wood below him, his eyes clenched shut in response to the agony radiating out from his shoulder and through the rest of his body.

The amusement had long since left the woman's face. Now, only anger colored her expression. "How noble you must have felt to have 'allowed' us to remain in the mountains, even after you had plundered it for your mining operations. Those few of us still in command of our minds were ever appreciative of it—and those without a mind to protest said hardly a complaining word. Some took years to be able to make so much as an affirmative nod; others have not even regained that capacity. Are we to thank you for giving us the smallest, most inconvenient piece of our own land to rebuild our civilization, even if it is only inevitable you take that from us as well?

"I've awaited this day for twenty-five years, Aritz." She paused, shaking her head. "Oh, how I've waited. To look into your eyes and watch you breathe your last, to prove that despite the lofty heights to which you have raised yourself, you can be brought back to our level. You've fashioned yourself something of a god, but you yourself have proven that to matter little. All gods bleed, and all gods die. Even those of our own making. You shall be no different, Aritz a Mata.

"But whenever the opportunity would present itself, and I assumed the stars had aligned, you would board your ship and traipse back home to your precious Acraria, to a family, something you had long stripped away from me. If it wasn't that, it was having to reforge the shards of my culture that you saw fit to grind underfoot until it was dust. Or it would be the constant care of the helpless, when you destroyed their minds as though it were nothing, or foraging when few among us had the capacity to fight or hunt as well as we once had. All of it, everything that you caused, everything that has prevented me from collecting on the time you have long overborrowed—it's all led to this."

Aritz squirmed under the blade's hold, pressing his head into the desk as much as he could, even as his shoulder roared in agony in so doing. "So, why..." he said, grunting through pangs of pain, "don't you...just...get on...with it?"

The way the smile framed the woman's angry face was unsettling. "It is the slow knife that cuts deepest, and the wise hand that knows when to strike. When your guard would be most let down—and when you would be most let down by your own guards, I'm sure."

Narrowing his eyes in confusion at the comment, Aritz opened his mouth again but felt the blade press once more against his throat, one false move sure to spell the end.

"Wisdom, prescience…I suppose it is to our own benefit that you did not kill *all* of our gods. The Owl's foresight is ever useful, loath as I am to admit it, loath as I have been to continue acting as its marionette. But…" She shrugged her shoulders, allowing a relaxed sigh to escape her lips. "I must inevitably play the role I was given."

Aritz's body seized as the steel dug into the flesh of his throat. A wave of panic overtook him. His eyes bulged, his fingers clenched, his bladder loosened and spilled its contents all over his legs.

But the blade did not cut deep enough. Only enough to draw blood. The woman stepped back, playfully balancing the hilt of the knife between her thumb and forefinger.

Unsure of where the next threat lay, Aritz rose to his feet with great caution and struggle, wincing at the burning still raging within his shoulder while also trying not to slip on the puddle of his own making beneath him. He pressed two fingers to the open wound on his throat, a surface level cut that still came away slick with red. Aritz narrowed his gaze, confused at the woman's demeanor, the air she carried about her enough to suggest she had played her winning hand. *Did she mean only to embarrass me?*

But then Aritz took a closer look at the blade she held, the waning sunlight attempting to glint off its steel, but meeting instead a glimmer that had long been dulled.

A shine stolen by stains of blood.

Aritz's eyes widened, his hand shaking as he brought it once more to the blood trickling down his neck. Twenty-five years had passed since last he laid eyes on that blade, one of the few fruits that blossomed from Kama's treachery and deceit. Sweat already began to pour down his forehead, his chest tightening.

"Is it not peculiar," the woman asked, "how lost items are returned when you least expect them?"

"You…" Aritz snarled, taking a violent step forward but crumbling to the ground in the attempt, his legs giving out from under him. He hacked up a wad of dense phlegm, the air burning against his throat. "Do you rea...lize...what—"

"I am doing? Of course, I do, Aritz. I have always known. I have known every day for the last twenty-five years." She walked away, carelessly whistling a happy melody, and returned with something dangling from her fingers.

Though his eyes were beginning to fail him, it was not lost upon Aritz that it was the pendant housing the images of the woman murdering his family and household. Sullying everything he was, everything he had built. The cold touch of the chain felt so distant as it was wrapped around his neck, the ornament pressed to his chest. He immediately felt something *pull* within him, a fleeting sensation gone as soon as it arrived, just as was the pendant.

"And soon," the woman continued, the smile wide upon her face. "Soon, all will know. All will see what you have done. Your story ends here, and with it, all its false words penned in your hand."

Choked breaths broke free from Aritz's mouth, his eyes watering. He felt nothing but agony, an inferno raging within, burning away everything inside him. "They'll..." he rasped, every syllable a struggle, "never...be...lieve..."

"I present to them only the truth. I cannot force them to believe it. But they deserve the opportunity to find that truth for themselves instead of the 'truth' you've forced upon them."

Though Aritz intended to growl, he could manage only a meek, nonthreatening croak. "Who...are...you...?"

Steel scraped as the blade was returned to the sheath along the woman's back. She held her head high, breathing a long, deep sigh. Within her eyes seemed to dwell a modicum of relief as though she had rehearsed this moment for ages. The light glimmering beneath her shirt faded away entirely, and her form shifted. Her skin tone darkened, her hair specked with grays and blacks, a light collection of wrinkles framing her eyes and lips. She appeared weathered, but not any more than Aritz himself was.

"My name is Tezalhat," she said. "But that, I am sure, means nothing to you. Were it in my power, I would ensure your death would be the punishment you truly deserve—that you would feel the pain of every single life you ended. But all I *can* do is take back what you took from me: you killed my father and sister. My mother and brother died because of you. For twenty-five years, I've played my role, waiting for the day the debt would be repaid." She paused, walking past where the few trickles of light still illuminated Aritz's world. Something scraped against the floor and she returned, holding his pistol once again. "And it gives me great joy to collect on that debt, knowing that this shall be your last memory. I do hope you enjoy your final moments, Aritz, wallowing in your own piss and blood, discontent in the knowledge that your legacy—and all the lies upon which you have built it—is no more. Goodbye."

Aritz reached out to grab Tezalhat's heel—or at least, he thought he did. His arms would not move. The creak of her footsteps on the floorboards faded into nothingness, and every breath was like a thousand daggers being plunged into his chest.

He stared at the puddles of blood forming before him, unable to look away, unable to remove it from his sight. All the strength had left his body. None were coming to save him. None had the power to dispel the lies that would soon be spread about him. But if they were keen to ignore the lies, to accept his "truth," then...

Then...

It was a hope. The faint thread of hope that his legacy would survive these flames. That from the ashes, there would still remain one to bear the Mata standard, to hold it high in reverence to a martyr undone by false narratives and obscene agendas. The name Aritz a Mata would endure. It had to. It needed to.

But whether it could was beyond his control. For the body of Aritz a Mata could not endure the shadows arriving to claim him, the inferno of pain at last dissipating, replaced instead with the icy grasp of death.

The Savior's Light did not arrive to claim him.

Tez was grateful for the soft soil providing a safe landing for her. Though it was only a two-story drop, her knees weren't what they once were. She had to remain in a crouched position for a few moments until her legs stopped shaking.

The pounding in her chest had at last stopped. The timing indeed had to be perfect. She had worried her cavalry would not arrive in time. She was happy to know her worries were unfounded.

To permit herself a moment to close her eyes and reflect seemed well warranted. The burden Tez had carried all these years had at long last been lifted. From the moment she had learned of Sen's death, it was her pledge to finish what her sister had started. *I couldn't save your ass this time, dear sister, but I also could not leave your work undone. It's over.* Glancing up at the window to Aritz's chamber, the shards of broken glass littered in the soil and grass around her, Tez could not help but allow a relieved tear to stroll down her cheek. She knew not what she would feel in this moment. It was not outside the realm of possibility that it would take time for her to know what to feel.

But even as the world remained dark for her and her people, it still felt as though a shadow had been bathed in light and cast from the world. And that alone was more than enough for now.

Her legs ceased trembling. Tez looked to her left and spied a figure sitting cross-legged on the shoreline, their attention seeming to be paid to the boundless seas. She allowed a tentative smile to crease her lips and walked after them. She did not bother returning her Illusion; the shoreline past Aritz's manor was deserted by design. It had not been uncommon for Ferrandans to "disappear" if they wandered too far into Aritz's view of the horizon. To no longer have to hide who she was, at least for a moment, felt invigorating.

The sand was soft underneath her boots. Tez approached the figure waiting along the shore, a man close to her own age, long locks of straight graying hair falling past his shoulders. It seemed he also felt comfortable without his Illusion cast.

"You certainly cut it a bit close there at the end, didn't you, Cin?" Tez said in a mockingly chiding tone.

Cin rose to his feet, spry as he ever was, and half-turned to face her. Much may have changed over the last twenty-five years, but his disinterested gaze was eternal. "Next time, you are more than welcome to climb up the side of a monument to Acrarian vanity and hang from a windowsill in anticipation of the perfect shot, Tezalhat."

"We both know you wouldn't have missed the shot. The Moon is still fond of you, for whatever reason." Tez lightly knocked her fist against Cin's shoulder. He humored it with the ghost of a grin, but nothing more than that. "And did I hear you give your name to Aritz as 'Nic?' You truly could not have come up with something more original than that?"

Rolling his eyes, Cin frowned and crossed his arms. "Didn't expect him to strike a conversation with me. Didn't even expect him to *look* at me. Guess I just caught him in a good mood."

"You'd be the first one."

The waves lightly crashed against the shore, gulls cawing in their persistent and grating chorus. A breeze provided a welcomed chill after spending so long in the dense and oppressive air of Aritz's chambers.

"Hey," Tez said, offering a half-smile and tucking loose strands of windblown hair behind her ears. "I know you don't wanna hear it...but thank you. I really couldn't have done this without you."

Cin shook his head, looking displeased as ever. "Didn't do it for you or the Tribes. Your sister simply wouldn't let it go. If it was something that'd quiet her, then all the better. I'd like to go a day without her voice in my head."

"That does sound like her." It warmed Tez's heart to know that Sen managed to annoy someone even in death. She had always thought the Haunted's communion with the lost extended only to their own Tribe, but perhaps Cin's connection to Sen as a fellow Eclipseborn allowed it as well. "Is she...how is..."

"I don't know how you want me to answer that, Tezalhat." Cin raised his brow. There was no malice in his glare. Just a modicum of concern and remorse, in his own way. "It doesn't change anything."

Tez frowned, but nodded, nonetheless. She cast her eyes aside. *To know she is well in the Otherworld would be good enough, but...*

Cin sighed. "So, what's next?" he asked, seeming eager to divert the subject elsewhere.

"Hmm?" she replied. In truth, she hadn't thought that far ahead. *I suppose I've become more like Sen than I thought.*

"You've killed Aritz," Cin said, outstretching his arms. "But this nation of Ferranda has not crumbled to nothing. What more has the Owl planned for you? It already bloodied its wings in the Acrarian homeland before flying back here, and I'd rather away before it speaks to me under the guise of the Moon's voice again."

Tez planted her hands on her hips, shrugging her shoulders. An avian shadow flew overhead as though listening in on their conversation. She watched it disappear past the rows of buildings and back to the north, wherever its watchful eye would lead. Reaching into her pocket, she withdrew the Memory pendant, grimacing at the weight of everything housed within it. "For the first time in decades...I really do not know. I feel as though I've now approached a branching path in the road ahead. Everything in here—" She shook the pendant to illustrate her point. "—has been a path with but one destination. My memories, Brin's memories...and now Aritz's memories. They're all serving to paint a larger picture. But what that picture means to those who would see it is another matter entirely."

"You don't mean this was for nothing, do you?" Cin inclined his head, smacking his lips. Grains of sand swayed into the cuffs of his trouser legs by the light strength of the gentle breeze.

She was quick to shake her head, her locks impeding her vision once again. "No, nothing of the sort. I want people to know the truth. But what they do with it...that is what I fear. Even as word reaches his King and Queen, who knows how long it will take for it all to take root?"

"Knowledge is a ripple effect." The Eclipseborn turned his gaze northward, to where the Owl had returned. A noncommittal grin creased his lips, his chest heaving with an accepting sigh. "Aritz did not establish himself as a god overnight, remember. It took years, a generation of tricking idiots into thinking he was something greater than he truly was. When the veil is lifted, the same idiots will cry foul all the way to their graves. But all it takes is one person to accept this truth for it to root. And from its roots, it will sprout and branch until we no longer have to hear the tales of 'Aritz the Founder,' and we can instead tell the cautionary stories of 'Aritz the Bloody.'" Remorse glinted in his gaze, his eyes downcast. "Trust me. I would know something about that. It just takes time."

Tez nodded, looking after the Owl's movements far away in the sky. "And if there's anyone who knows what to do with knowledge taking root, it'd be that bastard." She sighed, uncertainty still filling her heart, but she knew there was some truth to Cin's words. "We just have to be patient."

"You waited twenty-five years to kill him. I'd wager patience is something you know well."

"And it's its own reward, I can tell you that much."

A silence hung between them. Cin hunched his shoulders and dug his hands into his pockets, narrowing his eyes against a gust of sea winds. "And what will you do now?" he asked. "Now that you've no path set before you."

Tez kept an eye to the northern horizon, to the memory of the Heart far past the Forest, to its depths yet untouched by Invader hands. "I've spent the last twenty-five years just trying to rebuild what's left of us. I'm not about to stop that now. But now I can do so without as much fear resting in my heart. The Invaders might still take every inch they can get...but I can only hope that some of them will lose faith in their being here after they know the truth. And that is enough for me right now."

Cin grunted, nodding nonchalantly.

"I say this every time we meet, but..." Tez shrugged, crossing her arms as the breeze batted the end of her braid against her shoulders. "You're more than welcome to join us. There's...a home for you, if you want it. And...there's talk of an Eclipse coming soon, as well."

Seemingly without a second thought, Cin shook his head. "I'm disinterested in all that. Better off as I've always been, on my own, but..." He grimaced, paused, and began to walk away, stopping after five or six steps to turn his head over his shoulder. "If your sister ends up pestering me about something again, I suppose I know where I'll find you."

Tez chuckled. "Take care of yourself, Cin."

Cin nodded in response. "You as well, Tezalhat. Farewell." He sauntered off, hands still pressed into his pockets, his long hair fluttering in the breeze as he disappeared beyond the rows of buildings past Tez's field of view.

Deep down, Tez knew Cin would survive, just as he had for decades. She still held on to the hope that he would abandon his stubbornness and forego his life as a drifter, but as with the knowledge soon to be released to the people of Ferranda...it would just take time.

She looked down at the Memory pendant and put it back in her pocket. The weight of heavy burdens had at last been lifted from her shoulders, and for the first time in ages, Tez of the Stone Tribe felt a comfort at the uncertainty of the future. It would still be a difficult one, but the dread toward it had lessened. There was finally hope again.

Stars were beginning to glint along the eastern horizon as the night sky began its approach, and with it, the Moon's shine. In a few days' time, the shine would be blocked. But her people knew not to fear it. Not anymore.

Sea winds abounded amidst an air rich upon Tez's tongue with the taste of salt. As gulls called, circling the southern sea in search of food, she looked up to the flickering stars, content that the memory of her people remained, and so long as it did, always would the Tribes survive. In view of the Moon's light, Tez looked forward to the coming days when a new generation would be born—not cursed by the Moon, but blessed by it. It was what Sen would have wanted. Tez knew her sister would be smiling.

She couldn't help but do so herself. It was a wondrous thing, to hope again.

<u>End of the Final Book of</u>
<u>The Spellbinders and the Gunslingers</u>

GLOSSARY

The Stone Tribe: Occupants and landholders of much of the territories bordering the southern ridge of the Heart of the Land, the Stone Tribe has been considered the gatekeepers to the Heart. The most populous Tribe of the Land, they are a melting pot of multicultural roots due to the large number of adept warriors, hunters, and scholars who dwell within the Tribe's borders. Since the Invasion of the Acrarians, the Stone Tribe has offered land to the displaced peoples south of the Forest, most prominently the Sun and Arrow Tribes. Physically, they are easily identifiable by the braids they fashion at the nape of their necks and the face paint they adorn in adulthood in correlation to the Sign under which they were born: red for the Bear, blue for the Wolf, and yellow for the Owl. An adult bearing no face paint is considered an outcast not to be interacted with.

- **Sennalhat:** Also known as Sen. Second daughter of the Stone Chief Fannalhen and Dennalhir. An Eclipseborn previously traveling with a group of fellow Eclipseborn called the Children of the Black Moon, but defected from them. Survived the Battle of the True Heart.

- **Tezalhat:** Also known as Tez. Firstborn daughter of the Stone Chief Fannalhen and Dennalhir, eldest sister to Sennalhat and Brinnolhat. An adept warrior Bearsign who was granted the Boon of Endurance. Negotiated a cease-fire among the Lake Tribe and recruited the Arrow Tribe to retake the Stone village after Koelhe's coup. Survived the Battle of the True Heart.

- *[Brinnolhat]:* Also known as Brin. Youngest child of the Stone Chief Fannalhen and Dennalhir, younger brother of Tezalhat and Sennalhat. A bookish and shy young man who recently completed his Trial as an Owlsign and was granted the Boon of Memory. Executed by a firing squad in the City.

- *[Fannalhen]:* Also known as Fanna. Former Chief of the Stone Tribe, husband of Dennalhir, and father of Tezalhat, Sennalhat, and Brinnolhat. A revered Bearsign granted with the Boon of Courage. Killed by Aritz a Mata during a standoff in the Stone village.

- **Dennalhir:** Also known as Denna. Wife of the late Stone Chief Fannalhen, mother of Tezalhat, Sennalhat, and Brinnolhat. As equally revered a Bearsign warrior as her husband, her talent with the spear is unparalleled. Held captive after Koelhe's coup, but freed by her daughters during the Battle at the Stone Village. Fell after the Bear was slain during the Battle of the True Heart.

- **Tawandhar:** Also known as Tawa. A member of the Tribal council, a close friend to Fannalhen's family, and the father of Narvarho. An Owlsign of the highest order and a master of Knowledge. Accompanied Tez on her quest for allies to unify the north after Koelhe's coup. Survived the Battle of the True Heart.

- *[Narvarho]:* Also known as Narva. Sen's closest friend. A Wolfsign imbued with the Boon of Sound. Killed by Acrarians after attempting to rescue Brin.

- *[Rantalha]:* A member of the Tribal council and one of the Tribe's most accomplished hunters. A Wolfsign granted the Boon of Stealth. Took part in Koelhe's insurrection. Killed by Tez during the Battle at the Stone Village.

- **Sharrabha:** A member of the Tribal council. An accomplished Wolfsign imbued with Packmind who makes frequent trips through the

Heart on behalf of the Tribe. Accompanied Tez on her quest for allies to unify the north after Koelhe's coup. Survived the Battle of the True Heart.

- **Koelhe:** Current Chief of the Stone Tribe after waging an insurrection. Mother of Fannadhan. An Owlsign bearing the rare Boon of Foresight. Launched a coup to seize leadership of the Stone Tribe after Fannalhen's death. Fell into a catatonic state shortly before the Battle at the Stone Village.

- **Fannadhan:** Also known as Fann. Once a close friend of Sen, now a bitter rival. A Bearsign granted the Boon of Strength. Took part in his mother's insurrection and acted as an enforcer after she took control. Fell after the Bear was slain during the Battle of the True Heart.

- **Grafhar:** A mute Owlsign granted the Boon of Language.

The Lake Tribe: Settled upon the Big Lake north of the Forest, the Lake Tribe is a warlike group often more at odds with each other than with the matters of the outside world. There is wide infighting amongst the Tribe, specifically on opposite ends of the Big Lake. They are skilled naval fighters if only because they've constantly warred with each other on boats along the Big Lake, leading to the body of water to be nicknamed the Lake of Bones by other Tribes.

- *[Tenazt]:* Chief of the eastern Lake Tribe. A Bearsign endowed with the Boon of Courage. Killed by Hollow during the Battle of the True Heart.

- **Ket:** A healer of the eastern Tribe. An Owlsign with the Boon of Knowledge. Has become lovers with Tez.

- **Barrha:** Once a trusted Wolfsign with the Boon of Stealth from the eastern Tribe. Now rendered mindless after his Boon pendant was stolen by an unknown party.

- *[Yhaan]*: Chief of the western Lake Tribe. A Bearsign with the Boon of Fear. Killed by Hollow during the Battle of the True Heart.

The Keepers: Dwelling within the mountainous ranges of the Heart of the Land, the Keepers are the conductors of the Trial and the guardians of the Bear, the Wolf, and Owl. They are the only Tribe not to be displaced by the Acrarians nor have their territory occupied by displaced Tribespeople. The Keepers are the most prolific of the Owlsigns, with many of the Land's greatest scholars being born a member of this Tribe. They are bestowed an honorific dependent upon which Sign they were born under after they complete their Trial: Ko for the Owl; Ne for the Wolf; and An for the Bear. The Tribe is home primarily to Owlsigns and Wolfsigns, with very few Bearsigns.

- **Ko Zaran:** An Owlsign with the Boon of Knowledge who conducts Brin's Trial. One of the most learned scholars in the Land with an enormous collection of tomes in his personal library.

- *[Ko Endra]*: An Owlsign with the Boon of Memory. Ko Zaran's direct steward. Killed by Cin during the Battle of the True Heart.

- **An Rhan:** A Bearsign with the Boon of Strength. One of the most adept fighters in the Heart by virtue of being one of the only ones. Tasked with guarding the True Heart where the Animal Deities sleep. Fell after the Bear was slain during the Battle of the True Heart.

- **Ne Shanne:** A well-respected Wolfsign bearing the Boon of Pack-mind. One of the few Keepers who has ventured beyond the Heart.

- **Ko Seln:** An Owlsign granted the Boon of Language. Runs a tavern that can be found on the ascent through the mountain ranges of the Heart.

- **Ne Arsah:** An embittered Wolfsign with a Boon of Stealth. Spends much of his time at Ko Seln's tavern.

- **An Nara:** A Bearsign with the Boon of Restoration who spends much of her time at Ko Seln's tavern. Fell after the Bear was slain during the Battle of the True Heart.

The Sun Tribe: One of the Tribes displaced by the Invasion of the Acrarians, the Sun Tribe once dwelt along the southeastern coast of the Land, making a living off of fishing and other seafaring activities. They were the first to be displaced by the Acrarians after their arrival. At first resettling in the Forest, they were then further attacked by the zealously territorial Wood Tribe, leading to lingering animosity between the two Tribes. They have since settled in the Stone Tribe's territory at Stone Chief Fannalhen's offering, but many in the Sun Tribe are eager to retake their homeland. Members of the Sun Tribe are distinguishable by their hide garb bearing only one shirtsleeve, their long hair tied in two vertical buns at the back, and their tribal paint of two red lines crossing vertically over the eyes.

- *[Han'e]:* Chief of the Sun Tribe. A Bearsign with the Boon of Courage. Formerly party to an uneasy alliance with the Stone Chief Fannalhen, later took part in Koelhe's coup on the premise that she would help him reclaim his lands from the Invaders, but defected after she reneged on that promise. Killed by Fann during the Battle at the Stone Village.

- *[Tol'e]:* A Wolfsign bearing the Boon of Movement. One of Han'e's most trusted hunters. Killed by Rantalha during the Battle at the Stone Village.

The Wood Tribe: The de facto guardians—or rulers—of the Forest, the Wood Tribe is fiercely defensive and territorial, such to the point that they attacked the displaced Sun Tribe merely for trying to settle within their lands. Many Tribesfolk from the south who were merely passing through to the Heart to complete their Trials considered passing through the Forest a trial unto itself. The Wood Tribe makes its home high in the trees of the Forests in order to hold a strategic position against any would-be infringers of their territory. Leadership of the Wood Tribe is denoted by their makeshift crowns crafted from tree leaves and branches. Rarely is their skin kept bare; normally, it is painted in greens and browns to camouflage themselves amongst the trees.

- *[The Elder]*: A fierce old Bearsign with the Boon of Fear. In critical condition after a battle with the Acrarians. Perished due to his injuries.

- **The Matron:** An Owlsign healer bearing the Boon of Knowledge. Whereabouts unknown.

- *[The Chieftain]*: A Wolfsign often accompanied by a contingent of yeomen with Boons of Packmind. Critically wounded during the Battle in the Forest, killed by Sen in an act of mercy.

The Arrow Tribe: Hailing originally from the Plains encompassing the southwestern regions of the Land, the Arrow Tribe were a once-proud group of nomadic wayfaring horselords until the Acrarians displaced them and stripped them of their horses. Comprised almost entirely of Wolfsigns, they have since been allowed resettlement in the north within the Stone Tribe's territories.

- **Fen-Osenta:** Part of a triumvirate of Arrow heroes and brothers once responsible for quelling the Steppe Conflict.

- *[Fen-Detu]:* Part of a triumvirate of Arrow heroes and brothers once responsible for quelling the Steppe Conflict. Killed during the Battle of the True Heart.

- **Fen-Poven:** Part of a triumvirate of Arrow heroes and brothers once responsible for quelling the Steppe Conflict.

The Haunted: Perhaps the most mysterious Tribe of the Land, the Haunted Tribe bore the worst of the Acrarians' assault, and the few who remain have been forced into servitude by the Invaders. "Haunted" is not the true name of the Tribe, but rather a somewhat derisive term used to address the Tribe's fascination with the plane of existence after death, particularly believing they could commune with the souls of the dead.

- *[Shara]:* An escaped slave from the Acrarian City. Killed during Koelhe's insurrection.

- *[Ran]:* An escaped slave from the Acrarian City. Had never known freedom due to the Acrarian Invasion happening when he was only a year old. Killed during Koelhe's insurrection.

- *[Zarrow]:* A member of the Haunted Tribe who lived during the Pale Night four hundred years ago. Communes with Cin from beyond the veil of the Otherworld.

The Acrarian Kingdom: Labeled merely as the "Invaders" by the Tribes, the Acrarians hail from a continent far to the east. They laid claim to the Land after mistaking it for the mythical Great West before deciding to formally settle the island while displacing the native population. The Acrarians are subject to an industrial age with steam power driving innovation and exploration forward. To an extent, Acrarians are also religious zealots who follow the teachings of an unnamed Savior figure in whose name they have claimed the Land with the idea of spreading his will unto the world.

- **Aritz a Mata:** Leader of the invading Acrarian forces. The son of a lord in tremendous favor with the royal family.

- **"Red":** A soldier in the Acrarian army. See: Kamataa

- **"Dark-Hair":** A lieutenant in the Acrarian army. Also known as Gaona. See: Cin

- *["Blondie"]:* A lieutenant in the Acrarian army. True name Ludovico. Died during the Battle in the Forest.

- **"Pock-Face"**: A lieutenant in the Acrarian army. True name Ettor.

- *["No-Neck"]*: A lieutenant in the Acrarian army. True name Baltasar. Died during the Battle at the Stone Village.

- **Master Hernan:** A sycophantic Scholar.

The Children of the Black Moon: A collective of Eclipseborn from all throughout the Land, the Children of the Black Moon offer home and hearth not only for those born during an Eclipse, but also for those who were cast out from their Tribes. They currently live in the City amongst the Acrarians, serving in their army.

- **Kamataa:** Also known as Kama, Red. Leader of the Children of the Black Moon alongside Ziia. Formerly of the Lake Tribe. Due to choosing the power of the Draw, she has lived for over four hundred years.

- *[Ziiahlan]:* Also known as Ziia. Leader of the Children of the Black Moon alongside Kamataa. Formerly of the Stone Tribe. Due to choosing the power of the Draw, she lived for over four hundred years. Killed by Sen during the Battle at the Stone Village.

- *[Zara]:* Formerly of the Lake Tribe. Chose the power of the Touch. Died of a fall after being shot by Sen during the Battle of the True Heart.

- *[Hollow]:* Formerly of the Wood Tribe. Chose the power of the Draw. Killed by Aritz during the Battle of the True Heart.

- **Sha'a:** Formerly of the Sun Tribe. Chose the power of the Touch.

- **Vanta:** Formerly of the Arrow Tribe. Chose the power of the Touch.

- **Cin:** Formerly of the Haunted. Chose the power of Luck.

<u>RELIGION AND BOONS</u>

The Tribes revere the will of nature, and more specifically, the three Animal Deities: the **Bear**, the **Wolf**, and the **Owl**. Each Deity is represented in the fields of strength, community, and wisdom, respectively.

When a Tribesperson is born, they are born under a celestial "Sign" that correlates to one of the three Deities. When a Tribesperson comes of age at eighteen, they go on a pilgrimage through the mountain ranges of the Heart to receive a Trial from the Keepers, which tests their acumen in the fields relevant to their Sign. If a Tribesperson fails their Trial, they are exiled from their respective Tribe and considered an outcast. If they succeed, however, they are granted a specific Boon which enhances certain physical or mental capabilities. This Boon is later carved as a rune into a pendant or a weapon, such as a spear. Once inscribed, this object will hold the power of that specific Boon. In theory, this means that any who holds the object will be subject to those abilities, but this is a strict taboo, and those who break it are immediately banished.

Each Animal Deity offers five possible Boons.

Boons of the Sign of the Bear:
- *Strength*: amplifying power and force

- *Endurance*: increased stamina

- *Fear*: masters of intimidation

- *Restoration*: quicker recovery from injuries

- *Courage*: heightened bravery

Boons of the Sign of the Wolf:
- *Stealth*: muted footsteps

- *Packmind*: thought sharing within a group

- *Scent*: heightened sense of smell

- *Sound*: heightened sense of hearing

- *Movement*: can more easily detect movement in the earth

Boons of the Sign of the Owl:
- *Knowledge*: high intelligence

- *Memory*: storage of the history of the world

- *Illusion*: masters of disguise

- *Language*: quick to learn any foreign tongue

- *Foresight*: can observe glimpses of what is yet to come

THE ECLIPSE

Those born during an Eclipse are known as "Eclipseborn" and are looked upon with distrust and fear. Unlike those born under one of the Signs corresponding to one of the three Animal Deities, the Eclipseborn are granted abilities by the Moon that are deemed unnatural by the Tribes. If a person is discovered to have been an Eclipseborn, they are to be banished from the Tribe without question, though some take more violent approaches to addressing an Eclipseborn in their midst. There are three known abilities associated with the Eclipseborn:

- *The "Draw"*: The drawing in of life energy. Allows a recipient to extend their lifespan beyond natural means as well as heal from wounds that would otherwise be fatal.

- *The "Touch"*: The employ of death energy. Allows a recipient to kill another living being with just a touch.

- *Luck*: Manipulation of chance. Allows a recipient success more than is natural.

It is unknown if there are other abilities associated with Eclipseborn at this time.

A MESSAGE TO THE READER

If you've made it this far: you have my heartfelt thanks for reading THE LEGION OF THE LOST, and thank you for finishing this emotional journey with me.

If it's not too much to ask, I would very much appreciate you giving a quick review of THE LEGION OF THE LOST on Amazon and/or Goodreads. Reviews are incredibly important for authors (and indie authors especially!) as they enable us to expand our reach and let more and more potential readers know that our books exist! And besides that, I simply want to know what you thought of this book, whether your impressions were good or bad, and I do hope I'll see you in the next book.

If you'd like to keep up with everything I'm doing, you can sign up for my monthly newsletter at joseph-john-lee.com and/or follow me on Twitter and Instagram @joelee__ (that's two underscores!).

Thank you,

Joe

ACKNOWLEDGMENTS

Wow. Wow, wow, wow. What a journey it's been.

I first started working on what would become The Spellbinders and the Gunslingers in early 2020, before we had even the faintest idea of how all our lives were about to be disrupted by a global pandemic. Four years later, here we are at the end of the journey. It's bittersweet to finally close this chapter. I am truly bereft of the words to say to properly express those feelings. All I can say is thank you.

First, to you, the readers. It is because of you that I even had the drive to finish this series to begin with. When I first wrote The Bleeding Stone and found myself roadblocked by the trials and tribulations of getting it published, I wondered if I would ever find an audience beyond the few friends who I showed it to. But here we are, a whole-ass trilogy later, and I would not have done it if not for you. You're the best.

To Adam and Sammy: what more can I say to you both? You two are the reason I had the confidence to actively pursue this writing gig in the first place. You were the first to encourage me and make me feel like I was a "real" writer with some degree of talent. I wouldn't be sitting here, writing this acknowledgments section for the fourth(!) time, without you both.

To my editor, Michele Perry, thank you as always for helping bring my words further to life and for always validating me when I am unsure that what I have written is even worth reading. And to the dynamic duo of Felix Ortiz and Shawn King, getting to work with you guys on the cover arts for these books has been an absolute delight and always makes me feel like I'm doing something right to have your work be tied to mine.

To all my friends in the community, you all make navigating these publishing waters so much less scary, and it's always comforting to know I have so many peers in the same boat as me, navigating the same waters. I want to especially recognize João, Sadir, James, Katie, Michael, H.C., Christer, Joe, Luke, Bethany, and Morgan for being such wonderful people with whom to celebrate and commiserate.

And finally, to my dear wife, Annie. (Still feels crazy to say "my wife" now.) I am always indebted to you for your love and support; I may not have fully pursued this gig otherwise. It was thanks to you that the groundwork for this series started to build itself in my mind four years ago, so this series is as much a part of you as it is of me. Thank you for enduring the long hours I locked myself away to furiously write all this depressing stuff, and thank you for supporting me and all my weird ideas, even when some of it flies over your head. Having you in my life is wonderful for so many reasons, and you being in my corner and championing me and my crazy stories up is one of them. Thank you for being the absolute best.

Joseph John Lee is the author of The Spellbinders and the Gunslingers trilogy and has been a semifinalist in Mark Lawrence's annual Self-Published Fantasy Blog-Off. A true product of New England, he prefers Dunkin' over Starbucks, sometimes speaks with a Boston accent, and does not say the word "wicked" in casual conversation as much as one may think. He currently lives in Boston with his wife, Annie, and their robot vacuum named Crumb.